A Good Ending
for Bad Memories

Bold Story Press, Washington, DC 20016
www.boldstorypress.com

First edition published September 2021

Library of Congress Control Number: 2021911031

ISBN: 978-1-954805-10-1 (paperback)
ISBN: 978-1-954805-11-8 (e-book)

Text and cover design by Laurie Entringer
Cover art and author image by Preston Sampson

Printed in the United States of America
10 9 8 7 6 5 4 3 2 1

A Good Ending
for Bad Memories

To Karen)
I hope you
will have this
story.

Vailes Shepperd

**BOLD
STORY
PRESS**

Washington, DC

For my favorite sets of sisters
Patricia and Dolores
Raghida and Amal
TePo and Jope
and yours

And my three Shepperd men

Contents

Family Tree

Selsie, a slave known as "Two for the Price of One" suffers from undiagnosed Multiple Personality Disorder. Selsie loves and marries Lloyd Earl. Together, they have one daughter whose name is never again used after an incident in the woods.

"Daughter" has one child, Aberdeen. Father may be Scilla Landry's brother. *(Scilla is Selsie's former owner and best friend.)*

Aberdeen marries Henry Dagomire Macomb. They have one daughter, who inherits her great-great-grandmother's Multiple Personality Disorder, and one son.

Aberdeen's daughter, known as "Mother" to her children, alternately becomes Selma, Agnes, Berdeena, and/or Martha (always in the same order).

Aberdeen's daughter marries Clifton Thrace. Together, they have three children—Alley, Mirella, and Black Black.

Black Black has one son, Dag (Mother unknown).

Meeting Mostly Selma

Selma Macomb was beautiful and crazy, though she didn't spend time in front of the mirror, talk to herself, have fits, or see things that weren't there. She had never had a breakdown. She suffered regular "break aparts." Bits of her scattered everywhere like a Humpty Dumpty who could not put herself back together again. It was memory that left her in pieces, exploding in vivid flashes of the past followed by a destructive residue, leaving ashes of the facts, making them altogether impossible to order in any serviceable way. Memory made up the person which was Selma's riddle. She couldn't properly remember. She was merely one of five personalities housed in a single woman. Only one personality was present at a time and Selma wasn't always in possession of her mind or body, not when the others each had their own turn. Her disorder had less to do with true madness than considerations of space and time. She was only available one-fifth of the time and not by any ordinary scale or calendar. And yet, Selma had somehow intuited that the key to the fractured puzzle of *now* must be hidden in the odd reminiscences of *then*.

Fortunately, her responsibilities were shared, not only with her other selves but with her family and the household staff in the American-owned mansion in the western section of Cairo, Egypt, where they all lived. Selma was the wife of the American attaché and the mother of their three children, though the memories of marriage and birth did not reside within her. She was unaware of her disorder and so were the other personalities. Still, Selma was wishful and resolute: If she could order the past, she might be also able to anticipate and even invent her future. She could fix her memories and bring them back together in proper order.

For Selma, memories came up like stories and when they did, she told them to the children. After calling to them from the door, she crossed the expanse of her large bedroom, crawled back into bed, and then became undone. Fortunately, the horror of breaking apart was invisible to her children, and only temporary and mildly confusing to Selma who felt as if her arms were uncomfortably folded beneath the blankets. Her legs were indescribably twisted like a broken ballerina doll's, and the pain of discombobulation had fallen, unnoticed to the floor. Her disconnected hands danced from opposite sides of the large bed. Her lips moved but the words seemed to come in from outside and float about the room.

"When I was little we lived in a—" Selma paused to think of a better word than shack.

"Three rooms at the edge of a field," she continued. "My own mama sat in the yard on top of her stump, stirring her pot like an old witch. Yellow and purple flowers stood up on their slinky stems and when the dandelions arched and bowed in the breeze, the lawn looked like a tiny swaying choir with Easter-white hair." Selma chuckled a high sad line of *tee hee hees*.

"Wind-blowing grass was our orchestra. And along with the breeze went the scent of ham hocks that Mama said sweetened the pot. Mama still used Great-Grandmother Selsie's recipes and they could be dangerous. Selsie's recipes messed with folks. Her food mixed up with what was already in a person and depending on who was eating, it might be good or bad digestion. If you were dying and

2

wanted to, Selsie's potato tar would be the one thing you'd miss in the world. People spit her biscuit crumbs chasing their own confessions. Her pudding went down like it was the one thing that righted everything that was wrong. My mama's greens sat on your stomach like a soft blanket, covering hunger like it was cold. And Mama would have pulled up and washed down a truckload of giant collard leaves but after she cooked them, the greens barely filled her big pot."

Though it was 1958, it could have been 1934 because Selma only ever talked to the children about things that had already happened. She played in the past as if it were present and never once mentioned Cairo, Egypt, where the family currently lived. Pyramids notwithstanding, Selma's memory lived on the other side of the world in America, on the mountaintop where she grew up.

"'You have to feed the pig first,' Mama always said. That's who she said ate all the greens, some invisible pig that I told Mama should eat the kudzu and leave our greens alone. That invisible pig was my god when I was twelve—maybe before—but nothing too much ever comes to mind before I turned twelve." Selma paused.

"On a spring day, there wasn't anything better than Mama's biscuits, greens, and ham. She'd grate in a little true cinnamon that stayed on the tongue and pretty soon, you couldn't tell if the cinnamon was in the collards, the biscuits, or the person eating. We'd sit out, eating slowly, watching the moon come up and the stars turn on. Mama said we didn't need a man's light 'cause we got the sky. She said some things more often when Daddy wasn't around than when he was."

"'Little girl, today is one of your quiet ones. Tomorrow it'll be nonstop noise,' Mama said. Mama said I was like a tree that ran through all the seasons, all at the same time. Paying no attention to the real weather."

The three children crossed eyes at each other and giggled as they listened to their mother's strange fairy tales. These were good moments with Mother, and they would sit for hours if Mother would go on.

But then, her cadence changed. Mother sat up a little in the bed and began again. Only now, she was talking about herself as if she were the narrator in her own childhood.

"First, they said that little girl never spoke a word, then, they said she was a radio you couldn't turn off." Mother hunched one shoulder. "They were always confused about us. Truthfully, townspeople didn't care too much about folks who hardly ever came to town, but they wanted explanations they weren't ever going to get for all the stuff they thought happened up in the woods. They wanted to know why all the children never came to school at the same time. They wanted to know which children belonged to which family. And they wanted to know how many children my mama really had and how many children lived up in the woods. Mama said they were nosy and didn't need to know everything they thought they needed to know, one way or another."

Mother stopped talking. The children waited, she stayed quiet. All three tiptoed, one after the other, out of the room.

"Today" was always awkward. Selma couldn't count on herself to be in the day. Her life was more like having a bit part in a stop-action film: in a scene one day, then another scene three days later, or two years down the road in a slightly progressed future. The rest of the time she must have been traveling, though where, of course, she couldn't remember. She couldn't help being an odd tourist and guessed she must have been born this way.

When she wasn't telling childhood stories, she was the queen of not speaking until being spoken to. Communication was difficult because she never knew her lines or where she belonged. When she took the chance and said a few words, she knew that the others only pretended to understand.

Selma didn't mind her life; she wasn't unhappy, merely patient. Sooner or later, everything would make sense. She'd have a part in each day and the days would flow, one behind the other, the way they were supposed to flow.

She couldn't gather herself until the memories vanished. They came up like illness, temporarily derailing anything ordinary. Generally, the moments just after were not of reflection but rather empty of time and information—moments that would suddenly, or slowly, but always inexplicably, catch a thread of the day and reel her in. Then, just as if she were a regular person waking up in a normal way, Selma got up, bathed, dressed very quickly, and hurried out of the house.

Her feet click-clacked loudly across the marble floors. She raced out the door and the children, always on a stake-out of their mother, followed her, careful at first, not to get too close. Once, when Mirella accidentally bumped into Selma's back, she had turned and smiled oddly without uttering a single word. She looked down at her own daughter as if she were completely unrecognizable.

"Do you think Mother only pretends with us?" Mirella whispered as they skipped down the street behind their mother.

"Pretends!? You only pretend when you want something you don't have. Mother has everything," Alley said.

"Maybe she pretends she's back in the woods while she walks. Or maybe she pretends that things that happened didn't," Mirella said. "She's homesick."

"Wouldn't pretending be easier in a chair?" Alley asked.

"Where are we going?" Mirella asked.

"We're following Mother; she should know where we're going."

"What about getting back?" Mirella asked again.

"Doesn't Mother know how to get home?" Alley replied, sighing as if the question were completely ridiculous. But somewhere in her middle, fiddling around her stomach, Alley wasn't sure of anything about their mother, and that was what needed to be fixed. Alley was going to be the one to unprove that Mother was unreliable.

A while later, Umm Ridah, their Egyptian housekeeper, found the children walking on a busy side street near the outer wall of the Cairo Museum of Egyptian Antiquities. Sand and smoke were in the air, like all Cairene evenings. Sand from underfoot, smoke from the burnt husks of the corn sellers. The air smelled singed and agreeable.

"Your mother see you? She know you striet?" Umm Ridah shouted.

"We're with her," Alley said.

Umm Ridah made a big show of looking around in all directions and throwing up her arms.

"Well, we were!" Alley said.

"You come! You come." Umm Ridah grabbed their hands and turned them around.

She forced them home, all the while shaming their mother in Arabic. No matter because none of the children understood Arabic.

Umm Ridah had known her share of mistresses. Why some of them had to be mothers too, Allah a'alan! Umm Ridah recognized the peculiarity in her new mistress as soon as she met her. She had vacancy in her eyes. She looked at Umm Ridah's hairline rather than at Umm Ridah.

She'd been surprised to meet the Thrace family. They were her first brown Americans. Until now, she had assumed all Americans were white and all the other American families had been white, but people were people, mostly problematic, good and bad. It hadn't taken long to realize that the Thraces would be the same as all the other families except for Mrs. Thrace. Finding little American children alone on the street meant they had a careless mother.

Umm Ridah took the children home and pinched them though she called it a "tickle." She didn't want them to have bad memories of Egypt, so she tried to pour something else into their heads whenever their mother did something terrible. Of course, Umm Ridah couldn't be sure that her charges understood her, but she tried. She jabbered and pinched; then she would laugh so long and hard she'd have to sit and take deep breaths before getting up and giving the children a date-filled treat.

Her new mistress could not be addressed; she didn't seem to be the type with available ears. If Umm Ridah had anything to say, it could only be in response, after Mrs. Thrace had first addressed her. Days before catching the children on the street, Umm Ridah thought she saw Mrs. Thrace or a mirage of her, moving so differently and purposefully; Umm Ridah couldn't be sure. Mrs. Thrace on the sidewalk wore a tighter dress than she had ever seen in the house. Her hair was a loose mane, and inches longer than Umm Ridah would have guessed. Much more hair coiled down her back than seemed to fit in the neatly folded knot that sat like a fixture at the base of her indoor neck. Mrs. Thrace didn't look dressed for tea with other embassy wives. There was something serene and far too certain about the woman Umm Ridah saw walking. She called to her once without a response and wanted to call out again but did not. Disturbing her mistress on the street seemed too great an intrusion for such a woman.

Clifton Maxwell Thrace came home from work nearly every day at the same time and shortly afterwards, the family gathered at the table for dinner. This rule was never broken unless their father worked through the dinner hour, and often, he came home for dinner and went out again. Dinner was served at the same time and everyone sat in the same place except for Mother, who moved around the table from time to time, unsure of which chair to claim.

"I finally understand time," Mother whispered, as she spooned the rice, but before anyone could respond, she continued, "It's the waiting between events, all the waiting moments, and then," laughing gently to herself, "there aren't any events."

"It's not always easy to understand everything around one," she said.

Her conversations seemed to be taking place between her and someone unseen with the children and their father thrown in the middle and sometimes, after Mother had spoken, she might be silent again for days.

Other times, Mother might go on. "Even if all you have is uncertainty," she sighed, "anything can take the day."

"That's the trouble, isn't it?" she asked.

"Yes, yes, interesting, really," Clifton Maxwell Thrace answered. His wife could be her own monologue, and equally indecipherable to him and the children.

The children remembered their mother's conversations because she so seldom had them. Mostly, she told them stories but when she did speak to them or their father at the table, sometimes they would discuss Mother's words together after dinner, sifting for meaning.

"Mother doesn't have enough to do," explained Mirella. "That's what she meant about time."

"No, silly, she has too much to do. That's the problem: something comes up and she's got to do something else."

"Like what?"

"Everything."

After dinner, Mother disappeared, and the children had their father to themselves. As much as a preoccupied man could share with children, he did. Usually, he read to them. He'd start by asking them about their day and how they liked their new country. They, of course, were eager to respond and went on and on about the sights and smells of Cairo, but after a few minutes of no reaction from their father, they became quiet. Their father did not ask them to repeat themselves; he pulled out a book and read in as lively a manner as possible. Instead of children's books, to his nine- and seven-year-old daughters and five-year-old son, he read what was of interest to him: Richard Burton's books, history tainted by an outside perspective.

Later, Umm Ridah kissed and tucked the children into bed. She waited in the hallway shadows for one of their parents to come. Often, she would be the only one to send them to sleep. She would half read, half make up the story from their book of choice in the odd English she'd picked up from five American families, three that gave her classes.

Mrs. Thrace would disappear into her private room immediately after dinner and get ready for her husband. She stripped naked, wrapped her hair in a long colorful scarf, sat in front of her mirror, and smoked, taking in long drags, and easing out her thoughts. In the evening, her thoughts were always about whether she and Clifton would bed one another. He was the one to decide. Being touched by him was like going on vacation, removing her from the daily everything to the valley of his full weight on top of hers, the subsumption of her scents to his scent, her skin made to breathe in rhythmic echoes of him by his hands.

She kept Clifton waiting, taking a long time, perfuming all her scent holding places before walking into the bedroom where he sat in the chair beneath his favorite lamp. His cool glass tinkled with ice when she picked it up, stole one sip, sat down, and swallowed. Scotch—ugh—she sipped again and looked into her husband's eyes to see herself. Was her tiny, refracted face reflected in his eyes? She crossed her arms and subtly signaled her readiness for bed.

Thrace knew the precise dimensions of his wife's secret little room but never bothered to tell her. He thought every woman could have secrets even if she needed a room to keep them in, and though these weren't the kind of things he ever put into words, his wife could have a bunch of secret rooms as long as they were all inside his house.

Clifton Thrace considered himself lucky, but the truth is that he wouldn't have allowed for any other possibility. He possessed a distinctly individual world view, one he'd crafted from experience and hard work, eliminating what he considered excess. Everything that was important to him, was important.

He had wanted his wife from across a clearing on top of a mountain he had climbed looking for a family that had once possessed more land and property than any other family like them. From the looks of the shack where he found them, fortunes had changed. Before he had gotten close enough to smell her, Thrace felt his reason being eclipsed by the aura of a woman who looked as if she could effortlessly scale a tall pine. If they were the Macombs, her great-grandfather had been featured on a list he possessed titled, *"The Curiously Successful Negro."* Harvard University had supposedly initiated, compiled, and updated the list for more than a hundred years. The Negroes on the list had eked out far more than a simple living before, during, and after slavery. Clifton Thrace had been investigating privately over time. He had come across the list in his father and grandfather's things and wanted to know if the fate of these families had remained solid and their fortunes kept. In the middle of his investigation had been this extraordinarily beautiful woman, the great-great-granddaughter of Lloyd Earl.

Lloyd Earl was the first to amass what would eventually become the largest fortune on the list. He had purchased and owned land and property from Georgia to Washington, DC, including homes, churches, cemeteries, farms, and even a hotel where only Negroes stayed, where slave owners housed their slaves if the slave was lucky. Inside Mr. Lloyd Earl's hotel, slaves and all others were treated like masters.

Thrace found the last of the Lloyd Earl/Macombs on a mountain in Georgia. He had stumbled into a clearing directed by the church folks from the town who cautioned him that whatever he wanted probably wouldn't be found even if he spent a month with Aberdeen Macomb.

She had been sitting on what could only be described as an elaborately carved stool when he spotted her not too far from her front door. He glimpsed her behind the steam hissing up from the pot that sat between him and her. He moved closer, cautiously. Country people sometimes had dogs that only came into view when necessary.

He might have characterized her as an old witch living in the woods simply because of the setting, though she was an incongruently elegant woman. She stood gracefully and the wrapped dress she wore fell, revealing her shape and height.

"I'm Clifton Thrace," he stepped forward and raised his hand.

Aberdeen smiled as if she'd been expecting him. "To what do I owe this honor?" she asked as if she'd recognized his name.

"The honor is mine." He wondered how he would explain his sudden appearance, how he'd work into the conversation that he'd come to find out what had become of the family fortune.

"Surely, it is. We don't usually have city visitors up this far," Aberdeen said, clearly waiting for his explanation. "I'm Aberdeen Macomb."

"I—" Thrace hesitated, wondering why he hadn't already put his motives into an acceptable sentence. "I—"

"This is my daughter." She raised her arm in the direction of the woods behind her, and, as if conjured, out stepped the most oddly beautiful woman that Thrace had ever seen. Thrace coughed and grunted, clearing his throat, wishing he had planned something to say.

Her hair was wild and long; he couldn't quite tell where it began or ended. The mass of curly dark hair twirled in stark contrast to her paler reddish skin. She was slender and smooth with tight muscular legs that looked as though she could easily traverse miles. As soon as she came fully into the clearing, she retreated again and disappeared.

Thrace seemed to be struggling with his breath and Aberdeen said, "Just wait."

In the next few moments, her daughter stepped back out of the woods and then disappeared again. Thrace wondered if she was playing some sort of game or looking for something.

"If you let her, she'll be in and out all day."

"Your daughter?" was all Thrace could manage.

"She's grown a little too restless for this mountaintop," Aberdeen said.

"Has she been living away?" Clifton asked.

"Off and on but always back. She needs to be far enough away so she can't get back."

"Oh."

"Do you have a car?"

"Yes, in town."

"You have my permission to take her for a ride."

"Whe—" Thrace began to say and then caught himself. "Do you think she'd like to?"

She came out of the woods again, walked towards Clifton Thrace, brushed by him, and said, he thought, "I'd love to," in a tired alto as if speaking cost more effort than she wanted to expend.

"This one here is," Aberdeen turned and watched her daughter walk into the house, and said, "not sure."

Clifton thought Aberdeen had identical twins or something but was a little too shamefaced and tongue-tied to ask.

"She won't be long," Aberdeen said and sat back down on her stool.

Moments later, the daughter came out of the house in a beautiful dress, carrying her shoes and a bag. Her hair was now neatly slicked and tied back except for one or two strands hanging in front of her left ear. The shack must have had a magic room inside. She smelled like flowers, the woods, and homemade soap. Her dress clung to her lean body; full, large breasts sat high over her small waist. She had a bit of a boy's narrow hips with a little girlish flesh thrown on top. She led him back through the woods and at first, he wondered, then understood, that she'd know exactly where to go. It had taken him hours to climb but only forty minutes to get back down. They broke the tree line and she walked directly to his car. On the way, they passed a few town folks who looked at the two of them as if they were two-headed surprises.

"Which daughter is that one?" he heard one nearby man ask the other.

"They don't look that much alike, but you still can't tell them apart," the man answered and they both snorted.

Aberdeen's daughter stood by his car and waited. Thrace walked over and opened the trunk, pulled the bag off her shoulder, and put it inside. She reached for it at first, as if she might not want the bag out of her sight, but then relented.

He drove her to the county line and stopped.

"A little further please?" she asked. "I think it's about ten miles further."

He drove until she asked him to stop.

"We can go back now," she said, "if you'll come back."

"Of course, do you meant…" Thrace said.

"Tomorrow," she answered.

He took her on two more rides, each one longer and a little more joyful than the one before. The windows were down; air flew through the car and whipped around them. Each time, they stopped at a gas station and Thrace bought them different drinks. After the third ride, on the return, she'd leaned towards him and gently touched him right behind the shoulder.

Her hand on his back that first time stung him with heat he could still feel.

"Don't take me back," she'd said, again her voice tired but firm and clear.

He looked over at her to be sure. He was her rescuer, the one to take her out of the woods. He knew it to be true, yet something in him, even at that moment, had sensed more.

Maybe she was the one who had been in charge from the very first moment that he'd seen her step out of the woods. She had choreographed her own escape.

Later, he'd relive their very first moments together. The woman who had urged him to take her away, even the voice she'd used. He'd never heard her speak again in quite the same way. He told himself that he exaggerated their beginnings. Once he had her with him, he'd never seen or heard that same woman again. He toyed with the idea from time to time that maybe a switch had occurred, and that he had married the twin.

So yes, his wife was strange, and he did not know if the cause was the mountain woods where she had grown up, the burden of such beauty or some other family trait, and frankly, did not care. She was no longer a separate person but a consequence of his good sense and taste.

In his way, Thrace had anchored her and now she was free to float as she pleased within the great big sea of his belongings.

After a night of intimacy, Selma was still Selma at breakfast. The household was run so smoothly that it would have remained so, no matter what she did.

"Things run in families, you know," Aberdeen once told her daughter, who told Clifton Thrace. "The pickled-up head, peculiarities in the joints, particular disorders, and the medicine. A line runs through generations, things happen, and no matter when those things happen, two generations earlier, or in your time, they can mess and mark everybody."

Aberdeen, the great oracle, had also predicted, "Daughter, you're going to travel to the other side of the world and back to feel whole and straight."

Aberdeen had been right. Selma was stretched out on a bed in Egypt. She knew she had to get up. The children were supposed to start school. She stood up and figured there was time for a walk in order to prepare herself for dealing with the school. The trouble was she could only walk for hours which is how she missed most things, and specifically, the ones that had to do with the children.

Umm Ridah took the children and partially registered them, doing as much as she could as the head maid of the American attaché. That day, Umm Ridah practiced out loud the speech she wanted to give Mr. Thrace. She listed all the things that "Mrs. Il 'afritah il soda" (that devilish woman) Thrace missed. Umm Ridah never uttered the name she called Mrs. Thrace out loud.

"She no concerned to the children. She left them on the strieet! She no barely speak to them. Some days, she look them odd, like she not even their mother." Umm Ridah's planned speeches powered her work that day. She cleaned by herself without the other maids and put an extra sparkle on the kitchen. She was heading down the hallway when she caught her image in the mirror. The reflection stopped her argument cold. The quick flash of herself, an Egyptian matron dressed in her daily clothes, was an epiphany. Her words were true but in this funny little American household, she sensed that silence worked better.

Mr. Thrace wrote a note which his wife read, altered, and dropped off at the school after closing. She renamed the girls and made them twins. The fact that they were in the same class was a comfort. Mirella and Alley were in what was the closest equivalent to an American third grade. The "twins" were not quite two years apart but the class, teachers, and everyone associated with the school began referring to them as the "American twins." Alley was smarter, bigger, and slightly better looking. Neither of them belonged in the third grade.

When Umm Ridah picked them up after school, she told everyone several times that the bigger girl was older than the younger one. In the beginning, the staff would insist that they had no girls by the names that Umm Ridah garbled. Eventually, the girls came out of the school on their own. Confusion delayed the entire picking-up process, but after a week or so the girls knew that Umm Ridah would be outside. She had proven her reliability.

Umm Ridah walked the children home, all the while ranting and raving in untranslatable Arabic.

When Mrs. Thrace called her girls "the twins," Umm Ridah knew that her American mistress must be crazy. What she did not know was that her mistress had five separate personalities to prove it.

2

Meeting Mostly Agnes

Agnes didn't smoke but her body did. She felt used and it made her nervous. Bad nerves manifested into a tic but instead of involuntary movement, her tic displayed itself in a repetition of sound. Sounds strung together so tightly that they resembled a tune and, in some ways, she was happy to have a disguise for her tic. People thought Agnes's tic was a song. It'd been that way since childhood and most people thought her music was lovely.

Agnes took refuge in the top of the tree in her mother's front yard because she was always agitated when her father came home. He was the other problem. His coming and going unnerved Agnes. What right had he to give her irregular access to fatherhood?

"Why won't he stay?" she asked her mother.

"Just didn't grow that way," her mother responded as if Agnes was supposed to know what she meant.

"Seems like a father that is only here half the time is only half a father," Agnes said to her mother. Because to Agnes, it seemed like her father would come home one day with a doll's body, go away again, and a few months later, return with the doll's head. It wasn't true, he'd never even given Agnes a doll, but she'd get used to his presence in the house, his big smile, smells, noise, and his otherness and then he'd take it all away. So many questions and hugs would get lost in his absence. Agnes would have stored up all the things she wanted to share with her father, but he stayed away so long that she'd forget, and she never knew how to begin again when he returned. If she could smile and hug him, she couldn't speak. If she could speak and eat with him, she could not say anything nice. If she could say something nice, she couldn't look his way.

"Ignore her funny ways," she heard her mother tell her father. From then on, her father, Henry Dagomire ("Dag") Macomb, rarely spoke to her, unless Aberdeen was already talking to her. If her mother was insisting that she eat her greens, her father would mumble something about how good they were for a person, especially a little female person.

"One day you eat 'em, next day you don't. Changeable ain't all that good in a girl." Agnes remembered him saying this, but she didn't know what he was talking about because she never ate her mother's greens. She didn't like them, but she liked to hear her mother and father talking about her.

"Depends on from what to where, or to whom and how," Aberdeen said.

Greens confused Agnes, especially the way her mother cooked them. They were salty and cinnamony sweet. Saltiness mixed with sweetness annoyed Agnes because she liked both tastes. How could she enjoy one if the other kept intruding? The imposition of something sweet in between two salty bites was plain weird, like hearing "Once upon a time . . . the end," with no story in between. Agnes was not *that* changeable. Disruption made her cantankerous and if she had any sort of memory, she'd have remembered that eating her mother's collards was the same as relating to her father. Better to ignore everything and go outside.

She climbed the front yard tree or settled herself by the road to watch the kudzu grow. She'd spend a few nights camping outside until she felt settled enough to return home. Just when she felt like herself, her father would start his coming or going. Aberdeen seemed oblivious to either scenario. He'd either be there or not and life went on all the same. She cooked the same amount—a giant truckload of greens—sang the same songs and did the same things. And sometimes, she'd be laughing in the bed when she was alone as much as when Dag was at home.

Agnes couldn't remember too much before she turned twelve, but she remembered the night she was hanging upside down in the tree when Dag came out the front door and started rummaging around the porch, picking up a few things, including a shovel, which he hoisted over his shoulder. The moon was so high and bright that Agnes knew her mother would say "we don't need a man's light...," if she were still awake, but she had gone to bed early. Agnes watched Dag slowly stand up, pause, sigh loud enough to put birds in flight, and then walk towards the woods. She jumped down from her perch and crept behind him as he sloped up one of her mother's paths. Everything about the woods belonged to Aberdeen. Everybody else, including Agnes, was a guest.

Dag walked a long way, skirting Selsie's old stone kitchen.

"I heard your words," Dag said towards the old building, now nodding his head.

"Bury what you can't help but remember under something you can't stand to remember. Let's see if its gonna work. Selsie say you can bury things proper, the dirt will take them memories and maybe grow something new."

Agnes heard Dag, didn't know what he was talking about but followed close enough and when he'd passed the stone kitchen, behind him, Agnes rubbed her fingers along the walls, feeling the roughness against her hand. Aberdeen didn't like anyone around Selsie's stone kitchen, not without Aberdeen as guide and host. Selsie's place in the woods was hidden in an old grove so that Agnes could barely see the old place and rubbed it in passing, as if greeting her ancestor. She didn't know where Dag was going but it didn't seem to be towards town. He'd walked quite a ways when she heard him stop, take several breaths, and lean the handle of his shovel against a tree. Near enough to see his movement, she watched him take off his coat, and fluff it down. He stepped gingerly in half circles before he found what he was after and then he kneeled and pressed the earth with his hands. He put his ear and then his nose on the ground and stood up with a low rumbling sound that came from somewhere in him but not his throat.

He picked up his shovel and started to dig and as he dug he began to—was it sing? Agnes sat and watched. It seemed like hours before he pulled out some small white bones wrapped in a tattered colorful cloth. He set the bundle gently aside, then sat down next to it for moments, keeping his hand on it, tenderly, as if he were touching the knee of a child and then he stood up and put the dirt back in the hole.

When he was finished tamping down the hole, he grabbed his coat and swung it around his shoulders, he hooked his shovel to his coat, leaned down, picked up his bundle and carried it off down another of Aberdeen's paths, this one not so well used. He was still making noises as he went or at least that's what Agnes thought she heard. It also sounded like wailing, but she wondered if he weren't singing some church song they never sang at home.

The moon was dancing light like a lantern swinging between boughs, crossing over her father as he moved beneath trees. A little closer now, Agnes could clearly hear Dag. It wasn't a song. He was crying.

Agnes watched him dig another hole. This time, he dug up a bigger bundle of bones and he threw it roughly aside like he was sorry he ever had to be near whatever it was. Agnes saw more bones that clacked as they hit each other when he threw the bundle. They sounded hollow. The second bundle was much larger than the first. It had a round piece too; she hadn't seen the round piece in the first hole.

He picked up his sweet bundle, the one he treated better, and stepped carefully down into his new hole. He was wailing bitterly, jerking sounds out as if he were trying to keep them in and she could make out a few words. "Now maybe your mother will leave you alone. Maybe she won't be killing herself, wondering, searching, trying to love something she don't have, can't find, and maybe don't even believe. She needs a way to love the living. She needs to give up the dead, even the loved dead." He seemed to be performing a ceremony all by himself, with small clapping and hissing sounds echoing up out of his hole with the rhythm of the tears Agnes imagined pouring down his face. He'd taken the smaller bundle down with him first. Agnes was too scared to go close enough to see what he was doing down in the ground. When he came out, he looked wet, like the dirt had rained on him. Or maybe he'd dug up a water hole. He stood up and kicked that other pile of bones into the hole and buried it all again. Afterwards, he stood up, arched back, and screamed so loudly that Agnes fainted.

A few days later, Agnes tried to put her journey in the woods into words. She was agitated and not sure of what she'd seen but wanted to know.

"Mama, Daddy was burying bones in the woods. Whose bones are buried in the woods?" she asked her mother. "I thought you didn't believe that trees should stand over dead people?"

"Is anybody missing?" Agnes thought a little longer. "Is it where all the dogs are? Did Daddy bury the dogs you said ran away? Mama?"

Aberdeen quieted her daughter.

"Don't pick at wounds you don't remember," Aberdeen said, "and churn on the inside."

Right then, Agnes started to wonder if her mother loved something or someone that was in a hole and wasn't Agnes. From then on, she tried her best to do everything on the inside.

Agnes grew up without her mother's stoicism, only its appearance. She seemed like an emotionless young woman though she became entirely unhinged by the slightest change. Still, she followed her mother's advice. Agnes didn't even like to change clothes. Somewhere in between adolescence and adulthood she found a suitable rhythm which included her clothing, her affectation, her speech pattern, and of course, her mood—all constants. Her walk was fluid. Her hum did most of her talking. She could sometimes become anxious which revealed itself in the way that she rubbed two parts of her body together; her hands, her feet or often enough, her knees would do.

Agnes didn't remember moving to the other side of the world and didn't mind. She simply awakened to a lovely room, in a beautiful house, in an old city. She felt like a tourist who was fortunate enough to remain wherever she was as long as she liked. She toured and took to the American-owned mansion in the western section of Cairo, Egypt. Agnes always forgave herself for the things she didn't remember by consoling herself with the things that she did. It was hard not to appreciate the invisible hand that took such good care of her and everything else with limitless attention to detail and concern for her likes and dislikes. In her new closet at the end of her very large bedroom, in this house made of stone and marble, she found another version of the only dress that she planned to wear—a flowered confection in yellow.

Hugging was Agnes's primary attempt at motherhood. She didn't quite understand children, but she knew childhood to be all indescribable yearnings for explanations that never came. That was her childhood, in any case. The other thing that she felt sure about was that there had never been any tenderness. A hug would have solved many of her own problems, so she extrapolated that a great long hug ought to do wonders. She would hold first one and then another of the children in complete silence for an hour each and then start all over again.

When Alley came home from school and saw her mother wearing her yellow dress with the big peonies, she knew they would have to take turns sitting in her lap.

The longest hug spell that the children could remember lasted ten whole months. Every day after school, the children sat in their mother's arms, one after the other, love starved as Agnes guessed all children were.

"Mother smells lovely, doesn't she?" Alley asked.

"She does; the flowers on her dress smell real," Mirella agreed.

"Her arms are warm and soft," their brother whispered.

"My time's not up," he would beg whichever sister came to take his place. Then he'd grumble away, ever the loser.

Their mother and her arms were skinny but being able to sit and be held was magic and each engaged in their own silent reverie. Agnes did too. She pretended that they were babies unable to walk, talk, or be affected by the world.

Agnes hummed and squeezed them tighter in rhythm with her song. She never put words to her music, only music to her affection.

For the last week or so, all Mrs. Thrace ate was orange food: persimmons and carrots. She was growing thin but moved around slowly with a lumbering gait. Sometimes, Umm Ridah heard her moaning or humming but when she entered the room on the pretext of moving on with her chores, Mrs. Thrace would be sitting upright with a book or two, sometimes holding the book upside down, doing nothing at all. Even Umm Ridah prided herself on holding an English book right side up. What indeed was wrong with her mistress?

She had matching yellow shoes that she used to wear with her flowered dress. Umm Ridah had examined the shoes more than once because whenever Mrs. Thrace put them on with that dress, she said she was going for a walk. She didn't return for hours and the shoes never showed any signs of wear.

Eventually, "Your mother no wearing she yellow," Umm Ridah told the children. "You get dress, I clean nice." She had looked all over the bedroom for the yellow peony dress but couldn't find it.

To run the household, Umm Ridah had to take things upon herself. While Mrs. Thrace was out, her other duty was to teach the children to pray. She had long since had prayer rugs made for them. She couldn't find the yellow dress; nobody would be able to find the children's prayer rugs either. Umm Ridah was religious but her devotion was accompanied by a dose of superstition. Therefore, a prayer rug could only be handled by the person praying and the person who had given it to them.

She placed their rugs in position and guided them each to their knees. Prayers didn't need translation. The children simply needed to follow a ritual that might end with a treat. This particular ritual could not, however, be clocked as Umm Ridah was as lackadaisical as she was devout when it came to forcing it on the children. For one thing, their parents didn't know and, surely, Allah would grant forgiveness to the children of infidels.

"You know we're praying, don't you?" Alley asked her siblings.

"What should we pray for?" The boy asked first.

"Well, I pray for treats and toys," Mirella answered.

"Me, too, and I pray for us because sometimes I think we're going to need more prayer than most people," Alley added.

"Don't ask for too much. Ask for little things here and there, sweets but not bicycles; don't be greedy. We don't know which God we're asking," Mirella said.

"Any god'll do the same thing. The more blessings we ask for maybe the more we'll get," Alley said.

"I won't ask for too much," said their little brother.

Alley secretly prayed to feel safe, to understand things. She didn't know what exactly she meant but sometimes, she felt sure that a bad surprise would find them. Not all the time, but something about them and their household was ghareeb, like Umm Ridah said. One of the other kids told Alley ghareeb meant odd.

In school the next day, Alley and Mirella were asked exactly what kind of Americans they were. They didn't know what to answer and kept quiet. By the end of the day, the question caught up with them and they were being goaded for an answer. Several kids were standing in the hallway behind them, pointing. When their brother joined them on the way out of the school building, some of the kids started laughing and cried out in chorus.

"We know what kind of Americans you are. Fake Americans."

"Give us one proof that you're really Americans!"

Proof? What in the world was proof? Coca-Cola was American. They had had real Coca-Cola made from syrup. Maybe they had some at home they could bring to school. What about Aberdeen's greens or their father's parents? When they got outside, Alley asked Umm Ridah, "What's the best proof that we're American?"

"You come from American."

"Nobody at school believes us."

"Silly kids, no know American shoo."

They walked home and went into the kitchen to see if there was any food or anything else that was specifically American.

Umm Ridah followed their eyes as they gazed around the kitchen.

"Don't we have any American sweets?" Alley asked.

"Sweets not come from American," Umm Ridah answered. "We don't no steak burgers in this kitchen."

"Do we have any greens?" Alley asked.

"Lots Cairo greens."

"Maybe we can ask Daddy."

"No, no take your mother to school," Umm Ridah suggested.

"Would Mother really go to school?"

Mrs. Thrace was a foreigner everywhere. She had a strange look about her, so strange sometimes, so un-Egyptian that anyone on the streets of Cairo would certainly believe that she was an American. No one had seen her at school. She'd never been there.

Umm Ridah could look at the girls and tell that neither Alley nor Mirella had any idea how to ask their mother to come.

"Should we ask her?" Mirella whispered to Alley, who, for once, didn't respond.

At once, their faces melted together into the slow disappointment of knowing Mother would never come to school. She hadn't come yet. What would make her come now?

Umm Ridah busied herself about the kitchen so that she didn't have to see their little faces. She made an extra special dinner for the children that night though everyone ate it. She had to work very hard to make "plain rice" but that's what she did. She didn't know where it had come from but the one thing that Egyptians knew about Americans was "plain rice." If anyone ever said anything about America, it was immediately followed by "they eat plain rice." She made a big batch. Then she added chicken, lentils, and spices. Then she removed the lentils, bean by bean, and then the chicken. It would have been blasphemy to wash the rice after it was cooked so the spices had to stay. Then she put some lentils back in and removed them again. Preparing dinner took forever. She was so exhausted by the time that dinner was served that she slept late.

In the morning, the children were in the kitchen waiting for breakfast. Umm Ridah was not in the house. Fruit was left at each of their places. They sat down and ate. They were still sitting when their mother walked in. They were ready to go but didn't stand up.

"Isn't it time for school?" Mother asked.

"Yes," three voices answered.

"Well?"

"Umm Ridah doesn't seem to be in the house."

"Maybe she's waiting outside." Mother said.

The boy went to check and returned hesitantly.

"She's not there."

"Oh." Mother looked down at her yellow dress trying to decide its appropriateness. She looked up again at the children and then down again at her shoes. "Well," she said reluctantly.

"I'll,"—she hesitated—"take you," she said with surprised finality.

The children looked at each other in amazement. How in the world did exactly what they wanted to happen *happen*?

Mother put on a wrap and headed for the door. The children scooped up their bags and other items and quickly followed behind. Their mother's pace was a lot sharper than Umm Ridah's. Though Mother's hands fell casually at her sides as she walked. One jiggled and the other held a fist. Neither hand looked welcoming.

The children walked close behind, smiling and nodding at one another.

"Do you think she'll come in?" Mirella whispered to Alley.

"No."

"She might slow down a little. Maybe we could stop her in front of the school," Alley said. "All that matters is they get a look at her, but do you really think it's enough?" Alley was talking out loud. "She's American, isn't she?"

They continued behind their mother. When they had arrived within a few hundred feet of the school, a couple of other kids looked their way. The three of them looked at each other and simultaneously raced up to surround their mother. More kids looked their way. They were fifty feet from the school when they could no longer sustain their mother's pace without chasing her.

Of course, Mother kept walking. She was past the school when she heard one voice scream.

"Mother!!"

She couldn't stop herself at first, so used to her own momentum and then, "Mother! Mother!" Three voices were shouting so crazily that she stopped and looked back. It's the children. The children. Agnes turned around and walked back towards them.

"What is it, children?" she asked in a quiet calm voice, and right there on the street, in front of everyone, she rubbed Alley's face, and smoothed the little boy's hair. She touched Mirella's hand and waited right there in front of them.

Alley, Mirella, and the boy looked around to make sure that at least some of the children were watching and Alley

26

said loudly, "Nothing, Mother."

That was the last day any of the other children asked them about their origins and the first day Mrs. Thrace invited Umm Ridah to tea.

Umm Ridah came into the kitchen sometime after everyone left for school. She busied herself with her daily tasks, waiting to be scolded. In this household, it had not happened yet, but that didn't mean it wouldn't.

A few hours later, her surprise was physical when Mrs. Thrace leaned her head out of the sitting room as Umm Ridah came down the hall. Mrs. Thrace gestured and asked, "Shai? Would you like some tea?"

Umm Ridah continued into the room without altering her pace. She whisked her rag into her big utility pocket and stood on the threshold of the sitting room and hallway.

"Come in, please." Mrs. Thrace spoke in a heavier voice than Umm Ridah heard before.

Umm Ridah edged into the room but didn't sit down until Mrs. Thrace insisted.

"Please," she waved her hand towards the chair again.

Mrs. Thrace arranged the cup, plate, and poured the tea. She added spoonfuls of sugar with plenty of cream, a perfect cup of tea for Umm Ridah, who never turned down a good cup of tea.

Her mouth was already watering. Clearly, Mrs. Thrace could find and work her way around the kitchen and Umm Ridah. Some of her favorite English biscuits were on another small plate. Umm Ridah told herself she'd drink the tea and ignore her mistress. She sat down and was handed her cup.

Umm Ridah sipped slowly, bracing for the cruel words that she knew were about to come. The tea was so right that it caught her off guard; she might have even smiled a little and hoped the smile was one of those that she could feel but no one could see. She was three slow sips into the cup when she noticed that she hadn't heard Mrs. Thrace at all. At first, she congratulated herself on her ability to ignore her mistress but when she snuck a peek at her, she realized Mrs.

Thrace wasn't talking. She too was enjoying the tea and by the expression on her face, Umm Ridah guessed she'd made the tea just right for herself as well. Maybe better.

They drank slowly, in silence, each pretending not to pretend that the other wasn't there. Umm Ridah ate all the English biscuits before Mrs. Thrace balanced her cup upon her bottom lip, sighed, and spoke so quietly that Umm Ridah thought she was dreaming.

"Thank you"— Mrs. Thrace paused and then finished—"for taking such good care of the children," in a slow heavy tone.

Those were the first ten words of gratification spoken between the two women. Generally, Mrs. Thrace spoke to Umm Ridah with her back while she led her around the house.

Just now, for a few moments, Umm Ridah glanced at her front.

3

Berdeena

Mother lounged on the edge of their picnic blanket in the umbrella's shade and hardly moved except to unwrap the food baskets and lift her hand to mouth.

"Children, do you know which pyramid is which?" their father asked. "This one, Keop's, the Great Pyramid of Khufu is the oldest. Each block weighs approximately two and a half tons. You can see the differences in the smoothness of the stone."

"They are all lovely. Are they for sale?" Mirella asked sheepishly.

"I think the English and French might have borrowed them for a time," their father responded.

"Who'd want such a large grave?" Alley answered. "Imagine spending your whole life building your own grave. Maybe I'll make a monument to myself."

"You'll probably have to put it in our backyard." Mirella said.

"Why not? We should all be buried in our own backyards. The better to visit." Alley agreed. "But the Pyramids? Buy them just to say some fantastic piece of the world was yours."

"What should we put in the hole with you? You barely have anything," Mirella said.

"My suitcase but make it empty. Maybe I'll take some of

these cats from all over the place for company. But honestly, I think I'm going to travel in the opposite direction of most people. Instead of taking stuff with me, I'll bring it back."

"Good idea," Mirella, for once, agreed.

"The Pyramids belong to the Egyptians first and to the rest of the world after them. They belong to whoever has the luck to experience them," their father answered, moving the conversation back in the right direction.

Mother eased up on an elbow and ate another olive. Thrace cleared his throat and motioned to the young maid, who had brought the picnic goodies, to pour him a drink.

"Father, do you think pyramids were built by men?" Mirella asked.

"Yes, but no one knows how," Alley answered again.

"We believe we know why," Clifton Thrace began. The girls and their little brother sat back awaiting their father's explanation. His smooth tones cloaked the children, pulling them in a world that they could identify; they were a family with a father who knew everything.

Mother opened more wax paper packets of food, fingered off pieces of Roumy white cheese, wrapped flat bread around the cheese, and tore a large chunk with her teeth. She followed her first bite with another.

"Eat something, picnic," Mother's internal voice mocked and ordered her in its own flat tones. Often enough, food was her summons and by the time she had eaten a good two-thirds of the bread and most of the cheese, Mother felt better, more like herself. Good food restored her good nature. She eased up into a sitting position, stealing more blanket and sky, filling her corner with a different aura. She stretched, looked around, and slowly unwound herself, arching upwards which lengthened her shadow. Her bun collapsed in ringlets down the front of her shoulders, and she smiled wide.

Her stomach gurgled so loudly that the children wondered if Mother's stomach could talk but spoke a different language. Alley smiled and whispered to Mirella, "Musical mother." She recognized the gurgling.

Berdeena was a glutton just like her mother for whom she was similarly named, and their gluttony extended past food. She smiled at the children who blushed and looked at each other. Alley surprised herself with an involuntary clap of her hands and Mirella pinched her brother's cheek, pulling him closer.

"Let's circle these triangles," Berdeena laughed loud, stood up, and raised her palms.

"Come on, you. You're getting so big; I'm not going to know you."

Right in the middle of their father's lecture, the children jumped up and ran off with their mother, skipping and jogging around Egyptians and their Pyramids.

After the picnic, on the way home, Berdeena chastised them into singing some good old American songs.

In their reediest voices, the children sang with their mother.

"There's never a time when we can't find a song to sing," she told the children.

"Now, where were we?" Mother asked.

"When, Mother?"

"The last time we were singing."

"Ages ago," Mirella responded, looking up at her mother to gauge her reaction.

"Well, let's not waste any more time," she said. "Let's sing, let's eat, let's lazy!!" She swayed from side to side, next to the children in the back seat of the car.

Berdeena loved to sing, eat, cook, and lie under Mr. Thrace. These were the four things she most wanted to do in any order. Nighttime and bedding Mr. Thrace suited her temperament. She loved the sun, too, but she hated chores and the day always had a waiting list whereas everyone was expected to be supine in the dark.

Growing up, her favorite thing to do was "lazy" with her mother, Aberdeen, who was usually a very hard worker but whenever Berdeena was around, they spent their time together in the singular pursuit of more sitting around. Mostly, they "lazied," as they called their days of doing nothing. Or, at a certain time, known only to themselves, the two of them would jump up and cook enormous amounts of food. Every scrap of food in the house would disappear into a secret recipe. And then, though there were never any witnesses, they consumed everything they prepared, gorging themselves until their stomachs were distended painful arcs, and all they could do was breathe slowly and sing.

> Greens, greens, magical greens,
> the more you eat the more it means.
> Waxy, dark, fulfilling like wine
> A cinnamony thrill for an errant mind . . .
> Greens, greens, magical greens . . .

Berdeena's songs were mostly about food and conjured whenever she felt like singing. She taught her crazy songs to the children.

Mr. Thrace rolled up the car windows and sat up front with the driver. At times, his wife could be a marvel and a fright. She was a book that he hated to admit he was reading but couldn't put down. Every once in a while, he worried about the relationship between his wife and the children. Did she fill their heads with nonsense or with anything at all?

He sat up front staring ahead, ignoring the quartet sitting in back. Children were extremely adaptable creatures, he thought. He even envied them this skill. Two hours ago, they were tiptoeing around their mother; now they were dancing and snapping to the tunes of ridiculous songs.

Before now, Clifton Thrace had no idea that his children possessed such loud voices. They seemed mouse-like to him. Though he couldn't quite turn around and participate, he was glad that their mother could.

At home, they continued into the house with their songs.

"I'm cooking tonight," Berdeena announced and ordered the kids about the kitchen.

"You, Missy A, get the biggest pot you can find, fill it almost to the top with water, and put it on for boiling. We're going to cut up some things and throw them in the pot."

"Missy M, pick some good onions and celery."

"Don't just stand there, Little Man," she said to the boy. "You can read can't you? Tell me what's in the pantry."

"Not well," Alley answered for her brother.

"Well then, you get to be the double eye," Berdeena said. "Tell me the Missies are doing everything right!"

Banging pots and the clanging of kitchen drawers could be heard throughout the house. Clifton retired to his library. He could still hear their voices. How she could be a vulgar songstress one day and a picture of grace the next, Mr. Thrace thought, added to her charm. She seemed to know exactly where to put things. Her anger, had she felt any, she put away very quietly, as he had never been a witness to it. She was equally secretive with the rest of her emotions. On the whole, she was a very even creature, often quieter than he might have expected and he felt a little guilty patting himself on the back for sending up a thankful prayer or two about her nether parts. Pleasing and giving, she had never once declined his touch. She seemed eager—though never too eager—and never openly. She had been exactly the sort of wife he'd wanted, and he hadn't had to do anything at all except pick her up and drive her away from that mountain where he found her.

Honestly, he needed to pinch and remind himself never to disturb "what luck or the Lord had wrought," the supposed family homily that had been constantly invoked by his father, attributed to Thrace's grandfather.

"Son, respect what luck or the Lord hath wrought."

Clifton Maxwell Thrace's father and grandfather, one more severe than the other, liked to play with credit, giving and assuming as they pleased. Either God had provided or they had worked very hard. One statement precluded the other, but his father and grandfather used both. As a young boy, if he'd been overheard asking God for a hunting gun in his prayers, one of them would answer,

"Son, I do the providing in *this* house." But if he'd asked why they had meat every day when most of the other families didn't, one of them might answer, "Son, God provides." Then they'd want to know how he knew about other families and if he'd told other families about them. He'd never be sure what answer they'd want but "no" was generally a safe bet as in "no, he didn't know anything about any other families and no, he'd never said anything about his own."

They were confusing and unaffectionate men, especially to a small inquisitive boy. His father and grandfather hid everything—their affection, their smiles, their pocketbooks. Thrace had inherited the limitations of having grown up with men who were so closely akin in word and mind. They had managed to pass their skills onto Thrace through osmosis and he would have never noticed how very much like them he had become. In the end, death had opened their pocketbooks and yielded all their other assets to Clifton.

The confluence of his memories, like deep and shallow waters greeting each other, kitchen sounds, and his family's noise trickling under his door brought him back to the present. He was where he was comfortable—alone, sitting amongst his things, just as he had when he was a little boy. Commingled voices of his father and grandfather, scents of food, the women whispering, and kitchen clangs and bangs had swirled around his childhood bedroom.

As a young man, in the only household he'd known, he believed holding a little of the world in his hands might be possible. Before dinner, a young man should lie down with his thoughts. That idea came from his grandmother. They had spoiled him, not with affection and sweetness, but with what was and wasn't going to be, with the conviction of who he was to be in the world. He was a Thrace. Thraces did what they were supposed to and shut up about it. Thraces educated themselves, had owned and read books throughout the 1800s, and didn't think Phyllis Wheatley was a shock or a miracle. Thraces worked hard, played little—very little—owned property, married carefully, and produced children (but not too many). Above all, Thraces kept their own secrets.

Thrace had had no opportunity or reason to be anyone other than himself. His wife was his first mystery, and he knew enough to know that mysteries unfolded, and all a man had to do was let them.

His thoughts were interrupted by a call from the kitchen.

"Oh, Dear, come and eat!" Berdeena knew that no one could resist her chicken and dumplings even after they'd seen the messes she'd made, spreading whatever she was cooking all over everything. The children set the kitchen table and invited their father to sit at the head. They sang him into his seat, and he didn't have to remind them not to sing, once seated. Thrace remembered that they had only just eaten. He wasn't even hungry until he tasted a dumpling and then he couldn't help himself.

They ate with such abandon that hungry pigs at a trough may have grunted and snuffled with less noise. They ate every single scrap of food and then found themselves bloated, uncomfortable, and almost completely unable to move. The pile of dumplings had been so large that they hadn't been able to see over them. Now, they stared at each other over dough pieces and dripped gravy splattered in abstract droppings on the table between them. Each had eaten until the last dumpling was gone—reaching, spilling, chewing, and swallowing. Only the evidence of food was left sprinkled all over the table, the plates, their laps, and even the floor. The mad eating party had come and gone like a wave, leaving five Thraces pushed back in their chairs with stomachs so tight their legs wouldn't move.

Mr. Thrace was embarrassed but pretended that he wasn't. He hadn't kept count of his own intake until the food was all gone and then he reasoned he must have had more than anyone because he was larger than everyone. His immobility forced him to ponder how, indeed, he had managed to get himself stuck at the kitchen table.

Berdeena began to hum and then, ever so softly, she sang out in a steady contralto, eerily smooth and clear. She soloed first.

I have traveled from an unknown place, here to eat with
    you.
It's not easy, to understand or explain, but here we are
    once again …

She stopped and nodded to the three children as if her refrain was only introductory, and then they joined her when she signaled that they'd go back to the song they'd started together earlier, each of them taking a turn, making up their own verses until they sang the chorus together.

Greens, greens, magical greens
the more you eat, the more it means
Salty, lovely, cinnamony sweet
Whenever mom makes them, we love to eat.
Oh, how'd she learn to cook with such magic …

The boy chimed in when his sisters took too long.

Does this mean there will be a tragic?

Berdeena laughed and started again.

My mama stirred greens from her stool, sitting low.
Can you take us three to the picture show?

Alley added the last line and laughed.

Berdeena and the children sang and sang and then they got up.

"La la la la la's" floated from all parts of the house.

Berdeena ran water for one big bath. She liked the house empty of servants and generally and politely sent them away, even Umm Ridah. They were not always happy when they returned because the one thing Berdeena didn't do too much was clean. She loved to make a mess but didn't often tidy up after herself.

After putting the children to bed, Berdeena sat in the

bedroom a few minutes laughing, and rolling about on the bed before she went back down to the kitchen to rescue Mr. Thrace from his slow digestion. He was unable to move. Of course, he could have started singing with the rest of them. Singing worked. They had all been stuffed and now they were fine. Luckily, Berdeena had other remedies.

"If you could sing, you'd be free." She tried not to look at Thrace so she wouldn't laugh. She brushed some flour off his shoulder and smiled to herself.

Her dress felt a little tighter; she shimmied, pulling down the skirt a bit and thought Mr. Thrace's eyes crinkled. He smiled and gently moved forward.

It was against her nature but Berdeena began to gather up dishes. She reached across the table, exposing the smooth bar of her arm behind the delicate curve of her breast.

His right foot moved forward. She stood back up, her smooth flat belly at his side. Slim and tall, she was quite elegant, no matter the crumbs in her hands, or gravy stained on her dress. She carried the dishes to the sink, skirt swaying. Her tune breathed out and Thrace sucked in her music. She wiped flour off the counters and pushed crumbs into her hand. She moved about the kitchen and he slowly rose from his seat at the head of the table.

He walked across the kitchen, trapping her in the corner where the food cabinets met the ones with the dishes. He pressed himself against her and she let out a startled sigh. He leaned in and forced her to arch.

She knew he was coming.

In the morning, Berdeena was left with the children and the maids returned.

"Mother, will you sit with us for breakfast?" Alley asked.

"Of course," Berdeena answered.

When Mother was musical, she was given to excess. If she cooked breakfast, pancakes would probably be everywhere, syrup and butter too. Everyone would be compelled to eat them all and God knows when they'd get to school.

If the Mother who was in the mood to sing accompanied them to school, she'd probably start singing loudly, outside.

"Mother, would you walk to school with us again? Quietly, no singing?" she whispered. "Please?" Alley asked carefully, standing up.

"Of course we can," Mother answered and then she reached back, as if she'd forgotten something she needed to pull off the wall and headed out the door.

"Maybe Balloon Brother will come too?" Berdeena asked.

The children did not hear their Mother which was perfectly alright since she wasn't talking to them.

Berdeena's "Brother" was a balloon-like presence tethered to her arm, happily now floating high above her head. He was the ghost of her little brother who died young and grew up afterwards, Berdeena assumed, in a ghost family all his own. He didn't seem to know their family. She'd asked him about their other dead relatives like Great-Grandmother Selsie and Lloyd Earl but he didn't answer those kinds of questions. In fact, he didn't really answer questions at all.

On their first walk in Cairo, he asked if she still remembered how to cook which made Berdeena think of their mother.

"Daughter, you eat too well not to cook. At twelve, you ought to have a feast in your hands," Aberdeen said.

Berdeena had been reluctant to learn at first. Cooking looked easy enough to be difficult and the lessons began with her lying lazily on the kitchen floor looking up, listening to her mother. When she couldn't see what her mother was doing from her low position, she grabbed the rolling lounge chair so that she could comfortably watch. Generally, she fell asleep right after her mother began, as if cooking were some sort of lullaby, and then later she would awaken out in the backyard, or in front of the house, opening her eyelids to the fields. Once she found herself near the road where, if she had been awake, she may have seen the kudzu crossing. And there was even a time that she found herself on top of her lounging chair straddling the tiny creek that gurgled up only after days of rain.

"If a girl wants to learn how to cook, staying awake is the beginning part," Aberdeen had warned her.

That was a long time ago, when her brother had a few more talents than being a balloon. She was sure he was the one who had dragged her table all over the place after she fell asleep. Rolling her around and leaving her in strange places was his idea. What she couldn't quite get past was the notion that Aberdeen would be in cahoots with him. She'd never before exhibited any taste for practical jokes.

For a while, Berdeena was afraid to fall asleep for fear of waking too far from where she had fallen asleep in the first place. When she raced back to the house to eat, the food was always gone.

"Seems you might want to stay awake and stay home if you want to eat," her mother told her.

Childhood left her with an unending appetite and food became her constant. Berdeena was rarely around if food wasn't coming, hadn't already arrived, or wasn't being prepared, planned, or discussed. She had a bottomless pit for a stomach, an ache she was unable to sate, and she began to believe that her stomach fed someone besides herself. When he was alive, her little brother ate up everything. Now, she ate for the two of them, him with his invisible stomach, and nothing but a big balloon head that only she could see. And when she couldn't see him, she often wondered if the only place he had ever really lived was in her mind and memory.

Berdeena didn't trouble herself with too many whys. Who knew that the living could be so intimately linked with the dead? Anyway, besides her mother, whom she'd never ever spoken to about her brother after he died, she felt sure that no one else in the world remembered him and Aberdeen was on the other side the world.

Somewhere in adolescence, after brother stopped playing tricks on her, they had become the closest of friends. Berdeena didn't remember exactly when that was. Sometime between when she could see him running around and when she couldn't. He had adjusted to his state. After all, Berdeena wasn't to blame for his condition. Both invisibility and death had detractions but the fact that he couldn't walk and was totally dependent upon Berdeena to get around the world didn't seem to bother him one bit. She walked all over Cairo with him tethered to her wrist, soaring up behind, tarnishing the sky with his yellowed edges.

Berdeena walked towards the school, dropped off the kids, and disappeared for the rest of the day.

On those days, on any day, no one knew what she did all day outside her own house. She didn't have any friends. She never received phone calls or visitors and she never came back with anything at all except for her own exhaustion which made it impossible for her to do anything but retreat to the bedroom.

Every so often, she would lie in bed all day, motionless, letting the time go.

Vacation with Everyone at the Red Sea

Alley was becoming friends with another little girl at school, Hala, whom she thought, had a traditional family. Not that Alley knew exactly what that was and Hala, more than anything else, was interested in all things "American." Together, they were two little girls who were hungry for what they each thought the other had. The perfect ingredients for making a great friendship were present, yet each one wanted the friendship to take place at the other's house and neither of them was getting what they wanted which was a long comfortable look inside the other's home.

"Let's go to your house today," Hala suggested.

"We went to my house yesterday."

"And mine too ..."

"But only for a moment," Alley reminded her new friend.

"Why don't we spend this afternoon at your house and tomorrow at mine?"

"Because tomorrow never comes," Alley said.

"Alright, we'll stay outside and tell each other stories."

For one thing, to Alley, Hala's mother seemed extraordinary.

Hala spoke to her mother whenever she wanted and her mother answered. There didn't seem to be that barely perceptible moment of confusion and uncertainty that existed between Alley, her siblings, and their mother—the moments when they stood by and waited to see how Mother might move, indicating her mood, before they could act.

"What mother holds you for hours without saying anything?"

"Who cares? We like being held," Mirella answered easily.

"What about being talked to?" Alley asked.

"She talks to us," Mirella said.

"When?"

"When she wants to," Mirella answered.

"That's the point. What about when *we* want to?" Alley pressed.

"Well, what do you do when you want to talk to her?" Mirella asked, and Alley didn't want to answer but if she had, she would have said, "sulk."

One afternoon, and it was bound to eventually happen, the children came together to knock on their mother's door.

"Yes?"

Alley opened the door. If mother wasn't singing, cooking, or wearing her yellow dress, most likely she was in her bedroom. Alley confirmed Mother's shape beneath the covers.

"Come in, come in," she waved them over to her bed.

Undone by memory again, and though the children couldn't tell, Selma's head was resting in the corner where one wall met the other, so high up that had her body been beneath it, she could have been eight feet tall. Her waist, behind, and legs occupied a chair in the opposite corner. One hand rubbed the other at the small vanity table and her feet hid in slippers parallel to one another beneath the vanity chair.

Mother's oddness in that very moment made Alley wonder what possessed her to agree to asking if anyone could spend the night with them. One night, she thought, would be enough. If she could spend one night in Hala's household, she'd see the differences between their families. Maybe she could get her own night out and then postpone Hala's. Then Mirella surprised everyone when she spoke up first.

"Can we go to the Red Sea?"

"Yeah, can we?" the boy echoed. Then Alley butted in.

"Can I go to the mosque and spend the night with Hala on Friday?"

"Not really," Mother said.

'Not really what,' Alley wondered. Was she answering them or talking about something else?

"My mama said you never had to be lonely living in the woods. Trees were better company than most folk. She would come back from the woods full of stories. Mama always said one of her trees had something for me. Which tree? I asked. Then she'd describe a certain tree. Selma, walk straight down the cut path 'til you get to where the creek would be if it were to rain, step on by, and walk about thirty, forty feet. That old oak with the big west-facing bough got something to tell. He's got three twisted knots on his stomach and a sagging face. You can't miss the knots."

"I ran right off. Mama always made the trees' messages special. I found the three-knotted tree with the west-facing bough, but the tree didn't tell me anything. I ran back and told Mama. She asked if it was the same oak with the lightning scar covering a good three-quarters of his upper trunk. Some of her trees were ladies and some gentleman. Some seemed to be both lady and man."

"She'd always leave out a crucial detail in the first description. But if I didn't find the tree the first time, it was always too late. Trees never held onto their messages for very long. Mama would think and promise to try and remember to tell me what the tree might have had to say." Mother quieted down.

"Well"—having lost a little of her patience, Alley asked—"did the trees ever speak directly to you?"

Mother had started with the answer.

"You know," she said to Alley, "you always ask the right

questions."

Alley beamed, warmth shot through to her insides. She couldn't remember another compliment ever, from her mother.

Eventually, their father came to the rescue. He had decided on a trip to the Red Sea. He was going to surprise them and hadn't let anyone in on his secret except for Umm Ridah, who had been secretly packing all week. For this trip, she would join them as she had never before spent a month by the sea.

The drive to the sea from Cairo was dry and mostly flat. Hours after leaving Cairo, before them in the distance lay a shimmering horizon. Tiny spots of sun-reflecting glass slowly emerged in the distance as they approached. At first, the light hurt everyone's eyes but the very idea of spending time by the sea filled them all with an inscrutable and physical anticipation.

"Can we walk down to the water?" Alley asked first.

"Can we?" Mirella second.

Mirella and Alley grabbed their father's hands and they proceeded toward the sea, their brother behind them, Mother, last.

By early evening, some of the baked-in heat would have escaped. Egyptian sand was still warm in the early evening, several yards from the shoreline. The distance was a mirage and the sea was further than it seemed, particularly with such slow progress, except for Mother who passed them all, walking an even pace yards ahead. They watched her back, waiting for a sign that she had reached the sea. But instead of going straight she suddenly veered to the right and continued walking.

"Do you think Mother knows where she's going?" Alley asked her father.

"She probably won't go too far right now," their father answered.

"What if she gets lost?" Alley feared that Mother would start walking and never come back.

"She has an innate sense of direction. People raised in rural places often do," Mr. Thrace said calmly.

As they made their way closer to the water, the sand ground soft and fine. The sea had done all beachcombers a favor and they stopped at the edge, close enough for the sea to pass over their feet and ankles and retreat.

"If we stayed here long enough, the ocean would take us in and later push us back out," Mr. Thrace told his children.

Mr. Thrace was not on vacation. He had come to oversee some land conservation projects. So just as in Cairo, he would be gone for most of the day and the children were left with Umm Ridah and their mother.

Days at the sea were longer than days at home, framed by the hours the children spent conquering and naming sand dunes, building and destroying castles, and the time it took Umm Ridah to drag them away from the ocean and back into the house. Mother could sometimes be seen far in the distance or perhaps she passed directly in front of her family, always moving, her walk deliberate with some unknown purpose.

Mr. Thrace was surveying and so was she. He was surveying the land, measuring the rate of erosion; she was surveying the sea, weighing the strength of water, as water had sometimes figured in her own mother's constant admonitions. She could hear the percussion of water creeping through rocks.

"Wash out bad thoughts same as washing dirt out the dirty clothes ... wash through ideas with the dishes. Water down that hunger and the grass while you're at it." Aberdeen had a litany for Selma's every mood.

Water had soaked her mind away and hid it in a closed ecosystem. Maybe if she bathed in the ocean she would be able to retrieve her memory. The ocean was a sea of memories salted by the tears of people because the sad outweighed the happy ones. Selma was walking up and down the shoreline looking for a way into the water. She wasn't interested in the past; she wanted the present. So often, she seemed to wake up already in the middle of something she hadn't begun. Order had disappeared and if there were a time line, the minutes were separated from the hours and events from dates so that a month ago was as far away as ten years past.

She had been married for several years now and still didn't know how it happened. Selma had always liked the opposite sex. She had preferred the company of little boys from a very early age and could sometimes picture her old school room and most of the other students. Yet, she couldn't remember a single child that went to school with these three children who were supposed to belong to her. They were odd and amusing creatures but for someone more interested than she. They weren't bad company, and they weren't difficult to look at; they kind of had a warmth to them and honestly, she didn't mind having them around. Mostly, they sat quietly and listened to her stories, making them better listeners than anyone else in the household.

Back when she was young, Malty had been her chosen boy. They spent hours and hours, even whole summers together. She guessed people said they were friends because they both lived up in the woods and no one saw any of their other family members on a regular basis.

Selma and Malty used to touch each other up in the woods, usually up in one tree or another. It was always Malty's idea. For Selma, one day she was up in a tree with Malty and then she was under a man on a honeymoon. The first thing she had to do was turn on the lights and make sure that she hadn't married Malty. She loved him but she had promised herself, even after she licked him, that she would leave the woods.

Malty, lovely as he was (Malton McIntired Jessup, the Fourth was his entire name. His siblings had put the "d" on his middle name as a joke, and he had added "the Fourth," because he was the fourth child.), was such a natural fit, sitting in a tree, that Selma couldn't imagine him ever leaving the woods for good. He'd probably tease her with a little stay in the city and then force her back up into some mud-floored two-room. Malton was a song whose melody was so sweet she didn't notice, at first, how silly the lyrics were. She did wonder about him sometimes, sure that if he'd been capable of living outside the woods, she'd be somewhere living with him.

When she upped the lights and saw Thrace, she commended herself for a job well done. Sometimes, she wanted to know how she and Thrace got together. She told herself that Clifton Maxwell Thrace took one look at her and fell madly in love. But since she had been married to him, it seemed unlikely that he would ever act so haphazardly. Then she told herself "he looked at me twice." Sometimes, she didn't want to know, and the desire went away.

At the Red Sea, her first preoccupation was to get into the water. She would stand on her tiptoes, arched, a novice diver about to plunge. There, she stayed. Her hesitancy may have had something to do with the fear of bashing her head in the sand. Swim? She couldn't quite remember whether she knew how or not but guessed that what people said about riding bicycles applied to swimming. Equally unsure of her bicycling abilities, she reasoned that not owning one didn't mean that she hadn't learned to ride.

Her style of getting into the water kept her searching for an appropriate place along the shore. The water needed to stay deep and move slow. She imagined swimming through memory and catching hold. There would be the facts on her marriage to Clifton Thrace, the details on the birth of three children and perhaps the why of so many other things. She had walked up and down the shoreline looking for deep slow water. Her feet had grown calloused and easily scraped over the rocky hot sand.

Walking next to the sea, she realized how simultaneously playful and stingy moving water could be. She'd hear the rush of it going nowhere. The ocean bubbled and lathered like detergent but always left behind a dirty signature. It looked deep where it was shallow and shallow where it was deep. The waves played with her, same as her memory did without giving up one iota of information. The ocean sang, ringing out threats, "this water could salt and dry her." Up above, the sun threw out great yellow bars marking the sea with glimmering painful light. She couldn't look. The sea continued to sing, displaying only a small fringe and then sheltered three-quarters of the earth in an ever-deepening secrecy.

Selma was still looking for a place to get herself in when a body rolled up and had itself spun out of the waves and onto the shore. The sea had been a carpet and now unfolded its baggage.

4

Martha, the Detective

Then Martha showed up and took over. She called herself Martha, the Detective. She fancied herself good at getting to the bottom of things. Generally, she only stayed long enough to leave a bad impression. Her memory was chock full of her own dislikes and she disliked everything, which was the surest way to "know herself." Of course, Martha didn't like dead bodies and she didn't like the ocean either, or for that matter, sand.

Someone needed to move the body so that she could figure out what had happened. The victim seemed to be a young girl from the village. The victims were always young girls from the village and Martha wondered if there were not something clumsy about them that allowed them to keep getting themselves killed.

Fortunately, none of the authorities in the immediate vicinity understood English. Martha insinuated her way into the process of moving the body and was tolerated as the visiting guest, wife of the American attaché. No one had any intention of doing anything other than what had always been done. They were going to take the body to the British doctor who lived nearby. But they had never had a surprise death roll out of the sea before, and they'd never had an American family staying at the sea at the same time, so the coincidence of the two together, bodies and visiting Americans, didn't seem entirely unnatural.

Martha formed part of this strange entourage following behind a body on a cart being dragged by a donkey. She had the added authority of having been at the scene when the sea gave up the body. She had no idea where they were going or why, but she was sure that she would be needed. A couple of villagers were ahead of them. They didn't seem to be familiar with whoever it was that had ceased to be a person and became the body. They'd simply come upon Martha and the body on the beach. Why they already had a cart was clearly their other occupation. This small entourage made a first stop at a gathering of gentlemen drinking tea. They were hunched around a small table; delicately etched glasses sat in front of each of the three men. After an indecipherable exchange, two of the men quickly joined the crowd and they moved on to a second stop, just a few yards away in front of a small house where two women stepped out and another indecipherable exchange took place. Finally, the group wheeled further down the road in front of a very distinguished house. One of the party knocked and after a time, an old gentleman pulled the door open. He was so crusty that his origins weren't immediately apparent. He wore a knee length whitish coat.

"Good morning," he said in British accented English. He had a white cloth between his hands, and he wiped them, as if he had taken time to wash them before opening the door. He surveyed the crowd and changed expressions when he landed upon Mrs. Thrace.

"Yes, yes hello is it? I'm Dr. ???!"

Martha nodded. The gentleman lifted his cloth as his reason for not being able to shake hands. "Dr. ???" was so garbled that she couldn't make out his name. Was he British with the dust of Cairo, or Egyptian with airs of Sussex?

"Yes. Yes, well what do we have here?"

He listened as the other men explained about the body and motioned to the covered cart and to Mrs. Thrace. He walked over and pulled back the cloth.

"Why, what is this?" Dr.?? began carefully examining the body with his eyes, slowly walking around the table.

Martha was working out what happened in her own mind. Had the young woman tripped and been knocked unconscious near the soft sand next to the water? Then the waves picked her up but did not wake her up and sucked her in over the next few hours. Impossible. Martha expected nothing less than a cover-up. What's more, no one seemed to know who the body was, and no one seemed to be missing. Martha wondered why village girls always went to other villages to have themselves killed. The doctor needed to examine the body and find a means of death. Surely, there was a knife, a rope ring around her neck, or some hole or rather obvious disturbance in an otherwise young and healthy body.

In Martha's experience, these cases were always strange.

A few children had caught up to the group and were standing around. Mrs. Thrace stood in the middle of them all, staring intently at the doctor while the children stared more at Mrs. Thrace. The men carried the wet body inside, which took a little maneuvering without the donkey, and laid it down in the doctor's make-do laboratory. Then they backed their way out of the doctor's house, all except for Mrs. Thrace, and two of the little children, remaining too curious to leave.

The doctor removed the cloaks draped over the body, cut off some wet reeds that seemed to have wrapped around most of the body and said, "It doesn't seem to be human."

He left the body in the middle of his room while he walked around to his desk, rummaged through his drawer for a tape reel, and put it into a player. He pressed a button; the reel began a slow whirl, and he began.

"The carcass of an unknown creature has washed up on the Hurghada shore. Approximately human sized, oddly limbed, and . . . "

Martha didn't listen wholeheartedly. The doctor was talking too fast to be carefully examining the body and recording his results way too sanctimoniously. Mostly, he was talking and another thing that Martha, the Detective, disliked was "talking."

"approximately 60 to 64 inches long."

Martha was sure that she would be the one to remove the "approximatelys." Clearly, she was the one who wanted answers.

"no obvious cause of death. Perhaps natural causes, will have necropsy performed to determine . . ."

There would be no satisfaction in the truth, but it wouldn't stop Martha from getting at it one way or another. The one good thing about the doctor's report is that no one else would investigate anything. The way would be clear for Martha. While everyone else busied themselves lamenting the harshness of life, blaming God for the vagaries of what they assumed were accidents, Martha would unearth the truth.

Martha was never to be seen without a pencil in her pocket, the air of a question mark above her head, and a pad nearby. She was constantly scribbling something that she wouldn't let anyone see.

"What are you doing, Mother?"

"Working."

"You have a job?" Alley asked.

The three of them looked at each other.

"Of course I have a job. Who else is going to get to the bottom of things? No one else ever cares." Martha didn't like children any better than she liked anything else, but she knew them to be quite observant even if they generally had no idea what they were seeing.

"What kind of things?" Alley questioned her mother again.

"Mostly, the untimely deaths of rural people. Now, let me ask you a couple of questions." Alley looked at her sister and brother again. Mother plucked the pencil up into her left hand and turned toward them.

"Can you write left-handed?" Alley asked.

"Of course, can't you?" Mother asked.

"No."

"Well, it's always one or the other," Mother said. "Have you seen anyone walking along the shore?"

"Besides you?" Mirella asked.

"Yes, of course, besides me."

"Us?" Alley pointed at herself and her siblings.

"Not you. Anybody else?"

"Father?" Mirella spoke up quickly.

"Have you seen him on the beach?"

"He takes walks at dawn," Mirella answered.

"Have you seen him?"

"Umm Ridah told us he walked, too, but real early," Alley answered.

"Did you see him?"

"Maybe. Once we tried to get up early enough to go with him. We went to the door, but his boots were already gone," Mirella explained.

"His boots? He wears boots to walk on the beach? Did you see him?" Mother erased something on her pad.

"We think it was him. It is hard to tell from here. We saw someone on the beach and Father's boots were gone," Mirella answered.

"But we're not sure it was him on the beach," Alley mentioned, thinking it important.

"Now, let's take this one at a time. Girls first. Bigger one," she pointed at Alley. "What exactly did you see?" She attempted to smile encouragement.

"Nothing."

"What do you mean nothing?"

"Well, they got up and I was late. By the time I got there, Daddy or whoever was walking was just a dot."

"Would you recognize his boots?"

"Daddy's boots?"

"Yes. Were they gone very early in the morning?"

"Yes." Alley hoped she had finished. She didn't like such a strangely curious Mother, even if she was giving them attention.

"Middle?" she called. These children were three sizes.

"Yes?" Mirella answered.

"What did you see?"

"I don't sleep too well."

"Are you in the habit of seeing or hearing things in the middle of the night?"

"Umm Ridah says I sleepwalk and talk and don't know the difference?"

"Really? Did you sleep-hear or sleep-see anyone walking on the beach last night?"

"I only saw shadows. But I saw Daddy put on his boots and leave."

"Where were you?"

"I watched from the hallway, but it was dark between us and I didn't want to walk in the darkness by myself," Mirella explained.

"Did you see him leave?"

"That's when I went back to bed."

"How do you know he went to the beach?"

"Umm Ridah told us," in unison, Alley and Mirella answered.

Mother took one glance at the boy but didn't ask him any questions.

"She must have eaten something odd," Alley said to her siblings in her voice that purposefully could be funny or not.

Mother turned away from them and began writing even faster than when she had been talking to them.

Martha couldn't control anything except the fact that if a dead body appeared, so, it seemed, did she.

Shortly after she'd questioned the children, her memories began traveling to the surface from wherever they had been. Martha slid the pad and pencil in her pocket, sat back and let the past replay, accompanied by the children's voices.

"What did she mean 'deaths'? What deaths is she talking about?" Alley asked Mirella.

"Rural deaths, what's that mean?" the boy asked his big sisters.

"She means it as a symbol, an end of something," Alley explained to her brother and sister.

"An end? What kind of job is that? How do you get to the bottom of the end of something?" Mirella wanted to know.

"She must be very clever indeed."

"Stop making fun, Alley."

"Why should I stop? Isn't that what she was doing? Making fun?" Alley answered. "Scribbling with the wrong hand."

"She's ambidextrous."

"Sure she is," Alley said.

"Me too," their little brother said, "I can do things with both hands."

"You don't think Mother could be some sort of detective?" Mirella asked.

"Detective?" Alley repeated after her sister.

"What about a spy?" Mirella changed their mother's job.

"A spy?" Alley, and her sister followed by their little brother burst into laughter.

Then Martha's memory overtook all contemporary things.

Everybody talked about love but that didn't make sense to Martha. She remembered how crazily people behaved and how everybody in the whole town didn't want to do anything about the body she'd seen except hope it wasn't true. She didn't know what they meant by what some said, "something about passion or just plain cruelty." To Martha, the words sounded tasty, like a dish she was supposed to eat.

She had found the proverbial village girl's body swinging from a Sylph tree. She recognized the tree because her mother had described them before, though this was the first time she had ever seen one which was part of the reason that she could not leave well enough alone. She wanted to prove, for once, that she could identify a tree. Her mother had told her that knowing about trees was a special art. Her mother had told her that everything in the trees ought to be left alone. Aberdeen made tree stuff out to be so magical that Martha sometimes wished that she believed what the townsfolk said about Aberdeen being raised by the "Witch of the Woods," Martha's great-grandmother, Selsie. Most of the time Aberdeen and all her ways made Martha feel odd. She never could live up to her birthright. All she knew about the woods was nothing and most of the time she couldn't wait to get out of them to school. Hurrying must have been why she found the body all by herself. She had probably gotten lost and Malty, that weird boy, was no friend of Martha's. He had told her plenty of times not to play or come detecting around him. He said she gave him the willies with them names she named herself.

As soon as Martha saw the body, she started running and emerged from the woods at the edge of town rather than home. Whenever she veered off the tried-and-true path, she discovered something. Today, she had seen a body and if she had come to the clearing near home, things might have been different.

Running and sweating, she cleared the last tree and came up behind the school. Luckily, the teacher was still inside when she burst into the classroom.

"There's a body in the woods."

"What?"

"There's a body in the woods."

"Well, who is it child?"

"I don't know," Martha answered.

Mrs. Jefferson found it hard to believe. For one thing, everybody knew everybody—white, black, and in between. Mrs. Jefferson taught everyone, but if she could pick her class, she might have left out the strange ones that came out of the woods. They were truly odd and she didn't know whether they would benefit from her hard work.

"Now, who could be dead up in the woods? How are they dead? In the ground?"

"Hanging from a Sylph tree," Martha answered.

"A sif tree?" she never heard of a tree with that name, but she'd heard of lynching.

"Lynched?"

"Hanging," Martha repeated.

"Let's tell the Reverend."

Martha would always remember that conversation. Her memory of the rest of the words exchanged was probably a little fuzzy, but Martha could remember the gist.

The Reverend gathered the men that he could and asked her to direct them back to the body. She didn't have to go all the way, but she had to get them there. Martha began walking and thinking. She knew she was going in the general direction from where she'd come, but she wanted to explain to everyone that she was not good in the woods. More than anything she was afraid of the woods and as she walked further and further into them, she began to feel more and more unsettled, not just by the strange moving shadows of trees. She sensed her mother's anger. Aberdeen would be furious that she had led a pack of people into her beloved forest. She would be particularly angry that Martha had disturbed the woods with townsfolk, especially as she might have blamed the dead body on another one of Martha's what she'd called "PEEculiars," or was it the "family legacy?" Martha couldn't be sure which one. Aberdeen was always trying out words and she used to say that pure lunacy was either going to get Martha very far in the world or in trouble. The "PEEculiars" had something to do with her behavior. They said she was so "PEEculiar" from one week to the next and at the moment, Martha was thinking that right now she must have been in pure lunacy because she felt sure she was headed toward trouble. What if she couldn't even find the body? She plodded on, sloshing through the wet undergrowth, muddying her shoes, searching for a body that she couldn't even describe. The townsfolk kept asking her questions, Deacon Fielder more than anyone else.

"Who was it?"

"I don't know." She noticed that Mrs. Jefferson didn't come to her rescue.

"Was it male or female?" Deacon Fielder asked.

"I don't know."

"Well, what was it wearing? Was it a dress or pants? What color was it wearing?" Deacon Fielder pressed on.

"I don't know."

"What about its head? Did it have woman hair, long, or short hair?" Deacon Fielder asked.

"I don't know." All the questions just made Martha understand how much she had missed. She didn't know. As soon as she saw the shadow, she ran as fast as she could. She hadn't realized she was supposed to stay long enough to examine the body.

The Reverend finally bumped Deacon Fielder and gestured that he was to leave Martha alone. He whispered to the Deacon, "Surely the white folk hadn't lynched anybody so far into the woods. No, white folks probably hadn't done it 'cause they wouldn't take the trouble to carry no black man this far up into the woods. Then again, maybe a young black man had run this far before they caught him, and they lynched him right where they got him."

"What's a Sylph tree?" Deacon Fielder started. The Right Reverend bumped him again, but Martha had stopped answering questions. She was going to show them the body and then she was going home. She realized she was taking them in the right direction as she had seen a familiar tree, plus it smelled exactly the way it did when she ran through this section the first time, raw and rotten. Mama said that when the forest smelled, it was because it hadn't finished something it was doing. She hadn't noticed or remembered until now. Mama said the forest was composing, making one thing out of another. All Martha needed was the smell in the woods to point her in the right direction. In approximately ten yards, they'd be standing right where the body was hanging.

When they got there, Martha pointed up and they could see a rope knotted into a noose hanging a few feet down before it broke off. On the ground, they could see a depression in the mud where a heavy body might have been, and they could see a set or two of footprints circling about the tree trunk. What they couldn't see was a body.

"That's where it was."

As far as Martha was concerned, she had done her duty and she was going home. They'd look around and find the body or not, but either way, she was done. "Deed is done, deed is done," she repeated as she walked.

"Deed is done," she was alone again walking towards home. "Deed is done, deed is done," sounded fun and she enjoyed saying the same words over and over, making them true. That's what repetition did. It made things true.

Until the next morning, when she heard rustling leaves and branches and scampered up the front yard tree just in time to see townsfolk stepping out into Aberdeen's clearing. Mrs. Jefferson, the Reverend, Deacon Fielder, and others had stepped from the trees. Martha made herself into a tiny ball, squeezed close to the tree, and waited. The townspeople stood over on the side, brushing themselves off, straightening their ties, skirts, and shirts before they approached Aberdeen's door.

Aberdeen sensed the town before she saw them. She had known when Martha came home last night that some townsfolk were coming today.

Aberdeen registered her daughter's position and long since, all her moods. The one up in the tree was the strangest. Fortunately, she wasn't around too often. Grandmother Selsie once told Aberdeen that a whole lot of sisters could share one body. Aberdeen hadn't known at first what Selsie meant and wasn't even sure she did now. For Aberdeen, her daughter was one big girl, not tall or fat; her insides were just wide and different. The squirrelly one that always had questions was up in the tree now.

Aberdeen stepped outside so that she didn't have to hear a morning knock on the other side of her wooden door. She walked a few paces and stood directly under the front yard tree where the townsfolk met her with the Reverend, Mrs. Jefferson, and Deacon Fielder out front.

"Your little daughter say she saw a body up in them woods," Deacon Fielder started in and was interrupted by the Reverend's . . .

"Good morning, ma'am. Howdy do today?"

"She led us to—a what she call that tree—sif? Anyway, I ain't never heard of the tree and we ain't seen no body." Deacon Fielder confirmed what the town crowd already knew.

"There was a rope and some trampled-on mud," Mrs. Jefferson said.

"In fairness, a body coulda lain beneath that tree," the Reverend again.

"So, why are you here?" Aberdeen asked as calmly as she could manage.

"Nobody in town ain't not present," Deacon Fielder said. "Must be somebody from up here."

"We wonderin' 'bout the body. Whose body and where it is now," the Reverend spoke deferentially.

"You're looking for a body here?" Aberdeen asked her visitors.

"She the only one mentioned it so far," Deacon Fielder again.

"You know just like I do that these woods border two towns. Maybe everybody is alright in your town; maybe tomorrow morning the people from the next town will come knocking since I seem to be in the middle. Maybe it's their business and not yours."

Aberdeen had deftly removed the townsfolks' mission, but they had come to say a few things.

"We think it must be a young person."

"It could have been a crime of passion," Mrs. Jefferson said.

"Her name could have been Rosemary," Aberdeen offered just as confidently.

"Maybe there weren't a body atall," Deacon Fielder said out loud. They'd discussed it earlier.

"Maybe some giant foliage had just grown from the tree and made itself look like a body." Aberdeen wasn't being helpful.

"Little girls have been known to imagine," the Reverend spoke again.

"Bodies have been known to die." They could hear the edge in her tone. Aberdeen was a little tired of wasting her time especially if they didn't believe her daughter anyway. Then what was the point of their entire visit? She wanted them off her property without having to tell them directly.

"Folk have been known to be confused in the woods. Woods can be confusing," Aberdeen told her guests.

"Now, we just trying ta help," Deacon Fielder protested.

"Funny how two can be better than one, but five or six is almost always wrong when they thinking the same thing at the same time." Aberdeen was giving them some words to make them leave in record time.

"Six have been known to argue about everything all the way home." The townsfolk had already turned and were moving out of Aberdeen's clearing. She stood at the edge calling at their backs.

"Hate to see you leave empty-handed. Pick some berries as you go! Get a good handful." Aberdeen turned slowly and waited. She stood very still in her front yard, right beneath the tree.

"Girl, I don't know what I dislike most: them not believing you, or you guiding them right up to a Sylph tree."

"Mama they..."

"You lucky they didn't know better. You trying to share secrets that don't mean anything to anyone 'cept us."

"Mama, I—"

"I dislike everything so far about this morning."

Aberdeen turned her back on her daughter up in the front yard tree and walked into the house, calling back, "Get some kindling; put it near my pot."

5

Days at the Red Sea, Swimming

Selma cracked her eyes to the morning then refused to face the day.

A little later, Agnes awakened but her body didn't. She sat still waiting for it to catch up. Her arms and upper torso had twitched so much that her right hand banged against the chair and her left hand hit and closed the desk drawer where Martha had been sitting. The pain and the sound had startled Agnes into an edgy wakefulness. As usual, she had to figure out why she felt so frazzled and regain her normal calm. Clearly, she had spent the night uncomfortably in an unfamiliar chair which could have undone anyone. Secondly, she didn't know what she was wearing but the clothing wasn't hers. Agnes almost never knew what she had been doing but since she had just awakened, whatever she had been doing must have taken place in her sleep. Dreams were notoriously hard to remember and there needn't be any penalty for being inappropriately dressed while sleeping. She stood up, stretched, rotated her neck, and then noticed that she was not at home in Cairo.

By the time the children awakened, Agnes was ready to greet them, freshly bathed and clad in her yellow dress with the lovely flowers. At first, Agnes hadn't noticed that they were at a beach. She was slowly taking in her surroundings.

Umm Ridah came into the kitchen; she followed the low incessant humming that her mistress sometimes did. She buzzed.

"Morning, miss."

"Morning, Umm Ridah. When did we get here?"

The children awakened, happy to see their mother in her yellow dress. All three of them hugged her but the boy lingered in her waiting lap.

"Well, if there is an ocean nearby, let's go see it." Mother had a strange way of making the beginning out of the middle. They'd been at the beach for a couple of weeks, but Mother seemed to arrive only today.

The children ran off into the room they were sharing to get their beach things and so did Agnes. They skidded over the hot sand, down to the shore hand in hand, happily holding onto one another and their big beach bag. The children had a beach routine and unraveled the blankets first and put their individual towels where they each planned to lay.

Agnes took off her robe and beneath, she wore a yellow bathing suit. She sat down with the three of them surrounding her, put her arms out and managed to touch them all. The children curled up around their mother with their heads against her thighs, eyes closed listening to the surf, expecting to spend their day, one by one being held by her, until she slowly stood up.

Agnes could swim. She dipped her toes and afterwards bent over and tested the temperature with her fingers before taking a few steps forward and pushing her whole body into the sea. She went under and then turned and faced the children.

The three children stood up to see the sea between them and their mother. Hadn't she warned them not to get close? Mother went under and they strained upwards to find her and her head popped back up smaller than before. She began to swim, farther out into the ocean and at surprising intervals she would pop up and wave.

The children moved closer to the water, just to catch a bit

of their mother but none of them let the sea do more than touch their feet.

Mother swam from left to right and each time she changed direction she doubled the distance. She went way to the left and then way to the right. She headed away from the shore and then bobbed up above the glistening waves and finally, she held up a tiny still hand which stayed above her head.

Her tiny hand, the sun shadowing undulating figures over the horizon, the slight fingering breezes, altogether added up to an elaborately designed "good-bye."

The sea was going to eat Mother.

Alley started to cry. Mother went away and never came back on a sunny day in a Red Sea. To Alley, if any mother seemed capable of disappearing and never coming back, naturally, it would be the one with the lovely yellow dress, in the matching bathing suit.

Mirella began crying too. The sea could swallow anything it wanted and chose mother.

The boy ran home to tell Umm Ridah.

"Mother's drowning," were the loudest clearest words Umm Ridah had ever heard him say. He yanked her arm and she hadn't any choice but to run behind him.

They arrived at the beach just in time to see Agnes pop up out of the surf, laughing and smiling. She took in the absurd expressions on their little faces and, at once, decided to teach them to swim.

Alley and Mirella had partly recovered and though breathing jerked them up and down, they yielded to their mother's reach and let the cool water play gently over their toes. The boy started to cry now.

Umm Ridah quickly walked back to the house. "All drown now. Mr. Thrace no family any now," she said out loud. She gathered her things, walked back to the beach, and sat down to watch.

Agnes sat down between waves and motioned for her children to join her. They should get used to the water first.

She sat and they curled up around her. Agnes held first one and then the other in no particular order. When the sea was strong, it pulled the children and by the end of the afternoon, they would let themselves go, happily running and twisting into the waves, and then climbing up the sand to the safety of their mother. In a few days, the children were carelessly romping about in the waves, dipping their heads in and back out again.

Agnes could have turned them all into passable swimmers. She swam every day, and still held the children for hours both in and out of the water.

Umm Ridah could see them from the house, but mostly she watched from her chair twenty feet back—close enough to the water but between them and the house.

Mr. Thrace tasted the salt on the skin behind his wife's ear when he kissed her. The children told him that she was teaching them to swim. He hadn't imagined that she'd known how. He asked Umm Ridah who told him she watched from the sand.

"She'll do just fine," her mother had said, "and better if you let her be." Thrace hadn't known what Aberdeen meant at the time and guessed that he might never broach the understanding between mother and daughter, though he followed her advice.

In the early days of their marriage, he'd peek over at his wife and catch something strange. He quickly turned his head before she caught him, but not before sensing that she could harbor something enormous inside, something she did not want to share. Her face held a blank expression so intently that he knew his thought to be an odd one. He thought his wife seemed very tightly coiled around a very large emptiness. His ideas about her made him nervous; continuing with them gave him the image of opening a dark door which he shut very quickly. Thrace was the master of leaving alone what he did not understand. He took her mother's words to heart. She'd do fine if he let her be.

Thrace preferred to concern himself with things that he knew. He could turn a certain phrase or two and had been known to craft sophisticated documents. He could make dollars and knew what to do with them. He was well traveled and rather well put together with strong legs and sturdy feet. He held his wife above all else and assumed she knew of his deep affection. Certainly, he must have mentioned his feelings to her once or twice. Beside his wife, he sat admiring her as an abidingly pleasant attachment. From time to time, he gazed at her with what he thought was love in his eyes. She was the interior of his nice house, he lived in her, loved being inside of her but didn't notice that he rarely spoke directly to her and he almost never wondered what she might have said if she had been in the mood for conversation.

In the early years of their marriage, the quiet assumptions served them peculiarly well and with Agnes, things didn't change. The middle was exactly like the beginning.

To Agnes, Clifton Thrace was as irregular as all the other men that she had known and the same as he had always been. In the beginning, Agnes always felt a little out of sorts whenever she was in Clifton Thrace's company. How preposterous was it to assume that he loved her? He offered his irregular access only instead of periodically like her father; he offered his inaccessibility every evening as he always came home at approximately the same time. He greeted her nicely enough and always seemed to have a ready kiss which was as disconcerting to Agnes as her mother's collard greens. Either kisses were a prelude to bed, or they were just strange. Now when Mr. Thrace first came home, he kissed her though he wasn't quite ready to go to bed. Generally, he wanted to eat first and instead of asking her about dinner, he would put his nose in the air, a hound sniffing what she might have prepared. Agnes wasn't much of a cook and frankly, didn't quite understand that making meals was something she might have done during her day. If she hadn't prepared dinner, he was silent.

If she were sitting in the chair by the window, he would move a small lamp over to the sofa, seat himself, and pick up his book. Alternatively, if she were sitting on the sofa, he would sit in the chair by the window and pick up his book. If she were in the bathroom, he might be standing in the hallway when she opened the door. He seemed to wait for her to choose and then he would occupy the same room, in the other chair with his book.

One day, very early in their marriage, when Thrace came home, Agnes had hidden all the chairs. Mostly, she stuffed them in the nearest closets except for the kitchen chairs which she stacked and put outside just beyond the back door. There was one chair available in the bedroom which is where Agnes was sitting.

Mr. Thrace announced that he would not be staying. He had an unplanned dinner meeting and had just stopped home to freshen his shirt and change his shoes. Strangely, that same evening was also the first evening that Thrace mentioned Agnes wearing a very pretty, yellow floral dress. He admired her dress and Agnes thanked him accordingly. When he came home later the same evening, Agnes was still sitting in the chair in the bedroom.

He undressed, placed his clothing in the closet, lay on top of the bed, and picked up his book.

So he could find a place to sit even if there weren't any chairs. Sometimes, Agnes felt that Mr. Thrace's household habits were designed to give her something to do. If timed, in approximately three point two minutes, she could put fresh toilet tissue in the bathrooms. For a time, Agnes stopped replacing the tissue, but then Mr. Thrace seemed to stop going to the bathroom altogether and Agnes was afraid that he might explode so that she could see how long cleaning the entire house might take.

Mr. Thrace often gave her money and occasionally, some suggestions on how she should spend.

"I do love your yellow dress but you don't have to wear the same dress quite so often. I'd be pleased to see you in any dress." A few moments later, he had added, "I'm always pleased to be with you."

Agnes wondered what wearing the dress had to do with him. One perfect dress was adequate; she didn't need others—just a few copies of the one she had already chosen. When he gave her money, she bought another copy of the same dress. Now, she had several of them all in the same yellow with the exact same flowers. She either wore her dress or her pajamas. The wonder was that Thrace had noticed.

He hadn't noticed on the day that she had bought the extra dresses and left them in the closet, or on the day that she had found the very same fabric on dainty pillows in a specialty shop (she bought two pillows), or even on the day that she bought pairs of yellow shoes to match. But on the day that she had returned all his belongings, the ones that she had collected from the various locations where he had left them strewn about the house, and arranged them on the dining room table, he happened to ask, "Is yellow your favorite color?"

Having a favorite color had never occurred to Agnes. A favorite color was the strangest concept that had recently entered her mind and Agnes was beginning to believe that if she were going to have to live with Thrace, she was going to have to separate him from the things he did and said. If he asked her a question on Monday, generally, she could answer by Tuesday. She didn't really know this to be true, but if Thrace meant something he said one way, she would always interpret the opposite. They sat down together to eat, but she could only chew if he wasn't looking. But if he kissed her when he came home, they could make love later in the evening.

"I don't know how one would favor any one color or even, any one thing." Thrace smiled as if she'd warmed his heart. Truthfully, Agnes didn't make obvious decisions, not ones that taxed her thinking. Agnes did whatever seemed practical to Agnes.

She began to walk again. Same as she'd done her entire

life in the woods. She had been nervous at first without the woods to feel familiar. In the city, instead of silent trees, there was always the noise of people, people with machines, people without machines. Agnes thought she could outwalk the noises and began to leave each day right after Thrace went to work. To think properly, she needed calm and to become calm she needed silence and to get that silence she walked until she stopped listening or at least until the sounds coming through her ears got lost on the way to her brain and she stopped heeding them. After a few weeks, Agnes could walk without being intimidated by the sights and sounds of the city where Thrace had taken her to live.

Aberdeen hadn't given her too much advice. She said, "You could walk away anything," and always made herself clear by insisting that she had not said "walk away from," but simply walk away. "If you have something you need to think over, take a walk through the woods. You have to come back, but you can let the leaves babysit the worries for a time." Well, where was she supposed to put them in the city?

Agnes wasn't sure how she had gotten to the city in the first place and there certainly weren't enough trees for all these worried people to share. She liked the ratio better when there were more trees than people. Daily, she increased her distances, turning east and the next day west, and each time, she put a straight line between herself and the house she shared with Thrace until one day she had walked so far, there were fields and fields of grass rolling up and down in all directions. Agnes stopped going east but kept walking west.

She wanted to be in those fields every day and she finally walked far enough to find a great abandoned house. It was hot and she was tired. She had walked down an old overgrown macadam road with small spokes of grass poking up through the black like mini gardens defying lava. The walkway was columned by giant trees, boasting an old and silent elegance which now was merely silent. There were enough trees for a lifetime of worry for one.

Some of the trees had carved hearts with arrows shot through and letters that Agnes couldn't put together to form a word. A big wide porch fronted the house, but she kept on to the rear and found a long hedge row squaring a patch of yard filled with weeded gardens, dirty yard furniture, broken and split planters with no ordered growth, and the pool which invited her to sit. The water was cooling. Agnes chose the back steps leading up to the house and stared down at the water. Every day, she came back and sat and sat until time to turn around and shorten the straight line between the abandoned house and the one where she lived.

On Thursday, Agnes walked west to the old mansion, marched out back, took off her yellow shoes and her yellow flowered dress along with all of her under things and eased into the pool. She was completely submerged until the muck and slime threw her upwards. Floating clumsily atop, plying her arms through the greasy green, on her back, she gazed towards the house where she usually sat and saw an ancient lady making her way awkwardly down the stairs.

"If you're going to use my pool, get a bathing suit, and if you want to learn how to swim properly, you might ask."

Agnes was determined to accomplish something during the time she spent at the beach with the children. She hugged and petted them constantly and made all three children confident enough to mess around in the ocean. Then she went off on a walk and didn't return before the children slept.

In the morning, she slept in and the children left without her to go to the beach. Umm Ridah had taken up her usual post between the house and the sea and watched the children.

"Don't know water, after mama come."

"Come on, Umm Ridah. We can almost swim."

"No, stay, mama come."

They sat on the beach with their back to Umm Ridah, each slouching over in their own individual unhappy way, sticking their feet into the water, inching more and more of their bodies to get wet until they were practically immersed. Eventually, Umm Ridah would let them swim.

In seconds, the three of children were completely soaked. A few moments after, the ocean snuck forward, curled up around two little ankles, and slid Mirella's two little feet ever so playfully from beneath her and gently pulled her away like a big friend holding the hand of a smaller one.

She let herself go; she felt brave and adventurous without her mother, guessing that the Red Sea would do the usual and skip her backside against the sand. Emboldened even after she hadn't felt the sand scraping against her thighs, she let the sea give her a longer ride. On her back, with her head tilted forward, the sea was a fast-gleaming slide.

For the first time, she could see how far she was from dry sand. Panic overtook adventure, Mirella reached out to the shore which unbalanced her body, and just as she opened her mouth to scream the sea flew in. She wasn't smiling any more, and Alley and her brother knew she was in trouble.

"Umm, Umm, get Mother. Mirella's in the ocean." They were both afraid to say she was drowning.

"Shoo?" Umm Ridah jumped from her chair and started running towards the house, four or five steps before she knew the house was too far for fast help. She turned, quickly screaming at the same time as she lifted her skirts and apron in preparation for her own march into the ocean.

"Mrs. Thraaaaaaaaace, Mmmmm Thraaaace! What you done?" She began talking to herself in Arabic and slipped down onto her own behind before pulling herself up again and moving purposefully forward. She steadied herself on her feet, took a few more steps, stretched, grabbed Mirella, and pulled her so hard that she was next to her before she had a chance to blink. The child was coughing and retching.

"Put feet down. Put two feet down. You walk. No deep here. It's no deep." Mirella stood up without letting Umm Ridah go. She held on so tight that Umm Ridah could barely take a step. She pushed her in front, up the slight incline of sand, and out of the ocean.

Berdeena was running out of the house by then, running towards them alerted by Umm Ridah's cries. She got to the beach just in time to see a soaking wet and obviously upset Mirella walking next to an angry Umm Ridah.

"Didn't I tell you to stay out of the ocean?" Berdeena screamed at them all. "Didn't I tell you water is never safe?" Eight pairs of eyes looked back at her with such strangeness that for the first time ever Berdeena felt unwelcome. She backed away from the waves as they climbed up higher on the sand. Berdeena didn't even like getting her own feet wet.

The swimming lessons were clearly over.

"A l Uothou b'llah." God help me, Umm Ridah spat into her bosom—twice. Mrs. Thrace was not wearing yellow and didn't smell like flowers either.

Berdeena agreed with Umm Ridah that it was a good idea for the children to take a nap. She went into the kitchen and peeped into the refrigerator. She was kind of hungry and wondered what there was to cook. While the children were sleeping, she decided to take a walk. She didn't know why they had chosen to vacation near the sea. Didn't they know how she felt about water? For a while, she could barely drink it after her experience. What had Umm Ridah expected her to do? Thank God, the children were safe. When they awakened, she would warn them again. Water was dangerous!

Berdeena found the largest open-air market, full of unbelievable delicacies. She bought fresh chicken, lentils, loads of rice, eggs, spices, odd-looking fruit, and grape leaves. A young man with a cart wheeled it all home for her and Berdeena told Umm Ridah that she would take care of the kitchen tonight.

Umm Ridah didn't have anywhere to go but her own small room. From there, she could hear Berdeena singing. Twice she cracked her door to prove that a stranger hadn't come into the house. She hadn't known Mrs. Thrace ever to be so merry to want to make music. Even when she wore her lovely yellow dress, she had a quiet about her. Now, from the kitchen, a loud American was singing.

If you find some beans, you can't ignore them
but forget Jack with that bean stalk
don't put them in the soil.
Take them by the hand
Wash them up and put 'em on to boil.
Look around the kitchen
Look around the pantry
You'll find something that will make
those beans just dandy.
Throw in a chicken if you have it
Throw in a little beef stew
Stir it round and round
'Til the chicken mixes with the hound
If you have a little dog
Chop it up with the hog ...

Umm Ridah had no idea what the song was about but she put her eyes outside of her door once more after the aromas came into her room. Whatever she was making smelled wonderful. Mrs. Thrace could cook?

"Come on you three." The children had awakened. "Help me with my song."

"We don't want to eat hog or dog." Alley spoke up for all of them. She knew that she and her sister and brother wanted to but they couldn't be unhappy with their singing, cooking mother.

"Well, what about fish on a stick?" Berdeena requested.

"Eating it?"

"Singing it?"

"Oh I remember that song," Mirella coughed just to remind everyone for a minute that she had very nearly drowned, and then she began to sing.

Mr. Fish, Mr. Fish, how do I get you on my stick?
I can coax you up and into the air
I can whack the water and make you despair
If you take too long, I can bore you with a song.

I can loop an old worm but then two have to die
So come on fish just jump on in my big old pie.
I can clean you up and rub your scales
We prefer you didn't bring your tails
But we'll tuck you in a crispy blanket
A bed so neat, give you some tasty salt
And warm your feet.
We'll put you in the oven and
Heat it up slow
Chew you up and you won't even know
You're in my stomach 'cause it rumbles
like the sea, then you'll be back in the ocean,
Instead of me.
Mr. Fish, Mr. Fish, come on to my stick ..."

6

Remembering the Plantation (Every Black Family's Past?)

Cooking and singing were either getting Berdeena into or out of trouble. After she had been in the city for a little while with Mr. Thrace, she had almost concluded that one place was like another, depending upon the give-and-take of the sofa, where she would have been content to stay except for the continuing harassment of her invisible brother beckoning her to take him out into the world. In the end, he didn't have to beg too much because Berdeena's fourth choice was walking, but only if they had a destination. She was the opposite of her brother who hated arriving but loved traveling.

An abandoned plantation pulled her its way. Almost magically, the wind had blown her in the right direction as if all a house needed do was wait. She and her invisible brother headed straight out of the city toward the old house that had been through the turmoil of decades waiting for Berdeena. Once she discovered the house, she spent most of her afternoons there, far from the city in the quiet decay of an unruly garden. She sat out back and imagined she was in her own backyard. There was something welcoming and familiar about the house. Occasionally, she'd look up and feel as if she'd been sitting in the same place for a hundred years.

Berdeena poured her days into the garden. Mapping it had preoccupied her for such a long time that when she finally finished, she had to start all over again at the season change. Knotty little growths on the trees, greener pathways, and the slow rise of the stench in the pool all signaled the coming warmth. Spring hadn't yet caused too many changes, but she had finally decided which trees would be the singing trees and now in the afternoon, she would sit out back and sing to a long-leaf pine pretending it was her mother's "Singing Oak" from the woods where they lived between two towns. Daily, she sat beneath her chosen tree with her back up against the rough bark, singing her heart out. Aberdeen used to say they were from The Hill between Two Towns, no matter what other folks called the other two towns.

After Berdeena had been singing the same songs in a special order for a couple of weeks, she decided to go back to front, finishing her last two songs first. As she began the third song of the day, humming the first few measures before starting on the words, an old white lady came slowly down the back stairs.

"Keep to the original order. I always liked to hear those songs. Sing it in the usul order. I've been livin' by the order you usully use." She was missing a few teeth off to the side and overcompensated with strange pronunciation. Berdeena decided on an order and kept to it—in reverse, just as she had begun.

"You gonna backwards my day," the old white lady smiled. Singing was better than no singing and no company.

Berdeena decided to treat the old white lady as an imaginary part of the landscape. It was bad enough with her invisible brother; now what was she to make of an old white lady? The music evidently loosened up her inhibitions and the old lady started talking. She leaned over right next to Berdeena and started telling stories. Berdeena didn't like her leaning up against a singing tree talking but what could she do? The old lady started with a long list of complaints. That's how Berdeena discovered that she was real. Nothing she could imagine would complain around a singing tree.

"What did I know but spoiled and selfish?" She seemed to start with her own childhood but Berdeena also gathered that she didn't have to listen. Besides, it was impossible to listen while she was singing, and at the moment, singing was more important.

"My father was the second man my mama loved. She was saved from the wrong one and rewarded with my daddy. I didn't fit the mirror the way they wanted me to. He loved my mother and there was nothing else in the world and they spit me outwards, not between them. I'd diluted what they each saw in the other enough for neither one to bother with me 'cept on birthdays, when they could show off and get fancy stuff, invite all the neighbors and folks. One time, sshhh might have been the first time all attention was focused on me. They had about six or seven candles on a big pretty cake and it was time for me to make a wish and blow them out. I took as long as I could to make that wish. I was sneaking looks up at everybody looking at me and I wasn't even bothering to make a wish; I was keeping everything focused on me. Mama and Daddy were standing next to me. They each had a hand on my shoulder, and when I peeked up, they was looking at each other in between looking down on me, waiting to see when I might open my eyes and blow. I wasn't going to do it but Mama pinched me and I gasped and a few candles went out. I think Mama blew the rest of them but I wasn't ready to give up. Came time to cut that cake; I circled my arms around the cake plate. I wanted to keep that cake intact with all those eyes on me 'cause it felt warmer than anything I'd felt yet."

The old lady stopped for a bit, drawing breath like it might be difficult, pushing her old head down into her crooked hands and after a few minutes started up again.

"When they sliced it all up, I knew all that attention would go with them slices. As usul, Mama won. Real long time after that 'for I got any particular attention. From

then on, every time they had a birthday for me, we never had the blowing out candles part. Mama would bring me a cake privately with some candles and let me wish and blow but usally she'd come without Daddy and they'd have another cake for the party guests. Sometimes, they would sing the birthday song to me."

"You know that song?" She paused and looked over at Berdeena for a moment. Berdeena ignored her.

"One year, I had several cakes and Lord knows how many presents. I could get double everything except their eyes on me. Thing about birthdays is they turned me into this 'quisite little creature my parents dusted off for the public. Shine me up, take me out the dark cabinet, and put me in the display one, send me off to all the right places, and buy all the right things. They'd be sitting at the breakfast or dinner table planning what to do next, while I was listening. I was a well-used shiny suitcase that they liked to pack and send all over the world. Usully, while they were deciding where I was going, I was deciding what I wasn't doing. When they sent me to the best Swiss finishing school to work on my language skills and whatnot, I spent two years at that Swiss boarding school thickening and perfecting my drawl. Though I did develop a taste for fine chocolates, eaten at every meal, which turned my face into a pock-marked looking, paint-by-numbers set. One time, in the mirror, I numbered all my bumps. Numbered 'em backwards, too, so that they looked right to everyone else."

She wheezed in a few more breaths but once she got going, breathing seemed to come easy.

"That's my backwards memory for your backwards singing."

Berdeena was thinking that tomorrow she might sing sideways.

The next day, as Berdeena got comfortable, adjusting herself against the singing tree, breathing in and out, getting her lungs ready to sing, the old lady came down immediately.

"You know how two opposite roads can lead to the same place?" She must have guessed that if she started talking before Berdeena started singing they could have a conversation.

Berdeena didn't answer.

"Well, I'll tell you. I stopped liking my parents pretty much by the time I turned twelve. They didn't give me a choice. If they loved me they would want me around and since they didn't, they must not a liked me either."

Berdeena hadn't answered so she guessed that the old lady decided not to tell her about the roads.

"When they were around, they were nice enough. She might pull my head towards her stomach and when I was bigger, her shoulder. They asked me questions about where I'd been and they'd talk about the way I looked and how I'd changed since they had last seen me. They probably could have won me over easy, as I was more than willing to love them. But soon as they brought me home, they had to travel. They'd fly me home from Switzerland only to discover that they'd have to go somewhere else in Europe. By the time I was a real teenager, you wouldn't be able to find anybody meaner. The more things my parents sent me from abroad, the meaner I got."

The word came out like a hard period.

"Not just ordinary mean—prove to the world, show everybody—mean. It got so that I didn't even know how not to be nasty. My honest to God joy was to shock people with my meanness. I carried it around up above my head just waiting to stick a pin in and have all that festering garbage I'd been holding pour out all over some poor soul standing next to me expecting civility."

"My brother's a balloon over me," Berdeena said.

"Yeah, I see him up there. He's a strange looking fellow, isn't he?"

"You can see him?" Berdeena was shocked.

"I was wondering who he was and whether he was related or just a good friend."

Berdeena stopped singing for another moment. She was staring at the old lady trying to read whether truth was important to her. A sly smile started across her wrinkled face.

"Nobody in town talked to me if they could help it." She was thinking she might have a listener now and moved up to what she thought was the interesting parts in her story.

"Meanness needs an audience. In the US Post Office, I might pinch a baby 'til it cried, or hide an old lady's Christmas box. I had sway in the post office 'cause my mother and father were always sending packages home. Sometimes, everything in the back belonged to me and I'd pretend to be opening it when I was really writing mean notes to the townsfolk, labeling them and putting them in the appropriate boxes. I'd give the stuff my parents bought to people and then claim it had been stolen. I'd smash up some boxes, blame the post office, and try to sue them for favors. Then I'd insist that they carry some of my meanness around the county. That post office mailed more animal dirt and parts. My crowning glory was to rob the town of its name and pastime all the same day.

Pond-Beneath-the-Sun, Georgia, people used to believe God himself had come down, looked around the earth, chose the perfect spot to live and play, called them up personally, and recommended that they live there. Everything revolved around that stupid pond. All the right trees and flowers grew and everybody, but everybody picnicked and played, primped, and partook of the so-called loveliness. Some townsfolk even married out there and, in the spring they always held so many services around the pond that the townspeople seemed pagan and the pond their pilgrimage. All that ceremony should have been more than anyone could stand. In the winter, if it got cold enough, the pond would freeze over and folk would skate. That pond was the life of the entire town. Southern people could get attached to anything. You know what I did?"

Berdeena wasn't going to answer even if she was now somewhat listening.

"I drained that pond. Pond-Beneath-the-Sun, Georgia, should have been renamed "The Devil's Big Old Hole, Georgia and in a few weeks, the town could have been named again with "The Devil's Big Dry Hole." That was one of the easiest things I ever did. I never told anybody where I put that water either.

Every time I walked down to the town center, I snickered. Even years later, there would still be people standing around shaking their heads, wondering what ever happened to the pond. The Reverend thought somebody did something to make God mad and from then on they kept their services inside, which is exactly where they belonged and not out pestering people who were just trying to get somewhere on a Sunday without being bothered by religion. Getting rid of that pond lasted me a good long time. I stopped breaking up things at the post office and even brought some of the things my parents sent home.

I was a young woman before I ever wanted to do something kind. Right after putting my eyes on something and getting them stuck. That was when I first saw the man I married visiting some cousins who lived on the other side of where the pond used to be. I don't know how I even managed to see him. My eyes got opened for me a few times during that period. I'll never forget them days. I stood around long enough, right next to the hole until his folks had to introduce me. They snickered and whispered that I might look alright but I was mean as a snake. And then they turned around and didn't even bother to whisper and said that he wouldn't want to have anything to do with the old maid who might not have stolen the pond but was gladder than everybody that it was gone. Somebody piped in that though I was the wicked witch from the woods I lived in a mansion instead. For a time, they called me "Rich Wicked Witch," though I don't remember if I actually heard them or my husband told me later. They told him to listen at me talk, that I had lived in Europe for years but had a thicker drawl than a darkie that'd never even made the trip from "Pond..." to Atlanta.

He amused himself, risked his cousins' offense, reached out so charmingly, shook my hand in his, looked me right in the eyes, and smiled. That one moment made me twitch so hard my teeth went chattering, probably why they so broken up now. A chill skated down my spine and must have shaken the crust around my heart and cracked. All I could think of was how to give him a reason to extend his visit. For the first time ever, I thought about giving the pond back, but even if I wanted to I wouldn't have known how. Then I remembered the only other thing I had to offer and I hoped he liked his stomach 'cause one of Selsie's meals was all I could think."

"Selsie's meal?!" Berdeena shivered, moved out of the dull reverie of her music. She hadn't paid attention to most of the other rot that the old lady was going on and on about, but she heard "Selsie's meal."

"What do you know about Selsie's meal?" she asked the old lady.

"Plenty," she knew she had a listener now.

"She made it all the way down here from The Hill between Two Towns?" Berdeena asked.

"It ain't that far. You might have known her by reputation; I knew her food by fact." The old white lady had upped the ante and Berdeena couldn't let her win.

"I know her by blood."

"I knew her by ownership," old white lady claimed.

"You too young to have thought you owned somebody that couldn't be owned even in them times." Berdeena told the old white lady.

"I ate her food."

"I know what's in it."

"Me too—by taste and recipe," the old white lady boasted.

"Tell me?" Berdeena didn't know what she was going to do if this old lady could even name a fraction of the things that went into Selsie's meals. If she said she had a written-down recipe, then she knew she'd be lying.

"Keep secrets secret. That's what I know." The old lady measured her.

"I know what's in her meals. I can make 'em and I know where to get the magic that's in 'em," Berdeena topped the old white lady.

"If you can make one Selsie meal," she hesitated, already knowing what to offer, "I'll will you this house when I die."

"Show me your kitchen."

"Come on." The old lady climbed up her back stairs, opened the door, and stepped inside. She held the door and pulled back the floor-length drapes so that Berdeena could step in behind her. She went off to the right and Berdeena followed. The house wasn't at all the way Berdeena imagined; it was finer as if the outside and the unruly garden in the back were a disguise. She followed the lady into her kitchen and then asked her where the pantry was and whether the pantry had always been in the same place.

"No, the kitchen's been moved once or twice but everything that had been in the pantry traveled with the pantry." Berdeena looked around; sure enough there were some old, blackened jars, empty, but remarkably like the ones she remembered Aberdeen showing her. Supposedly, Selsie smoked the glass on all her jars. That way, even if someone watched her closely, they still couldn't see what she put in the food.

"So you might have eaten it. But you don't have the ingredients to make it now."

"Do you?" the old lady wanted to know.

"Yeah, at home."

"Well then, it's an acceptance of conditions?" she extended her wrinkled, spotted, curly-fingered hand.

"I make a Selsie meal, without you watching and you will me this house?"

"Yep." The old lady answered, thinking if this woman could make a meal—a Selsie meal, if she could—she was related to Selsie and the house where they were sitting already belonged to Selsie.

"When?"

"Tomorrow?"

"Alright," Berdeena said.

Berdeena walked back home, remembering the things that Aberdeen had told her about Selsie. Selsie was Aberdeen's great or regular grandmother and she had been a slave. There were stories and stories about Selsie and most included food. Aberdeen not only could tell a Selsie story, but she might also mix up one of Selsie's dishes. Berdeena had loved her breast-growing potatoes but was afraid to eat too much. Sometimes, she even wondered if she were supposed to eat Selsie's food or rub it into her hair or skin. Aberdeen had laughed and said it would work either way. Aberdeen had filled Berdeena's childhood with stories of Selsie.

"Anyway, it touches you, it'll do what it plans to do. But if you want some real pleasure along with the plan, you'll eat it. You eat it once, you'll eat it again. Even if it makes you sick, you'll eat it knowing exactly how it'll do you." Truthfully, the magic wasn't in the potatoes but in the spices and the timing with which Selsie whipped them. Although known for many many things, including being the Queen of Secrets, Selsie was also known as a slave the white folks called "Two for The Price of One." Some people said that she worked hard enough to be counted twice or even three times. Other people said they called her that because one day she was one person and the next, she was liable to be someone else. Amazingly, all those Selsies could cook and each had a specialty.

Supposedly, the white mistress was given Selsie (wrapped up in a pretty pink dress with a big red bow on her head) as an early birthday present by her daddy. Upon first encounter, Scilla Landry brightened and gave Selsie such a complicit smile that Selsie decided not to tamper with the food she knew she would have to prepare and carry to her—not at first. Scilla came to know all the Selsies and just how to approach them. A true friendship began when they were children, grew swiftly and solid, and lasted all their lives. Scilla welcomed a friend that she would not have to share and when she discovered that Selsie had some hidden talents, she wanted them all for herself, but was forced to compromise.

Scilla might not have been the real witch but she could harass Selsie until Selsie gave in and then pretend the magic was her own. Selsie displayed her many moods and conjured up meals. Silent Selsie had cured the cat that had been sick for months and diseased the slave overseer who had been cruel for years. Selsie had merely traded their constitutions and Scilla had seen her sneakily dusting and stirring things into both their food. Soon, the overseer couldn't keep anything down and began to slink around scratching himself behind his ears and legs. No one could understand him when he spoke with his raspy high voice and no one could find him without first finding a patch of sun where he would generally be curled up, sleeping.

Meanwhile, the cat grew fat, healthy, and mean. Scilla hadn't ever liked the overseer. He had a peculiar fondness for her older brother which seemed to be returned. Scilla wouldn't have minded if Selsie's powders made the overseer disappear altogether and quietly told her so. Selsie gestured to Scilla that she could get rid of him, probably piece by piece rather than all at once and, anyway, she needed to sleep over it a night or two.

The next day, Scilla had moved on. Now, she wanted a little sister and got one the day her father's mistress gave birth to a little girl that looked a lot like him. Her father's lover had never been healthy and childbirth pushed her right up to and over the threshold of death's door. Indeed, on that very same day, a singing Selsie baked a cake for Scilla's mother and only Selsie and Scilla knew that the cake was baked with enough sympathy-activating spices to make Scilla's mother offer to bring the baby girl home and keep her.

When Scilla was fifteen and wanted her prettier cousin made ugly, she had to sweetly coax the ugly out of a Selsie who'd been wearing the same flowery dress she'd made for days. Scilla wanted her to change clothes because she was easier to talk to when she was wearing something else. Next, she wanted her cousin's beau to propose, but she was so young and fickle that soon after, she wanted him to go away. Daily, she wanted something and daily, she invented new ways to beg Selsie for the corresponding food. She had eaten plenty of breast-growing potatoes and would absolutely want more subtle hip-dancing stew along with shining long hair and beautiful skin.

Eventually, Scilla wanted the fiancé that she'd rejected to come back and be the fiancé who would become her husband, so she attempted to charm the indifferent Selsie, with a strange sounding tic and a left-legged limp, to make and spice the right kind of chocolate. First, a big boy-child and then a pretty girl shortly afterwards, were stirred up and served by Selsie. Naturally, when she finished having children, Selsie's strong cider left a small crack, but closed Scilla's door. If Scilla wanted to sleep for two days or be awake for more; or if she wanted to rearrange her shape to fit into a Paris frock, she went into Selsie's kitchen.

Everyone came to Scilla Landry's parties. They knew that Selsie would have cooked the food. At times, Scilla wanted her friends near so that she could solicit their secrets as they drank Selsie's sweet tea, though she had stopped offering biscuits because the urge to confess began with childhood and didn't wait until the cookies had been consumed. Her guests would spit out inane secrets simultaneously with moistened biscuit crumbs that stuck to the furniture. Occasionally, even Scilla ate too much and did not know how to quit Selsie's food. For many years, she had eaten nothing else. Even the fruit that came from the trees passed by Selsie before reaching Scilla.

Selsie never gave anyone a recipe though everyone asked. Hers was an emotional science and the food was always better if she were left alone. In her part of the world, she was a free-floating piece of property. Instead of staying put, she could forage in the woods to gather and grow spices.

Sovereign in her kitchen, slave to a woman with unlimited caprices, and also the free and clear owner of a spirit that no one could harness, Selsie circumnavigated the roiling storms of her own complex inner world.

Scilla Landry was her one constant and every day for twenty-five years, she woke up and decided whether or not today ought to be the day that she should poison Miss Scilla. But her mistress amused her. As every day, Scilla needed a particular meal for an even more particular purpose and more than anything, Selsie loved to experiment. Without the mistress, Selsie knew she'd be someone else's underappreciated cook.

After all, it had been Scilla's idea for Selsie to make some crumpets for the two of them to eat that, no matter what, would make them laugh until they cried. Into their funny pastry went some orange-colored spices and together, the two of them walked hand in hand while anticipating the happy effect. They had a secret hiding place up in the woods where no one could find them, and they laughed in tandem with one another especially on the day that they were both saddened by the death of Scilla's father. Their friendship was strong, foddered on the mutual manipulation of the people around them and yet each held a hammer over the other one's head. The mistress could always sell Selsie and Selsie could always sneak a potion, and sometimes did, into the mistress's food. Selsie would sicken her and then provide the cure.

The mistress was always sifting the difference between whether the way she felt was natural or not. Selsie ate exactly what Scilla ate and sometimes first. Supposedly, whenever Scilla thought Selsie was angry, Scilla lost weight as she was afraid to eat. Selsie never stayed angry long as she thought Scilla was so silly. For one thing, spice didn't only work with food.

Selsie tried to pass her harvesting skills, recipes, lessons, and everything else down to her own daughter. Selsie hated waste and she hated when they ate the meal faster than the time she took to cook it. Food ought to be slowly savored over long periods which Selsie had built into her recipes but time, four sets of hands, and two heads changed, warped and, diluted them.

What came to Aberdeen went to Berdeena and Berdeena, for now, mostly kept them to herself. But like her mother and great-grandmother before her, Berdeena did learn and love to cook.

She gathered her jars and wares and walked back out to Pond-Beneath-the-Sun, Georgia, to add herself to a family tradition and cook for an old white lady. This one, with a bunch of missing teeth and probably only two taste buds left.

The old lady's nose brought back memories and she could smell that Berdeena must have had Selsie's touch. But what she recognized as she ate was the erratic sensations that the food caused. She was full but could not stop eating. That was the part she had forgotten and now she knew as surely as she remembered being told, the darkie had poisoned her. She wanted to run to the telephone but was unable to move. Berdeena wanted her house and saw no point in waiting for her to die of natural causes. People said that Selsie had killed her great-grandmother, too, but no one could prove it.

"I am already old enough not to live too much more." The old lady squeezed out words, "You didn't have to kill me. I don't mind dying, granddaughter like grandma. Just another southern family tradition."

"Start singing. Hum first and then sing," Berdeena told her.

"I got more to say before I go. You know, I got twin boys and a girl. You'd never know even if you hung around here long enough to see them because they don't come." The more she talked the larger her stomach seemed to become. After a moment, it hurt so much that all she could do was groan.

Berdeena kept right on singing, ignoring the old lady's first talk and finally her grunts. She was leaning way over sideways, almost with her little white head on the table. Stock-still, suspended, with a most taciturn expression etched across her face and despite a tightening stomach, the old lady seemed peaceful.

Berdeena wondered if she had put too much spice in the food. The spices ought not kill her, maybe she'll sleep better, but if she wanted to get back to normal, all she need do was—sing.

In their days together, the old lady had only mentioned one song. Berdeena thought it may help and she started humming and then singing,

"Happy Birthday to you, Happy Birthday to you!" The old lady started humming along with Berdeena and they hummed the whole song through about forty times before the old lady eased up to sit properly in her chair and sang,

"Happy Birthday, dear Thenia Landry, Happy Birthday to me!"

After the first time, they began to cook and eat together regularly or more exactly, Berdeena fed Thenia and always took a plate home to Thrace. She got so that she liked the Pond-Beneath-the-Sun kitchen better than her own and generally cooked there and carried half the food home and left half for Thenia. Liking Thenia's kitchen cast a little like Thenia's way but didn't make her trust Thenia or for that matter, Mr. Thrace. She pretended to hide her spices within the kitchens but mostly carried them back and forth with her every day.

Thenia and Berdeena ate lunch together and Berdeena would leave dinner atop her stove. After lunch, they spent their afternoons outside. As the days grew warmer, Thenia's garden began to overflow with blossoming weeds, the bright green stems of future flowers, buzzing insects, and right along with the normal pleasantries of spring, the pool kicked up a nasty stench. Berdeena decided to surprise Thenia and clean out the pool so that they could refresh themselves by sticking their feet into cool clear water. Berdeena pictured them sitting side by side, one singing, one talking, feet cooling together, splashing each other with small waves, their skin wrinkling up as they soaked.

She arrived a little earlier than usual, picked up an old long-poled net that she found in Thenia's shed and began to drag the mesh across the pool, collecting brown leaves and drowned bugs. She was making piles on the side not too far from where she was standing. As usual, she was singing, but not loudly enough to wake Thenia or even for her to hear if she were already awake.

Berdeena didn't expect to be heard and neither did Thenia as she carefully came down her back steps, intending to startle Berdeena and stop her from poking around the pool, especially if she was intent on cleaning it up.

She had wanted to sneak up behind Berdeena to prove that if anyone could sneak about her property it was her. Berdeena could sneak around as much as she wanted on the property when the property became her property but that wouldn't be until after Thenia was dead. She was going to let her know, in no uncertain terms, not to ever mess with the pool.

On the last step, her foot got caught in her own nightgown; she tripped, lunged forward, and knocked Berdeena into the slimy stinking water. Coughing, panicked, and gagging on her own disgust at the water in her mouth, Berdeena was churning in the pool like an old washing machine as she struggled towards the edge where Thenia was making a cough-like noise. She gulped mouthfuls of air so that she would not choke on her own laughter as she made her way towards the edge to save Berdeena from drowning.

She had knocked Berdeena into the pool, but it was not Berdeena whom she finally managed to help out of it.

Selma came out of the pool and after drying off demanded cigarettes.

"You smoke?" the old white lady asked.

"Don't you?" Selma asked with a scowl that would have never crawled across Berdeena's open singing face.

"Yes." Thenia went into the house to grab her cigarettes.

"You could swim a little the first time we met." Thenia was old and unsure but still asked, "what happened? What happened to all them good lessons I given ya?"

Thenia sidled up next to the woman she had known as a singing phenomenon, hoping to resume the afternoon camaraderie to which she'd become accustomed.

Instead, lighting their cigarettes was the first sign that things would not be the same. For one thing, smoking and singing weren't compatible. Still, they sat next to each other intermittently puffing. Smoking, at best, was an unreliable pleasure. They didn't exchange music, food, or words, at first; they simply polluted the garden.

The next time Selma walked out to Pond-Beneath-the-Sun, Thenia was out back waiting. No greeting passed between the two as Selma sat down close enough for Thenia to give her a cigarette, lean over and light it.

"Did you marry in a church? Has your union been blessed?" Selma asked Thenia.

"Well, if you mean dedicated to something, I guess I can say yes. Ordained, as it was, by awfulness," Thenia answered and continued.

"My union was started in a church alright and who would have known that God would let the devil marry a mortal woman right inside one of his temples. Any good Baptist would have thought if the Lord were paying any attention, he'd a struck down my husband the moment he set foot across the threshold and me for bringing him into the sanctuary, trying to pass him off as decent. He was a troll, a mean old bastard that should have been stationed under a bridge by himself." Thenia made some odd-looking gestures as she sat next to the pool calling up her husband's memory.

Selma couldn't tell if her movement was invoking or banishing evil or maybe she was forgiving herself for speaking badly about the dead or praising God that the evil was gone. Thenia got up, walked around the garden until she found a rock, came back, sat on the edge of the pool, closed her eyes for a minute, and tossed the rock with a "thwump" smack dab in the middle of the pool.

Love notwithstanding, Selma had wanted to be away from The Hill between Two Towns, Aberdeen, her ways, and everything else about home though she desperately missed everything too. Mr. Thrace had been the fast car that picked her up and drove to the city without any ceremony that she could remember. She was missing details, but she wanted to preserve her ability to live in the city and away from her childhood home.

"What would make a marriage last?" she asked the old lady.

"Silence. Bad hearing, ignorance of who the other is and if you want it to last, you've got to just pretend that it's alright to live in a house and share your bed with a total stranger. As little conversation as possible, as much sex as possible, again that's if you like anything about him at all. If he's a sorry son of a . . . what might keep you going is 'laborate fantasies about how to kill him."

"Are you still married?" Selma asked.

"Till the day he died, though I took my own name back. I've always been more Landry than anything." Thenia got up, walked around the garden again, found a larger rock, sat down next to Selma, made a more elaborate gesture, and threw the rock smack dab into the middle of the pool again. "Thwwunkump!"

"You must love your husband," Thenia figured and said so.

"I love the smell of trees, my mother's food, and probably Malty who lived in my childhood with me." Selma said, and, "Maybe the warm chill of what's to come from Clifton Thrace's body on mine," so quietly that Thenia didn't hear her.

"You think you might cook something, any time soon? You can get to him with those meals you been makin'," Thenia said.

"I don't cook."

Thenia looked over at the woman who had been cooking

meals for weeks and wondered whether Negro women were plain weird.

She remembered talk about Selsie and her grandmother being the best friend each other ever had. There had been lots of talk about Selsie in Thenia's growing up, odd talk. Selsie was "two kinds of rice in one kernel or all the rice blends in the same bag." Mostly talk about her amazing food.

Surely, this woman was Selsie's relative. One day, she was making Selsie's amazing meals and the next claiming she couldn't cook. First, she sang all day and never smoked. Then she smoked and never sang. Thenia looked at her. She did look kind of different, but she knew she was the same. Truth be told, Thenia didn't always feel the same way all the time either.

Thenia's own mother had been moody. What would her children say about her? She chuckled to herself and knew she'd hang with whichever of these women wanted to hang out by her pool.

"You'd still be married to him even after he's dead. Or even if he'd divorced you secretly and was living with some other lady in the next town. Plus, if he had anything, you get to keep it. Some of our best moments of marriage happened after he was gone," Thenia Landry claimed.

"Sometimes, I'd run to the window and check to make sure he was still dead. He's in the pool and from the top of the house with a flashlight, I used to try and see him anchored at the bottom with the giant rock I rolled in to keep him there."

Selma looked over at Thenia to see if she were making up stories.

"Even now when I throw a rock in the water, I make all them wishes I couldn't make when I was little. First, I thank God that he's dead and that no one ever found out that I'd helped, then I wish I'd known another kind of man just to see if it'd make me different, then I throw the rocks right in the middle to make sure none of his bones get to see the sunlight." Thenia started laughing as she looked over at Selma. She kn ew the woman would be deciding whether to believe what she said. She also didn't know what had possessed her to confess but it was the first time and she figured she might as well tell the whole story.

It was way too late to send her to prison and that is, if there was anything still at the bottom of that pool but the rocks she had thrown in making wishes, like her pool was a tourist fountain, collecting payment for wishing. Nobody would believe the Negro woman anyway or more likely, no one would care. Most of her husband's family was gone and she didn't even think her children would be shocked. If they thought real hard, they would probably remember their father's meanness, but they wouldn't because most people made saints of the dead. The thing that she most regretted was that since he died, all the meanness that he left behind jumped back on her. She hadn't realized it at first. His meanness took hold of her, one tiny bit at a time. She kept away from people because she didn't want them to know she'd turned back nasty.

"I knew I was going to kill him when I had the twins. He took one look at my beautiful baby boys and said, 'They monkeyish babies but we'll make the best of it.' There wasn't anything monkey-looking about those boys but his words made them think they were no better than apes. I couldn't ever shake it off them. What those boys had was a monkey monster for a father and that was the only thing monkey about them. I didn't start smoking 'til the day he quit. He used to smoke out back on the patio. Every evening, after dinner, he'd smoke and drink by himself in what he called the sacred hours. The hours where he was finished with all of us; we were the worse part of his day he said. He wouldn't even let the kids play in the backyard after dinner. This entire garden," Thenia gestured with her two skinny old arms, "wasn't room for him and his children together. He drank the same drink all the time. I had so many fantasies about killing him I don't even remember if I poisoned his whiskey, pushed the urn out the upstairs window onto his soft white head, or smothered him while he was drunk and asleep on the patio. Think I did all three. What I don't remember is the order. To make sure, I'd been practicing pushing heavy things out the window which was hard work 'cause I had to pick it all up again or at least hide it from him. I didn't want anything to fall right next to him so he'd know I was trying to kill him. I wanted him to be surprised he was dead. I dragged him mumbling and slobbering near the edge of the shallow part of the water, kicked him in and watched him roll down into the middle 'V.' Wasn't too much he thought well of. He'd always said that the pool, whole backyard was stupidly built. All the crap that fell into it got stuck in the valley where the shallower end met the deep one. He always said it didn't 'precipitate proper- ly.' Never mind the rocks I stuffed into his pants. After he sank, the first thing I did was go back to the table where he'd been sitting and lit up one of his cigarettes—first time I ever lit up—then I sucked down the last inch of whiskey he'd left in the glass. You know I got so sick, sicker than I'd ever been my entire life but not before I struggled with one of them decorative boulders and levered it down into the pool right on top of him. Then I threw up right into the pool, same time as I realized how stupid I'd been finishing up the poison that I'd killed one-third of him with. One- third poison, one-third rocks in his pocket, weighed him down, final third drowning. Never did get the thing to fall on his head. I was sick so long that people thought I knew he was leaving me and that's why. When I started laughing out loud from my bed, they guessed I was coming all to pieces but I'd realized that it was a good thing that I had gone ahead and killed him three ways. One way might not have worked. They all figured he'd left me for whomever it was that he might have been playing with. But it wasn't true, he didn't leave, he wouldn't have because he liked being mean too much to give me up. If I thought he would leave, I'd have let him go. I think he liked to see the shock on my face every time I got a taste of what real meanness really was."

Thenia got up and started fumbling around for another rock.

Selma became quieter than she already was. An old feeling, one she almost never had, of not being where she belonged swept slowly over her right before she disappeared and left Martha sitting next to an old white lady in a garden that she'd turned into a confessional.

The old lady was talking up a storm. Martha simply listened, tried to identify Thenia, but wasn't too uncomfortable sitting on the edge of a funky pool, knowing she'd get to the bottom of things eventually, wondering why the old woman wanted to talk up and take the blame for something that surely, she couldn't have done. Martha could look at the frail old thing and tell she liked to make up stories.

Thenia Landry wouldn't stop confessing and when she finished her own, she went back a generation or two. "My grandmother and Selsie killed somebody too. They say once murder gets in, it stays and runs in the family. So maybe they killed somebody together and then Selsie killed my grandmother but Selsie killing Scilla don't really make sense. They loved one another, plus nobody ever seen Selsie again after Scilla died. They probably went on up in the woods and laughed themselves to death. Both their husbands had already died." She paused for a while to let her companion take it all in.

Thenia thought her friend was wearing another expression she'd never seen but she'd probably never heard a confession before either, because Thenia had never made one. She was feeling like a different woman today too.

"People said they used to have a special place. You know after we heard Selsie died, we waited and waited for someone to show up and claim everything. We figured her relatives would take what was rightfully theirs. My grandmother already left this house to Selsie. But no one came."

"When you first showed up with your sultry voice and crazy long hair, I thought it might be you. 'Bout time. You looked straight out some strange woods, that first day."

The name "Selsie" was a little familiar to Martha. One more formidable, inexplicable woman, she figured. This family seemed to be full of them. Looking around at the house, stinking pool, and weedy garden, she figured Selsie must have saved herself some trouble.

7

Aberdeen's House

Selma awakened in a little bedroom next to Thrace. Before she felt the moist stickiness between her legs, or the salty breeze coming through the window, she could smell that they had made love during the night. The room seemed full of pleasure and she only needed to wake up fully to pull it off the ceiling and hold on, but the room was unfamiliar. She sat up quietly, looked down at the shoes beside the bed, and slid her feet in. They were a comfortable fit. She stood up and stretched.

The children were already in the kitchen when she entered. "Morning, Mother."

"Morning, children," she replied, grouping them together.

The Thraces were finishing up their last few days by the Red Sea.

"Will you go to the beach with us?" Alley asked, knowing by her Mother's expression that the singing, cooking, big eating, and swimming were all cancelled.

Mother reached for the coffee that had already been made, sat at the kitchen table, and smiled as the steam rose above the cup.

She hadn't said "no" to the beach which turned out to be a "yes." She accompanied them, walking easily beside the children and Umm Ridah. Even Thrace agreed to join them in the early evening.

The children had their favorite spot between the house and the sea. They flattened and ordered their blankets and towels, not too close to the water.

"Look at Mother," Alley pressed her siblings. Mirella lifted up on one elbow, and the boy turned around.

"Her head is walking a foot above the rest of her body." They laughed, including Umm Ridah. Their mother was a mirage that the sun made in cahoots with the glassy sand and reflecting sea.

Once again, Selma searched for a place to enter the water and swim with memories through the details of her life. She got her toes wet but never both feet before she lost the ocean's door and the confidence to swim. She never managed to get into the ocean, try as she might. The children built castles with small bucket-shaped layers and made up stories about who lived inside.

"Two mothers live in my castle. One of them spends day and night pushing up the walls, making sure they don't collapse. She runs from room to room packing sand, making sure the house stays moist. The other one takes care of everything else," their brother said.

"Like what?" Alley asked her little brother.

"Cooks, cleans, takes care of Father. She never leaves home. She holds her son for hours and tells him stories and all her stories are about him. Who he is and where he came from," he whispered this last.

"Your mother sounds way too normal. Don't all mothers walk? A little?" Alley asked her little brother.

"Nope, he answered, "she doesn't like to leave home. She gets homesick."

"You know what I think Mother's doing?" Mirella asked. "Our mother?" Alley and her brother looked over at Mirella.

"Yes, our mother."

"When she walks, she's reliving the past like an old play in her head, only she's changing the end, setting things right. She misses something and I think it's in America," Alley explained first.

"No, she isn't. Mother is shopping for highly particular shells. She's making us a necklace," Mirella said.

"Maybe she's looking for lobsters to feed Daddy for dinner," their brother said.

"No, not today," Mirella said, "She will not be cooking today. Maybe she's looking for a place to put all her secrets."

Umm Ridah snickered hearing this last.

"If you mother put away secrets she be disappeared," Umm Ridah added to herself.

"If she's not singing, she's *not* looking for food for Daddy," Alley reminded the younger two.

"She's not singing."

"Allah a'alan. She cook nice, veby nice," Umm said, nodding.

"She has a cast of family in her head. Sometimes, when we interrupt her, they all get confused," Alley said.

"How can she remember all the parts? Mirella demanded. "Mother is walking a wall around us. She means to protect us, but it also hems us in."

"What do you mean 'hems us in?'" Alley asked.

"I mean shelters us from the world so we won't be hurt by anything. The trouble is that while she keeps away the bad things, she keeps away the good things too."

"What things?" Alley asked.

"I don't know, just *things*," Mirella answered.

"Name one."

"Friends," Mirella spat out.

"Friends?" Alley asked, surprised.

"Well, you don't have any, do you?" Mirella pointedly asked. "It's not because of Mother's magic wall."

"Then why?" "I have a friend. And anyway, you can only blame Mother at home, not school." Alley was a little annoyed. She did have a friend.

"Who's your friend?" the boy asked his older sister.

"MY FRIEND is Hala and you have to make your own. It's not so hard, you know."

"How would you ... ?"

"You might push out something that's interesting about

yourself. If someone wants to know about you, they'll ask you things and you can be interesting." Alley anticipated the question.

"Easy peasy," he mumbled.

"You don't want to seem too odd," Alley said, afraid that they were.

"Are you going to bring your friend home?" he asked.

"Well, that depends. I'll see when we get home. There are lots of ways to make friends. There's the accidental meeting. This kind of thing happens all the time. Parents could also have friends that have children, and the children know each other from birth, so naturally the children are already friends and then you could always have a natural way and people want to be near."

"Are our parents' friends back in America?" he asked.

"Probably," Alley answered.

"What needs constant motion?" Mirella asked and sighed, "A lesson painted in a parable."

"Parable?" asked their little brother.

"A pretty song."

"When is anybody going to see this work?" Alley asked.

"All will be revealed," she said in exasperated tones mimicking their Arabic teachers. Alley got quiet.

"How long did it take Michelangelo to paint the Sistine Chapel?" Another question they had all heard before.

"Mother magically paints an invisible mural of teachings and history for us. One day, we'll all sit down and she'll unscroll it. We'll stare at her wall for weeks and weeks to see it all. That's what she does every day; she adds to her wall," Mirella said with a great flourish. "The Misunderstood People's Wall," she called it.

"At the end, there's a giant painted understood period." Alley finished Mirella's mural, twirling, dotting the sky with a period. She rolled over Mirella and their brother, back and forth between their towels, like one giant wind, smashing all the castles.

Thrace didn't make his pilgrimage to the beach as promised on the first day of their last few at the Red Sea. The children weren't surprised until the day he did arrive before sunset. He was even wearing beach clothing. He sat down on all three of their big towels after pulling them together.

"Why are you so far apart? You didn't make room for your father?" he teased his children. "Where's your mother?"

"She's rehearsing," Alley said first.

"She's painting."

"Son?" Thrace waited for his son's idea. He looked over at him but the girls answered for him.

"His mothers are inside their wet sandcastle shoring up the walls."

"So you make up stories about your mother?" he asked. "None about me?"

"You're always working," Alley said.

"We know what you're doing," Mirella agreed.

"But Mother's here and we still don't know what she does."

Mr. Thrace realized that he was the uninteresting one, the one not worth imagining.

"Where is your mother?"

"Walking," Alley said.

"Still walking. I've never known anyone to walk so much. Do you children like to walk?"

"I don't think anyone likes to walk as much as Mother," Mirella stated.

In their entire six weeks at sea, the longest time the whole family spent together was in the car on the way to the Red Sea and back. On the way home, Selma rode up front next to Mr. Thrace who drove. They were leaving behind the first vacation that the family had ever had that they were all old enough to remember. They could have celebrated birthdays at the beach, they had lived in Cairo for more than a year and the children were now twelve, ten, and seven years old.

Father tried conversation, but Mother always made him a little quieter.

"What was your favorite part about the beach?" He threw

a question out into the air. No one was sure who should answer. He glanced at his wife and looked at the back seat through his rearview window.

Mother took such an inordinate amount of time to answer the question that the expectation hung in the air and then disappeared. Asking mother anything was a slow, unyielding pursuit.

Their father only asked his family questions for which the answers rarely mattered. He was an easy conversationalist and would have picked up any thread with them superficially, now that he was a part of the car-trapped audience. He was just as curious as the children about their mother and sensed that they would not answer before her.

"Walking. Walking around the edges of the sea," Selma finally answered.

"Our first swimming lessons before the acci…" Alley nudged Mirella. No one had mentioned the "almost drowning" to their father.

"Picnic seafood," Mirella said.

"Playing in the sand," the boy was polite enough to let his sisters go first.

"What about you, Daddy?"

"Having you all there," Father's answers always had to do with the goodness of being together which seldom ever included him.

Adjusting to being home again was most difficult. It wasn't the house so much as the fact that she had gotten used to walking on sand. Back on the hard-stone streets of Cairo, her feet could feel the difference. Her first walks were shorter which meant she spent a little more time at home. She found cigarettes in her little room. She had taken a paper clip and carved her name onto the foil pack. She wouldn't read the name, not out loud in these odd moments when she seemed to float, not quite tethered to anything at all.

She picked up the pack, held it to her nose. Stale tobacco was plain sad but didn't taint her ease as she warmed to her room, relaxing in her perfect seat in a private box. She caught a whiff of familiar scents from a small bottle of perfume on the low table that nested right under a taller one. Three small mosaic tiled tables, one right beneath the other were next to the chair. On the shortest table lay a pretty hairpin and as she reached over to pick it up, her foot hit the edge of a shoe poking out from the decorative curtain that skirted the chair where she sat. She pulled out the shoe, a comfortable after-walking shoe with double pads, and slid one foot in. This little room was her gift to herself. Only she would have known herself so well to provide such suitable things. The chair felt a little more welcoming and she eased back in her padded shoes and smiled. Dabbling a little perfume onto her neck with her index finger, she used the other hand to push the cigarettes away after she had put the small perfume bottle exactly where she must have left it. She was so comfortable that she forgot how long she had been sitting. She heard some sounds and followed them.

Four children were waiting at the kitchen table while Umm Ridah ladled something into bowls and passed them around. She stole glances at the unfamiliar little girl. The children were chattering and peering into the kitchen from her vantage point made it impossible for them to see her. They were too busy to look in the direction of their mother's quiet apparition. She liked being invisible to the children and wondered how she might stay so and still eat. She didn't want to disturb their obvious pleasure. The little girl fit in so easily at the table, she wondered if she too might stay. This one didn't have any freckles. Her skin was plain.

She turned and quietly walked back down the hallway into the bedroom. Plan B perhaps. She stood in the corner, near the window, looking out into the back garden when the children came bustling in. They stumbled into the room against the unclosed door.

"Umm Ridah is taking us with her to the bazaar." Alley spoke up, none of them looked at their mother.

"We need a little money please Mo—Mother." Alley closed

her eyes and held her hand in the direction she guessed her mother was standing and turned her head in the opposite direction. She was afraid to look. Maybe the Mother standing there wasn't the one who would reply in a normal way.

Mother looked over at the four children; three of them had the most ridiculous stances. Clearly, they were playing a game and she had forgotten the rules. One girl looked directly at her. Perhaps that one was it, and she quickly imitated a position somewhat similar to the children's with her hands reaching towards them and her head turned in the other direction.

'Money,' she thought 'did they ask her for money?' She made sure to stay frozen as she tried to figure out how money fit into the game. Children were such odd creatures.

Umm Ridah stood outside the door waiting for the children. In minutes when they hadn't returned, she knew they must have run into one of their mother's snags. She peeked in and noticed them all in poses, playing while she was waiting for them and just before she became perturbed for the useless waiting, she noticed a curious expression on their mother's face. Right then, she whispered, "Money?" and Umm Ridah knew she had no idea where she'd left her purse.

Umm Ridah had hung the purse in the closet after finding it in the bathroom and Umm Ridah knew exactly how much money was inside. She quickly crossed the room, turned the knob on the closet, and unhooked the purse from the inside back of the door. She walked to her mistress and handed the purse to her.

"Thank you." She looked inside the purse and saw quite a bit of money. Newly exchanged Egyptian money lay stacked next to a used ticket, an unopened bag of sweets, various old receipts, a couple of pens, another small bottle of perfume, and a pack of smashed cigarettes.

She lifted some of the money out of the purse and before she handed some bills to the children, she spoke.

"Mr. Thrace built a house for my mother."

The children didn't see her body parts come loose and take up various positions around the room. They hesitated, remaining near their mother. She was about to tell a story. In preparation, she cleared her throat which was now sitting on top of the bookshelf, flexed and pointed the toes on the foot that hung off the bottom of the bed.

Before she spoke again Umm Ridah took the money out of her hand and put the purse back in the closet. She grabbed the arms of her two girls and circled them with their friend around and out of their mother's room. The boy followed and she escorted them out of the house to the waiting car.

"Just because they give you money, they think they own your ears," Hala whispered as they climbed into the car. "Money always has a price and for children; it's ears. They pay you to listen to their old stories," Hala reiterated to her audience of three. "We love Mother's stories," Mirella said, sadly.

An empty bedroom didn't matter. The memory wanted out, coercing her into being its passage. She aired it like a radio playing on whether there was a listener or not.

"The house that Thrace built for Mama was a present. Mama didn't really want the house for a whole lot of reasons. Number one, she said she wasn't moving. Two, people couldn't be exchanged for presents. She hadn't given her daughter to him and her daughter wasn't hers to give, and she definitely wouldn't take me back and she told him so. Mr. Thrace said they would build it right in her woods; she could pick the site, anywhere she wanted. He refused to have his mother-in-law living in a three-room shack. It was just not proper, that's what he'd said over and over again.

Mama wouldn't kill a tree just to use it dead and she told him so too. The easiest place to build a house on her land was right next to the three-room where she already lived and that seemed ridiculous, especially if they weren't going to tear down her shack. Of course, Mama wouldn't let anybody touch her house. Somehow, Thrace got her to let him measure and he put some stakes in the ground calling them, and the rope he wrapped around them, the foundation of her new home. The new one, if built, would be three times as large as her old one, just the first floor would be larger. Thrace planned two, even three floors and he had decided to use brick, which cost a lot more than timber.

Maybe to him, the more he gave, the more he would get in return, but I was only one small prize. Comparing myself to a house seemed strange. It could shelter Mama at least, but what was I going to do for Thrace. He said 'nothing,' he said his gift was an expression of his joy and to let him worry about the building and the paying. All I had to do was 'be,' but I wasn't even sure I could do that. 'We're a family,' he said. 'Families share everything.'

Mama said 'NO,' one way and the other. Her clearing was big enough for a pretty large house but that's not what it was going to get. Maybe the land would get some more planting and harvesting. She'd be better off with more food than a larger house. Thrace said she could have both and for a time the standoff ended all conversation. He stopped badgering her and Mama wouldn't say nothing either.

The townsfolk were talking it up and Henry Dagomire Macomb got wind of another house, right next to Aberdeen's on her mountain, and when he did, he came back from wherever he was. He thought a house would be good for her and for him, it'd be a better place for the 'comebacks' he knew would be coming, but he told Aberdeen, 'Let him build woman—just to have it.' Mama had heard those words before; those were exactly the words that Selsie used to describe her freedom.

Mama told me that story long ago when I was little.

'Just to have it,' Selsie said. 'Not too many people even knew 'cause I didn't want nobody to mess with my freedom. I bought it, put it away, and kept right on doing what I'd always been doing. Maybe some days I'd smile more than I used to but mostly, I didn't.' That's what Selsie had said about her freedom and Aberdeen remembered, and once she told me, I remembered it too. It was a fact carved into Mama's spirit and mine.

Eventually, Mama told Thrace, 'Go ahead and build your house, right here next to this one.'

For months, Aberdeen watched and listened with absolute horror. She spent most of her days up in the woods until the house was finally built. Thrace said that hardly anyone who worked on the house ever saw anyone in the woods and asked him why he was building a house in such a strange place.

When it was finally done, Mama was amazed and so unsettled that she sat out in her field for hours gazing up at the house and talking to herself without ever going inside. That's what somebody from the town said. Her brick house had somehow acquired four numbers and neither Aberdeen nor the towns folk knew how they'd come up with an address for the woods. Was this the four-thousandth one-hundredth and twenty-seventh house that Clifton Thrace had built? Did it have four-thousand one hundred and twenty-seven bricks? Did it take four-thousand one-hundred and twenty-seven trips carrying the parts of the house up that makeshift road? Were there only four thousand one hundred and twenty-seven houses like this one in the world?

Aberdeen endured the waves of townsfolk who came up through the woods to visit her new house. She'd not let one of them inside and she didn't go in either. After a bit, she stopped minding them staring from the field. Sometimes, they stared together.

"Sure is fantabulous," somebody said.

"Aberdeen, now you done got yourself an address," the minister implied.

"An address? Why did I need an address?"

"Now you can get mail and people will know how to find you."

"Seein' as you've been in my yard more this year than ever before, doesn't seem like I was lost."

Aberdeen had a new house just to have it. As the minister said, she started to receive some mail. Not surprisingly, the first envelope was from the minister, inviting her to church, only Aberdeen didn't know because she never went inside the new house, and the mail when it came, once a month or every two months, was shoved through a narrow slit in the door. When it rained, the mail was dryer than she was and when the winter came, it was warmer too. Aberdeen liked the new house surrounded by snow and she began to grow used to the noises it added to the air.

The new house with the numbers hummed and clicked. Once, she thought the brick house sneezed. Her old shack merely shivered in return. Wood and mud houses like hers made noises too. Wood shrank and expanded, breathing, real, real slow. Mud dried. Together, the two structures were their own neighborhood and Aberdeen thought it particularly funny that one person with two houses could constitute a neighborhood. Her humor or maybe it was loneliness up there on her mountain mostly alone. She told folks it was her humor and her hearing that was responsible for having her believe her ears. The new house, hummed, grunted, creaked, sneezed, and finally began talking to the old one.

8

The Consequences of Mother's Oddness on the Children

Clifton Thrace came home early and interrupted the solemnity of his wife's afternoon. His intrusion startled her into a kind of involuntary cohesion. Her head came off the top bookshelf, and her heart out of the closet where she hadn't even noticed it had gotten to. Something was missing as she propelled herself towards the door. Her hand and Mr. Thrace's each held one side of a doorknob with the flat wooden door between them. Her liver scampered to catch her from beneath the bed.

"Are you wearing a different fragrance?" Of course, she took her time answering while Thrace listened for the merriment of children and heard none. She was as he'd left her not a few hours ago except that she had changed shoes and was now wearing some padded things that he hadn't ever seen.

She had been remembering and the leftovers muddled her brain. Something had come to her that she must pass on, a "hot potato game" of information. Some history had passed through her and left before she could hold on. Thrace's early return had bumped into her consciousness and she lost the temporary light of focus.

"Where are the children?" Thrace asked.

"Not new, old," she answered.

Thrace considered her very strange answer for a few seconds until he remembered he had first asked her about perfume. Now he was off on a different tangent altogether, thinking about her infernal habit of taking so much time to answer a simple question. Everything didn't require so much effort.

She didn't do anything else as slowly as she answered questions. Direct speech clearly rattled her. Thrace wondered if he spoke to her without intonation, merely talking, if she would respond more easily.

"We're going to dinner tonight at the home of the Ambassador. It's Jonathan Porter's farewell," he said without the raised inflection at the end that made a sentence a question.

"In the bazaar with Umm Ridah."

"Not in any bazaar, at the Ambassador's home." She certainly seemed stranger today than usual, which put Thrace more on edge. He imagined her at dinner, sitting beside someone that didn't know her, answering questions ten minutes after they had been asked. She would make a very strange conversationalist. For a moment, he entertained the idea of putting out a dictum—no one is to ask the attaché's wife any questions.

"Do you think you could respond more quickly when someone asks something of you?" Surely, the easiest thing to do would be to leave her at home. Then he looked at her standing in the middle of the room, looking so well put together for nothing. She hadn't known about the dinner, so except for the shoes, she had dressed nicely but simply. He attempted to measure the effect that her presence would have upon his reputation. If she were silent or answered questions quickly, she'd be nothing but an example of his ability to make good choices. But what could he expect from a daughter of The Hill between Two Towns? Truly, a preposterous name for any place!

Thrace needed a cocktail. "Can you be ready by six o'clock?" He left the room without waiting for her to answer, made his drink, and returned.

Jonathan Porter's retirement could have a major effect on his own tenure. Not that any new ambassador would have reason to change the terms of Thrace's stint, but that he might wish to change it himself. Working with Porter was spending a little time every day with a very good friend, or the way he would have imagined it would be if he'd ever liked any man more than Porter. They had been a team here in Cairo and Porter's usual ease would smooth over any wrinkles that his wife might cause with her odd and slow responses. What Thrace was truly feeling was sadness, which for him, like any other emotion, could be misinterpreted.

Jonathan Porter may have been the only man Thrace knew with whom he'd share a secret. He'd already told Porter about his father and grandfather's aspirations for him and had even let slip a childhood story or two. Porter was probably the only other living human being who knew that Thrace's father and grandfather had died together. If he'd felt inclined to whisper his suspicion to anyone, he would have told Porter that he'd always wondered if their deaths had been a choice and not an accident. Thrace hadn't believed they'd done anything so unthinkable as suicide, but he'd often guessed that if one of them had gotten into trouble, the other would have sacrificed himself easily, never giving a thought to the rest of the family. Each would have chosen first and foremost to sacrifice himself for the other. Thrace, his mother, and grandmother had been treated to kindness and even tenderness, but the two men were heart and soul to one another, and their closeness had provided a barrier to Thrace's. Mostly, he felt unwelcome between them and growing up without his father and grandfather's affection had eliminated the need. Thrace had never had many friends.

"Sure," she answered and Thrace sat down with his cocktail while she began her ablutions.

A short time later, Selma stepped out from her side of their bedroom, "Ready," she said. Thrace took his last sip and looked up at his wife. She was so simply elegant that he found himself wondering if she'd always been a foreigner, a foreigner to the mundane things and ways with which most folks concerned themselves. Absolutely, she had no business being from a town in the hills. All the guests, he understood now, would forgive her no matter how long she took to answer if she bothered with any answers at all.

His thoughts were all over his face. Selma smiled and held out her hand for him to collect.

Hala turned out to be quite the judicious friend. She had a cousin and advised Mirella that they should be friends with one another. Her cousin attended the American school and in Hala's mind, was closer in size and sensibility to Mirella than Alley. This way, each would have their own friend and when there was a need for a foursome, one would be available. Daphne, Hala's cousin, had been equally unpopular as the American girls. Secretly, Hala had been jealous of her cousin's half-American-ness. Now that she had a whole American friend, Daphne had been reevaluated. Hala could have an American best friend along with a half-American cousin, but one would not do without the other. Something about it was unseemly, though she could not have explained. Perhaps the answer lay somewhere in her mother's voice always denigrating her sister's American husband not for anything other than his lack of wanting to be or even understanding what it was to be an Egyptian.

Furthermore, Daphne's family seemed to enjoy more of what it was to be a certain kind of Egyptian than Hala's. They lived in a larger house with a nicer courtyard. They spent more time in the Prime Minister and other important people's company. In her own way, Hala avenged her own mother, as now she had her very own American, the prettier, taller of the two and had gracefully given the other one to Daphne. Hala had never disliked Daphne; she had only disliked feeling inferior to her. Now the two older girls could dictate to the younger ones.

Mirella instantly took to Daphne as it was true that they

were approximately the same size. Neither of them liked being told what to do by their older counterparts, but neither of them had the guts or the gumption to start a rebellion.

Daphne's halfness had always been held against her. Furthermore, even she understood one half and had no clue about the other. Her white American father had returned to the States ages ago and though there were always promises of his imminent return, she hadn't seen him since her second birthday, and she had long since grown indifferent to his biweekly telephone calls. The last thing in the world that she could have imagined wanting was an American friend. They didn't make good fathers. They moved back to America.

Maybe the darker ones would be different, but she doubted this too. All the same, however, there seemed to be no other choice. She took her place and walked next to Mirella, a couple of paces behind Hala and Alley, but she wasn't crazy about it.

Mirella didn't have any sort of gauge with which to measure friendship so Daphne's quiet indignation over everything, she guessed, was part of her character. Daphne hadn't even known that something called a Black American existed and she wondered aloud more than once, "If you're supposed to be Black Americans, why are the three of you so light?" Also, she was supremely jealous that Mirella had been back and forth to America and had the gall to barely remember. "Who wouldn't remember going home?"

Oftentimes, to Mirella, friendship felt akin to being sanded then smoothed as she would have to endure so much unprofitable chatter before they could settle down to a nice game of jacks.

"It smells funny in your house."

"Don't you have an Egyptian cook?"

"Is your maid American? I can't sit on a dirty floor and get stains all over my clothing, you know," Daphne repeated herself.

This nasty little monologue took place every day but only

at the Thrace home. At first, Mirella took the time to answer her friend's terrible memory or lousy ritual.

At Hala's, Daphne had another set of fussiness.

"Your family doesn't buy your bread at the proper bakery, do they?" Only Hala knew that Daphne was referring to the so-called American bakery which is why on this note she ignored her.

"Did your maid finally get those glasses she needed?"

"You know perfectly well she has always worn glasses. Yours does too as they are twin sisters."

"Are we going to be having the same tea?"

"Last week's tea is being saved especially for you." Hala wondered why in the world Daphne had picked up her own mother's habits. Their subjects were different, but the intent was entirely the same. Maybe biliousness was like thickness, nose size, and hair color that spilled into the baby whether the mother liked it or not. Their family was always hoping that no one got their grandmother's nose, though they referred to it as a throwback to their ancient Pharaonic ancestors. To her credit, Hala knew how to shut up both her cousin and her aunt, but sometimes let them go on.

"Is it English tea?"

"It's Father's favorite tea. He has it every afternoon right here in our garden in Egypt. I think I'll wait and have my tea with faather," she said, stretching the vowels in her imagined American way. She would use her so-called American accent if Daphne turned particularly annoying.

"Father will be here soon and stay the night. And maybe the rest of his life too," Hala said and snorted in her cousin's direction.

In the beginning, Mirella spent a good bit of her time with Daphne engaged in petty disagreements weighted by the game of jacks that held them to a small circle on the floor. Each insisted that her own version of jacks was the original and each claimed that her culture had invented it.

"So what really is a Negroa?" Daphne asked

"A Negro," Mirella corrected her. "I'm a Negro."

"But what does that mean exactly?" Daphne hadn't satisfied her curiosity at all.

"What do you mean exactly?" Mirella asked.

"Never mind that really; there are lots of words that describe people in Arabic, but were you poor, were you slaves? How come you look like you look? Didn't American slaves come from southern Africa. You don't look African," Daphne went on.

"We look just like other Negro Americans. What are you?"

"Most of us are Cairenes; we're descendants of the Pharaohs."

"Did the Pharaohs play jacks?" Alley butted in to help her younger sister.

"They invented them," Daphne answered.

"My mother played," Mirella lied and continued, "when she was a little girl in the mountains."

"My grandmothers played—both of them." Daphne one-upped her.

"You have the same grandmother as Hala, don't you?"

"On one side."

"That was the grandmother that only sat and was served?" Mirella repeated what she'd heard from Hala.

"So?" Daphne asked.

"So, she didn't play jacks."

"So?"

"The grandmother who played was your American grandmother, right?" Mirella was setting her trap.

"My Egyptian grandmother ordered her servants to play in front of her." Daphne had to go along with Hala about her mother's mother even if it wouldn't win her any arguments. Hala was mean and bossy.

"Where were the servants from?" Mirella guessed that Daphne would say some darker part of Africa and of course, she was waiting for what would be a sweet victory.

"The Sudan."

"Aha!" Mirella sighed extra loudly. "The Sudanese got it from the Angolans and the Angolans took it to America and your American grandmother learned to play it from her mother, who learned it from her mother, who learned it from a slave."

"Your ancestors were slaves!" Daphne said.

"Of course they were," answered Mirella, quite proudly. "The past is part of the whole that makes us. If you love yourself, and you must, love your history too." Mirella sang out and even Alley turned toward her. Surely those lyrics came from one of their mother's songs. Where was the food in it she wondered? The song was probably about bananas.

Daphne sat momentarily quiet.

The jacks game went to foursies in silence, which is just where Alley and Mirella's little brother hid. That is, he did when the games took place at home. No one had a little brother for him to play with, so he played by himself in the silence and shadows next to his sisters where he could pretend to play with them without their notice. Generally, he spied on them from behind the door of the next room. They liked the formal front rooms though they were hardly comfortable, chock full of hard silver furniture inlaid with mother-of-pearl, tall standing silver and gold filigree screens leaned against two walls, and a calligrapher's tapestry on the other. The highly polished floors were bare behind the sofas and all four girls preferred to play on the smooth tiled floor, surrounded by ancient luxury. Together, they had chosen the grandest of rooms for the simplest of games.

Little brother eavesdropped upon their nonsensical arguments and their ever-continuing game that no one seemed to win or lose. He heard the delicate jingle of the jacks scattering and the tap of the ball as they bounced it, scooped jacks, and caught everything in one hand. He lay back on the carpet in the other family living room listening. He didn't know what the girls were talking about, but the sound kept him company, letting him pretend that the choice to be alone was his. If Umm Ridah or one of the others happened to pass through the living room, he would pretend to be reading, upside down like his mother. He lay comfortably across the carpet with a decorative pillow under his head behind the slightly opened doors between the living room and the front hall. After school, his was a daily pastime of spying, sucking salt, and splitting squash seed shells with his teeth and tongue.

"Iswid, Iswid," he heard a male voice in badly accented Arabic, peeked around the door to check his sisters and their friends, then slowly looked behind him into the living room. No one reacted but him. He sat up, very still. He waited to see if the voice would say something else. When it did, he jumped up, and stepped into the middle of his sisters' games.

"Did you hear that?" he asked.

"Hear what?"

"Someone calling," he answered,

"Calling what?

"I'm not sure. You didn't hear anything?"

"Get out of the game," Alley gently pushed his leg. "You're in the way."

"Like all boys all the time," Hala said.

Brother stepped back away from where the girls were playing.

"Further," Daphne said and rolled her eyes at him.

"Iswid, Iswid," he heard the whisper, "step away from the girls. They don't want your company."

He again confirmed that he was the sole listener, peeking behind all the doors, kneeling to look under the sofas and behind the screen in the corner. He looked out the windows, out the doors, opened the closet doors in the hallway, stood stock still, and waited. The voice spoke again and then, like legions of folk from time immemorial, he pretended he hadn't heard a thing.

"Aswad, Iswid, little brother, you've nothing to do but watch girls."

It was not a question nor was it untrue. The voice must have been somewhere close, and following him around because besides school, all he ever did do, was watch the girls. What else did he have to do? Umm Ridah went to the movies every other afternoon but she only occasionally took the children. Anyway, he wasn't too comfortable watching films that he didn't understand because they were too similar to the rest of his life. He went to school and then he watched his sisters. But it all felt the same. Clearly, the voice would be an odd addition to his day and he already sensed that it might not add any fun.

The voice couldn't exactly be timed or expected. And from the very beginning, from the first time he heard the voice until the next ten times, he'd already guessed it probably wouldn't be around when wanted or needed.

"Iswid, Aswad, today is a different day." The voice said suggestively. The audacity to speak at all was an achievement, little brother guessed, though not on all occasions. Frankly, its first utterance had proven its ability and since then, even when silent, little brother sensed the voice near, biding time. More than anything, he was simply curious and thirsty for words aimed directly towards him. What would the voice say and when? Would it always be right, how did he fit in? Was the voice kin to him in a way, would anybody else ever hear?

The voice never grew predictable but did grow into comfortable company like an old radio that was always on whether it aired music, commentary, or merely buzzed, and over time, it ceased to matter whether the voice said anything meaningful or not. For one thing, one glorious thing, the radio had named him and he was eternally thankful.

The voice always called him Iswid or Aswad. He knew "Iswid" meant black and maybe slave depending upon who said it and so did "Aswad." His voice pronounced the same word with two different accents. Little brother didn't mind one or the other. The voice always called him twice and he began to think of himself as "Black Black," which was better than "son" or boy or little brother. He had always wondered if his father had forgotten his name and only vaguely remembered their relationship when he called him son.

"Iswid, Iswid, why don't we do something? Something, together. Let me think of it. There are wonderful things for a boy to do in Egypt. Welcome in Egypt Iswid. Iswid? Did I ever welcome you?"

The voice talked and basically, *talked*. After a few months, Black Black realized that that was all it could do.

"So you're not God, but another little boy? Where's your body and what's your name?" Black Black whispered.

"Iswid, Iswid, I'm godlike; I don't need a body and you can call me, today that is, today you can call me Karim, *generous* in English."

"Karim?"

"No, not in your American way, *Kareem*. Say it right, or I won't answer."

Black Black finally had a friend, albeit an unreliable one but that did seem to be the nature of friendship. If he were very very quiet, he could sense the voice's presence which was all he needed for a little comfort. Because he was used to being the invisible friend himself, it was easy for him to let his voice be. He never knew for sure, but assumed his talking radio was around, especially when he was alone. Not daring to talk to him out loud, he had no proof that his friend could hear his thoughts.

Their communication tended to be one-sided. Neither of them was the least bit bothered and so began and continued the friendship between a disembodied voice and an unvoiced boy. His friendship with his voice helped him understand why old Egyptian men fancied their radios. Next to each other, buffered from conversation by the worlds they carried with them—bearded, draped, and wrinkled old men with faces like breathing statuary in a disorderly museum, drinking mint tea in the cafés, smoking atop the ancient walls along the pathway the children followed between school and home. Old Egyptian men were holding, shaking, and cursing their small transistor radios, listening and berating one another about the news. Black Black began to wonder if the radios weren't stand-in bodies that old Egyptian men purchased for their secret voices.

Sometimes, he didn't listen for what his voice said so much as where the sound came from. Was the voice inside his head or right next to it? Sometimes, sound gurgled up his middle, hidden inside him and he wondered how words managed to get in his belly, and at other times, sentences were whispered into his ear. Something invisible stood right next to him and expressed itself. No wonder no one else could hear. The tones were far too low and close.

Karim didn't say obscene things and never offered new information.

Black Black was considering that his voice didn't have any wider world than he did. Evidently, he was stuck in the same place. Occasionally, he did say things that Black Black wasn't necessarily thinking but they weren't things that he couldn't think. His friend was no smarter than he was. Like the old men, he had his own radio, but for now, he decided not to waste the money on buying it a body.

Mirella had to endure Daphne's constant complaints and Alley was always fighting with Hala about where to play. Black Black, of course, preferred for everyone to play at home but the girls were often at their friends' houses after school and on those days, he was left completely alone. So far, to Black Black, all relationships seemed rather odd and unreliable. Other people were never quite manageable, and he bet if he bought the voice a real transistor radio, it would only use it to become more unmanageable. With the girls, the jacks game was automatic and so, too, was the accompanying argument. Friends were good and troublesome. His voice was the same as everyone else's friend only better because he didn't have to watch him doing whatever he wanted to do.

"Iswid, Iswid, Allah! Allah! Do they ever get tired of jacks?"

"The taller one is pretty pretty even with that nose. She could smell you coming."

"Iswid, do you think the races mix well? That one's always

fighting with herself. She's a nuisance to humanity. She's a testimonial that races shouldn't mix."

Rather than argue, for months and months, Black Black's friend kept him full with nonsense which suited him better than the give-and-take in conversation. He was a good eavesdropper, though the voice spoke only to him and he tended to think in long uninterrupted rifts, if he were thinking at all. Black Black's tendency was to watch and listen. He could probably describe the girls in far more detail than would be healthy and far better than the four of them put together could imagine. Naturally, he noticed when the four of them, all at once, began to change.

"Iswid, Aswad, look at the girls. Now you've really got nothing better to do than watch them. Growing nicely, growing very nicely. Soon dates won't be just for eating." It was an emphatic statement. Black Black didn't need him pointing out something that was already perfectly clear. He'd been listening and ignoring Karim Iswid (as he'd decided to name the voice) for quite some time now. But he had always disliked it when Iswid trampled upon his thoughts, which occurred in one of two ways. Either Iswid distracted him by alighting on the very same subject in a more interesting fashion or he started talking while Black Black was thinking something he truly wanted to remember.

Most of Black Black's thoughts about Daphne, he wanted to remember. Yet, she was the girl that Karim Iswid disliked the most, so they often found themselves on the very same subject. Just when Black Black was imagining her looking at him and smiling.

"Iswid, Aswad, that one's eyes are crooked. One is American and the other is Egyptian. She's going to be cross-eyed when the two halves want to study each other. She'll be smiling, but really Allah, Allah, she's all frown. She'll grow up to be a contortionist, but no one will notice. She won't be paid. It's a good thing that her American father has money. She'll need it to attract a husband."

Spying on his sisters hadn't changed too much over time except that the girls had changed the venue. Hala and Alley spent the afternoon in Alley's bedroom, seated before the large mirror at the vanity table. In between taking turns in the bathroom, Daphne and Mirella sat on the floor behind the two older girls waiting for their turns to take in their own images. Black Black lay just on the other side of the door to their adjoining bedrooms. Before the girls had made friends, the door was always opened, now the door was always closed until Black Black creaked it open to listen, and sometimes peek.

"I'm going to be just like my mother when I grow up," Hala said with relish.

"What do you mean? What is it about her?" Alley asked. "What does your mother do that you can do?

"She's been educated abroad. She's very well rounded and intelligent. She's so many friends and is so talented. She calls me her Junior, that's what it means in English," Hala explained.

"My mother calls me 'the one with the active mind!'" Alley pulled that one out of the past.

"When did Mother ever call you that?" Mirella asked.

"Once," she told her quietly and made the "shut up" face.

"Well, she called me 'pretty little one.'" Mirella had to be in on anything about their mother.

"Once too?" Alley whispered back and they both laughed. Neither one had any more claim on their mother.

Later, after their friends had gone home, Alley said to her sister, "Remember when we asked her about our birthdays, when we were born? How long it took, was it the morning or the evening. I think she tried really hard to answer."

"But did you ask the right mother?" Mirella hesitated then asked anyway.

"I tried all of them, in yellow, when she's singing, even when she's just quiet."

"Neither of them? Every once in a while, for a moment, she seems so real and then it's as if she's never been here,"

Mirella answered.

"She doesn't remember anything about us at all." Alley said what she'd guessed.

"We see her every day. Why doesn't it seem like she's with us?"

"She's involved in other things and we just don't know what those are. Maybe she is a spy, but her subject is herself," Alley said. "Maybe when she gets to the bottom of the end of things, she'll tell us from the beginning."

Black Black listened no matter what they talked about. To Black Black, all the girls were alike in the sense that they had all the necessary parts: eyes, noses, cheeks, lips, and mercifully bodies. But his opinions about the girls were decidedly different than his voice's. Of course, his opinions were superior which he attributed to his being part of the same physical realm. He knew that Karim must see the girls as he referred to them whenever he wanted, but he was sure that the voice could not be in the same room with them, at least not physically and he thought there was something to be said for being able to look at a girl who could look back, even if he spent most of his time staring at them without their notice. Hala did have a large nose and it drew the eyes unnecessarily in its direction except if she were wearing her navy blue short sleeved dress.

Something about the navy blue made him look at her other parts, not so near her face. Black Black actually liked Hala's nose and the fact that to get to know her face, the nose came first which was probably a good thing. Her overwhelming feature forced him and anybody else that looked in her direction to slide sideways off her nose and meet the frank expression that waited in her eyes. He liked her more for it. Her expression was as steady as the sky and anyone who liked the sky would like her.

Daphne, on the other hand, had nothing to "unrecommend" her. She was so easy to look at that Black Black found it almost impossible to look away. His eyes didn't claim one feature either; they meandered. Over her two small brown piercing eyes to the grooved area between them and the true side of her face that met her black crooked hairline. Her high forehead generally let him begin an easy ride over her face as it gently sloped towards her pear-shaped nose but that was only when he took a frontward projection. If he looked at her profile, the nose was seemingly long until it met a plump short end. Between her fruit-like nose and the tiny jump to her always dry, pursed lips sat an asymmetric mole. Here Black Black always lingered, at the oblong beauty spot which lay three-quarters of the way between the center of her face towards the end of her lips on the right-hand side of her face, and waited for the secret message she might send him. When he was full of silence, he headed on downwards to her rather pointy little chin.

His own sisters were harder to look at, or at least gazing at them always required an uneasy adjustment on his part, like finding out that breakfast on the moon was the same as it was on earth. It was supposed to be different but wasn't. Where he expected to be startled there was an unsurprising sameness, and all three of them had nice little noses so that when the sun shined over them in the afternoon the same small shadow fell over the middle of their flat lips. Lips that were neither large, nor thin, nor reddish, nor too supple. They were all a little stiff-lipped which showed up in their Arabic but not in their English.

Alley's eyes were shinier with a slightly lighter tone than that of her two siblings. Lately, she had a readier smile that came often enough for no apparent reason and again, Black Black was a little dismayed that all their smiles opened to reveal the same slim gap between their two front teeth. Surely, his gap should have been stronger or wider to illustrate their difference of gender, but he and Mirella also shared the same brown eyes with lashes so thick and long that they sometimes obscured their vision.

Black Black viewed through them a gloom that hovered over everything while Mirella told him they were cover.

They could hide under their lashes and be protected by the fact that unless someone were standing very close, their lashes could hide their true expression. For Black Black, mostly it was a chore to throw his eyes open.

All three of the Thrace children's eyes might have been the same size, but Black Black's were always the ones—the most wide open.

9

Walking towards Childhood, Birthdays, Past, and Home

Selma had been walking the streets of Cairo a few days after Jonathan Porter's farewell party when she first noticed her company, the funny little man who had sat across from her at dinner. Clifton Thrace had been the attaché for Jonathan Porter, the US Ambassador to Egypt, for many years when Porter surprised everyone and announced his retirement. Selma guessed the man worked in some capacity at the consulate or embassy. He had stared at her most of the evening, sneaking his eyes her way from behind pillars, large vases of flowers, and even a person or two. During the meal, he sat diagonally across from her and spent much of the time peering between the tall water and wine glasses. When she looked at him, he obscured his face back behind the centerpiece, offering the side of his head and his right ear. She looked directly at him, proffering the smile he may have wanted. He was shy she guessed and a little strange. It was his choice, but he would not give her the pleasure of receiving her nod. Instead, she was treated to his profile and three-quarters of the back of his head. It was a game of cat and mouse he played, and she was amused.

Jonathan Porter himself had been her true dinner companion. His baritone voice musicalized everything he had to say, and Selma admired his cadences even when his speech was not directed to her—and most of what he said was not. Porter sat next to her the entire evening, much of it with his arm draped over the back of her chair, sheltering her, speaking to everyone as if on behalf of the two of them. Selma was silent and included. He'd enveloped her in his easy manner and for moments she felt confident and longed to expand her time in his company.

"The trick to changing countries is . . ." he'd said but she hadn't heard Porter's words and thought her own—not knowing any tricks.

On the street, walking near the high wall break of the Cairo Museum, she caught a glimpse of the funny little man when she turned around after feeling eyes on her back. He had given her an odd sensation once before. Somehow, at the end of the party, he had managed to be the one who delivered her wrap to her. He had insisted upon draping it over her and even went as far as to straighten the cloth while pretending to brush lint from the top layer. He had ever so carefully touched the back of his hand against the bottom of her cheek.

How utterly odd it was to be touched by the soft hand of an absolute stranger.

Mr. Thrace noticed too and interrupted by clasping his hand on her arm just above the elbow, gently ushering her forward.

Now, on the street, Selma caught sight of the man with his temporarily frozen face sitting too purposefully amongst the haphazard Egyptians in a café on the edge of the Khan al Khalili. She skirted the bazaars in search of as much solitude as possible on the crowded Cairo streets. He could not follow her surreptitiously any more than he could stare. She could feel his presence and wanted to alert him that being followed amused her, she wanted to let him know that she was in on the joke. Selma couldn't remember when she had had such fun, playing hide-and-seek in the open.

When she felt him, she didn't always look, giving him the privilege of the illusion of invisibility. Other times, she'd glance back immediately assuring her own suspicion. Sometimes, she liked to give him the guts to talk. She imagined him having a message from Porter, rushing to catch up to her, stopping her. Most of the time, she left him alone, glimpsing him here and there, taking the place of a familiar tree that she looked forward to seeing. Some days he was more disheveled than others. The sidewalks changed too. More burnt corn husks to step over, more sand.

The children's game of trailing their mother began again too. Where there had been one silent man, now were three often noisy children. She'd see her followers on the same day but never together. Maybe her two sets of followers ought to band together in an alliance of common goals. The children were eager to have her do something for them. She couldn't quite remember what she was supposed to do or where she was supposed to go. She was equally uninformed about the man from the consulate; she wasn't even sure that he worked at the embassy or for Porter but assumed that he must.

Selma walked as she always did—with energy but without a destination. Rounding first one corner and then the next, she didn't know if she'd caught glimpses of the children or merely imagined she had.

One early evening, when she arrived back at the gated front of their entrance, she saw them all. The consul man was standing amongst the children until she came closer and he rushed off.

"Who was that you were talking to?" Selma asked the children.

"No one, a nice man," they answered in a surprised unison.

"What did he say?"

"Nothing, really. Just hello." They looked up at her, as if she had come to life from nothing.

"Why should I go to the—what was the name of the place?" Selma asked.

"Mother, will you go please, to the Ramses Lily?" Alley asked.

"Please, Mother, will you?" Mirella joined her sister.

"Why?"

"We need to borrow their special room," Alley answered.

"What special room?" The children were determined not to use the word "party" as they couldn't reveal their surprise.

"Oh Mother, we can't tell you why. It's for something we're planning," Alley pleaded.

"It's a surprise," Mirella put in. She had given away more than they had discussed and her sister sighed angrily, blowing air her way. But somehow "a surprise" worked.

"Alright," said their mother.

"Today?"

"Tomorrow," she answered, soothing the children at once. They smiled and she had put off with a promise what she still did not understand.

There were several different ways to get to the Ramses Lily Hotel and Selma had chosen none of them; still the children were a short way behind as she continued to walk. She turned down the narrow lane towards the ancient Coptic Church and as she passed the old doors, she glanced backwards over her shoulder to see if the children followed. A few steps forward and they were still nowhere in sight as Selma continued onwards, simultaneously somewhat relieved and disappointed. She had grown used to distant company and the accompanying noise. The street was narrow and sloped with uneven stones and without the noise of her entourage, she had no choice but to hear her own clop-clopping. Downwards, then left, she counted twenty footsteps before she allowed herself to look back. She took forty more steps then craned her neck and looked to the right, feeling the searing poke of two eyes on the center of her back. The consul man had turned the corner. Relieved, she walked on without ever looking back again.

The next day, she headed out the kitchen door, raced across the compound, and veered to the right, the exact opposite direction of the day before. Fleet and tricky, she had an amazing number of walking speeds and didn't need to be moving very fast to leave her four followers behind. Smiling to herself while thinking that she preferred secret company to be invisible, she tripped and almost toppled completely over. Quickly righting her stance, glancing around to assure that no one had seen her momentary loss of dignity, Selma stood up taller and moved faster. She'd almost felt the sensation of being chased when she turned, stopped, and realized that she was alone. Christ, she must be taking leave from her senses. Then laughing to herself, she decided to let them go, pretending to wave away the ephemeral little beings scampering to freedom.

She walked on until she suddenly knew why the kids and the consul man were together, why they wanted her to secure a room at the Ramses Lily. How in the world did they remember what she never did? Surely, her birthday was coming. The kids and the consul man were together to plan a birthday party for Selma! Thrace must have put them together for such a preposterous mission.

She would endure it, for their sakes, honestly pleased that they had remembered. How wonderful to be considered. Selma couldn't remember ever having a birthday party.

She eased her pace, and still walked long and fast enough to leave her thoughts behind in the passing squares. Walking opened her mind, cleared the nagging, and left her empty and calm so that she could enjoy the subtle pleasure of moving. Back to the comfortable solitude of moving without the weight of waiting chores or the burden of history. She walked until the mechanics became automatic, her entire body so light and effortless she was free-floating through the city, boundless without map or destiny.

She was unnaturally tethered, however, whether to the house, impossibly to the children, or to her husband; it didn't matter. Selma eventually made her way home—the long smooth rope of the day first unraveled, grew slack, then recoiled, tighter than before.

Agnes woke up, put on her yellow dress, and wouldn't have smiled except her lips curved upwards. She had joined her body with an emotion already in progress, a leftover that she would be unable to fathom, making her wonder who had cooked in the first place.

When the children saw her, coordinated in yellow, they were disappointed.

"She might go out," Mirella said.

"Doubtful," Alley answered. Yellow Dress Wearing Mother did not go out as much as the other ones. "But we can ask her while she's holding us. Maybe we can talk her into our party."

Black Black didn't say anything. He dreamt his own dreams in the warm circle of his mother's arms.

Agnes preferred to hug in silence. This time, while she held each of the girls, they talked and talked about themselves and their friends and something they were all planning together. Agnes could hold them but not listen, enjoying the physical closeness and easily ignoring the noise. She began to prefer the boy as he was still mostly silent; however, the few things that she did hear came from his mouth.

"Other kids have parties. Big ballroom birthday. Ramses Hotel?" Surely, by now, he spoke in whole sentences, but Agnes could only pick out a few words. The children seemed overly excited and holding them didn't immediately calm them the way it always had. They were growing—right before her eyes despite her wishes—growing and changing, cooperating with the world and not Agnes. Trying to hug them prickled her. She'd had to change her hugging position and soon the hugging chair. Two could no longer comfortably fit.

Instead, she began to walk more, and one day she saw the children behind her. An hour later, a funny little man seemed to be following her and she ignored them all. She understood the children wanting to be with her all the time though she was unsure of the disheveled man. He seemed vaguely familiar and walked as if he had forgotten something, something that she might be able to provide by mere proximity. Agnes never thought of herself as an aid to anything; generally she was the opposite—disjointed as ever. Her clothing was a foil as she was always precisely dressed. She told herself that change was mostly an illusion, a thing or things she must ignore until they went away. In time, the funny little man would disappear.

Each morning, after Agnes hugged the children for a few hours, she went out. She thought she was alone until she spotted the man yet again. Ignoring him hadn't worked and she had no idea why he would keep following her. Thoughts kept bubbling up in her consciousness, making it very difficult for her to move with ease. Agnes could either focus on being followed by the queer little man or walk. She could not do both. Seeing him stopped her in her tracks. She would manage just fine until she turned and spotted him. She tried not to look back and if she could not gaze backwards, she could not cross the street and walked around the same block over and over again. If Agnes walked the same block repeatedly, she would become so exhausted, she could barely think or move. On the other hand, if she walked two hundred different blocks, she would become so refreshed both mentally and physically that she could walk two hundred more. The disheveled little man was a hindrance, and she could not continue to be followed by him. He must want something. Agnes stopped so that he could take whatever it was, or possibly give her something? The little man approached her, he raised his hand a touch, she thought he was about to speak but he hurried away.

Agnes had an inkling that something was about to happen. Her entire life, she'd always believed that one day, some stranger was going to arrive and bring with him a very large package. He would hand it to Agnes and inside would be her very own story. She would unpack her box carefully, putting everything where it belonged, neatly arranging the past. It didn't matter how it arrived. Maybe it wouldn't come in a box, maybe not with a little man, but Agnes was open and would be accepting.

In childhood, Agnes had once been cited for reading the most books in her entire town. She had taken more from the library, borrowed more from families around town, and generally seemed to have more interest in books than anyone else in from The Hill between Two Towns.

There had been some question as to whether the prize should be awarded on Agnes's birthday. Of course, she hadn't read any of the books. Better, she had imagined them. She had held each and every one in her hand for as long as it took to imagine the entire story. She had turned all the pages too.

Finally, she understood. In Cairo, she was to be given the party she had never had. Those cheesy bundles together with the funny little man were going to give her her long overdue award and a party at, where was it they said? The Ramses Hotel?

Agnes hurried home. She was so excited that she could not sit still to hug the children and if Agnes couldn't hug the children, then Agnes wasn't Agnes.

Actually Leaving

The house had grown quieter as if weighed down by the children's disappointment. A few days into the new month, they heard loud uneven singing coming from the kitchen. Berdeena was trying to teach Umm Ridah a song.

Fish from the sea
Fruit from a tree
Nature provided sustenance suuusteeenannce
Man rubbed sticks for fire

Grain from the fields
Birds from the sky
God provided beauty
Man shaped iron.

White crested green waves
Flowers dancing on weeds
Crickets and butterflies

Man hooked traps and nets

To see color, man needed womankind
Sweetness ridin' on a slow breeze
Music in the morning light
A man will always need a woman . . .

Umm Ridah's heavily accented alto stumbled over "breeze" and reached its pitch on "always needin' an woman." Clapping, Berdeena laughed and began the whole song over again.

Mrs. Thrace always wore her yellow dress with the flowers for long periods before she took it off and showed up dressed any kind of way, cooking and singing. It was one thing that Umm Ridah felt sure about. She must be saving her flowered dress from the smells and stains of cooking. She was an odd mistress, probably the oddest. Umm Ridah liked the fact that she didn't have to get involved with her mistress. Mrs. Thrace kept her own secrets and her own counsel and Umm Ridah knew that she was appreciated as much for taking care of the house and the children as for leaving her alone. They were perfectly capable of sharing a house, even closely, even when Mrs. Thrace decided to sing and asked Umm Ridah to join her.

At these times, Umm Ridah didn't know what to make of her mistress or her songs. The children enjoyed them and that was enough.

Sweetness in a slow breeze
A man will always need a woman.

Raindrops fall out of the sky
Sand rubs off rocks
The Earth follows the earth's melody
Man grows hair in his ears.

A woman will hear nature's song
All men will always need a woman.

Not particularly musical, Umm Ridah couldn't hear the beauty in most music. With her very large fleshy ears, she claimed to have a heightened sensitivity to sound.

"ilragel diaman mihtag li habibti."

Alley translated Berdeena's words for Umm Ridah.

"A man did always need an woman," whether the man knew the truth or not. Umm Ridah didn't try to sing too much because English tasted funny in her mouth. She swished her hips a couple of times and hummed as she worked. Together, she and Berdeena made a mountain of food. A hybrid of Egyptian and American flavors, a first for the Thrace household. Both Berdeena and Umm Ridah enjoyed themselves immensely and Umm Ridah stayed in the kitchen long after she was used to because Berdeena insisted that she sit and eat with the rest of them. When they were all stuck in their chairs unable to move, Berdeena got up and sang around the kitchen, wiping, brushing crumbs, and finally, she passed out the back door and went for a walk leaving the rest of her family to hum themselves out of stillness.

Singing happily to herself, she wouldn't have noticed one way or another if she were being followed. Not at first. She knew she was supposed to find the Ramses Lily to lease the ballroom for one night in approximately three weeks. The children had asked her more than once. Trouble was, no matter which way she walked, she couldn't find the hotel. She had passed it several times but had yet to see it. The hotel was one of the largest modern structures in all of Cairo and still the sight of it evaded her.

Berdeena moved around entirely in her head. Amazingly, she hadn't had an accident or fallen, or bumped into any of the crowd on the Cairo streets as she was generally in conversation with Balloon Brother, a most powerful master. Whenever they walked, he was the look-around which was why Berdeena never noticed where she walked. She had fully accepted the description of their surroundings as Balloon

Brother's unassailable duty and therefore as she walked, she listened to his voice and walked in his world. Balloon Brother had marvelous powers of description, so much so that since Berdeena wanted to believe him, she refused to look when he described extraordinary things. When he insisted that they were being followed around by a funny small man with sticky hair, a roundish belly and one run over shoe, she simply imagined him.

"His suit, however, is very well made, fits him just right. Either he's grown into it or he never takes it off; the cloth has no choice but to move with the rest of him."

"His clothes could use a good cleaning. All of him could use a cleanup. Not just his outside, his inside too. His thoughts should be rinsed."

Berdeena laughed. Having Balloon Brother was like having a live storyteller following her around, taking in the world, twisting it and giving it back.

"He looks dishonored by deed, and a little unloved to go along. Love returned may have made him fix his hair. Unrequited love would have required him at least to clean his suit, but absent love, love expected and not given would leave him unkempt as he is and you know, in the middle of all of that obvious-looking despair is a coming peace."

This is where Berdeena peeked because Balloon Brother's descriptions often included "peace." Never mind the fact that he couldn't possibly know anything about love. But "peace," she needed to see because frankly, she wondered if he meant peace as a color.

"The dog's face had a lovely 'peace.' Plants stood around in the dirt in complete 'peace' and occasionally even a very large edifice with people running in and out exuded an air of 'peace.'"

Berdeena used to think that Balloon Brother probably had no idea what "peace" meant. Or maybe what he meant was a kind of inevitability and she supposed that buildings, dogs, and plants could possess a sort of "inevitability." Certainly, a man could. Maybe that's what everything living seemed like to the dead.

To Berdeena, life was one big series of inevitable events and if she could accept an invisible brother floating up above her head bodiless, tethered to her wrist, expounding about love, then she could accept his descriptions.

"One of his shoes is brown and the other one is browner. Half of him feels one way and the other half feels something else."

Berdeena was wondering if Balloon Brother meant that the shoes fit differently, one was tighter and newer and therefore less comfortable or.... He interrupted her thought knowing exactly what it would be ...

"His feet are fine. He's of two minds." Now he imitated their mother. Aberdeen had always said people were two headed.

"What do you mean then?" Berdeena asked Balloon Brother.

"Look, he's standing right there in front of that hotel and can't seem to decide whether to go in."

"What hotel?"

"What's it called?" he said talking to himself. "The Ramses Lily."

"Where?" Berdeena had turned around immediately and walked back to the hotel. She'd never seen the little man and didn't know that she was walking into the hotel almost directly behind him. Berdeena read the signs and realized that she'd have to take the elevator up to the ballroom but first thought she'd find out how to lease one.

"Should you be renting a ballroom for yourself? I mean if the party is for you, why would you have to rent the room? Shouldn't you just arrive?"

"Who said the party was for me?"

She began thinking about the possibility; she was standing in front of the concierge with a strange smile distorting her beautiful face, but she was silent, and the concierge was unsure of how to proceed.

"May I help you?" he asked.

She was wondering why in the world the children would

be having a party for her.

"It's your debut," Balloon Brother said.

"Debut for what?" Berdeena asked out loud.

"I beg your pardon?" the concierge asked.

"Your music," Balloon Brother declared. Berdeena could be so trying.

"Ask him if the room has good acoustics?"

"Does your room have good musical acoustics?"

"Which room would that be? A guest room or a ... ?"

"Your main ballroom."

The concierge was a little surprised.

"Our acoustics are incredible," the concierge insisted. The woman facing him was an English-speaking foreigner. He simply asked, "May I show you one of the ballrooms?"

"The hotel has more than one?"

"Three," he answered rather condescendingly.

"Show me the largest one first and then the others, please," she shot back.

"If you were to invite everyone you know, it would just be me," Balloon Brother said, "and maybe the children." Berdeena ignored him.

The main ballroom at the Ramses Lily was entirely too large for Berdeena's debut. In the end, she'd looked at all three and settled on the third and smallest. She would make her singing debut for a small audience with an intimate party where she imagined she'd also cook the food. That way, she could certainly assure herself a captive audience. She began to concentrate on the event. She even wondered if she could persuade Umm Ridah and the children out of the audience and onto the stage and had to laugh at herself. She was quietly humming, to Balloon Brother's exceeding annoyance, when they were once again crossing the lobby about to exit after having reserved the room.

The concierge had provided his rapt and kind attention, especially when they were detained at the door along with everyone else when word spread throughout the staff, amongst the guests and into the lobby that a youngish, unkempt white man was hanging upstairs in a guest suite reserved for use by the American Embassy. No one currently in the hotel could identify the man and no one had even noticed him entering the hotel. Upon checking, they discovered that the suite had had a standing reservation for several afternoons, sometimes overnight but mostly just for a few hours. The standing reservation had been on the books for a few years.

They let Berdeena and Balloon Brother leave. The concierge could testify that today was the first time that he had ever seen her, and that she had remained in his company the entire time that she was in the hotel. He had noticed her arrival. But he had not seen the man who had gone upstairs and hanged himself or alternatively, gotten himself hanged.

Many stories came out about the little dead man without any evidence to prove anything. One hotel employee said he thought a woman had used the suite often enough, but imaginations ran over facts. Everyone was mostly satisfied with the version that indicated some man had come into the hotel and gotten himself hanged. It was an accident with the heavily roped curtains. Generous folk said it was a true story of unrequited love. The authorities found an altar to a woman in the man's apartment. More room for her likenesses than for his belongings. All the images of the woman were drawn by him. Whatever his talent may have been, it was not for drawing.

First Selma, Then Agnes, Berdeena, and Finally Martha—Flying Forward, Remembering Backwards

Ten days later, Clifton Thrace was wearing a smile that would not leave his face. He moved his arm so as not to crowd his wife but did not speak to her or the children as they sat in the first-class section of Panam Airlines, headed back to America. Thrace's surprise had worked exceptionally well, and he felt ecstatic at having pulled it off and more-so, at the thought of going home. They had spent years living in Cairo, Egypt. If the rest of his family had noticed his face, they would have all felt mocked by its undisturbed pleasure as they rode to America in an undisguised state of stunned horror and surprise.

Behind in Cairo, they left a party that they would neither be hosting, nor receiving, nor attending. No cake, no cooking, no singing, no prizes, no dancing. Nine of them sat very quietly in four seats.

For the first few hours, Selma rode in a stupor of memory, but not her own. She had come undone again. Outside on the wings, her eyes were surveying clouds. Her lungs she left behind breathing the dusty burnt air of Cairo. Her hands were at her throat cautioning her to swallow. A few tears were on the marble near the front door where the girls used to play interminable, unwinnable games of jacks. Her stomach, acidic and churning, heaved up and down in her suitcase.

Only Selma's heart and mind sat thumping and thinking back and forth in the narrow, belted seat. Rather than Aberdeen who generally came to rescue her from her sorrow and fear, this time, it was Selsie. Selsie's stories were waiting up in the clouds mixed with the horror of leaving, ready to accompany Selma to America. If anyone could come to the rescue, it was Selsie, Selsie who shared her disorder with her great-granddaughter.

Selsie was having a party, too, only she was giving it, hosting it, and holding it for herself and her gentleman friend, that is, if they could come to some sort of agreement. Mostly, they were arguing about freedom. Selsie's friend had always been free and Selsie had just earned hers, partly from hard work and partly from knowing that it would have been hers whenever she asked. She'd asked. She was ready and she had wanted to celebrate. Her gentleman friend decided to put in with her and celebrate his self and his freedom, too, and that's how they got to arguing. Selsie wanted to know what was the point of celebrating something now that he'd always had. He had wanted to know what was the difference between celebrating now, yesterday, or tomorrow. Selsie accused him of wanting to celebrate with her because he just learned the value of his own freedom by measuring it next to hers.

He looked at her in such a serious way that she knew why everybody called him Lord Earl instead of Lloyd Earl. Really, they mostly pronounced it "Loyderl" as though it was one word.

"Freedom ain't nothing we should be fighting over, seeing as we both got some; boundless ain't bound to be measured."

"You just want to celebrate now 'cause a mine. You ain't wanted to celebrate before. Now you know how good it is 'cause you know the difference."

"Woman, if you tellin' me that I ain't ever had a day to celebrate, you tellin' me wrong. I knew the worth every morning when I never forget the price of forgettin' that paper I got in my pocket to prove my freedom's true. I carries my freedom wit me every day, an extra coat in the cold, more sweat in the summer, ideas in the springtime."

"A piece of paper in your pocket ain't nothin' 'gainst a lifetime cooking the food of love for mouths you can't stand to eat with. You full a ideas, alright."

"You lyin' if you say you ain't sometimes love them people."

"Love like a pain in the knee you get used to," Selsie answered him.

"Like when you massaging that knee so's to make yourself feel the pain you know you love whether you used to it or not."

"My freedom deserved to be celebrated, 'cause it's new," Selsie said.

"Mine is old. Don't old folks still get birthdays?"

"Mine make me smile sometimes, while I'm still in the kitchen cooking for the same people I done always cooked for making the same pay I done always been paid."

"Girl, smiling ain't improved none on them potatoes?"

Now he knew she was the best cook anybody had ever heard of, including him, whether he traveled around or not. She liked him and she didn't like him. She loved him but she didn't like loving him because it made her listen even when he was talking the nonsense he was now and like he usually was.

"Your freedom seem to like nonsense. Mine ain't sure," said Selsie.

"You ain't had yours long enough to know what it like."

"It don't like being told," Selsie knew that much.

"Neither do you. Maybe it'll be as stubborn as you. Stubborn freedom won't git up and move, don' care what's comin'." She was having second thoughts about sharing anything with him—certainly not a freedom party, not the way he was talking like he knew everything about it. But he could read the question in her face and it was a good thing too.

"I'll bring the meat. You make the cake." Now there he was telling her what to do again. He just happened to be right, like he always was, most of the time. He knew it would be a party for two. Just them. She'd cook his meat alright. What he didn't know? She was making him a special cake, a "Shut Up" cake. She had just decided on it. He was going to like it so much, he was going to keep eating it and all he would be able to do was smile. What she didn't know? It would have the same effect on her.

The two of them sat on a blanket in their finest clothes out in the field all by themselves, blushing. Lloyd Earl and Selsie were immobile, stooped over the cake, stuck in with the wildflowers and weeds blowing around them as if they belonged to the landscape. They had chosen to picnic on the rise without the shelter or comfort of trees. Other folks could see them up there, sitting way out in the field looking crazy, especially when it started to rain. The talk was that freedom made Selsie crazier anyway.

Selsie was a little wet when she started thinking that freedom let her sit out under the rain as long as she wanted to and that a Shut Up cake made a person quiet so a person could use her time without the imposition of her mouth, which gave the brain a little steadier work. Then she started wondering what Lloyd Earl was thinking. She looked over at him.

He could see her still covered in as many smiles as she had started with, only now they were all wet. He knew he'd been poisoned, she was always poisoning him with whatever it was she put in the food. It seemed like it must have worked on her, too, this time, as she was smiling crazily and neither of them could get one word out whether chewing or not.

Maybe freedom was going to separate her from her food. She used to be able to eat it right along with everybody else. She'd be sitting right there doing nothing while everybody else was writhing, confessing, frozen up, or changing in some way. Maybe freedom was going to free her in one way and bind her up in another.

Lloyd Earl wondered if she was going to have to change her recipes, but he hoped not. She was always up in the woods picking up secrets and weeds and putting them in her pockets. She didn't know that she didn't need to poison him for his feelings. He'd already loved her before he said one word to her, so he didn't need any of her potions for that. He'd loved her from across the road, in his own field and even in town, especially when she came sauntering by ignoring everybody but knowing nobody could ignore her, not if they wanted to eat peaceably.

He loved her before he ever tasted a thing from her hand. Folks made up stories about her. They said Selsie didn't know anything about the other ones. They used to bet on which Selsie could cook the best. She was the whole town's topic of conversation, more colorful than a cotton field full of rag-wearing slaves picking it—a used-to-be slave woman.

Even Lloyd Earl had seen a personality or two, that is, before he got to know her well. For one thing, they had completely different strides and he used to wonder which one might be easiest to approach. The limping one moved slower but the haughty one once winked. One of the first things he ever said to her was that she could try "all them women" out on him. She told him that if he was the right man, she wouldn't need to share him and he wouldn't even need to meet any of them other Selsies.

"If you ain't, don't matter who you get to know." After they started living between her house and his, all the other Selsies moved out for good. Lloyd Earl asked for explanations, but none were forthcoming.

People used to wish that somebody in their own house would die just to get a piece of Selsie's "take this to the dead house" chicken with potato tar.

That's the one thing she thought her freedom might change. She wouldn't be cooking up any more meals for dead people's family. She thought it might be better to cook something for the people about to die and send that around in time. Then people got scared because they began to understand that if Selsie was sending them food somebody in their house was bound to die. Most of the time it wasn't who they expected, so Selsie started sending the food around way before anybody was going to die because it made them all nicer to each other.

"You don't know, I might be the one dying."

"Tell Selsie to send some more food." The second time, they'd have to pay for it. Sometimes, they'd send the raw materials and ask Selsie to make something of it. They'd load up Lloyd Earl with chicken, poke salad, eggs, and potatoes and tell him to give it to Selsie. One rumor had it that Selsie could turn kudzu into a turkey dinner. They never knew what they were going to get back, but it usually didn't matter.

Lloyd Earl would be pulling his old horse which would be pulling his old cart through town. He could be smelled long before he arrived carrying everything that anyone wanted. He was a concert of exquisite parts packaged in his ever-present paraphernalia, an old carpenter without a waiting job but all the necessary tools. He had ideas on paper wadded up in his jacket pockets. Other sensations gurgling, jostling, echoing around in his big belly, whispering rags pinned to his tattered clothes. Atop his head, a soft worn cap lurked sideways covering the music in his head. Thin-kneed corduroys over his powerful thighs rubbed against each other in four-four time; threads unraveled trailing behind him, the longest strands hung over his sturdy suede boots, falling under his foot and dipping into the soft caked mud that smoothed the grooves and flattened his boot print, leaving it unrecognizable in the dirt. His boots covered plenty of road without ever leaving a readable print.

His cart, on the other hand, was as clean as Selsie's kitchen, which was the first project that he knew she had given him. He had always been a project man, but he was unsure now whether he invented them or whether they were fed to him.

He'd have carried three-quarters of Selsie's food into a house before the subject hung in the air, quivering like a giant cloud about to burst. Leave it to Lloyd Earl, who would always know exactly how and when to get Selsie paid.

Everyone knew that Selsie sent four things: a meat, a starch, a vegetable, and a dessert. Lloyd Earl always knew which family liked which item best. That would be the one left in the cart.

Usually, he was in a room with something he wanted but didn't own. Sometimes, it would be a book so he could keep his tool bench from wobbling. Maybe it'd be that big thick book to block up that draught coming through the big hole in the wall. Some of that wood to steady Selsie's front door. One time, he'd taken some glass as Selsie could maybe use it to seal a crack between her shelves. Lloyd Earl never left empty handed. Nobody minded and not a soul wondered what in the world he'd do with all the stuff he collected.

Not even when it was finally done did everyone know who was responsible. The Hill between Two Towns had the first combination "Negra Library and Laboratory in America" and it was entirely thought up, scavenged for, created, and conjured by one Lloyd Earl. He still thought Selsie had poisoned him into it, but when he showed her his final product, she was too surprised to have known it was coming. His building was nondescript on the outside, same as him. But inside, it was one of the finest, most orderly collections of books in neat stacks on precisely built shelves on one side and a pristine-looking equally measured kitchen on the other side with cold storage baskets set beneath the earth and blackened glass jars waiting for Selsie's powders and herbs in cabinets affixed to the walls. She only needed to touch the wall in a particular place to open them up. It was somehow manufactured so that the books did not mingle with the kitchen and vice versa. Selsie stood in her kitchen, looked to the other side, and thought to herself. She couldn't do nothing with those books but imagine what was inside.

An unappreciated skill, incidentally, passed down to her great-granddaughter Agnes, who could also imagine what was inside a book but could not read. If Agnes understood the words, she couldn't put them together well enough to extract meaning. When she wanted meaning, it wouldn't come with words, but through touch with her hands and fingers or her arms and occasionally, in scents that found their way to her nose. Words were songs to be enjoyed; just the sound of voices soothed her, but to depend on words for understanding was something she could never do.

Memory traveled and must have crossed odd boundaries as it reached Agnes where she was, on the same airplane, sitting somewhere beneath Selma's beating heart on route to the United States of America. Agnes's body was there but not her mind. Agnes was thinking that here she was—robbed of her party again at the hands of the nearest man. Men were antithetical to togetherness as far as she could remember, which wasn't too far. The only other man she had ever known was her father, with his intermittent doses of fatherhood. Even the memory of him put her in pieces, not violently so much as necessarily. How could she remember him whole if she'd only had him in pieces? Thrace was seated nearby, a stand-in, serving another unintelligible purpose, but that was the nature of her relationships with men. Thrace had put them on this plane much like her father had removed her from the scene of her only other party when she was very young.

Her mother had tried to explain, "Your father's saving the family pride. Sometimes the things you can't touch are bigger than what you can," Aberdeen had declared. Whatever it was she was talking about was something they could all share. Agnes had wanted something for herself and one thing didn't seem too much to ask for in the universe she shared with her parents, though clearly it was more than what was going to be provided.

A representative of the town council had asked Agnes to read a passage before they would hand her the trophy for having read more books than anyone else in the entire town. Unfortunately, her father didn't trust her to read even though she had already formed her own plan. Only Agnes knew that she could tell them whatever it was in whichever book they chose with plenty of detail. It might not sound the same as the story in the book, but it'd be as good or even better. So what if she pretended to read while telling them a better story than any of the ones they knew, plus, what if they didn't recognize what she was reading one way or another? Agnes was already disappointed because they had given her a slim tome and she had imagined an epic. She had prepared a magnificent tale with big sounding words for reciting and was ill prepared for anything else. Her father was ready to put down any challengers to his authority, including Agnes, so as she attempted to make her way to the podium, he grabbed her by her arm and yanked her in the opposite direction in front of all who had come for the announcement, the pageantry, and of course, for the promised refreshments.

The town council, which had chosen the book for her to read and had arranged the program, was always more interested in ceremony than anything else and thought a small recital appropriate. They had chosen a book that no one had ever read. No one would have known if Agnes were reading the book or not and if her father had only snatched the book after Agnes had recited a passage or two, no one would have been the wiser. Agnes's father didn't save the family dignity; he insulted the entire town by not having the grace to keep his strangeness to himself and for reasons that they were wholly unable to fathom, dragging his crying daughter off the stage and back up into the woods.

Dag had, however, quieted his daughter, so that rather than being celebrated as the "readingest" girl, Agnes returned to hardly existing at all. Her father had upstaged her with his own act and disappeared her altogether. Afterwards, Agnes began another readjustment to her usual disjointedness.

She wouldn't be heard. Maybe she could be unseen. Agnes began her dedication to revenge with a campaign of accidents. She dreamt big but had the sense to start small. The early successes—pins in her father's favorite seat, salt in his sugar, dirt in his shoes—propelled her forward. She had even mixed and crushed up some weeds and dipped his toothbrush into the mixture. Hours after he brushed his teeth, he still had such a terrible taste in his mouth that he had to immediately coat his taste buds with something and the only thing that would ease his tongue was bread dipped in molasses. He began to put on weight and Agnes enjoyed the fact that something she had done had a long-term effect and she imagined herself giving him permanent souvenirs.

She imagined rubbing his comb with a salve that would make his hair fall out or if she could put some poultice on the right side of his seat that would be absorbed through his pants and cause one leg to draw up shorter than the other. He'd have to limp, and people would constantly annoy him with their questions about what had happened to him, especially since he had no explanation. Eventually, he would start to explain his limp with lies. One lie would lead to others and in the end, he would die, be barred from heaven, and forced to haunt them. Agnes and her mother would not be frightened; they would take pleasure in ignoring his ever-present ghost.

The trouble was, as usual, that Agnes could never get her entire body to participate in any one thing at the same time so only little pieces of her enjoyed the pranks. She was sitting in the front yard tree when her father sat on the pins left in his chair. She heard him scream only once and felt a warm wave in her stomach. Oh, to have eaten something lovely but the bitter taste in her mouth made it hard to accept. When he tasted salt in his coffee, spat it out, cursed and shivered, Agnes felt her leg fly up grandly and hit the top of the table, but the joy of flight was short-lived as she stubbed a toe. She was sitting on the front stoop when he came out of the house with one shoe in his hand, walking on the back of the other one. He hit the shoe in his hand against the house, furiously shaking dirt from first one and then the other. Agnes bent over and laughed but it didn't feel good. It was painful because of the force it used making its way out of her stomach without mirth and without the participation of any other body parts—more like a motor rumbling up through her throat and out into the air without the ease of an accompanying feeling.

Dag took one look at her and it hurt him too. His poor little skinny dejected daughter might be trying to laugh but looked sickly, more if she were throwing up sound. Sadly, he shook his head. How in the world could a little girl not even know how to laugh? He picked her up and hugged her hard and Agnes felt herself getting smaller, losing her wind, erasing all her schemes and finally relenting. In his arms, he disappeared her again. She became smaller and smaller, which left seat 3A on flight number whatever to the United States of America available for Berdeena, now crushed beneath Selma's beating heart and Agnes's dull memories.

Berdeena was far more anguished from having to listen to Balloon Brother's nonstop tirade over not being able to attend the party. Berdeena wondered why in the world he was carrying on. The party had nothing to do with him. He would have merely been a floating bystander. She was the one whose debut had been hijacked. Here she sat on an airplane crowded into one seat next to three sad, silent children. They were certainly pitiful looking.

"Christ, Christ, Christ!!" Balloon Brother screamed until he caught himself and regrouped. He did not want Berdeena to know the real source of his anger, so he pretended to be angry on her behalf.

Berdeena, however, wouldn't have fallen for his so-called sympathetic anger one way or another. He was far too self-centered to expend any emotion on anyone else's behalf. Berdeena didn't have a clue why he was so angry, but she knew it was not because of her cancelled debut.

Normally, he was only with her when she walked or occasionally when she worked around the kitchen, though coming onto the plane made sense. How else would he get back to the United States of America if he had wanted to? Berdeena wondered if he might stay in Cairo; he truly loved Egypt. Perhaps that was the real reason for his disgruntlement.

He'd probably have to come up with an entirely new vocabulary to describe "peaceful" Washingtonians.

She peeked over at the children wishing she could think up a song that might cheer them. Frankly, with her stolen debut on her mind, she didn't feel too musical but if she didn't put her mind or her mouth on something, she'd be compelled to listen to Balloon Brother's furious ranting. He went on longer than usual, so long that it took her back to his beginnings, triggering the past, and how they'd come to be as they were. Something about flying forward made Berdeena go backwards in time.

She was twelve when Balloon Brother died but she wasn't sure how old he was. Aberdeen had never been good at remembering her children's ages so if either of them wanted to know how old they were, they had to keep track of it themselves.

He was the first and only boy from Selsie's line. If there was talk about the woods, her little brother would have come up because that boy spent all his time in the trees. Aberdeen said he was "monkey in a good way!" He had long arms for swinging from upper branches, superior intuition, and the know-how to move around the woods without anyone being able to detect him. These kinds of skills were more important to Aberdeen than others. He could hide and follow her all around the woods, stumping her when he popped out in her most secret haunts. Convincing animal noises were his specialty, and he could make anybody believe they were being chased by wolves or flown over by exotic birds. Aberdeen grew exceedingly proud when she discovered that *he* was the noise, footprints, and all evidence of the "Monster" that spooked the town for a month or so each fall.

Balloon Brother wasn't ever at home; he was always in the woods and they grew used to feeling that he was around without ever having to prove him with their eyes. For Aberdeen, the joy of having the two things she loved most love each other filled her up, her happiness expanded and eased over everything. The brightness dazzled everything, including the household in its fiefdom and for a short time, all was well.

Then, one Sunday, Brother crawled down from his last tree, came into the house, and climbed into bed. In a flat, emotionless way, he had already finished grappling and now accepted the facts. He told his mother, "I'm never getting out of this bed."

"I'm going to stay here and never get up again."

Aberdeen didn't want to believe him. Her little son told her he was sick and took one full week to die. She took forever to pretend that he had lied. Plus, she could never forgive a God that would take a boy on Sunday. Her son could not be dead and certainly he could not have died without a remarkable explanation. Aberdeen kept coming up with alternate schemes and stumbled through the house thinking them up and rehearsing out loud.

"What if he'd been accidentally poisoned, stepping on one of those black tail weeds? Or he sniffed one into his nose, those toxic Magnolia smelling petals. Was it a black tail that killed so quickly? Are there any around here? Maybe he's just run away. That boy's run away again." She'd get a little happy when she could suspend him somewhere in the world, just out of eyesight.

"That boy found a tree that he loves more than his mama. Who is he scaring with his monster foolishness? He could be three towns over messing with new folk!" She'd get excited when she believed herself. For moments, everyone would be relieved, a little happier that Brother was playing tricks on people they didn't know nor would ever see. Aberdeen would smile for a bit and then stop.

Happiness had merely stretched Aberdeen, but sorrow spread all over everything like a moist fungus, twisting the house and the air into an ugly oddly unchanging thing.

"He wasn't born. I imagined him, brought him to life, watched him get away," she'd declare and silence herself for a time.

"He's been lynched. That's it! That boy's been lynched."

Aberdeen would carry around her gun until Dag came home and wrestled it out of her arms. In one quick snatch, he'd take away the weapon so she couldn't point her hate, but not having a target for her feelings was far worse than having one. With a target, she could at least take all the hate she had for whatever took her son and aim. Without one, her emotions were all over the place. They sat on her and made movement impossible. Some days, she couldn't get up and other days she got up but could only walk through the house conjuring ways and whys for her son to have died.

The stench was more than anyone could stand. At first, she wouldn't even let him be buried. The awful smell was the proper accompaniment to the plague of emotion that swallowed Aberdeen whole. Stench was a reminder and a memory all in one.

Aberdeen's grief was irresponsible and took over the rest of her life, covering everything else with inattention. Was it a mistake; she wasn't meant to have a son? There hadn't ever been one from Selsie's line. God took him back. Or maybe it was a punishment for a life Aberdeen had taken, one that hadn't belonged to Aberdeen.

Berdeena began to live right when her little brother died. It was as if his death gave her purpose. At twelve, she became the reservoir of grief and everything before turned vague and remote, as if it occurred in another life, some other girl's life. Everything after would somehow have her dead brother in it if he'd wanted to be there.

Berdeena had come into the bedroom to grant the little boy a wish. Instead of a dead boy, he told Berdeena he wanted to be a balloon floating up, up, and away. But when Berdeena opened the window and tried to release him, he grabbed onto her wrist and would not let go. She had planned to watch him fly. She never saw his body again but began to hear his voice.

Sometimes, he answered when beckoned; mostly, he only came when he wanted. At first, she listened to all the nonsense he spouted and cooked up loads and loads of the food that he requested, and she ate. Berdeena and Aberdeen together climbed through the woods and gathered the spices they needed to feed the dead and the living, with a different effect.

Dag took his little boy's body and buried him in the woods.

"I imagined him. Imagined him," Aberdeen often mumbled, pushing the words down beneath her chin, caucusing within herself. Berdeena heard her mother and then thought 'if she could imagine one, why not imagine another and next time, imagine his name too.'

For Martha, the idea of a party was an idea she'd never have. Martha hated the woods. Events in the woods supplied her earliest and worst memories. If she was in the woods, she was lost, twisting between trees, her fear running wild, moving too fast to see where she was going. Years and years ago, when Martha was twelve, trying to get home from town, she had inadvertently stumbled upon a dead stranger. She toppled out from the trees onto the site of a murder in a small clearing and always wondered whether her mother, the murderer, resented the intrusion. She stood not three feet away from her mother and a body and surely, more life had come into her as it left the dead little white man. Aberdeen could have dragged a mule if she'd put mule-dragging in her mind, but since Martha was there, she might as well be useful. Martha's were the only other pair of hearing ears present, but Aberdeen's words were not for Martha. Perhaps they were for God, more likely they were for her own keeping.

Aberdeen talked as they dragged the body away.

"That library kitchen is mine, passed to me from my grandmother on my mother's side, built by my grandfather for us and no white man is going to be allowed to take it. 'Especially a dirty white man talking about miniment domain. I've watched you coming in and out. Visiting would have been alright but you outstayed your welcome. You kept leaving and always came back. You asked me what I wanted like you're the one in position to offer me something of mine.

I told him, seems I should be asking him, seeing as he's in my place. He laughed and said "what you say? Your place? This gonna be my place. All I got to do is stay here one straight week to take advantage of the law. The law's on my side. It's called 'Miniment Domain.' He said it and started laughing, laughing real crazy. Fact, he started dancing around showing himself, saying he was in front of his place and can do what he pleases.

Dancing like the little white man he was, singing about what used to be mine is now his and all he had to do was spend another couple days sleeping beneath the books and then it would all be his. He said he didn't know why no nigger need a kitchen and some books as if niggers could read. Then he said ain't nobody but a nigger gonna put his books next to his kitchen.

Maybe now that he got to be the owner of so many books he might just take up and learn to read himself. He said he know don't no mountain nigger like me know nothing 'bout no books. He say if I did it was all in my 'magination.

As they began to dig a hole, Martha imitating Aberdeen's movement without instruction, Aberdeen went on talking— but not to God or the sky—she was talking to the dead man.

"Any other building, you could probably take with your domain. But this thing is my family, not just a place for you to sleep, not with your dirty head and no reverence. Bet you think a mountain nigger wouldn't know that word either." Martha could not see any, but she heard the tears in her mother's voice.

"Now you messed in. You got in and mixed in my family's legacy with your silly death. Seventy years my family had this place, seventy years ago Lloyd Earl built this building. Scrimped and saved, begged and worked for this place." She kicked the dead white man. Martha startled. Aberdeen looked over at Martha and for the first time addressed her, pointing to the dead white man.

"He was a thief. Death wasn't a surprise," Aberdeen said, but all Martha could see was a dead little grayish man with a peaceful looking face. From then on, though she didn't know it, Martha would always be wrong about death and the dead, one way or another.

Death kept confronting Martha—death and memories—and she hated them both. One memory always brought another and they were generally filled with horror or dread. Martha preferred facts. She had seen a little body swinging from a Sylph tree but both body and tree disappeared before she could bring the townsfolk back to see them. Sometimes she remembered without purpose; other times she knew why things had occurred. She brought the townspeople to that tree, but not by accident. She wanted to save her mother from herself, her grief, and whatever she was grieving for. For once, she thought that maybe someone that lived off the mountain could help the ones who lived on it. It didn't work. Martha hadn't thought it through. Just seemed like for as long as she could remember, if she were around, something or someone had died. Maybe, Martha kept the death memories so no one else had to.

If she could, Martha stayed away from the woods and most people. She was only riding back to America because she was squeezed in with the rest.

Martha, the Detective heard about the Ramses Lily and the death of the funny little man who had been walking around Cairo. She was the first one on the plane to speak to the children when she flipped back her notebook cover, pencil in hand, and asked them.

"Why the Ramses Lily?"

The three of them looked at each other and then looked at her.

"Had you booked the room?" Alley wanted to know.

"The room had been booked for ages by someone on the embassy staff."

They felt a momentary shot of that same attention, sharp and warm. So, their mother *had* booked the room and they could have had their party after all.

"Ramses Lily has the nicest party room," Mirella assured

their mother.

"According to Daphne and Hala," Alley continued.

"Who?"

"Our friends," Alley answered.

"Which friends?" Martha asked.

"Daphne and Hala, our friends," Alley answered again.

"Did they know the man found in the room?" Martha asked the two little girls.

"What man?" Mirella asked.

"The de—," she realized she was talking to children. Maybe she shouldn't use the word "dead." The man no longer living in the suite."

"There was a man living in the party room?" Mirella asked.

"Why?" asked Alley.

"Not living there, he died in there." Martha explained, impatience in her voice.

Mirella, Black Black, and Alley glanced at each other again.

"You think that's why we're leaving?" Mirella asked.

"No, leaving had probably been planned for a while," Alley answered, "but a death in the ballroom might mess up a party."

"We could have changed the location."

"Mother doesn't look any happier than we do," Mirella said.

"Why should she be? It's not as if we're going to her mountain. We'll be closer but . . ."

Alley's voice trailed off; she didn't know anything about their new home.

Black Black decided to put away his disappointment, which was smaller than he thought, and look forward to the future. Though he hadn't ever had a birthday party, maybe America would give him one. To Black Black, the United States of America loomed on the horizon with great promise and he began to enjoy the idea of going home, welcoming the new boy that he would become with the friends to go with him.

Alley sat between her siblings, squeezing them on both sides, making herself available to mediate. She felt a sudden need to up the ante, to focus her attention on them. Though truthfully, gazing at her brother, she sensed that he might need more than she possessed. He fidgeted so.

"In' shallah, In' shallah. Ib'id an ach 'issharr w'ghanilo," Alley said, trying to comfort her younger siblings. "L'bab ill biy gheelack minno l'reeh siddo w'istireeh."

"Get away from bad things and sing. Close the door on the ill wind and relax."

"You think we'll always remember Arabic?" Mirella whispered to Alley.

"Let's try," Alley responded. "We'll remember Umm Ridah, we'll talk her like a language."

11

Arrival in America

The Thraces arrived in America, each with their own individual baggage. Standing in front of a revolving turnstile waiting for suitcases hardly seemed necessary.

Their new house was a brick colonial with six bedrooms, a finished basement, two fireplaces, and several bathrooms, and sat on a large surrounding lawn. A fine house that could easily become a fine home.

After Thrace showed them the first-floor powder room, Selma stepped in, dropped the walking shoes that she had packed in her small carry-on bag, and slid into them. While her family toured the house, Selma opened the front door and quietly slipped outside.

Thrace continued to show the children around the house, ignoring the fact that his wife was not with them. In the commotion of arriving, how could she prefer to venture outside before seeing their new house? He told himself to be ready for her appreciation when offered. He had thought of everything. The bags were brought in and left in the large front entryway. Alley, Mirella, and their little brother stood quietly just inside.

"Come in, come in," Thrace told his children. "Come look at your new home." He walked further into the space, stopping above the two steps that led down into one large room.

"To your left is the den, in the middle, the living room, and on the right, more living room. We'll look at the kitchen and den later.Let's go up." The den, living room, and other living room shared a wall of windows. He didn't bother to tell them that the kitchen was full of food, didn't brag about his careful attention to every detail.

Thrace lost a little of his bluster, unsure how to bring a smile to the three sad faces that looked up and held onto his every word.

"I thought you'd like this view," he told Alley who was confused at first, not realizing that her father was delivering her to her very own bedroom. "You all go ahead and unpack your suitcases."

"Mirella, here you are across the hall. You have a light in your closet and a bit more space for your clothing.

"Son, your room is up here where no one will even know you're at home if you don't make too much noise."

"Go ahead now, you've seen your rooms, get your bags and unpack them, put your things away, put things in your room where you want them."

The girls walked down the hallway and stood between their rooms.

"Let's switch," Alley whispered, and they smiled and did.

Black Black went down the hallway by himself, head down and shoulders up.

"Put your things away," she called after him, "you can sleep in my room with us."

They'd have their own rooms, but they'd do what they always did when they were upset. They'd climb into one bed and stay together.

Thrace glanced toward his own bedroom, sure that it would be a good warm host for him and for his wife. He had provided mahogany furniture, the set like one his parents had owned, befitting his notions of the marital bedroom.

After settling the children into their rooms, he retreated to his study, sat down in his big leather chair, and imagined where he would put the rest of his things. His small bronze figures would line the desk. The larger pieces would be arranged atop the two tallest bookcases across the room, separated by windows. Gently rocking himself to and fro in his elegantly squeaking chair reminded him of his good sense. Leather in a closed room with polished wooden floors smelled of a confident man, a man who could relax in surroundings manifested by his own hand—a level-headed man, who had followed the most reasonable dictates of his father and grandfather and could simply ignore the whims of a moody wife.

His father and grandfather ignored the things that didn't agree with their worldview and in most instances, that meant his mother and grandmother. With gentle tut-tuts and silence, the elder Thrace men addressed most of the chatter that came from the women's end of the table. Clifton Thrace had been in the middle which to him meant they ignored half of what came from him and further, they had kept the women from spoiling and softening him.

Clifton Thrace had taken on a wife much in the way that would have pleased his male forebearers. She was beautiful and had given him a son and two daughters.

"The things a man built and amassed would protect a man, his line, his family" was something Thrace had heard all his life and had come to believe and live as a personal credo.

His father and grandfather had amassed a small fortune. They had hidden everything because all too often property belonging to colored men had been taken by white ones. Secrecy was the only way their wealth could survive in the world they had known. They had worked hard and together to protect their wealth and family. After they died, his mother and grandmother presented Thrace with separate keys to different boxes hidden in the attics of the two houses where they had lived.

They were hard, beautifully carved boxes with five numbers burnt into the center backs of each. His father's numbers added up to one more than his grandfather's, as if one had been the 137th and the other the 138th, but of what, he didn't know. They hadn't left a decoder or clue to the boxes. Inside lay a keepsake or two, property deeds to more property than Thrace had known about, and the strange sets of paper, dated 1860-something. They were a few pages long, faded, and delicate, each headed by ***"The Curiously Successful Negro."***

They had circled certain family names and listed figures in columns to the left and right of the printed text. There were several different addresses on the backs of both sets of the carefully copied, almost identical lists in each of the boxes. The Macomb name had been underlined twice. Otherwise, in their mutual boxes, his father and grandfather had hidden sums of money, deeds, and other keepsakes. There was a gold watch in his grandfather's box and a carved wooden owl in the one left by his father. Each had also left a small iron figure, not quite fully formed but close, almost as if the carver had known exactly how to form the metal but stopped before he'd finished.

Over time, Thrace had decided to at least find all the addresses though they were spread from Connecticut to Arkansas and further west. Guessing at first that the addresses belonged to other family members, he had asked his mother and grandmother who responded by naming their own family members and trying to make sure that Clifton Thrace also knew them. Second families seemed impossible for the men he had known; they barely had enough affection for the two women he knew, and he couldn't imagine them having enough space for a second family in some other town with more children. One woman did not seem to amuse them enough to want two.

The first address had no yield and whatever had been on the land was long since abandoned. Thrace walked the perimeter of an old fence and even searched the yard, walking over the grass and stone, scraping his foot as if pushing a few blades aside might yield a bounty of information, relics of a family who had once had a structure and lived inside. He had gone to the black side of town and asked questions.

Folks told him stories of a real fine house that had been burnt down and the family gone. No one knew the family's name or where they had gone.

There were years between the individual visits to the addresses his father and grandfather left. For one thing, Thrace was busy with his own fortunes. Secondly, not knowing what he was looking for or how to find it, and not being sure that he'd like what he'd find didn't propel him forward. Proximity was a consideration too. Of the next three he visited, three were small, well-tended places. The people that lived in each of them said they hadn't been there that long and that the property wasn't theirs anyway. They were renters.

The fifth place was somewhere in Connecticut and Thrace had waited until providence, so to speak, sent him to New York. Eastlend, Connecticut was far north from New York but near enough for him to take the time to find it. Thrace rented a car and drove almost through the entire state of Connecticut. He'd gotten to the center of Eastlend, a whitewashed municipal building with parking spaces for three cars, none of them being used. He opened the door and walked inside a self-service postal facility. No one was inside, but the boxes were named and lined, and the keys sat in the lock as if everyone came in at the same time and all left their keys. A basket sat on the floor in front of the metal wall with a few things inside, but what caught his eye was a note that read:

"When crowded with mail, anybody going near take this up the bi-road to Old Lady Jack. Front road ain't cleared." The "ain't" was crossed out and replaced with "isn't" in a neater hand.

Thrace took the contents of the basket and headed out for the bi-road which he easily found. It looked like an ossified trail that very few traveled. He bumped along the road, frightened for moments that he might disappear in a Connecticut ditch and no one would ever know. The road narrowed for a long stretch and then suddenly widened. After he'd gone another mile or so, the road opened to a well-tended house with flower boxes in the windows. It had a neat and widespread front lawn. He stopped and waited before opening his car door just to see who might come out of the house to greet him. When no one did, he stepped out and took a couple of steps forward. Then a dog came barking and wagging its tail from the back side of the house.

The dog came to the car, sniffed him back and front, then pushed his leg forward with his nose. The dog ran forward, leading the way, running back, circling him, urging him toward the house. When he headed towards the front of the house, the dog barked and turned his head, telling him that it was the rear of the house that he needed to get to. Thrace covered the side, following a grassy path that wasn't well worn but meant to be used. He touched the house and tried to look in the windows, but they were set too high in the wall for him to be able to see inside. When he reached the corner of the house, the dog jumped up, barking more excitedly as if announcing the arrival of someone his master expected.

"You must be new, or old Clark wouldn't have warned me." A very old but hearty lady said in a clear and strong voice, then she looked at him.

"Earl, Macomb, or Thrace?" she asked, and Thrace was shocked.

"Thrace," he responded, "How did—?"

"Who else was going to come down this road that I don't already know? You get to know some things by the time you get to be my age. Them three I mentioned helped my daddy."

"My daddy earned it, they banked and insured him, helped him keep his place. Them Thraces traveled for Macomb, who traveled for Lloyd Earl. They was light and people didn't bother them so much 'cause everybody knew they probably close to their masters though they never had none. They was what we used to call free blacks," she said it like one word and breathed a little and took a sip out of her cup. On the front of the house, she had a larger porch. At the back, she sat under an awning on top of the wide set of cement stairs that led to the backyard.

"I'm drinking my morning whiskey. Like some?" She rose before Thrace could stop her, and now he was too embarrassed not to take her offering because of the effort it took her to fulfill it. He waited. She came back outside, pushing a block of well-carved wood, carrying a glass in her hand and a bottle in her apron pocket which Thrace hadn't noticed she was wearing.

"I could just as easily sit on that stool or in this chair. Which one you want?"

"Please," Thrace said, "allow me the stool."

"My daddy's," she said, and Thrace sat down, lower than he remembered sitting even as a small boy. His knees rose to his ears.

"My daddy liked the stretch of sitting low," she said. "Me too."

They sat quietly for a while and Thrace tasted his whiskey. The first time, the taste surprised him, smooth, strong, slightly sweet, and warming. The second taste was even better.

"Some were afraid of the whiskey my father started making. The Thraces more than Dagomire Macomb. They thought it would bring trouble. Thraces more careful than Mr. Macomb. Mr. Macomb trucked in imaginary white men. That's what my daddy said. Daddy said he got the know-how from Lloyd Earl but he had to teach himself after Lloyd Earl died. He could create 'em and he did, for all us that needed 'em. At one time, this land was almost a hundred, now it's on about 47 acres. Daddy didn't ever want to sell no land; neither did none of them but Daddy gone, and troubles did come. Not too many but trouble is trouble."

"Daddy didn't call himself no bootlegger 'cause the whiskey wasn't his or that's what he supposed to pretend. And you know, they kept all this know-how, everything from the women. Only reason I know, I was the only one left when Daddy had to talk. He had to tell somebody something 'fore he died. He gave me his box and said if I ever married, I's to give it to my husband but I never married."

"Do you still have the box?" Thrace asked, trying to shutter his curiosity before it exploded and scared the old lady.

"Burnt it up one winter, accidentally," she responded and Thrace felt the loss.

"Well, maybe not so accidentally," she corrected herself. "I was mad at my daddy that time. Stayed mad a long time after he died though I knew enough to keep making whiskey and doing what he always done and hiring that bank a' men to seed, plow, and farm this land. Last harvest now. Just my kitchen garden, but you can do what you want with it now."

Thrace didn't know why she was telling him about the place as if he'd come for the land. Quieted, he thought it best to just listen.

"No questions?" she seemed to sense his dilemma. Thrace was still thinking about the box.

"I didn't burn the papers," she said. "Just the box. I got the deeds, and you can have 'em. No more Jacks around that I know. Did you try to find any others? Daddy had a brother and a sister one time."

"I'm not sure why or what or who you believe I am . . ."

Old Mrs. Jack interrupted, "My whiskey make you tell the truth. It'd be just like the next generation not to know what to do. That's why the menfolk were wrong, wrong to keep everything away from the women. You know, my daddy and all them men, Thraces, Macombs, and whatnot could read and write but they kept it from the women same as the whites. Didn't make no sense and I told them so. Begged Daddy for years till I sat back and reminded him that he didn't have no son and wasn't likely to. He didn't have no choice if he'd wanted things to go the way he wanted them to go. Daddy lived to be a hundred and something, though he didn't know his real birth year. Ima get those deeds." She stood up and turned.

"You hungry?" she asked Thrace.

"I'm fine. Please don't trouble yourself for me." Thrace said and Old Mrs. Jack sat back down. She didn't say another word. Thrace didn't know it, but he had made a crucial mistake. Turning down her food turned off her words. Refusing her generosity meant he was refusing all she had to give and after a few moments, she told him.

"Come on back in a couple of years; I think I got it in me to live a few more years. I ain't quite a hundred yet. Clark gonna take you back to your car. But if I don't got a hundred in me, the comeback is gonna come back. Don't you worry. The come back is gonna go back."

Thrace had no idea what she was talking about and he hadn't ever gone back.

A knock at his door brought Thrace out of his reverie.

"Come in." Thrace squeaked upright in his chair, hoping for Mrs. Thrace but it was his daughter, Alley, more and more often now, speaking for all his children. They were hungry. He interrupted his reverie to tend to their stomachs. He made sandwiches and tea.

Afterwards, back in his quiet study, Thrace still didn't know if his wife was in the house or not. He had had the good sense to hire a company that delivered and unpacked all but their most personal possessions. His house—*their* new house—had been ready for the family before they arrived. Selma had not noticed because she had not come inside. Thrace rewarded himself with the knowledge that he had done the proper and right thing and that his wife should be happily surprised that all her things had come with them to the States. In the mood that he admired most, she was agreeable and appreciative of her husband's decisions and though she was not emotionally or vocally effusive, she let him know in the way that she was always ready to receive him. The way she cooked and sang at certain times, the way she went about herself in her own ineffable way. Thrace's good quality in his own marriage is that he had no expectations and could live next to her and their children happily ever after without a single contribution from any one of them.

His wife's appetites matched his for no better reason than the only appetite with which he was completely familiar was his own and it was large enough for two. And Thrace was neither selfish nor self-absorbed, just altogether uninterested in anything outside of the quiet pursuit of wealth and the provision of goods for his family.

Thrace lived in the everyday of his life which provided a kind of faithful, intractable happiness gleaned from the details of a good dinner and a properly working toilet. Unnoticed by Thrace, his wife spent all her time in memory. The marriage was marvelously symbiotic with the past bumping into the present every evening in their bedroom.

Everyday decisions needed to be properly made and dispensed with which is how Thrace managed to look for, find, and purchase a house without ever bothering to mention it to his wife. The fact that they were returning to the States, moving to Washington, DC, had also remained a mystery for Selma and the children.

With this same tact and skill, he hired the new housekeeper.

Together, the children invented a game. *Scare Thrace's maid.* They locked their bedroom doors when it was time to clean, misplaced the mops, emptied the cleaning fluids on their own individual projects, and kept the kitchen immaculate. They placed things precariously on upper shelves in closed cabinets so that when the doors were opened, cans of beans, bags of flour, and boxes of cereal would fall. Mirella did a one-footed scraping walk in her pink tap shoes; Alley rolled her dresser back and forth causing the house to make strange unwelcoming noises and then they would hide. If the maid were in one part of the house, they'd make noises from the other. When she came to investigate the noise, one of them would go disturb whatever she was doing. For instance, if she had been dusting, they'd take the furniture polish and her rag, the broom if she were sweeping, the mop if she were mopping.

They'd scared one maid by draping themselves with sheets and turning off the lights in the hallway. Mirella and her brother mewled like cats that had gotten caught in the house and when the maid came up, they silently began floating towards her on their skates. The woman sneezed, dropped her bucket, and ran.

"She's allergic to cats," Alley said, and they all laughed. But they had to clean up the mess from the bucket and put it all away.

When Selma returned from her first walk, she could not find their house. In her haste, she had not bothered to identify any address or distinguishing feature. She looked up as she turned the corner and caught the name "Hamilton," and somehow remembered that Thrace's house was on Hamilton Street. She made her way back without the assistance of any one thing and now stood on the corner underneath a green Hamilton sign with white lettering, wondering to which house they had moved. None of them looked or felt familiar, none looked well used or had visible remnants of family life. The Thraces now lived in America, in houses behind groomed lawns with well-tended façades. The "Joneses" were hidden and no one would be quite able to tell, at least from the front of the house, whether they were striving to keep up or laying the standard down. Selma stood on the corner taking in the individual characteristics of each of the houses. The corner property sat at a sideways angle toward the front of the street and was erected from a pale sand colored brick. Next door, the house faced frontward and because of the four shaded windows on the second floor and four shaded windows on the entering floor, nothing separated it from the others. Adjacent to the four-windowed brick house stood another unattached sand-colored brick house with an even more austere façade. The family had troubled themselves with the extra effort to clear the house of any evidence of people. As Selma was no surer of one side of the street than the other, she took both in.

A little man bent over, shoulders tightly hunched, shuffled past, tethered to his lumbering white-whiskered dog. Both man and dog, caught up in the slow rhythm of advanced age and equal pace, paused next to Selma. The old man waited while the dog sniffed Selma's ankle, "New people moved into that house. Coloreds, I think," he said to the dog, "Right there," the old man hadn't pointed, but the dog looked over at the brick house with the plain very large square garden. Selma walked the rest of the way home, opened the door and went inside.

In Washington, DC, on her first walks, an accidental clue led her home. First, a dog, then a stranger running away from the house with a broom.

The maids often came on the days when Selma walked early, so even if they had been adventurous and went looking and calling for a mistress, they would have missed her. Each had a slightly different reason for quitting though none had blamed the wife, the children, or the eerie noises.

Thrace kept getting notices and kept requesting maids. He thought them all generally capable as the house was quite clean. He assumed that the exiting maids had all cleaned the house once before they quit, finding something disagreeable in the interim. Though he could never discern the problem, it did not occur to him that the disagreement could be placed with his wife or children. For one thing, when he asked the agency why each of the maids quit, he got everything from "The house is too quiet" to "An unoccupied house does not need a housekeeper." He even heard "Brand new brooms standing in a clean hallway corner were bad luck." They seemed to be a superstitious lot. "An unused broom would sweep good fortune straight out the door for all who entered." Exactly half the maids took the new brooms with them.

"Why do these housekeepers keep leaving if they are so good as to keep the house spotless and prepare such nice meals?" Thrace asked at dinner.

"The house is already spotless." Big mouth Mirella made a mistake.

"How is that?" Thrace asked, more curious than anything else, "Each of them cleans the house once before deciding not to keep the job?"

"Not one of them has ever really cleaned once," Alley said.

"Who, may I ask, has cleaned?"

"We..." and Alley knew she shouldn't finish her sentence, even without her father's change in facial expression and tone.

No wife of his had to know about laundry or cleaning supplies, and certainly not his daughters. He'd only allowed his wife to cook because she seemed to like it—occasionally. When she didn't want to know her way around a kitchen, she did not have to and the fact that they were performing as maids was a failure on his part. What had possessed them and how had they become so talented at cleaning in such a short space of time? He wondered if the Egyptian had been teaching them to clean and it angered him more. Young Negro girls did not have to know the inside of a broom closet. Not a Thrace, not one of his daughters. Thrace would take this up with his wife. His daughters were not to be engaged in cleaning this house nor any other.

But the conversation would have to wait because Thrace had been delivered the opportunity he'd expected. The sugar, the refinery, the kitchen, and their manager were ready, and so far under the price of the same small operation in Louisiana. This was to say nothing of the aggravation of doing business in the south, in 1965. Thrace could do nothing else but abandon the immediate and mundane needs of his family in order to do a site review and sign the papers on what would become his small factory in Mexico. Thrace planned to leave first thing in the morning, so he asked his wife, after bedding her, to keep the new maid at least until his return.

12

All Kinds of Flowers
in Mexico

Thrace had nothing to compare to riding alone uphill in a small, rickety roofless car. In his mind, he listed what little he knew of Mexico: lovely weather in the North American winter, an amazing variety of tropical plant life, more land for his money, no extradition to the United States. Distracted, he looked outside at the most colorful variety of marigolds and dahlias he had ever seen. The air was so heavily scented with a sweet fragrance, he felt coated and wondered if he would seem overly perfumed when he arrived. The posturing floral brilliance stung his eyes. Garish bright orange petals with a smooth waxen beauty were almost grotesque. Under the clear, blue sky, beauty didn't comfort Thrace but rather unbridled his normal resolve, replacing it with a slim foreboding. He assuaged himself by thinking of the disarming nonsense the children might say if they were riding with him surrounded by such a sight.

"Father, I think it's for us," sweetly offered he thought by his younger daughter.

"She thinks we're the only people in the world when we're all together," the other would have answered with her ready competition.

"Wouldn't the world be alright with just us?"

"No."

Thrace wouldn't always know which daughter finished the conversation and it didn't matter. He laughed at himself for going along with the farce of the girls being twins. He liked them twinned, easily wrapped in one bundle. His son might not participate in the conversation, nor his wife. Reluctantly, Thrace put his mind where it belonged and rode the rest of the way up the hill deciding how he would manage his new "hacienda," complete with a sugar mill so that he could grow and refine the sugar he would need to make his candy.

Thrace would be a landowner in the Michoacán State of Mexico. His neighbor was the former presidente, Lazaro Cardenas. Thrace had to thank Jonathan Porter, who had retired in Mexico, and got bored of doing nothing. Porter told Thrace that he had remembered his plans and discovered a place to begin. Porter offered to manage the operation. Thrace had been surprised and delighted to hear from Jonathan Porter on the eve of his ending mission in Cairo. Right when he was ready, Porter came up with the goods.

In some ways, Thrace hoped that Porter would be just an adequate manager. He knew not to hope for more. His friend's excellent skills came with the certainty that his term would be short-lived. Eventually, Porter's gifts would be overwhelmed by his restlessness and Thrace didn't want to grow dependent on a manager that would eventually be consumed by a desire to move on. The State Department had been perfect for Porter and Porter had been perfect for it, especially in the days when a truly charismatic diplomat would have been appreciated. Porter had served as ambassador in five countries under three different presidents and each of them had wanted more service from a man who refused. One thing that Porter knew too well was when he'd reached the end of his interest. That restlessness figured into all aspects of Porter. He'd been married once for a short time and afterwards, had been passionately in love over different continents for many short periods. In love with women, in love with the cities where they lived, and cities where they didn't.

Thrace was the opposite, clearly a man addicted to the long haul which showed in his meticulous competency, and carefully measured movement. Thrace had been like a distant apprentice until he moved to Egypt where he and Porter worked together for the first time hand-to-hand in the same embassy. When Porter retired, Thrace felt the difference. Rather than seek a plum assignment abroad, Thrace had moved to Washington, DC Porter told him that he could probably choose an ambassadorship anywhere in Sub-Saharan Africa and Thrace didn't mind the truth, knowing that Porter wished to tell it. One could reinterpret Porter, but it would be a mistake. Porter's honesty had been a part of him, another arm, freely extended. The other person might be disturbed or disgruntled when greeted this way, but Porter exuded truth and fairness in all his dealings. His manner suited and served him.

Thrace and Porter sat on the rear porch of the hacienda which overlooked Thrace's property. Porter had taken possession of the hilltop house that overlooked eight hundred acres. Porter's other highly prized talent was to set up a graciously appointed house. He'd put a house together many times in so many parts of the world that he seemed to have always lived wherever he was. Visiting Porter at home was always a comfortable treat, very close to, but not overly defined by luxury. It was a perfect experience, from the scent in the air to the temperature of the room, no matter whether the house belonged to the tropics or the tundra. In the middle would be Porter with his same sure manner, his khaki pants, his expensive shirts, his outreached arm, and his confident smile that did not convey happiness or the lack of it; rather, it betrayed an ability to take whatever had come.

"Porter, how long have you been here?"

"The moment I saw this place, I knew it was perfect, especially when I learned of the sugar. They bring every foreigner out here in search of a buyer."

"Was it furnished?"

"Empty."

"Empty?" Thrace was so surprised that he stood up and looked into the rooms again, at least the ones that he could see from the outside.

"My confession is—"

"Surely, this extraordinary table has been here for a century?"

"Open-air market a few weeks ago. I came upon it after lunch. I'd had a few drinks. The table was too right for this place so you probably paid more than you should have."

"I am indebted to your good services, sir."

"You'll find all the receipts with the other papers. You'll need to look over the worker contracts which I've had newly drawn up. They are a formality that was insisted upon by Alana, for practice perhaps. You've given raises to everyone." Porter smiled. "Though the mill has been without an owner—a Mexican foreclosure—they have never stopped production, harvesting, and taking care of the cane. We raised them for their show of good faith. How good is your Spanish these days?"

"Rusty, in a few days—maybe a little more certain."

"Fortunately, my assistant speaks English."

"Where did you find him?"

"Her."

"Her?" Thrace asked, surprised.

"She is a relic from another time. I think she may have had something to do with El Presidente next door."

"Is she as old?"

"Timeless. I have no idea what age she could possibly be, but you'll meet her tomorrow. She works like us, very early."

Thrace stood up and stretched, twisting his back one way and then the other.

"Sit again," Porter requested. "Please, I have a confession."

"You're not going to give me the preemptive speech about your intentions, are you?" Thrace sat, smiled, and looked over at his friend, glad to be so comfortable.

"I've been on your clock a little longer than you know as

you'll see from the receipts. I committed to buy this outfit before I sought your blessing. I didn't do it all overnight. I've been working for a couple months now, researching sugar production and refining. I remembered a little from Cuba, and it's different, but not too much."

"Are you saying you want a retroactive paycheck?" Both Thrace and Porter laughed.

Porter suspected that Thrace probably had more money than he'd ever know socked away. They had always discussed matters openly and Porter understood Thrace's necessity for wanting to believe that money would protect him and his family. Thrace's tie to America was different than his own. Porter was a white man living abroad, a foreigner. Thrace was a black man living at home, a foreigner in his own country. Theirs were different stories. Porter's great-grandfather had been the one who had been seen to his ignominious end by a prosperous former slave. Thrace's great-grandfather had been a prosperous black man. Their history, Thrace and Porter's, had, in a way, prepared them for the possibility of friendship and each had taken it up.

Thrace brought a cashier's check and the ability to wire into the state-owned Mexican bank they had already chosen. He knew that Porter would do what was necessary, including paying and reimbursing himself and he knew the receipts would be catalogued and kept for him to peruse which is exactly what he'd do.

"My confession is that this place, more than any other, seems to hold me. Are you prepared for me not wanting to leave?"

"I'm prepared for things that one would never expect could happen," Thrace said.

His friend looked at him and smiled.

The next morning, Thrace was the third person to arrive in the kitchen where the other two were already working. They had matching cups of coffee and their heads close together eyeing a long roll of graphs that encompassed the entire table. Another waiting cup sat next to the stove across from where they were. Both startled and Thrace could see that they had been used to working together without the imposition of a third party. She stood up immediately.

"Alana Morote," she extended her hand and welcomed him. "There is coffee."

Thrace walked over, poured coffee into his cup, and used the tiny sugar rocks in a dish nearby. He opened the small thin refrigerator for milk and poured a little into his coffee. He sat near the counter and took his first sip. At the same time, without altering her position at the table Alana announced, "Your first taste of Mexican sugar." She knew without bothering to look up that he would be smiling.

Thrace was filled with an incomparable sense of well-being and in his own mind, he was already expanding his business. He'd make all sorts of specialty candies with this, his own sugar. As he looked down at the cup in his hand, he smiled again. Had he always lived right here in a Mexican kitchen?

He liked Alana immediately and picked up on the time-lessness that Porter had mentioned. He also wondered to himself if she were the reason that Porter might stay and almost instantly knew that she would not be. Even if they were intimate, Porter would not bank on the longevity of his own feelings.

The three of them spent the day in the kitchen. All three meals were served there. The cook arrived and worked around them, restricting herself to the countertops, serving ample plates around the perimeter of the papers laid out on the table. By the end of the day, Thrace almost had a complete narrative of every transaction that had been made on his behalf.

As Alana was leaving, she announced, "Tomorrow, the dining room. Dinner will be served in the dining room." She smiled, turned, left the kitchen, and then the house.

Thrace and Porter headed back out to the porch with stiff necks and backs and soothing drinks.

"Where does she live? Far away?" Thrace asked Porter.

"She prefers to walk, wherever it is."

"You don't know?"

"Let me say that she is far too competent a woman for me." Each added their laughter to the others. Thrace told himself he would evaluate her on that basis tomorrow.

The three of them toured the property very early the next morning with Alana and Porter explaining to Thrace the intricacies of the machinery, the ages, uses, and dates of acquisition. Rather than old hands, they seemed to be full of the kind of enthusiasm one comes to from sharing new information. Some of the talk of sugar refining was new language for Alana. For Thrace, the language was familiar, but the machines were not, and they had a kind of reunion of people who had arrived at the same conclusion from different directions. Thrace had always liked to listen to technical information, and he appreciated the fluency of his compatriots in the sugar business as he now thought of Porter, Alana, and himself—an expedient threesome.

Porter mentioned the pan evaporators, or as they were also known, "multiple effect evaporators" and told Thrace that they were probably twenty-five years old but still produced as clean a liquid sugar as they always had. Particular attention had to be paid to cleaning them and they had instituted another sifting feature between crushing the cane and putting it into the evaporators. First, they cleaned the cane and removed as much excess plant material as possible; the extra material the villagers dried and used for God knew what. They carefully washed the cane before putting it into the wringer, an old-fashioned looking washing machine. After crushing the cane and almost pulping it, they sifted it again through a sort of makeshift contraption that neither had a name nor a patent and then put it into the pan evaporators. There were three evaporating machines. Afterwards, they put the sugar through a couple of different processes. In one, they mixed the raw sugar with a little more molasses which was a sugar by-product, poured it into molds, and let it dry, turning it into loafs to be used in whichever way Porter saw fit.

When they had completed the tour of the small refining factory and showed Thrace the end product, Porter announced that he had scheduled some personal appointments and that Alana would take Thrace on a tour of the surrounding town.

Thrace noticed that most of the liquid by-product of sugar refinement was neither stored in the factory nor in one of the outer buildings that were slated to be used for processing. He wasn't sure whether to ask Alana about it or to wait and let her tell him. Her efficiency so far suggested that he ought to wait; however, to him, the perfect time for her explanation had arrived. They were leaving the small refinery and the business of it behind them as they headed down the slight incline to the road where a buggy awaited them.

"I hope you don't mind but for a tour, I prefer the slower transportation." She gestured toward the buggy and waved the waiting boy into the driver's seat. The buggy was a re-tooled open-air vehicle dressed down for the local tourism industry if there was one.

"This car can't go any faster than 20 miles an hour and this young man has mastered the art of driving it." Everything had been carefully considered for the new boss.

"Most of the workers cannot read, but that is not what's important. I believe the important thing is that they hold something tangible that represents their relationship to the company. For me, a contract is a big hand; it can be held, squeezed, or also thrown away." Thrace wanted to ask how she learned English but decided to wait.

"My feeling is that the village can wrap itself around sugar producing, especially if it feeds them and not just food, but feeds their joy, their souls."

"Do you know what they worship?" Alana continued and pointed at the small stone building used for something church-like.

Thrace didn't like the use of the great "they" but at the same time, his eyes hurt because of the way the sun bounced off her shiny black hair.

"I feel it's a simple religion, much like . . ." she said and Thrace understood that he was to be her captive, buggy-trapped audience.

". . . Well, I think worship is simple like morning ablutions; it's what you wash yourself with. Do you know what Michoacán means? I've forgotten to tell you." Thrace didn't answer right away and reminded himself of his wife's most difficult habit.

"Michin means fish, Hua means 'those who have,' and Can means place."

"Fish for those who have a place," Thrace liked his own juxtaposition.

"We are proud of our fish," she said and Thrace laughed heartily.

"I didn't mean that literally. I meant in the way that our village was chosen to be a place of abundance—fish life easily available to us, a God-given place."

Alana said "we" a lot with what seemed to be her own conclusions and Thrace wondered if she were misrepresenting anything.

Porter looked upon her soliloquys as more evidence of her complete ability. She could clearly think through anything and easily determine the most efficient plan of action. Porter also felt that when she dug in too deep with the details and stayed too long and often, the best tactic for him was to ignore her. He trusted the outcome and Alana enough not to have to listen to ins and outs of the circuitous paths she'd taken to arrive at a decision.

To Alana, life was religious, especially the rituals that she practiced to make alcohol. She spoke of them with a kind of reverence that scared the men. Neither of them knew about the still that she operated with the leavings of the liquid sugar. She had mentioned the still, but they had not heard.

Thrace, Alana, and Porter were seated at the promised dinner in the dining room. The two men had rejected the idea of sitting end-to-end and sat across from one another with Alana at the head. She felt this was an attempt to spotlight her and decided to pontificate accordingly. But the two gentlemen seemed to spend several moments in their own worlds, and she was impatient with being ignored.

"To Norbert..."

"Rillieux," Porter joined Thrace in announcing the last name of the man they were toasting. Norbert Rillieux was the son of a slave and a wealthy white father from New Orleans who had been freed by his father and sent to earn an engineering degree in France. Upon his return, he had invented the pan evaporator in 1846.

Only two men such as Porter and Thrace would have these details codified and compacted.

"Good-bye to the 'Jamaica Train,'" Porter raised his glass a second time.

"Patent 4,879," Thrace joined him.

Alana felt compelled to listen when the two of them talked. Yet, she could see when their eyes glazed over, and their ears stopped working while she was talking. Porter was overt and outright with the fact that he was not listening and from time to time even interrupted right in the middle of her ruminations. Thrace, on the other hand, quietly turned off and with him, she eventually sensed when she had talked past his listening.

"Can you imagine, Alana? Before Norbert Rillieux, cane workers had to ladle steaming hot sugar from one cauldron to another with a long stick, a full heavy bowl on the end of it with an even hotter pot to pour it into? If you splashed it, you were burned. If you spilled it, you were whipped."

This, Alana took as her clue to invention. "My product is a very efficient one. You see, an efficient worker can design a useful instrument for the company, which is why my method of production is probably the best for turning the surplus sugar into a potable liquid for sale here." She avoided using either "spirit" or "alcohol."

"In neighboring towns—in the capital and further—what we sell in the village should be subsidized and somewhat diluted. It's true that I have done this alone and in secret, but with the full support of the factory, production can grow. This brings me to my most worthy idea. What about a yearly festival to launch each year's yield? We will dress up the whole village and host the world! Imagine us a stop for tourism." Alana was excited and detailed her hopes for the festival with colors and flags, stages and music. She'd planned everything for the entire village. Plenty Fish State Festival, she'd said in deference to her new boss.

Thrace and Porter were perplexed. They ate heartily, treating Alana's plans as something to be freely ignored, so much background music. Both, however, complimented her on the planning of such a lovely meal.

Later, when they were alone, Thrace told Porter, "Maybe Alana can run the house, the factory, and the town."

"I told you she was supremely competent," which for some odd reason made Porter think of Mrs. Thrace. "Will you bring everyone when you return?"

"Maybe just the Missus, she hasn't really been away from the children since they were born."

"In all these years? Was it choice or necessity?"

"Neither. Just the way the festival of life has fallen." Again, Thrace and Porter had a chuckle over Alana. If anything, Thrace thought his candy should be the symbol of the town. Porter had one other thought, 'Mrs. Thrace at the festival.'

13

Getting Used to America— Selma, Agnes, and Berdeena Try Gardening

Two weeks after leaving, Thrace arrived back in Washington, DC; the first thing he thought approaching home is that his yard must have hosted a festival of inept gardeners. Each gardener must have had a little plot for himself and exercised his most disturbing fantasies in plant life. Dug up in places, tamped down in other spots, something had been freshly buried and the yard had gone wild. What flowers there were looked wan and rather unsettled, and the grass needed mowing. His next thought 'Alana's garden would be carefully planned and finely executed,' surprised him more.

He shoved such an oddity away and walked into his quiet house.

The girls heard his footsteps and together peeked through the railings at the top of the stairs. Often home alone, the two of them were generally together and it just so happened when he arrived that they had been engaged in a game of their own design called, "We-Still-Live in-Egypt." The two of them would pick a room in their old Cairo house, sit in one corner of the room and together describe everything in the minutest detail to the right or to the left. Each would select a side of the room and the one who won, by creating the most detailed layout of the room, owed her sister a favor. If one of them remembered something that happened or had been said in the room that both sisters remembered, one could preempt the other and win. Alley had just made Mirella remember the day they discovered the face hidden in the marble floor.

"Remember when Mother froze with her foot in the smile?" Mirella asked her sister. Alley remembered but held out because she knew it would cost her the game unless she could add another detail.

"She was like a statue waiting to be placed. We walked her to her room, pushed her inside, and went back downstairs," Alley added.

"We thought Daphne and Hala might have noticed," Mirella laughed.

"Hala didn't say anything. That's one thing I liked about her. She always left well enough alone," Alley said.

"Daphne didn't," Mirella added. "She said when her mother talked about Americans being people without laughter, she thought she only meant the fathers but maybe it included mothers too."

"Daphne was a pain," Alley admitted.

"Mostly, but my only friend," Mirella said. "She had some good things too."

"A nice house and good treats," Alley said.

"That was the first day we went to Daphne's house, remember? We thought Mother might come out of her room," Mirella added expecting points.

"Same incident—no points," Alley told her sister and then they heard the front door open.

Their father stepped inside. They stood up and ran down the stairs, Alley yelling.

"I hug Daddy first. I won!" She didn't have to call it as she had reached their father first and jumped into his arms. Truly glad that he had come home, they hugged, squeezed, and barely let him go until he held one daughter in each arm, then leaned her back so that he could see her face. He couldn't remember such an effusive greeting from his children before.

"Where are your mother and brother?"

Alley looked at her sister and signaled to keep hugging him.

"Mother's walking and," Alley guessed.

"Maybe they're together," Mirella said. These days, the two of them kept the same hours.

Unbeknownst to his sisters, Black Black had once again taken up following his mother. At first, he used to watch her from his window. He watched until she became a tiny stick moving away from their house, but it depended upon the direction she had chosen. Sometimes, she dissolved into a small bobbing head; other times, she would go headfirst and he could only see tiny feet but that was when she walked down the back alley. Other times, he'd hear the door, and no matter which direction he looked she couldn't be spotted. He watched for days until he felt brave enough to follow her and he followed her until he felt brave enough to select his own direction and by then, he had learned enough of the city to get himself home. Strangely, no matter where he went or how long he stayed, he usually ended up at home the same time as his mother.

Black Black and his mother discovered Rock Creek Park. They breathed in soil over laden with the perfume of crushed and moistened leaves, dropped from the branches that shaded their way. They traveled to the music of disparate chirpers above the constant rhythm of a solo woodpecker that intermittently tapped the bottom to droning insects and mingled with the slap and slide melody of leaf upon leaf when the trees swayed. The two of them, Black Black and his mother, felt the sweet push of coolly tinged breezes as they meandered around tree trunks, drying the sweat into salt on their necks and arms. Indeed, they heard each other snapping and shushing through the underbrush, each working out a path close to but not with one another, yet something bound them.

There didn't seem to be any available boys in America

either, at least not for Black Black to play with on a regular basis. He was excruciatingly lonely as even the voice disappeared for a time, and then only returned occasionally. When it did make itself heard, he was wholly unpleasant.

"Iswid, I didn't have to come, you know. America is overrated. I don't remember being invited or even asked to come. You should be happy I volunteered. Who else do you have? Iswid?" Black Black was thinking that if his voice had wanted to talk to him, he'd had to come to America; furthermore, he ought to know that no one else was listening, so if he'd wanted to be heard, America was the place, invited or not. Black Black had mastered the art of listening and so did, never feeling he had to argue, essentially with himself, at least not with words.

Once while he was still walking behind his mother his voice quite clearly told him. "You probably only need one 'Black' for America." On that same walk, while Black Black was still following his mother, he'd come out strongly again.

"Iswid, still in your mother's pants? Where's your father? Better still, your grandfather. You don't need standing up information; you need sitting down."

For the first time in a long while, Black Black thought his voice had a good idea—perhaps more than one. Black did have a grandfather. His mother's father was somewhere, and he knew where his grandmother lived. If he could get to his grandmother's house, surely after all his trouble, she'd point him in the direction of his grandfather.

Black had a mission; now all he needed was a plan, and he figured the right plan would probably come up with itself while he was walking in the woods.

Selma had started the festival of inept gardeners to help her find her way back home. She was generally very tired from the mix of emotions that overcame her as she walked and quite frankly, guessing where she lived had grown rather nettlesome. Selma had fallen in love with the rocks, the creek, the trees, the paths, indeed, the idea of having a park at her disposal. So many trees, so few people. She had only wanted to come home to eat, rest, and take herself back to the nature she loved. The house hadn't rendered anything that caused her to feel herself back to it, so she decided to create a marker. In the corner of the yard, she took three sticks, hammered two straight into the ground and nailed the third one crosswise into each of the others to steady them, and only then noticed that she had created a two foot "H." She left it bare for the first couple of days. Twice, she returned home before she added some plant life. Gathering vines and leaves while walking in her beloved Rock Creek Park, she brought them home and draped them, twisted them, and even nailed a few to her homemade "H." Finally, she would recognize, maybe even come to accept, or merely get used to this new place.

Days later, Agnes awakened hungry in a strange house. It wasn't the first time that she'd been inexplicably transported. Moving was incredibly unsettling. She guessed she was alone and honestly, she'd just as soon have the house to herself as have Thrace in it, especially as a house was not something that one ought to be moved into by surprise. The house looked acceptable, so far. Familiar things were in some of the rooms. She even liked the main rooms. She found a window seat in a back room that didn't have an obvious purpose and decided that it would be her spot. She'd sit next to the children, hold both their smaller hands in hers and stare out at the yard. Mostly, she stayed in her pajamas and her imagination. When the girls appeared, she told them that she had been unable to dress as she could not find one. The girls went upstairs with their mother, opened her closets, and pointed to all the hanging things.

"Mother, there's plenty to wear. Look at all these things." Alley touched several of the dresses with the back of her hand.

"You're right, they're merely things. Someone else's who doesn't have particularly bad taste, just not my taste. They must belong to the former owners."

"Mother, these are all yours," Mirella assured her. "I've even seen you . . ." Alley stopped her sister with a quick shove for she had registered the fact that her mother was still holding her hand. They had crossed her bedroom together arm in arm.

"Mother, it's the flowered dresses that aren't here. Maybe we can ask the maid to find them."

"Is Umm here too?"

"No, but father has hired another one. She'll find your dresses."

"Umm didn't pack them, did she? I suppose she couldn't find them. Well, different flowers for different gardens?" She attempted cheerfulness.

"She'll buy you new ones," Alley comforted her.

While Agnes waited for new dresses, sure that they'd probably be unsatisfactory, she thought of her mother's love and care for her flowers. Aberdeen tended her garden for hours every day. She pruned and weeded, poked, and talked to her flowers. She smiled, proud and happy, finding so much pleasure among her groups of irises, petunias, jonquils, peonies, and pansies. She seemed perfectly content. Agnes was the one always trying to find her place in her mother's affection.

Agnes was so concentratedly needy that she wanted every ounce of Aberdeen's attention. She preferred to vie for Aberdeen's consideration and hoped Aberdeen would not notice her hungriness, see her seethe while fidgeting, waiting for the warmth of Aberdeen's glance to coat her with validation, to confirm that Agnes truly existed and was not just little legs wagging and stirring up the dirt beneath them. In her mind, the only competition for Aberdeen's attention seemed to be the flowers.

Aberdeen was too stubborn to be beholden to Agnes's silliness, and focused on her flowers. Usually, Agnes stayed close and when she wasn't underfoot, she was nearby and when she wasn't, she heard her mother tell her father that maybe she finally had something to do besides be needy.

Agnes decided to become a flower. A flower beautiful enough for her mother to straighten, prop up, push things away from her feet, and stare at her in a surprising way, full of awe and love—that's what Agnes had seen as she watched her mother care for her flowers. Agnes wanted the gazes, her mother's hands, all the attention that her mother used on her garden to be used on Agnes. She began collecting walnuts, ochre, herbs, colorful weeds, and spices. She ground them up and mixed them with oils and God knows what other substances that she found between her mother's kitchen and the world outside. She stayed up in the woods in her place not too far from the house and painted flowers on every inch of her naked self. She painted as much of herself as she could reach with her right hand and then painted the rest with her left. Her back and butt, she reached by painting the ground and first sat on then lay on and gently rolled and then remained still until she dried. When she was finished, she walked home in her newly resplendent skin, flowered nakedness for her mother.

Catching sight of her across the yard, Aberdeen filled the big rusty wide-mouthed bucket to the top, waited for Agnes to come close, then, all at once, threw the water on Agnes. She refilled her bucket and threw it over Agnes a few more times. Her father had been there too, she remembered, sitting on the three front stairs that led into the house.

"Those were some pretty flowers," she heard her father saying.

"Yep, but those were poisonous haycocks that she'd crushed to make them colors," her mother replied.

"That girl gonna kill herself for your attention, but them flowers she painted were some pretty. I might as well be invisible. She'd like to suck you up through a straw."

"You be the straw," Aberdeen laughed and said to her husband and then turned to her daughter.

"Little girl, paint them flowers on your clothes, let them dry out and then you can be a flower. Flowers don't just get to be flowers overnight. Takes time. Time, hard work, nature's choosing."

Temporarily restored order in the world, Agnes had succeeded. Quite pleased with herself, she'd caused her two parents to have a conversation about her, even if her father had a little trouble expressing himself because of the glutinous substance she'd left in his snack.

While she was curled up around her memories in the window seat, the new maid walked in with the flowered dresses in a variety of four colors. Agnes was pleasantly surprised—one of the dresses imitated her childhood garden. She asked the housekeeper to trade in the other three for more of the one she favored.

For the first time in Washington, DC, after hugging each of the children for an hour by the window looking out over the backyard, Agnes walked out the front door. She noticed their very strange garden and told herself that she would remedy it as soon as she had a moment, and that moment took another week or so while Thrace was still in Mexico. By then, Agnes had walked around Washington enough to know that all sorts of wonderful flowers were abloom.

Unfortunately, Agnes had never focused her attention on the toil it took to create a garden. Aberdeen's gardens were a wild profusion of all the possibilities that God put forth. Her garden was a mix that had found its order through the skill of Aberdeen's hands and grew beautifully and seasonally as Aberdeen had known how and when to plant and those skills had been passed down to her directly from Selsie.

People said Selsie had known how God would have planted his very own garden. But Agnes was clearly not the daughter to whom she had given these skills.

Agnes clipped the stems of flowers from any garden that she happened to pass, pocketed her clippings, and then came home and replanted the transported flowers. She considered her gardening parallel to her own plight. Indeed, she was a recently transported flower, too, and as she watched her clippings each die at their own pace, she wondered about the future and then began to focus a little renewed attention onto her garden. She dug the holes deeper and wider and at first, collected more flowers. Where she had tenderly taken one stem in the past, now, she took two, and continued in the same way every day.

The old man with the old dog gave Agnes her first piece of advice on gardening.

"If you cut off the heads of any more of my flowers, I'm going to report you as a vandal. Once you cut them, you kill them. Why you planting dead flowers is a mystery to me but do more of it and the mystery may be where you end up."

Agnes stared, not having the faintest idea what to say.

"Now here," the old man reached out and handed her an entire small flower, dirt and all.

"This is what you put in the hole. Flowers have to have roots to grow. You already made the hole the right size; now just put this in and cover the roots back up. I don't know what city you came from, but in this city we don't cut off the heads of our neighbors' flowers and I can't think of no city where a dead flower can grow again." He and the dog walked away together.

Though the old man's manner puzzled Agnes, she accepted the lesson and from then on began digging up entire flowers from different places, bringing them back and replanting them in her yard. She wished to have no further encounters with angry old men though she appreciated his advice. She planted his gift near the old one-rung ladder, hoping that soon enough the old-man flower would overgrow the ugliest garden ornament that she had seen in Washington, District of Columbia.

She hadn't been surprised, however, that the ugly piece of ladder could be found in their yard. Agnes seemed to remember that there was always a little ugly hanging around. One broken up piece of ladder—a beat-up letter "H"—stood crookedly in the front yard inviting bad luck. Agnes dug a few holes, figuring that flowers could hide the letter. If no one in the household would tend to such things, perhaps she had better. Every time she returned home; the ugly "H" greeted her. "Hey lady, hey lady," she imagined and hoped the flowers would grow very tall, very soon.

Weekly, the old man would come by, walking his dog, stopping to give Agnes pointers when he found her in the yard.

"When you stopped stealing from your neighbors, things began to shape up. Flowers are sensitive you know. They don't just grow anywhere. Time, hard work, nature's input. Situation has got to be right." Agnes guessed he was right; she hadn't stopped stealing her neighbors' flowers but her garden was truly taking shape—a rather strange trapezoid (now protected by its own scarecrow as she had come to regard the "H" which she had also christened "Harry").

Only one more person added her energy to the Thrace yard before Thrace came home. Berdeena's was the wildest of all, yet she was the most competent gardener. Berdeena didn't want to grow flowers, especially ones that could not be eaten. She wanted to grow herbs, food, and for good measure, she generally threw in a little of what her mother used to call "helpers" which were almost always poisonous. She hadn't had command of a patch of earth in ages and was exceptionally happy to have some earth now. She liked the new house, and she loved the new kitchen and when she found out that the yard came along with the rest of it, she began humming and whistling and finally went into full booming song.

Every lady needs a garden
To make her feelings grow
Every woman needs a garden
To make her feelings known
Little girls need flowers and grass
To romp and churn, giggle and burn,
To play when the moments come
while the moments last . . .

Little girls can grow petunias

pluck, and throw them away
A lady might Susan for a few days in May
Her garden will change as the seasons already know
But a plot—wild, yielding strong,
Sweet truth, and edible fruit—needs a
woman to plow its song
Long, green, haycocks and holly
Matching extractions, strange or jolly

Every lady needs a garden
To make her feelings grow
Every woman needs a garden
To make her feelings known
In her gardens live her secrets
Roots beneath the dirt, winding round and round
Undiscovered yearning hidden in the ground
Unheard words, not attached to sound

The kids let their mother sing a few verses before they came down, loving her music from the warm comfort of their beds. If they waited, Berdeena's scents would greet them and they'd know she was singing and cooking. Alley had glimpsed the fact that anticipation from her bed may be as sweet as actually seeing what was being served. She was always the last to appear, the one who most savored the moments.

They met their mother behind her mountain of stuffed muffins. There were sweet ones and meat ones, and both mixed with cheeses. They did their usual—sat down and ate until they couldn't move, poised around the table like statues in an installation when gently and slowly, they hummed their way out of their mother-cooked stupor.

"We're going to garden; we'll need every crumb." Berdeena decided to use the crumbs as her presents to the soil. Aberdeen had always told her, if she were first kind to the soil, kindness would be returned. She excused herself from the kitchen, asked Umm II (their name for the new maid) to help and slipped away and poked into her secret stash. Putting her hands in the seeds gave her an indescribable surge of memory mixed with pleasure. Berdeena's hands had always known which seeds to plant where. She gathered what she needed, headed out to the garden by way of the kitchen, collecting the children and Umm II.

She gave them all jobs. "Girls, dig precise and random holes. Make them as deep as two muffins and wide as one."

"You, sweetie," she pointed at Black, "get some buckets of water. Get them from the house, mix the hot and cold water, make it warm, and bring it out."

"After we fill the holes with these seeds," she held her hand opened for him to see, "you pour one cup and a half into each of the holes and then I'll fill the holes up with dirt."

"Girls don't dig right next to each other; move away, turn your back to each other, and always dig in front of your body." Berdeena would only use the holes that she liked, so it didn't matter where they dug, but she liked having more choices than less. She would lay each seed upon its own bed, a soft pillow of sweetened herbs atop muffin crumbs so that the seed would break out, helped along by the insects that would consume the crumbs and the worms that would cleanse their bodies by letting the soil travel through them, spreading opened spores about the soil.

The girls dug holes all over the yard like moles in yearning. They worked diligently and intuitively. For moments, they truly were their grandmother and even their great-grandmother's daughters working the dirt, methodically sharing in their unknown legacy. Mirella and Alley pulled dirt up into their hands and let the dirt fall though their fingers into little mounds like castles for bugs.

Berdeena stood by the front walk and surveyed the holes dug up by the girls, each marked with a pointy little hill. She hummed to herself as she chose the holes and emptied her pockets of seeds. When she was finished with the regular seeds, she stood in the corner near the funny little marker and buried her most prized possessions. She put the helpers in the ground all around the things that were already there. They would eventually overgrow everything in the corner both beneath and above the dirt. She liked having the marker, even though she knew she'd never forget where she put secrets in the ground.

"Help whenever expected," she named this part of the garden. Happy that she had managed to plant her secret seeds without the others' eyes. They had all grown tired from being bent over digging holes, carrying water, awaiting instruction, and retreated into the house.

Proudly, Berdeena surveyed her triumph over the small patch of land, pleased about all that would come. She was smiling and just about to start a song for the plants when she was startled.

"Looks like you've finally figured out how to garden. If you like random."

Berdeena wondered whether the dog or the man had spoken, neither being particularly welcome, and if they'd watched her work.

"I've always known what to do in a garden."

"Not a few weeks ago."

"I've only just arrived," Berdeena answered.

"Then your twin without the gardening skills has been here before you."

"Well, you'd better be careful just right here and not let the dog eat grass from this part of the garden."

"Dog knows where to get fed." He continued down the sidewalk, talking to his dog. "Least she can work the dirt, even if she makes a crazy foreign garden."

14

Black Finds His Grandparents on His Mother's Mountain

"Umm II takes very good care of us," Alley said. She had read her father's mind.

"Umm II?"

"She doesn't mind it, honestly. Mommy asked her."

Thrace wondered if he'd ever had a conversation with Umm Ridah outside of household function. He had liked and respected her; her presence in the house was a panacea of cleanliness and calm and she had presided over everything without ever making a presentation of it. This, in a fashion, was the way he thought he liked all unfamiliar women. They should be capable but without presentation—their likes and dislikes all tactfully unapparent. These days, his previously disparate, abstract thoughts about women were coalescing and he didn't understand why.

He was pleased to be at home. After the girls had temporarily sated themselves with enough of him to leave him alone, he sat in his office breathing himself in, welcoming himself through the subtle aura of his belongings. He liked the man that sat at this desk, positioned the items, and read the books upright on the shelves. In his office, due to no effort on his part, dinner would eventually be ready, and they would all gather around the table. Before the night turned over, he'd be abed next to the woman that belonged there.

Thrace was shifted out of his daydreaming a little earlier by his wife's noise and movement coming from the direction of the kitchen. Her most rambunctious self had arrived. She hadn't knocked upon his door. Part of him wanted to run and put his eyes on her, but he willed himself still, both his emotions and his hands. He occupied his chair enthroning himself. Everything in its time, a man whose queen should have known to be around when he arrived, even if he hadn't told her precisely when that would be. He listened to her singing, soon after could smell her cooking. He vowed not to eat so much and promised himself he'd make love to her slowly. But it was against his will that he always lost because he ate until he froze himself at the table and later, when he could move, he made love to her so furiously that he lost all his ideas and then found himself wondering what they would do together the entire summer before he returned to Mexico.

It would be a summer of odd sensations for all of them. Along with the heat, there would be the particularly unsettling feeling that came from not having known their son was outside the house until someone brought him home. Generally, the Park Rangers returned him, warning, of all things, that he had been found once again asleep in the park.

"The park is closed at dark." So, they returned him and he looked at his parents and the Rangers asking, naturally, without words, what in the world was wrong with camping in America?

There would be the peculiarity of being watched, as there seemed to be an old man poised at the fence, peering into the garden. And then there was the maid, positioned like a sentry, who for the life of her could neither make heads nor tails of the Thrace household.

Their first summer in Washington, Thrace went to his State Department office, Selma walked, and their boy disappeared and reappeared. They made love often, sweating, sliding off one another—and all with a curious kind of detachment. For summer picnics, they spread their blankets in the backyard, sat around the feast, and watched the food be partially consumed as a banquet for insects. Mirella came, Alley didn't.

Somebody brought the boy home from somewhere, but it was after they had cleaned up and put away most of the food. They carried food up to Alley. Washington wasn't easy to get used to.

Thrace attempted to take over the family's well-being. He did as he always did and began to arrange sightseeing tours. They visited the memorials and the Capitol, the Smithsonians, the reflecting pool, and the zoo. They sat on the grounds, stared up at the Monument, and pretended to be tourists. Washington was clean and pretty with no real dust to speak of or wipe away. In short order, they were so caught up in the frenzy of tourism that they could step away from their own peculiarities at least for a month or so. They made it to the inside edge of the summer and happened to have just returned home after spending the day walking around and sitting through a mass at the Shrine of the Immaculate Conception. Though they were not catholic, they had enjoyed the ceremony of the Latin high mass.

Each of them had retreated to their own corner of the house when a knock intruded. Umm II answered the door.

"This boy's been found trespassing in the Park again."

His mother came to the rescue.

"Come in, Dear; lunch is just about ready."

"Ma'am are you aware that he's breaking the law?"

"Law? We've just come back from a mass. And it's daylight."

"Evidence was that he'd been where he was for a couple of nights," the Ranger added.

"Impossible," she seemed to say to no one in particular. "We were all just at mass. Shrine of the Immacule..."

"Ma'am, is there a father, a husband?"

"How else..." she had walked back into the interior of the house leaving Umm II with the stranger.

"If the boy is found again, we're going to have to keep him.

I mean arrest him, and someone from this house, a relative, will have to bail him out." Umm II listened until the Ranger was finished and quietly closed the door.

After that day, she never saw the boy again. They must have sent him somewhere on her day off. From time to time, she checked his room for evidence of use without ever finding any. She had once asked her mistress who answered with only a strange and long stare that she'd been unable to interpret. She dusted, increasingly less often, and wondered where the boy had gone.

Black had only been practicing his escape in Rock Creek Park. Now was his time to travel to his grandmother's house because she could tell him about his grandfather. He had been using Rock Creek Park to see if he could survive in the woods and discovered, to his delight, that it was easier than expected. Rather than be afraid under the moonlight, he had come to love, close-up, the stillness beneath the crunches and whispers of a night in the woods. He mapped his journey, gathered tools, food, shelter, some favorite snacks and, set off to grandmother's house. Two and one-half days later, hitchhiking, walking, and one short bus trip later, he arrived nearby.

His grandparents' house wasn't on a predictable road.

He didn't know exactly where she lived, but he knew the name of her town and he only needed to ask once for them to point him towards the woods. He came up upon both her houses and sat out front wondering on which door to knock. He saw a little movement in the newer-looking house and tried the door. The new house seemed the most welcoming.

An old man opened the door and motioned for him to come inside quickly.

"She still pretendin' that she don't know I'm here."

Black was too afraid to think that it had been this easy to find the man he was looking for. "Are you Mrs. Aberdeen's neighbor or is this her house or . . . ?"

"We'll get to that, boy. Come on; make some noises that

sound like a house. Can you squeak or something?" Black laughed and tried. He had walked in on something else he didn't understand.

"Now, boy, you ain't got to arrive all easy like, your grandma's been expecting you." Black was even more astonished that the old man seemed to know him.

"She gonna tell you that the trees told her you was coming. But the truth is she just wanted it so bad. She been wanting to see you all ever since you been gone. She ain't seen you since you was a baby. Did you come alone? She's gonna say she was just expectin' you but she'd a taken what she could get." The old man caught his breath.

"'Round about now, I like to go up and then back down the stairs, make it sound draughty, wind blowing through an empty house. Now you go on and tiptoe back and forth 'round the top of the house."

Black did what he was told, peering into two empty rooms and a third one that was being used for storage. The room had all manner of boxes, all unopened—big and small boxes, some torn a little but mostly still wrapped the way they must have arrived. There were letters as well, but only the boxes interested Black. He was looking at the labels when the old man called up to him.

"You're not tiptoeing. Make some creaking noises. You can do it with your mouth if you can't do it with your feet." He could hear the old man chuckling in his old-man raspy voice and he didn't know if he thought something else was funny or if he was making fun of him. He heard him talking.

"She's gonna think the house got married and brought a spouse home."

More importantly, he heard him moving around and when he peeked down the steps, the old man seemed to be moving about with such contagious glee that Black couldn't help but be infected. He tiptoed downstairs and skipped behind the old man, following him on his rounds from room to room. He had a special arrangement in each room. In the kitchen, he tapped the pipes in the corner with a spoon. In the living room, he pushed an old chair in a circle with his knee. Everything he did, he did while standing completely upright. He used his foot to push an old rusted iron back up against the wall. Then he just began to laugh and clap.

"She'll be coming along soon. I just announced you, boy. Come on, let's sit down." He grabbed Black's hand and held it and then began to shake it.

"Howdy do?" he asked him. "Boy, I just don't know what to…"

Sure enough, both the old man and Black heard something at the side of the house.

"Look! Look out the window." There was an old woman rubbing a circular hole in the outer stains on the window and then putting her head close so that she could see into the house. She put her hand above her brow and stared. She stood motionless for a very long while looking into the window. When she disappeared from the window, they both waited for her to come through the door.

"Boy, you might 'a done something nobody could get your grandmother to do." He paused to give the boy time enough to think about it.

"She ain't never entered this house yet. She open it up with her key when the mail man deliver things but she ain't ever stepped in or opened a single one of them packages."

"Why?"

"She ain't made up her mind yet."

"About what?"

"I like the way you speak, boy." He reached down to shake his hand again, still without bending. "She don't rightly know if she likes the house and then if she were to like it, how that would obligate her, so to speak."

Black looked around. "It seems to be a nice house, still seems new, no one uses it much?"

"That's the truth, up 'til now."

"She hasn't come in yet."

"Might take a while. You can't just tell by looking at her, but she's a great big woman. Big enough so you can take some of her with you, too big so's you can't just live next to her all the time."

To Black, she looked about the same size as everybody else. Bigger than him, but so was everybody for now. Even he knew that that would change. The one thing Black loved though was that this old man talked directly to him. There was no one else in the house and he wasn't going to give it up just because he didn't understand what he was talking about. He was willing to listen, he could listen and listen to a voice that had a man that was standing right there all upright and everything, talking to him. He didn't mind how big his grandmother was. Right now, Black felt as big as anyone.

"Takes a big woman a long time to change, so much to move." They waited a while, and nothing happened. They both looked out the window but didn't see anything.

"Well, it might take her a while yet, boy." He caught his breath again. "Houses have legacies, stories for you, gifts that you might be unwilling to accept."

Black looked at the old man because of the changes in his speech. His lips didn't seem to be moving. The old man was a ventriloquist and the words were coming directly from his head instead of being countrified by his mouth.

"She's even more afraid of the legacy she might leave."

"What's a legacy?"

"I'll let your grandmother explain yorn."

"Maybe we ought to go out and get her."

"Boy, that's the best idea you've had yet."

Black liked the way the old man talked to him like they'd already been together a long time.

"I bet I know where she hidin' too. Come on 'round back." He gestured with his hand and Black followed.

They walked up in the woods a little bit and Black felt familiar. He already lived here. He didn't want to think about the possibility of his grandmother sending him back to Washington, DC His return had never occurred to him and what a funny time it was now to have to think about it before he'd even met her.

"A little bit further, we're going to her evening tree."

Black wanted to tell the old man that he wasn't afraid of being in the woods at night but didn't. He kept up easily knowing how to walk over uneven paths in the dark. Finally, they came upon one of the thickest trees that he had ever seen, the trunk was so large and round that if he ran around it twice, he'd be almost winded and definitely dizzy. The boughs' reach so great and full; a tree house roof hovered over them. There, he first spotted his grandmother close-up. She was sitting against her tree crying, crying so many tears that she was completely wet. All Black could think to do was crawl up next to her and put his arms around her, whereby she put her arms him and the old man joined them. There the trio sat, well into the night, hugging each other until Aberdeen stopped crying.

"This is your grandfather, Henry Olmstead Dagomire Macomb."

"Dag, this is your grandson, Clifton Maxwell Thrace, IV but let's call him something else."

He was a Junior? No one had ever called him by those names.

"How about Max the Black, a brave pirate?" She had accepted the name he had given himself and added one he already liked.

Grandma Aberdeen was a miracle, and he couldn't imagine what might happen next. For a long time, nothing did—nothing he could see, but his grandmother was indeed a miracle. She worked right there under the tree, pushing around her memory, moving out the bad, making room for Max the Black in a crowded, unwelcoming place, in her mind amongst the bad memories. Simply because she'd longed for a moment didn't mean she was prepared, nor did it mean she'd know what to do when the moment arrived. But taking the most troubling memories and putting them out of reach seemed right. First, she had to savor them and then move them.

No man could take the things he didn't want to remember

and put them away. The secret was to unearth them, lay them bare on the surface, examine every detail. Afterwards, they could be pulled apart and put back together without the emotions and pain that tried to hang on with permanent fibers, catching on uncertain facts, linking memories that had absolutely nothing to do with one another, and refusing to let go. Love didn't have to hurt, but everyone remembered it that way. Rather like butchering an animal, one removed the innards and tendons, cut up the loins, and preserved only the choice pieces. What a person chose was individual. Aberdeen cleansed her memories of pain.

She'd been taught by Grandmother Selsie and she could remember the facts of her own murder the same as she could remember when her Selsie told her the details of the murder that she too had had to commit. Selsie had insisted and plied into her that there was a right way to put and keep things in the head.

On that morning, many years ago, Aberdeen rose slow and lumbered about, moving more pounds than she weighed. She washed herself using soap she had perfumed the day before with flowers she had grown specifically for their fragrance. More than anything, Aberdeen liked the sweetness of freshly made soap and flowered air. She washed her whole self, washed because Dag might be home that evening and smiled, thinking her ablutions might predict the night. She was big and heavy whenever she had to make a decision and back it with action. She'd been pondering over what to do for a few days and though she still did not know, she knew that by the time she'd gotten up in the woods, if her mind didn't know her hands would, and one was enough to warn the other. She wore a comfortable dress, the one with the V-neck and the easy waist. She pulled it over her head and when she smoothed it and slapped her hips, she approved herself and slipped on her shoes. In the kitchen, she lit a fire, brewed the proper black tea with courage, strength, sweet leaves sprinkled with tiny flakes of ground dried mint, and one dried bud from a flower that only Selsie bred. She finished the tea on her front three steps, washed and dried the cup, and stepped away from her house.

Only once she made her way to the old path, did she receive the full honor of Selsie's company. Beside her, she felt her presence. Thankfully, she heard her voice. She'd tell her story again, just as she had many times before. Aberdeen could hear Selsie easily, Selsie still alive, holding her hand, telling her the things she needed to know. As a child, when Selsie was still amongst the living, Aberdeen could tell how serious the story was based on how tightly Selsie gripped her hand.

"Lloyd Earl took that place out of thin air with a kind of magic that only a nigger man had or could perform. What it gave to ourselves was immeasurable, but it ain't the same for you now. You don't have to embody that old building and them books with your soul 'cause we done done that. There's room, but it ain't no necessity. You could be part of the town. Negroes got a few things in town now. Church and all. When Lloyd Earl built that library, it was the first thing any of us ever had public besides trying to claim ourselves and I was mighty particular as to how I let that thing be used. You ain't even usin' it.

Sometimes in families, things just need to pass from one generation—two forward. You can use Lloyd Earl's library to know what's possible. You know what a nigger man can pull out of thin air like a tree from nothing? That's a powerful lesson to pass on even if you don't need it, living up here in the woods apart from people. Maybe your children could need it. Aberdeen, you big and whole," Selsie told her. "You don't need nobody. People say you big, but it's only your aura. You let yourself glow and it make a small woman grow. That came from me; your mama wasn't the same. She small and small and take herself apart, making herself smaller. She made herself suffer for the deeds I done. You know, making somebody die is easy. It's the afterwards that counts. In my case, it wasn't the law or nothing like that, just the way I was going to be with being a murderer, somebody who taken life from some other. I'm the one that made the poison. Most nobody know I'm the one that administered it too. I made him thirsty.

You don't know who I'm talking about 'cause me and Scilla done made it all go away. He was her brother-in-law, came to town one day to see his brother and wound up staying. He came with his nasty religion and tried to spread it on people. It wasn't no good-tasting sauce. But all he really worship was his own pleasure and that pleasure he took whether anybody agreed or not. He liked to sneak it out of you, telling you it's something else, like the thing you need to sacrifice for the God that made you. Scilla wanted him gone from the git-go but she didn't have no real reason, but her sense. And her senses always been close to right. Waiting, and waiting for God knows what, is what we did. Things in her house start to turn sour and her husband turned silent on his brother. If his brother left the back door open and honey all over the counter, he told her to leave his brother be. He clogged the well, he tied the dog up in the woods, and let Scilla's favorite horse outside the pasture. He did things to take Scilla outside the house, take her long time up in the woods. One son was saying weird prayers and the other one seemed to be struck dumb but it was alright with their daddy.

Her daughter and her daughter's best friend followed her brother-in-law around like he was Jesus, and they were disciples.

They did whatever he asked, which included laying down next to each other naked, the two girls giggling, letting him touch them. They was about the same size in most ways but he said Scilla's daughter had breasts made for touching and her best friend's were best made for sucking and he aimed to prove himself right. He was clever, this brother, coming into his brother's house with a coating of need and nicety. He put on the family ties with tales that Scilla's husband didn't remember. He told up things about their grandparents and parents, he told them where the money had come from and where there might be still more. He told him he was too religious to be subject to earthly man's petty cares. He put his brother's mind outside his house though he let his body stay.

The only reason we found out about the girls is 'cause they got to competing and my daughter planned to win. You know your mama and Scilla's girl best friends since children, thrown together in a better way, than me and Scilla. But me and Scilla always competed, and I won. I won only 'cause 'a what God gave me, knowin' about Earth and life and such. Your mama had to win, but she don't know what I know. She ain't ever open for me to put things in her that way but she wanna win same as me.

She told that man to meet her. She know a place where they could be alone for a good long time, a private place. And I found out 'cause she up there tendin' to the library, pickin' my flowers, and placin' them around. First time she ever cared about that place. But he so special, she done made a mistake. She primpin' up the library the day before so's to give me time to plan. I told Scilla what I suspected, and she made a lie to her girl, telling her her Jesus-like uncle done founded a church in the next town over and didn't need her no more. Made her mad enough to tell, mad enough to burst open and let it all out. He couldn't find no others besides them.

They was the only and special ones and she the most special and gon' prove it no matter what Scilla or anybody else say. She the one told about their breasts and how touching ones was better than sucking ones 'cause sucking is what they's made for and anybody and everybody's got those kind but not the touching tenderly ones. Scilla had to bite her tongue and hold her hands not to slap her for her stupid. But it gave me time to plan and now I knew what your mama was planning.

I primped up the library finer than she had. In my kitchen library where I'd sucked the meaning out of them books, I couldn't even read, where I whipped up recipes and fed the whole town. Now my daughter want to turn our special place, not just turn it into something, show it to them, let the white people know where it was. Even Scilla didn't know about the kitchen library. She want to defile herself in my kitchen, make it a place of sexual assignation, a word sucked out of them books and in the process, she gonna suck the pride out of us. I prettied it up and made them tea and if I'd have been wrong it would have killed my daughter too. But it didn't.

He went home without touching her, and without a memory of where he'd been. He might a stayed that way but Scilla wanted the job finished. She fed him my pudding on top of that tea. Scilla knew never to give anybody that pudding after they'd drank enough liquid, and she knew I'd given him tea. But then again, I'd given her the pudding. Greedy, he ate more than most people and Scilla wished him a pleasant good night.

She was the first one to find him dead the next day, but she went back to her room and slept late into the morning. His own brother found him, made arrangements, put him in the ground, and went on with life. Scilla went on with life too; one of her boys stopped praying and the other one started talking again.

Ours is what changed. My daughter closed herself to me. She told me never to call her name again and I still haven't. In some ways, wished I'd waited for that man to show her his evil, but I was too scared of the other things he'd show her along with evil. I'd seen enough cruelty in my girlhood, to never want to see no more.

Neither one of them ever questioned the fact that he was working the same spell on them both. Scilla and I figured my girl still needed to win something. She needed to crash herself against something. So Scilla and I planned it. She crashed herself against Scilla's son, against the wind, against one of them Indians in the woods. That's how I got you, but I didn't know that your mama would spend the rest of her life pulling herself to pieces and putting herself back together again. She been backwards and sideways but never straight.

Aberdeen, when you kill somebody, all the bad in them takes away their one chance at good. You never get to know if they could a redeem themselves. I ain't recommendin' taking somebody's life. You can't just kill evil; good go along with it, all the dead's and some of yourn too. You'll be struggling to shore up good for the rest of your time. You don't always win and you used to winnin'.'"

On her morning, Aberdeen moved steadily up the pathway into the woods and five seconds after she heard her victim singing, Aberdeen realized that she didn't believe in redemption, not for every man and particularly not for the one dancing out in front of her property telling her that it would soon be his. She wasn't giving up her library, preferring to live with the specter of possibility like her grandmother before her. Selsie and Scilla had cleaned up one mess. Aberdeen and her own daughter had cleaned up another.

She put it all back into her mind and told her grandson, "The first thing we have to do is tell your mother you're here and seein' that you took all this trouble to arrive, you might as well stay."

Max the Black jumped up and ran around Aberdeen's tree. He ran until he was dizzy and out of breath. He fell and what laughter was left squeaked out of him and joined up with that of his grandparents, the two of them, sitting under a tree, looking right at him.

"That boy might just might be one of ourn," Dag said and laughed again.

When she had almost come to the conclusion that there hadn't actually been a boy in the house, that boys just weren't permanent, that the one that *had been around*, that the Rock Creek Park Rangers kept bringing home, was all in her imagination, Selma received a letter. It had been weeks since a ranger had brought him home and threatened to keep him, which was one of the other scenarios that she had been imagining. His grandmother had told him to mail the letter, but he had been afraid. Aberdeen knew he would mail a letter to his mother when he felt ready, when he overcame the fear of them coming to get him.

But the tiny bit of Selma that might have been his mother was so happy to get his letter that she slipped it under Thrace's door and went out for a walk. Pure happiness, the little she felt of it, had always made her too fidgety to be still. Happiness was a big interfering emotion, hard to get a real hold on, and while walking, she could let it go.

Thrace picked up the letter and read it. Boys still had to run away did they? Only now they wrote back. He guessed what he was doing in the woods from the very beginning. Well, it wasn't going to take him back to where he'd already been. He wouldn't let it. His boy was safe, living in a house that he built. He was still sheltering him and that would do.

He could recall the freedom of running away without the reason, the delicious feeling of the breeze dropping just below the heat of sweat, cooling his nervous wetness, drying him before he could become too moist, pushing him forward the way Fall tipped in on the edge of September and October days, gently warning of the coming months. The first sweet taste of cold, heavenly after the boxed heat of a humid summer, promised the end, and opened the beginning of something. Thrace thought about what promise would yield and decided on "possibility." He too had run away from home at the far edge of summer. His son had followed in his footsteps and though he knew it had a touch of absurdity, he felt prideful. Like father, like son he supposed, and one other weird thought pierced his fatherhood drama. 'Alana had probably been a runaway too.' Here he was, this late in the summer with a thought of her.

He'd be back in plenty fish, Michoacán State, Mexico, soon, right after the girls started and accommodated themselves to their new school.

15

The Twins Go to School in Washington, DC; Mother Goes to Mexico

To Selma, only yesterday she had registered the girls as twins in their Egyptian school. Now here was a task that she had to perform all over again though once should have lasted for their entire school careers, she thought. They were the same girls. If their records followed them, why wouldn't all their information travel with those records? As far as Selma could tell, schools liked to trouble mothers. The girls had grown and had done so in opposite directions. Mirella had grown tall and Alley wide, not in the sense of being fat, but rather in requiring more air and space. She wasn't as easy to ignore as she used to be. Mr. Thrace had chosen the school and Selma had only to show up and do whatever was required to enroll the girls.

"Tell us a little something about your daughters?"

"One is littler than the other," Selma said after a time.

"Have they adjusted?"

"They'll have to. Children seem flexible, don't they? Still forming, they can leave out the unwanted parts," She answered.

They asked her all sorts of questions that she found herself unable to answer truthfully or in a timely fashion and as she had been totally unfamiliar with their previous schooling, she couldn't make any sense of the papers that she handed over to the new school. She had one thing in her favor. Thrace had already visited, chosen, and paid in advance for two full years of the private school for Negro girls. Enrolling them was merely a formality and quite frankly part of the satisfaction that the school would derive, getting a look at more of the family that had entrusted them with the education of their very special daughters.

Selma was rather odd and uncommunicative, proving once again that there had not been any formula or similarities between the Negro families wealthy enough or concerned enough to make a certain kind of commitment to Madame Wallace's for American Negro Daughters (they'd left "school" out of the name to save themselves any undue harassment from the society at large). Selma didn't seem like the type to take up a collective body of teas, meetings, or drives but she had paid and frankly, it was the requirement that superseded all others. It set her above many other families who participated far more than they ever paid. The school also offered boarding and when asked, Selma had at first been unsure and then reasoned that they lived close enough to the school to walk.

"Are the girls fraternal or identical twins?"

"Oh, they aren't really twins at all," she answered and the school ladies waited for more. And wait they did, because for the entire four years that the Thrace girls were enrolled in Madame Wallace's for American Negro Daughters, they only ever met one Thrace daughter in the classroom. Mirella entered the ninth grade and stayed until graduation. The other daughter never arrived and after questioning Selma Thrace once, there wasn't any need to do so again.

From time to time, the subject of the second daughter would come up, particularly after they noticed that Mirella had completely different handwriting on her homework than the handwriting they had seen her make use of at school. The English teacher believed that Mirella took her time at home and was therefore neater. Other teachers believed that her twin sister did her homework. They must have made a bargain that one should come to school and the other would remain at home. There had been rumors that the girls were truly identical and could not be told apart, and that some days one came to school and some days, the other came.

Mrs. Wallace was graceful enough to stop the speculation. There was one Thrace daughter attending her school. She had not unearthed Mr. Thrace's reason for educating one daughter for the price of two, however, another man's business was simply not the thing on which to waste one's time. Mrs. Wallace, if nothing else, had always possessed the ability to get on with the necessary and a deserved reputation for soundness in not only reasoning but in the choice of how to expend her qualities of reason. If the Thrace family had enough discretionary income to pay double tuition to educate one daughter, so be it. All other explanations were simply time consuming. Even the rumor, however riveting, that the Thraces had only ever had one daughter who had two personalities and occasionally included a phantom son was not worthy of her time or consideration.

Alley had taken to her bed and refused to get up.

At first, she was simply amusing herself, whiling away the time between now and whatever was next. She'd stick a toe out on one side, testing the air. She crawled under the covers so that her head lay where her feet belonged and wondered if anyone might enter and notice. She stretched as far as she could with her arms.

Deciding not to get out of bed hadn't happened suddenly but rather gradually. In the beginning, she would still get up and then slowly more and more parts of her would stay in the bed. For a few days, she'd hang her head over the side. A few days more, she'd lay sideways, alternately swinging her legs. On her back, she'd stretch all four of her limbs into the air. Finally, she had spent an entire week, body on the floor, feet on the bed. On Saturday, after a full week in bed, she concluded that there was no reason for her to get up. Her state guaranteed a good decision as blood rushed to her head, giving her a superior thinking dynamic. Upside down with her head on the floor, she had told her mother about her decision. A few hours later, her mother, who had been sitting in the room next to her, commented.

"Welcome," she told her, "to what hopefully will be a very nice rest. You must need it." She touched the side of Alley's face and went out of the room. What Alley had needed her to say was, "Get up out of that bed, right now," and when she hadn't, she knew it was all the same to her mother whether she did anything or not, exactly as it had been with their brother. They let him run away and stay away, and neither of them cared. She had known before that neither of the three children were important to her parents, still; she had wanted to be certain. She and Mirella were going to have to finish raising themselves. They were orphans, children of practically dead parents, and she had decided to raise herself and Alley from the bed.

"Are you really going to stay there?" Mirella asked her sister from the side of her bed. Alley had made pronouncements before, but this time she seemed more resolute. After the first couple of days, Mirella accepted the fact that she'd be a lone walker to school and back.

She'd have only herself as she hadn't bargained on Alley's having any sort of role from the mattress. She hadn't known that not getting out of the bed during the day, meant spending a busy wakeful night. Eventually, Alley would run the entire household and more from the bed. Mirella had indeed begun walking back and forth to school alone. She listened in class, took notes, collected text books and syllabi, came home, and put them all in the front hallway and promptly and purposefully forgot about school. The next morning, she would find her books, and notes appropriately arranged and waiting near the door. When she arrived at school and opened her bag, she'd see that her homework had been done and precisely packaged for delivery to the teacher.

Something invisible and steady began to grow between the sisters. The thing that allowed Mirella to ignore her homework kept Alley in bed all day and let the two of them dine together each evening at dusk sitting in Alley's bedroom, twinned them more than an accident of birth or the whim of their mother. Loneliness in a big, parentless household roped them with its noose; circled around them; provided order and sameness, thereby joining the sisters in a routine which would last into adulthood. Their funny little world had never had any practiced rituals—the world that included their mother, father, and brother was slowly ebbing away.

"Take me with you," she said in a tired alto. Thrace startled. He'd heard that heavy voice and tone before, but so long ago he had trouble at first remembering. A hypnotist's voice, those tones elbowed his first memories of his wife riding in his car, the way she had tapped his back, a light hot touch. He eyed his wife, catching her eyes because she refused to look away. The woman from the woods, the one who had appeared through the trees like a beautiful witch sat draped over the chair in their bedroom, watching him pack. Resolve wasn't one of her ordinary postures.

Now, it was Thrace's turn to take forever to answer. She had never asked for anything that he could remember and now, in such an incongruous fashion, she had demanded. There was a time when Thrace worried about the odd things that concerned his wife—moments when she became far too preoccupied with things that had nothing to do with her. He remembered being happy when they moved away from Atlanta. She had been drawn to several stories about an old woman whose husband, a supposed strong swimmer, had drowned in their backyard pool. At the Red Sea, she had taken an interest in some strange folly and for the first time, in a very long while, he wondered what would be next. Taking her away might not be a bad idea at all.

Selma had come upon some odd sensations. She felt a draught coming from the direction of her daughters' side of the upstairs hallway. Not that it had ever before mattered, but Selma realized that the thing that she may have intended, the thing she knew she wanted to get to, no longer needed her attention. The fact that an old man and his dog were following her around ruining her walks was one reason to travel. The dog had started trailing her. He sniffed something, and his man followed the slight tug of the dog. After a few days, Selma imagined the imprint of the old man's body next to his dog's buried near the crazy "H" in the front yard which provided an even more pressing reason to head off to Mexico.

Thrace eventually answered and that night, they made love like travelers. Selma packed her things, something that she was unaccustomed to doing especially as she had no sense of where she was going or what she might do. Should she take her fears or leave them behind in Washington, DC? She left a smile for the girls. She wondered about laughter and whether Mexico was a place where one might need some and thought better of taking something that had always made her uncomfortable. Walking shoes were a must and, too, there was the fragrance of Washington flowers that she'd like to have with her. If she could evade the old man, she'd cut a basket full of flowers to put in her suitcase. In the end, she left the fears behind and took fortitude, in case walking in Mexico proved to be steep rather than flat.

Selma arrived in Mexico with a couple of pairs of shoes and not even an extra sweater for a cool evening breeze. They rode up the hill in the open car beside the flowers, both in silent appreciative awe, happy that the other hadn't uttered any useless, poorly timed words.

Thrace knew that this was just one of the reasons he loved her, the absolute idea of her which was all he had.

Porter and Alana had waited dinner. Alana had alerted the cook and Porter had asked her to make sure the bedrooms and bathrooms were ready for the Thraces. Alana left all conversations about the Thraces to Porter. She peeped into their ready room and quickly pulled the door behind her. Porter was reading just as he always did before dinner.

When he walked across the room and shook Thrace's hand, he knew that he was as happy to see Thrace as Thrace was to set eyes on him. He genuinely welcomed Mrs. Thrace and hoped they were hungry. Selma stepped towards the century-old table, feeling its grooves with her hands, she stood at the chair next to Porter's rather than close to her husband. Alana approached the table and was introduced to Mrs. Thrace and the four of them sat down. Thrace and Porter went right back into their shared esoterica and the two women listened raptly to the men, the evening's only entertainment.

"I have something to show you, Clifton. Moving to my place here, I went through some very old boxes. I want to show you a set of lists that I found, lists of..." Porter said.

"They prove that I was right, of course," Thrace smiled. "Right about how the lists actually existed," Thrace said quickly, keeping Porter from saying aloud that he had a list of *The Curiously Successful Negro*.

"These may be copies, but how did you know they existed?" Porter immediately understood Thrace's hesitation.

"Part research, part gift, most of what I've read sends you directly to the archives of Harvard University. Have you looked over them?" Thrace wondered if Porter had seen his grandfather's name listed in every year that the list was compiled. But he did not ask.

"The writing is small and difficult as if whoever created it wasn't sure they wanted anyone else to see. Without my magnifier, looking at them reveals nothing to my poor eyes," Porter said. "Almost as if they were coded."

"They were a danger, a welcome and a danger. I was told that certain people coveted the list, just to know it was true, happy that men were doing well, and that men doing well enough had company. But it scared people. A list provided easy means of identification. In 1862, a successful Negro was a rarity, but a careful Negro was the status quo. Imagine the two combined. Most successful Negroes were already afraid of disappearing; they'd never call attention to themselves. Most of them hid their abilities or what they had accumulated because of their ability," Thrace paused, and continued, almost breathless. "To find themselves on a list must have put them in a tragic spotlight. At the same time, no one believed the list. But I've also heard it was used to confiscate their possessions." Thrace also didn't want his wife to know that following the list was where and how he found her.

"There were women on the list as well. Supposedly, it was intended as a study created to do some kind of fact-finding. I think it began as a Harvard study or research paper, sort of the study of small miracles. How in the world did these men and women succeed despite such odds against them?" Porter asked.

"Might have started as research and then wound up something else."

"I may have 1842–1865," Porter indicated.

"I'd like to see them," Thrace said.

"Strangely, a Moses Fitzlough or Fitzhough comes to mind. They found him in his slave shack sleeping the sleep of the dead on top of his coffin of cash. He had bought each and every one of his children out of slavery, built houses for their mothers, and sent his children wherever he could to educate them, but never left his old master's shack himself. No one ever unearthed how he did what he did. Imagine? It is amazing!" Porter shook his head gently from side to side.

"I remember hearing the list was longer than anyone expected which changed the way it was viewed. A few was all right but too many frightened some," Thrace said.

"What would be the reason or even the criteria if it were still being kept today?" Porter wondered.

"Use it as a census or a lesson in history. Do these families still exist? How are they now?" Thrace laughed at himself, thinking of these family heirs as potential clients, husbands to his daughters, wives to his son. A kind of financial purview came automatically with him. Money was a buffer to gird up the walls, keep his family on the inside, warm, coddled, and topped with luxury which was quite funny for a man whose daughters were on the other side of the world in a big, yes, nicely appointed, extravagantly lonely, house.

After dinner, they briefly discussed the morning, and everyone went off to bed.

The next day, when Selma arrived in the kitchen, Thrace could smell nonnative flowers. She wore the same dress as last evening but somehow managed to look fresh.

"Here is fresh coffee and your husband's sugar." Both Porter and Alana seemed to offer simultaneously. Selma looked at the coffee, moved slowly towards it after acknowledging them both with a gentle nod, then stopped before lifting a cup. She slipped a small rock of sugar on her tongue, however, and smiled—the happy reaction that both Porter and Alana had come to expect.

"I'd rather walk before drinking anything. Is there a path?" she asked, and Porter realized he hadn't heard her voice last night. Her smooth measured tones, distinctly clear, and unaccented, didn't attach her to a place.

Porter did not know anything about Mrs. Thrace.

"If you leave the house from the back, you can wander through the gardens and if you walk long, you'll still be on your own property though the formality of planting ends. If you take the front door and follow the road, when you see houses close together, the town is near. The walking road is different than the driving road. The walking road is narrower."

"Thank you," Selma answered. She left quickly and Porter didn't see her until dinner. Again, the dress appeared to be the same but oddly different and her skin was radiant, even in the dull light of the large dining room.

On the third or fourth night, when the men were alone after dinner, Porter asked "How is Mrs. Thrace liking Mexico and where in the world does she find to walk?"

Thrace answered simply, "She manages," and felt that he

had sounded too short without meaning to. "She has walked the world wherever we've been. I think it's a childhood admonition, something her mother told her: Walk, walk, walk. It will fix everything. Mind you, her mother was equally capable of disappearing into the woods and returning days, even nights later, more beautiful after she'd returned than before she left." Thrace hadn't planned to say this last out loud, but the truth won its way.

Porter had already seen the evidence but did not permit himself the admission. He didn't feel it was too personal to say to Thrace but refused to give himself away. He had seen her and he had certainly noticed that she had worn the same dress and become more beautiful in it, every day.

"Thrace you've married 'a walking mystery.' Have you heard of them?" Porter had put on his best about-to-impart-information tone.

"No."

"Neither have I," they both laughed.

Maybe their lives would have remained even and static, nicely calibrated if Alana had heard the admiration for his wife in Thrace's voice. If only Porter had kept himself from walking through the town and back gardens of Thrace's estate. But honestly, he wanted to follow the woman who appeared so different each evening while wearing the exact same clothing. Porter told himself that there were subtle changes that he missed, yet he didn't believe himself as his powers of observation had never before been so inadequate. Porter wanted to know if she went somewhere specific or if her walks were a kind of endless meandering. Why didn't she appear exhausted or overwrought from the Mexican climate? Walking rejuvenated her; there was something in it, something that she went out and tasted that wholeheartedly agreed with her.

Porter didn't at first want to accompany her; he wanted to follow her, a few paces behind. He felt like a sheriff casing a potential miscreant without knowing or even being able to ascertain the crime. There were a few days that he missed her altogether as she must have changed her schedule or route in the morning. Porter also skipped a few dinners, too afraid that his new chore—following Mrs. Thrace—might appear in his expressions or words.

Selma had lured him inexplicably and hadn't noticed. Not until she the morning she tripped and almost stumbled onto the road, had Porter reached out and caught the inside of her arm. He had been there, close enough to help.

The very next morning, Agnes woke up but wished she hadn't. She was dreaming that she was being followed, only she liked the man behind her. She hesitated, then put on her flowered dress and went out into a house and garden that matched the one in her dreams.

This time, Porter had followed her because he couldn't be sure that she was the same woman. Her dress looked different. He thought he'd overheard Thrace and Alana discuss taking her shopping because she hadn't brought any other clothes besides the tightly fitting dress that she had worn since the day she arrived. He knew they hadn't shopped yet, but the familiar body was moving about with an altered step and pace.

Porter couldn't imagine that the same woman could move so differently. She favored her left side rather than the right, she was no longer subtly slew footed and could it really be possible that her waist was smaller and her hips just a touch fleshier. He had never followed a woman before, and surely, it had to be impossible that he had followed two different women for the first time in his life in the same week.

He found himself drawing very near without disturbing her. He needed to be in front to glimpse her face and then behind so that she could lead. Then, she sighed, turned her head slightly and smiled which gave her away. Porter recognized the grouped gestures because he had seen them before. Mrs. Thrace had a slight sway in her walk when she had been walking before today. Each time she reached the dead end in the garden path, she forced herself to go right, as if in an afterthought. She had barely concluded that she could no longer move forward, and finally when she had, she clumsily rescued herself and moved to the right, catching her dress on the thorn of one or two astrid flowers.

After glimpsing her face, Porter followed along much more comfortably. She was indeed Mrs. Thrace with a new gait and a soft emotionless expression. Though he desperately wanted to hold the hand of the woman, he was shy of a welcome and didn't know if he had grown closer to her simply by his proximity to her or if she had somehow subtly signaled welcome. Each day, he followed her a little more longingly and a tad closer. Porter felt he could hold her quietly in the garden for hours without words being uttered between them. He was already communicating with her as he moved synchronously behind her, speaking in a silent language that the two of them had somehow drawn up between them, both content to circle one another in gossamer threads of expectation, awaiting the coming absolutes of a shared future. She let him stay and he viewed her silence as an assent to pursuit. She had turned and looked at his face only once, sighed again, but never parted her lips widely enough for words to slip out. Porter imagined whatever he wanted.

A week later, Porter was wounded to the quick on the morning he came into the kitchen trailing an unusual sound. Mrs. Thrace was humming. She had thrown over the secret of their silent communication in exchange for humming a dirty little song that everyone could hear. Porter hurt himself on her music and vowed not to look at her as she sang.

She was a background radio that he needn't bother with, especially now, as he understood that she hadn't been saving her voice for him, but invited anyone, even the cook and maids, to hear what he thought belonged to the special place he had created for the two of them to share. Moreover, she was back to moving the way she had at first, and strangely, bursting at the seams of her dress. Somehow, the same dress had become sizes too small. Maybe they had washed the dress. She leaked and when she opened her mouth and let the words fall out, Porter held his breath.

"Is it the coffee or the sugar that needs a song?" she asked and then went back to humming for a few infinite minutes before she sang again and segued back into a happy little hum.

Porter exhaled, sure that his face was red hot, and then she passed behind his chair. With plenty of room between him and the wall to spare, she brushed him with her dress and smell of imported flowers. Something in her song was his and he felt a slight hint of satisfaction followed by the gentle tug on the beginning wave of unanswered longing, the state to which his stomach was becoming accustomed.

No one noticed any changes except for the maid. Porter swallowed his meals and then privately chased them with her special mixture of herbs in milk for an uncooperative stomach. He had asked her to prepare the mixture for him.

Neither Alana nor Thrace had seen the residue of Porter's red face or the dust on his newly worn shoes from so much walking. For them, nothing at all seemed different about anything else because they were engaged in a sort of eerie waltz all their own, which began with the rhythm in the way Alana held her pencil. She wrote straight up and down with a bobbing pencil and Thrace thought the way she measured lead on paper. Magic.

Never mind that she was copying charts, or making lists, or brainstorming ways to broaden the town festival to include Thrace's candies, and eventually her liqueurs. Perhaps her efficiency is what he admired, though strangely Alana seemed to be the only one in Mexico who possessed it. They were together daily in the kitchen drawing the company on paper, and then going outside to translate it into a factory with machinery, parts, and labor. She knew exactly what he would want as his ideas were perfectly aligned with her own planning. Alana had always been a planner, right down to the very tiny details, so she could oversee the meticulous reconstruction of a second pan evaporator and yet be available to remind the cook exactly when to add the herbs for a perfect fish Saltado dinner.

In the tiny details was where Thrace found the things to admire. The bobbing pencil, the smooth hairs that ran under her ponytail and ventured down her back, the small absent chip from the side of her front tooth that she tried to hide with her tongue before and after she spoke, offset her otherwise perfection.

They had the same idea for the inaugural candy—a speckled mint with a liquid chocolate, subtly anise-flavored center—and Thrace softened to Alana's idea for an adult alcohol-infused version. One would be a "mint chipped" and the other a "chipped mint" and they toyed over ideas for how to market them and which candy would be which. His feelings for Alana quietly and easily grew in tandem with the variety of flavored candies that they invented. Her mind worked so much like his that his respect and affection for her grew like a baby inside him. His sugar consumption notwithstanding, he nurtured his feelings for her without any real outer manifestation except a shiny glow on his skin, and a stomach where he could now rest his hands.

He had provided no definite sign, but he felt sure that she knew. Didn't he smile more, seem happier, eat with more relish? Alana was open and available to be loved and he found it so oddly different from what he felt for his wife that loving one of them was an antidote for loving the other.

The strangest sensation of all was not seeing his wife all day, spending the day with Alana and then bedding down next to Mrs. Thrace, their backs to one another at night. There was a quiet between them that was lovely, reminding Thrace of their trip up the mountain.

Neither Thrace nor Selma minded; in fact, they both craved the infinite possibilities in silence. Subtracting words from their encounters became a kind of shared passion. True anchors for one another, the Thraces stilled their panic, a by-product of the things that they were feeling.

Nightly, Thrace and Selma floated side by side in the murky depths of surprising emotions. They had never before slept far apart from one another in the same bed. Now they climbed in at exactly the same time, each turning over, letting their backs rub but never reaching out, one for the other, sleeping as soundly and happily as they ever had. The resurgence of feeling that both were experiencing had the strange consequence of spilling out and filling the entire house with goodwill.

For Porter, Mrs. Thrace seemed now like three completely different women and he wanted to lose himself in her crowd. It was the reciprocation of Porter's feelings that for the first time in her life, made Mrs. Thrace want to keep things she easily gave away. She wanted to put things where they belonged rather than where she might like to try them. She wanted to remain in the day, so she could take Porter all in. She desperately wanted to remember.

To Mr. Thrace, the perfection in Alana's details suffered in the befuddlement of her being in and returning love.

Frankly and fortunately, it was time for the Thraces' journey home.

On her next to last day in Plenty Fish State, Mexico, Mrs. Thrace found the post office and mailed the largest package yet home to her mother.

16

Mother's Packages?

Max the Black was there to receive the giant box that his grandmother would not let him open. There was also a large envelope with small crooked writing addressed to Lloyd Earl and H. Dag Macomb. Max was too excited about the big box to notice the envelope that his grandmother carefully cradled, walked back to the room behind the kitchen, and put away. On top, the envelope had a return name only. Somebody named "Comeback" sent it. Aberdeen put it where he kept the other "Comebacks."

"Store that box with the others," she told Max. If he wanted to open them, he had to start at the beginning, open one box at a time, and wait for Grandma Aberdeen's explanations. She had to uncover and move around years' worth of boxes to find the very first one and since moving boxes took her the better part of two days, she was tired.

"You can open this one first in the morning, after breakfast." Max the Black wished his grandfather were about. Surely, his grandfather could have persuaded his grandmother for him. But H. Dag Macomb was not at home, and Aberdeen remained immovable. The order was more important than what was in the package. Max the Black had grown more and more impatient with a huge box sitting in the middle of the floor. He put his ear to it, tried to rock the massive gift back and forth, and even kicked it hard once to make sure that whatever was inside was still alive if indeed it had arrived that way.

He went up into the woods when he didn't get his own way. He fiddled around in the clearing near the kitchen/library though rarely went inside alone even though Grandma Aberdeen welcomed and encouraged him to pick up any one of the books and read them all the way through. He sat out front on the stoop whittling wood waiting for Jessup. Jessup was the daughter of the other family that lived on the mountain. She went by her last name. She always showed up a few minutes after he did, and Max the Black figured she either followed him from home or never had anything else to do except hang around clearings. If she wasn't in this one, she'd be at the other one Max the Black had found.

"She still didn't let me open one box."

"What's in 'em?" Jessup asked.

"That'd be the reason to open them. My mother sent them."

"Did she send them to you?"

"Maybe." Max wished he were sure.

"Maybe? Maybe them boxes don't have nothing to do with you." If he didn't like what Jessup said, she changed it. "Maybe the boxes are gifts for the future."

Jessup spent a lot of time imagining hers away from this place. The future was always on her mind particularly with Max as she thought they should be fine-tuning their getaway. As far as she was concerned, him thinking about his mother wasted their time.

"Are they travel ready?" Jessup asked.

"What's that mean?" Max asked.

"Well, if your mother were truly thinking about you, she'd be giving you useful stuff that you could take with you," Jessup answered.

"You ever think that I just got here and you're already leaving?" Max questioned her.

"I been here long enough to know it's a place to leave not,

to come to. Your momma's gone, mine too. We're following in their footsteps." Honestly, Jessup wouldn't follow her mother to a candy store.

"My grandmother has never left this place."

"How old is she?" Jessup asked.

"What?"

"I mean, grandparents want their children to go out in the world and do big things." Jessup didn't want to ruin her one chance to get off the mountain. She didn't want to admit she was scared to go alone either. It was more that she wanted to lead, but from behind. Jessup was going to get out in the world and name herself, get the mountain off her as soon as she could, and Max the Black was her comfortable ride. They'd bonded as soon as he turned up at the school.

"My father knew your mother." The declaration had instantly claimed his attention. She'd let out a little here and there after she saw how he ate up her information like fresh honey on a stick.

"She and my daddy, Malton, used to lick each other in the trees. Nobody knew the woods better than them two. My grandma used to say that there was always a Macomb on top or underneath a Jessup." Max the Black didn't care what she meant so long as she kept talking.

She started out telling him the truth, but when she ran out of truth, she told lies, except about herself. To Jessup, one person in the world ought to know all her blemishes; she'd see how he might react and that'd tell her whether she should tell some things and not others.

"I'm just Jessup 'cause my Momma named me something my daddy forgot. He don't want to step in, in case she return and he already got me all used to one name when I got another. My momma parks babies and then go on about her way. She parked two for my daddy and one time, I heard them say she mighta' parked another baby for some other family."

Sometimes, when Jessup told stories about herself, she took off some of her clothes but that wasn't anything new 'cause she and Max undressed together all the time. Sometimes to get in the creek after a hard rain, sometimes to cement their friendship by touching their parts together. Jessup said to call her Jessup. Sometimes, Max could call her Malton's Jessup. She loved her father she said, he was always kind and nice to anybody.

"He still waitin' on the mountain to change things and this ain't no mountain, Max the Black. We live on a hill."

When his grandmother finally did come to him with a box he could open, the box was so small it hardly seemed worth the wait.

"Mountain people seem simple," she told him "but with people and mountains, there are always complications."

Max the Black felt the beginnings of his foolishness paying him back. As soon as Grandmother Aberdeen opened her mouth, he knew he was wrong. She'd never done anything but steer him right and amuse him along the way.

"Knowing it didn't ever stop nobody from being it. I'm talking about foolish but I'm not talking about you," she smiled. "You excited and how could you help but be? You're going to learn all about your family, you're going to learn what everybody should know without having to learn. People ought to be born with whatever history they can handle and nothing else, 'ceptin what they need." She gave him the first box, a fraction of the size of the big one.

"Open this one first."

Max the Black opened the package and found a tiny broken music box. At first, it didn't look broken, but when he lifted the top to let the music out, he knew it had to be.

"Open up, keep listenin' 'fore you start decidin'," Grandma Aberdeen said.

The music box didn't have a mechanism to twist; he had held it upside down, searching for a knob. Finally, after a few moments, noises hissed then lurched forward and stopped again, then restarted. A most amazing sound came out of the tiny little box and repeated over and over again, reminding Max of an animal calling out one single thing to another animal.

"Boy, that's your mother's song. She mailed that box back the first time she ran away. Had I known, I might have . . . well I might have . . . She started mailing stuff back here the moment she went away. No matter how they were addressed, my name or house at 4127, boxes seemed more for safekeeping, sending them here for me to hold and sometimes I think she was just sending stuff away from her. Clifton Maxwell Thrace, the Black, they're yours, them boxes, one at a time, over time."

Max the Black wasn't listening to his grandmother anymore. He was listening to his broken music box and at first, he thought that's why the music sounded the way it did; but the more he listened the more he knew. The music was his mother's pig song and he wondered how in the world she got the song into the music box. He wanted more but now he didn't mind waiting either. When Grandpa Dag came home, he showed him the music box and then lifted the top and let him hear.

"I ain't heard that song in more than thirty-some years. Sounds painful." He wondered if his grandson would ever get sick of playing that song because wherever he was, was that so-called music. He and Aberdeen had never figured out what had happened to their daughter's song. She'd run away with her music and came back quiet. Maybe she took that song out of herself and put it in a box so that her kids could have a choice of whether to sing.

"It's telling me something, Grandpa; I don't know what yet. I'm 'a listen till I know."

"Maybe just memorizin' the sound is enough."

Box number two Grandmother Aberdeen gave Max the Black not too long after the first one. Maybe she gave the second box to him to stop the music as he had kept that first box opened so that the music was incessant, exactly as it had been when his mother was little.

Aberdeen and Dag had felt younger than they had in

a long time. One night, when Max the Black had climbed up the front yard tree, he could see in the window of the old house and they were dancing, holding each other close, laughing about something. Aberdeen still didn't spend too much time in the new house, but she did go inside from time to time and Max got the sense that each time, she stayed a little longer. Whatever had kept her out of the house shrank and what pulled her in, grew. Max and Grandfather Dag mostly slept in the new house except for when his grandfather slept with his grandmother. His grandparents slept together when Grandfather Dag first came back from wherever he had traveled to and most of the time when he had finished sleeping in the old house and came to the new one, he'd bring Max the Black some cake. Grandmother Aberdeen must have had a bunch of cakes in her old bedroom.

In box number two, his mother sent back the reason why she had run off in the first place. She had followed her father, curious to know where he traveled. Box number two contained another box and when he opened one, he found another and another, each as carefully wrapped as the one it had come in. Max the Black carefully and slowly opened boxes all afternoon to the tune of his mother's music. He was afraid he'd miss or break something. But at the end of the day, there were many streams of colorful ribbon and prettily decorated paper, but no present.

Selma arrived in Washington, DC, stepped across the threshold, and splattered all over the house. Thrace went to his office. Mirella noticed the arrival first because for some odd reason, as she came home from school that day, she felt something amiss. She tiptoed into Alley's bedroom after having seen the suitcases.

"Mother's home."

"Is she hugging or singing?"

"I haven't really seen her, just the evidence of arrival," Mirella told her sister.

"Oh." Then they heard her calling them and looking at

one another, they tried not to go, but Mother compelled them with her tone. They slinked inside their parents' room, each trying not to look but neither of them could command their curious eyes. Glumly and quickly, they scanned the room trying not to see anything but when their senses took over their sight, their emotions crept out as well. They hadn't seen their mother for a month and deep down inside, though they were angry enough to pretend it wasn't true, they always held out hope for closeness and understanding. If they just listened to her one more time, maybe they'd understand their mother, why she was as she was and why whatever she was didn't include them.

"I'm not an only child. I think I had a brother who disappeared too." Her voice came from outside the window and ricocheted off the walls because her lips were near the ceiling on the far side of the room and her throat with her hand gently attached sat upon the big bed's headboard. Her voice had to bounce around a bit before clearing her throat, finding, and then coming out of her mouth.

"For a short time, we were a family: children, a mother, and father. I was the oldest; the little ones were always dangling from my sides, holding onto my skirts, and following me around. Sometimes, the three of us were alone together, but mostly we would sit in an arc on a picnic blanket outside my mother's garden, watching her work. She let us stay as long as we weren't too noisy. All of us had pieces of one old blanket because the little ones fought so much. Truthfully, the blanket was mine before either of them arrived. They'd fight and then I'd sit between them and roll both ways till I rolled them off the blanket from opposite sides, pretending they fell into the creek and the blanket was the only boat. They'd scramble back on and we'd rock, riding the conjured waves.

But boating might have made too much noise because one day, Mama tore the blanket in three and gave us each a piece. She tore it up perfectly. My piece was bigger; my brother had a mostly blue piece and the girl, my sister, had yellow. They were twins for a while, but the boy grew bigger and faster and he would tease her about how his body knew better what to do with food than hers. If she discovered that she could do something that he couldn't, it was an all-day contest. She could braid grass and find the sweetest honeysuckle and get more sweetness out of the weeds than him. He could run faster, jump higher, laugh louder, roll in one little ball down the hill more tightly wound than she could. She once leaned against the tree longer and he could hold one eye closed. Neither of them could climb a tree too well. They ought to have counted how many times they fell down in one day. They were two of the clumsiest things ever. They couldn't eat or drink without spilling and the real contest could have been on the clothing with the most spots or the blankets with the most dirt 'cause they did everything on their blankets. Sometimes, they'd place their blanket pieces back together and sit so close to one another that they were two halves of the same kid, whispering to itself. It was the only time they tempered their one-upmanship. Maybe they were setting up the rules for the greatest contest of all. Who could out swim the other? She started it, telling him that she could swim more like a fish than he could. Neither one of them knew how and for the longest time, they were content just to argue. She'd glue her arms to her sides and jerk about like she was in the grips of a full-blown seizure. He pedaled his legs furiously, riding something but never water. None of their jerking around looked the least bit like swimming. We all ignored the two of them when they started upping the ante. She was going to cross the lake, swim to the other side, run up to the top of the mountain, swim around in the mountain pool, then head back and help him across the lake. He was going to speed swim across an ocean, once he found one, swim around the world, mail home souvenirs from each port, and then come back and find her sitting on her piece of blanket still opening and playing with all the things that he sent home. She was going to swim to Africa, ride down some waterfalls, bring him back a drink of

African river. Their feats were so outlandish they were funny. When we paid attention and actually heard them, we'd laugh, but the twins didn't like being laughed at because they took their contests very seriously."

A smile might have entered her voice. Mother's voice changed as usual when she was nearing a new destination. The girls knew she'd soon be finished or she'd be changing the subject.

Naturally, the girls didn't see it, but one of her legs walked across the room and joined up with the other one. Her legs could probably walk alone, all the walking she'd done. Small wonder her legs hadn't taken off and run away and met up with some circus to get away from her.

"Maybe I made them both up for company, except my memory insists." Mother began again and they wondered how much longer she'd go on with things that had nothing to do with either of them. Alley thought the least she could do was ask whether she was finished resting and Mirella thought she might make one mention of school.

"They're so clear and unmistakable. My imagination has never been trustworthy. Feelings don't go away either. My, how I know I loved that little boy."

Mirella and Alley both stopped listening for a moment at the word imagination. Alley should have stopped listening when she mentioned how much she loved her invisible brother. Mother must have wasted all her love when she was a little girl.

"My mother nor my father ever talked about it but I think all that fighting about swimming made them go to the creek. They must have decided while they were sitting so close to each other that no one else could hear them. I think they planned a secret swimming contest for two. They were going to make their own first secret to keep from the rest of us."

Her voice came on in from outside the window and she swallowed with her throat, which simply meant that her voice fell onto the bed then found her lungs on the floor near the closet door. The rest of her seemed to be gathering together as Alley and Mirella took the opportunity to slide out of the room.

When their father came home, life was only marginally different. To the girls, the household seemed shaken. Someone had picked up and shifted the placement of everything. It hadn't taken long, just a few weeks, but their parents had become kindly disposed, not too troublesome, not especially needy guests. The girls were the proprietors of a strange hotel with one efficient member on the housekeeping staff, no other employees, and two dotty guests.

Umm II took the visit in stride, added more steaks or potatoes, but otherwise did exactly as she always did. She took care of the household and whomever might be in it. The only other difference was that she served food in the dining room rather than the bedroom where the girls generally ate. She liked her job. Simple and unchanging is generally how she liked a household, the same. Her checks were regular and she was too. She kept all the rooms clean just as she always had so there was no special preparation for the Thrace's arrival. Even the boy's room was clean. She assumed the parents would return, though she did have a fear or two after a month passed without seeing them. Now that they were here, she had the distinct feeling that they were not staying and frankly, she couldn't quite discern the girls' feelings—not just about that, not about anything. She knew their favorite foods and even their favorite underwear, judged by the amount of times they requested each item, but determining how they felt about anything else hadn't been her concern. One went to school, the other didn't seem to go. Umm II used to sleep in the house, but Alley had given her the option of going home and returning early. Umm II took her option and Alley ceased to be disturbed during her nightly pursuits.

"Well, you both look wonderful. Everything agrees with you. Are you well?" Mr. Thrace asked his daughters, treating them as fellow travelers on the same ship and before they could answer, he continued, "Your reports from school are more than satisfactory, but then we knew we had only very smart ladies in the house. Mrs. Wallace must be highly gratified by having such special students." Credit was always an indeterminate issue for Thrace, in spite of his preference for assuming most for himself.

Indeed, they were his daughters, though they now were two distinct entities rather than the little things that used to barely let him go when he returned. They had hugged him perfunctorily without any of the free unyielding neediness that he remembered. He preferred them as young ladies on the verge of womanhood and wondered if Mrs. Wallace's place had anything to do with their obvious maturity or if it had, as he suspected, been a matter of age. Children grew up overnight and his had changed quite a lot in one month.

"You are quite the young ladies, I see," he smiled very warmly as he said so.

Umm II had been in the room at the time. What she saw was the two saddest little girls she had ever seen. They were closer to being anything other than confident young ladies. She swept her eyes towards Mrs. Thrace. There wouldn't be any help there for these two girls. Mrs. Thrace had a whole world living right in her facial expression; anybody that looked her way could see that she was occupied, but not with the outside world, within.

"You're getting along so nicely." Clearly, everyone at the table and Umm II who was serving the meal, wondered what that meant. "It makes it easier on a father when he has to spend so much time away from his girls. I'll have to be back in Mexico soon."

"Will we be moving?" Mirella asked.

"That would be a good target, yes, a very good target, not just yet." Their father answered and Alley had been instantly sorry that Mirella asked. Now she couldn't even pretend that they would soon be where their parents would live. Their only measure, the Thrace childhood tradition—wait and see.

Their parents hadn't spent more time in Mexico than they had in Washington, DC, but they had obviously left something happier behind. Alley couldn't imagine what could be in Mexico and for a moment wondered if her parents could have other, different children down there. Livelier ones that made them laugh? It was too silly to imagine but she could use her imagination any way she wanted, even on herself. Cautious as a rule, not quite confident enough to conjure what she may have wanted, Alley imagined in a tiny arc beside reality. Her jolly, fatter mom baked sweets every Sunday, held them every Monday, took them on walks all the time, and talked to them about current events whenever they were near. That's when her imagination included her mother. Mostly, Alley imagined things that did not include her mother and now, maybe not her father either.

Mr. and Mrs. Thrace didn't stay too long in Washington, but still longer than either of them seemed to want to be there. Mother took up walking again and Thrace spent long hours at his office. The girls went on as usual with a few minor inconveniences. Alley ran into her mother at night and Mirella bumped into her on the way to and from school. Her mother acknowledged her in the street, smiling a very warm smile, as though she were admiring someone else's little girl.

Mirella was almost happy she hadn't made any friends at Mrs. Wallace's for American Negro Daughters. How in the world would she be able to solve all her mother's unsolvables? It was awful enough when someone from Mrs. Wallace's made a request for something from their mother. Alley generally handled everything with tactful negatives and future promises, but somehow the school had figured out that Mrs. Thrace was currently available, and they were determined to have her participate and attend the Mrs. Wallace's for American Negro Daughters' November Ball.

17

Untethering Carefully Placed Ties

Agnes woke up in Washington, DC, but her body stayed in Mexico. The weather turned cold, yet she pulsated with inner heat and couldn't quite keep on a sweater. She didn't like climbing ladders and hanging crepe paper streams from the ceiling but that's what she was doing, decorating Mrs. Wallace's for American Negro Daughters' party room. She wore a thin flowered frock and nothing else but sandals as she stood atop a ladder reaching upwards. Something about hanging paper streams from the ceiling, like dressing the sky, felt familiar. Standing high, hanging things in the air took Agnes back in time, an intrusion from the past. Maybe memories hid in the joints and stretching released them.

She was twelve and a half years old when she cut an old quilt into long streamers and tied the pieces to separate branches in the front yard tree. She had a little recitation to accompany every piece she tied. She couldn't remember them all...

Papa left the hill today. Mama cried her eyes away,
He snuck a package on his ride, Boy, I wondered what's inside?

And another...

Rain, rain dropped all over the mountain's crest,
Teacher said put them ugly stories to rest?

She thought they were like nursery rhymes or songs to the sky before she suddenly realized that they were not songs at all, they represented an odd calendar events: places, people, and things she's tied around a tree branch rather than her fingers. The only thing that she could remember was wanting to remember. Blue was for masculine things, yellow for Mama. Together on the same strip meant something for both her mother and father. The tree was leafless at the time and as dusk ceded to night, the yellow and blue strips of cloth drifted separately, each one moving alone in the breeze. Agnes had stayed out most of the night watching the pieces twisting about. What had possessed her to decorate the front yard tree, she didn't know, and she couldn't quite read anything in the pictured view of her mother's face the next morning, when she came out of the house, looked up, and cried. The quilt was old, and Agnes didn't believe the old cover she used to sit on had ever been beautiful. Pieces hung off the branches, plaits beribboning the tree in faded colors. The knots she tied weren't pretty like bows. She had known her mother to cry at the sight of something beautiful. But the tree looked like a tree with rags tied to it and as far as Agnes was concerned the crepe paper on the school ceiling looked as unnecessary.

Paper hanging from the ceiling looked like paper hanging from the ceiling which did not make Agnes feel festive. She wasn't even quite sure how she'd been dragged inside this school except that the school stood on the pathway between her house and where she meant to walk. She had awakened before the rest of the Thrace household and decided to walk. There were a few other ladies standing out in front of the school and they corralled her. In truth, she had let them. They spoke with her, sharing a common goal and sensibility, and Agnes didn't mind quite as much as she might have.

They had gathered a bit too close, believing that the cold would harm her more than their unused to closeness. Finally, another lady had arrived with the key and they all went inside and set about doing various chores. Agnes went along especially as they were so thankful to have her. They told her that her husband was a very generous man and he had covered the entire cost of the party, which was very kind indeed. The ladies told her that Thrace had thought of the dance as a parting gift to his girls as he would soon be traveling again. Instantly, Agnes warmed to the occasion and volunteered to do whatever they might need. The sooner they had this party, the sooner she'd be back in Mexico.

Agnes arrived home in the early afternoon, sat in her window seat, and waited for one or the other of the girls. Neither of them came and the disappointment of not getting to hold them left her saddened. Still hopeful, but saddened, not hugging them was like undoing something necessary. Not hugging was not Agnes.

A few nights later, on party night, for the first time, everyone from Mrs. Wallace's had the opportunity to see the entire Thrace family. Both daughters, their mother, father, and even the housekeeper, Umm II, attended the party. All around the room went talk of Mrs. Thrace's elegance, despite her near nakedness in the "dead of winter," the other day while helping out at school. The girls were quite dissimilar; however, twins didn't have to have any particular likeness. Mrs. Thrace looked almost as young as her girls and was far livelier than both. Thrace should be quite proud of such a family.

It was Berdeena who had put on the dress and attended the ball. She danced with every man in the room and did so with such energy and happiness that the ball wouldn't quite have been one without her. Her swirling gray and blue garment and the streamers she pulled off the walls and wrapped around her partners livened up the room's dull countenances. Mirella and Alley's eyes never left their mother. They had never seen her dance or smile so long to so many others and seem happy. The evening was capped with a long slow dance between the Thraces.

At first, the other couples had cleared the floor, but Mr. Thrace invited them back and asked the musicians to play a few more songs. They seemed to be doing a round, switching partners until Mr. Thrace moved off the floor, walked over to the table, reached for the hands of both his daughters, and brought them to the floor. They were both awkward and Alley, the prettier one tried to sit down quickly, but her father wouldn't let her. He motioned to a young man sitting at one of the nearby tables and put Alley's hand in his, the strangest thing that Alley remembered her father ever doing. He bent down and whispered in both their ears, "Just a dance, a dance or two." He danced with Mirella who laughed out loud. She couldn't keep her cheeks from shaking and felt sure her face was bright red. Her father swirled her around the dance floor and remarked that she was quite a little dancing lady. His hands felt warm and strong until he switched, placed her hand in a boy's and once more took Alley's. She stumbled, her father waited, and she righted herself, looking up to catch such warmth in his eyes. The evening ended all too soon. Thrace picked up the wraps for all his girls, wrapped them up tight, and together they walked home.

The other girls came over to the Thrace table simply to be in the aura of such a lively woman, smiling at her and wishing to be nearby. Alley guessed that for a while, at least, school might be a happier place for Mirella.

Unfortunately, it was a very short while because Mirella had acquired a knack for "ruining the party." Her parents were traveling to Mexico in two days and Mirella was so angry that she couldn't bear to listen to any more anything about her family. As the English teacher began to speak, intending merely to start with a small compliment to Mrs. Thrace for making the party, Mr. Thrace for his generosity with the ball, which had by turns allowed them an earlier purchase of new books, Mirella screamed an interruption.

"My mother is silly and always changing and frankly not the least bit interested in anything, especially not this school."

The teacher chalked her tirade up to sadness. Poor girl, she told all the other teachers, both her parents were traveling and leaving them with only a maid. Anyway, it closed the door that had briefly opened between Mirella and the rest of the girls at school.

Mrs. Thrace

Alana and Porter were unprepared for the Thraces' arrival and were absolutely caught off guard when they heard voices in the entryway. They were, as usual, in the kitchen drinking coffee, going over the endless amount of paper that cooking candy seemed to create.

Alana, Porter, and the Thraces stood in the hallway staring at one another, mildly embarrassed at the goofy smiles that skated uncontrollably across their lips when either of them looked up at the other. Even Thrace looked silly and out of place standing in his own hallway. For endless seconds, he did not look into Porter's face. If he had, the two of them could have helped one another gain a measure of equilibrium. They stood in four corners of the hallway smiling until the housekeeper passed by and gave witness to her own surprise. She immediately walked outside to gather the bags and came back in puzzled when she hadn't found any.

Alana translated her questions and both the Thraces realized that in their haste, they hadn't bothered to claim their own bags. Laughing out loud to mask the fact that they had gotten off the plane and run straight through the airport to the taxi stands without bothering to collect their belongings. The Thraces looked at one another, each a little surprised at their shared foolishness. Their gaze, especially at one another, finally gave Porter his tongue.

"Welcome, my friend," he reached out and grabbed Thrace's hand and then his shoulder, pulling him into a mutual embrace. "I think we may be able to scratch up dinner for four."

"I am hungry," Thrace said.

"Me too," Mrs. Thrace said in a smooth, slow, alto, and everyone followed Porter into the house, the women behind, trailing the men with the clip-clop of heeled shoes on the stone floor.

Thrace didn't come to bed that night and Mrs. Thrace had stayed in the room to avoid having to sit with Porter in a crowd. She could not let him think she was any more ridiculous than she had already betrayed, flying off to Mexico without claiming the bag that she had for once, carefully packed, standing in the hallway unable to do anything but foolishly smile. She lay down and mercifully slept a little and when she awakened, she was still alone. She had gotten up and wandered about the house, taking it in little by little. She liked the stone floors and muted colors and eased her hands along the grooves aged into the table on her way out to the balcony where she looked over their domain. Here she was where she was so anxious to be. The night scents of the flowers brought the familiarity of walking amongst them. Their scent made her think of Porter walking behind her and she knew that she had wanted to craft their first meeting. It should be alone whether in the dark on the balcony or in the garden during the day. She could not share him, not until she had the confidence of what privacy might render. If he had touched her, she could carry the memory with her into a room full of people, but she had used up her ideas of him in Washington, DC Now she needed more. She stood on the balcony a long time before she felt the full weight of fatigue and went back to bed.

Thrace was there, having spent an entire evening unable to do anything but talk about the company. Surprisingly, he hadn't wanted to touch Alana, not yet. Part of him wanted to practice which seemed absurd and left him temporarily unable to touch either one of the women he thought he loved. For the first time in his life, Thrace was stunned into inaction.

Mrs. Thrace moved into the garden first thing in the

morning, ready for Porter to pick up the thread and begin right where they had ended. She pretended to unravel skein after skein to be sure that Porter wouldn't miss her trail, she moved slowly, repeated arcs, tried to stop and wait but Porter had promised himself to stop following her.

Somewhere, wrapped up in his ruminations of her was one fact that kept showing up, no matter where he put his imagination. He would be holding her, caught in the astrids, being pricked by thorns when the fact that she was Thrace's wife bled out from his skin where the thorn had stuck.

On the sidewalk, when he pushed her against the plaster of the old church wall and put his lips on hers, the fact that she was Thrace's wife would assert itself as clearly as if it were written in large letters on a sign pasted to the curved back of an old woman who passed by. The third time, the words were written in the sky as they lay on the balcony while Thrace and Alana had traveled to another town in search of a special flavor. Porter could not follow Mrs. Thrace and he was also relieved that she hadn't appeared at dinner.

While Mrs. Thrace twisted amongst the blossoms in the garden, the very few glances that Porter allowed himself, each time, she seemed impossibly certain and ethereal, and the longing that he had to assure himself that it was her hurt more than he ever expected.

He finally decided to approach Thrace the very next time that they were alone and after the first couple of days, the opportunity presented itself every night at dinner. Neither of the women seemed to be eating; however, each evening they were expected and therefore privacy between the two men couldn't be assumed. Consequently, the lack of certainty didn't allow them to speak candidly to each other. Both were being haunted by the spectral possibility of the women showing up at dinner.

After a few days of silent encounters when Thrace began to believe that his ears were fading, Porter said something. Thrace didn't hear it and because he was unsure of whether Porter had tried to speak, he refused to ask. Then he could have sworn he heard Porter say, "Are the women well?"

"How should I know?" Thrace answered, fully annoyed.

"How should you know what?" Porter asked.

"About the women?" He had slipped now and doubted whether Porter had even asked a question. "Did you not ask if the women are well?" Thrace threw it out, sacrificing his perceived dignity.

"I would certainly like to know, even if I haven't asked," Porter confessed, hearing the anger in his own voice, but frankly relieved that he hadn't burst. Then Porter was almost sure he heard himself mumble "I'm in love with your wife."

When Thrace didn't utter a word for an excruciating amount of moments and then said, "Have at her," Porter knew he must be hallucinating.

"I think I've eaten something peculiar," Thrace said.

"Do you mean really or in the sense that you're just feeling rather odd?"

"I mean that I'm feeling rather odd. I don't suppose I've ever felt this way and I hope that it's something I've eaten, something temporary, something that will pass right out of the system." Thrace didn't know what he was talking about and hoped Porter didn't either.

"Things do pass," Porter said uneasily. He'd hoped the thing that might pass might not necessarily pass.

Thrace was reminded of the conversations he used to have with his wife. He couldn't make heads or tails of them and he thought it was funny now that he was playing wife to Porter. He laughed, halfheartedly at first, then with full gusto. Porter did too. When they had finished laughing, they began to drink.

"To your return," Porter tilted his glass.

"Safely if not soundly." They raised their glasses toward one another, swallowed all the liquid, refilled them, and drank again.

"Invisible women!" They both looked behind themselves and laughed."I hope it wasn't anything I said," Thrace snickered.

"I haven't spoken one word to Mrs. Thrace since she arrived, I haven't seen her." Porter tilted his glass again.

"Well, you can't blame yourself, she's rather . . ." Thrace stopped himself.

Porter was relieved because he couldn't bear to hear her spoken about by another man, and especially one with perhaps more to say than he could.

"Why haven't you spoken with her? Go ahead; say whatever you like. She's probably heard everything you'll have to say," Thrace said to Porter but he was talking to himself.

"Candy, candy, candy," he said, scolding himself for talking about his factory.

Porter took it as a suggestion for topics to discuss with Mrs. Thrace. Well, at least he was given the go ahead for conversation. Really, he could talk to her. What was the harm in it, Porter asked himself?

"Honestly, you could talk about anything," again Thrace spoke to himself, but Porter was listening.

"Yes, it's true," Porter answered, thinking of himself too.

"To titillating conversation with a point!" Thrace sealed the subject. He and Porter polished off more tequila.

Porter raised himself thinking of standing up at once and going in search of Mrs. Thrace for purposeful conversation, but his legs felt heavy as boulders. He remained at the table with his friend.

"How's it going?" Thrace asked, figuring there was no point in not talking about the factory with Porter.

"Everything is as expected. We're ready for a first line of production."

"Yes, yes, just deciding on the flavors to make first. What should we taste first, Porter?"

"Something exquisite and fine, perhaps a little sweet and very savory, strong and worth remembering," Porter answered.

"Translate Porter, what flavor would that be? Would that be chocolate or tart lemon, peppermint?"

"Combinations seem more sophisticated, sweet peppermint with a very tart lemon center. Maybe the taste should change, the longer the sweet stays on the tongue. Sweet and mild at first and the closer and closer you suck toward the center, the lemonier and stinging the candy becomes. Sadly, it's over; the candy is finished but the stain remains on the tongue."

"Porter, we're only going to borrow the tongue, not keep it."

"When I was little, I liked the kind of candy that always threatened to escape. The taste and the texture were slippery. If you tried to talk, it might fall out of your mouth and naturally land directly in dirt," Porter said.

"What kind of candy was that?"

"The kind that made you salivate; the candy was always sliding about, hard sours, but you didn't want to chew for fear of breaking a tooth or finishing too quickly."

"Was this the way the candy worked in everyone's mouth or just yours?" Thrace was full of smiles when he asked Porter, who was now moving his tongue about his mouth like a fish or snake or something amphibian.

Porter's tongue was messing around in a conversation when his clear preference would have been for another kind of involvement altogether. He refilled their cups; they clanked together and drank.

"Candy should be universally slippery, sweet, and well liked," Porter answered through wet lips.

Thrace had mostly been talking to himself from the very beginning and Porter's answers were incidental. Thrace wondered how he could lift the conversation out of the realm of candy and into intimacy, preferably with Alana; perhaps a drunken Porter could be useful. Porter had always been a good drinking partner. He had always remained sensible and never seemed to remember the evening any better than Thrace. No loose ends with Porter.

"Lingering on the tongue might be a good start," Thrace could say to Alana. "Perhaps I could linger on yours."

"How do you mean that, in sentiment, or as an advertisement? People that eat the candy should feel that; or do you mean linger in the mind really, rather than the tongue?" Porter asked his friend.

"For instance, if we were going to sell candy romantically," Thrace began.

"To children?" Porter sounded startled.

"No, no. Between a man and a woman?"

"You mean if a woman were to sell to a man or if a man were to sell to a woman?"

"Oh, either way, either way would do," he paused, "wouldn't it?" Thrace could again feel his annoyance rising.

"Marketing is not my forte." Porter waved his hand in front of his face as if something putrid had passed his nose.

"Sell yourself Porter, what if you sold you?" Thrace asked.

"To whom?"

"Anyone," Thrace answered.

"Well, who exactly?" Porter wanted to know.

"How about an invisible woman?"

"If she's invisible how will I connect to her?" Even a drunken Porter could be far too literal.

"Oh for goodness' sake, sell yourself to somebody's wife or mother."

Surely Thrace didn't mean his own wife. Did he?

"To Mrs. Thrace?" Porter again sounded hopeful.

"She'd take far too long to respond. Well, if you could quicken her somehow. But everybody wants candy. Forget about selling, let's let everyone have some. It's delicious and if it is delicious enough, they'll come back for more and keep coming."

'Was he taking back his offer or leaving the offer out there? Once said, was said', Porter thought, 'said was said.'

Thrace couldn't sell himself to Alana. 'Wasn't she his already?' he asked himself but had no idea how to move forward.

"Porter, can you fly?" Thrace asked.

"I'm a pilot without papers. I'm currently unlicensed."

Porter thought about the last time he was up in the air fly-ing without papers and somehow, like everything else these days, he conflated the memory with his of Mrs. Thrace. He'd been up without proper credentials, so he loved her without being married to her. Emboldened for moments, he thought, who was going to stop him at one or the other?

Thrace wanted to go to bed but not to his own. Anyway, the only bed that he knew where to find was his.

Porter was ready for bed too. Unfortunately, he passed out right where he sat for the entire household to witness. His head fell back, his mouth opened wide; drivel, both the silent kind and the kind with words, ran down the side of his mouth before he began to snore as loudly as possible.

Mrs. Thrace was in the garden very early that morn-ing and caught her first glimpse of Porter in days. He was oddly disheveled and bent forwards, falling home instead of walking. He didn't look capable of following her around. She followed him. She had never pictured Porter outside of his togetherness with her and the idea of him having a pri-vate domain made her curious. Maybe that was what he was waiting for, for her to take a step in his direction.

She followed him down two or three narrow streets and tried to remember them to find her way again. He could have easily seen her if he'd wanted to because no one else was on the streets beside the two of them. She click-clacked over the cobblestones loudly, not taking the least bit of care not to be heard.

Porter didn't have the strength to turn around. He heard the noise but decided that the echoing footsteps were walk-ing through his head. He preferred phantom noises to real ones now, and realized that he wasn't in any condition to judge between the two. His bed called him, and he wished he'd had the energy for a long hot bath first, knowing he'd sleep better. But all he could do was climb the stairs, open his door, and stagger towards the bed.

She sat on the stairs outside his door waiting for noises

that she could identify. None came. She pushed on the door, creaked it open, and peeked through, but all she could see was a very pale blue wall. Tipping inside, she invited herself to see more. She'd come this far.

Porter possessed the orderly rooms of a sober individual. That he was currently abed with a hangover surely was an aberration. His walls were not pale blue as it turned out. The light bounced off the stone floor onto the blue carpet and reflected itself onto the walls.

Porter's largest room was awash in light from the wall that sat over the street which was covered in windowed doors and exited onto a balcony. She hadn't noticed the balcony from the street, but she could look out onto it now. A potted garden of astrids covered one end and on the other, a small handmade fountain trickled water. Porter's rooms were a lesson in Egypt, Mexico, Europe, the United States, and Southern Africa. The room proved harmony could be produced from disparate sources. She wanted to stay with his things but felt she needed permission. The room hadn't been set up for strangers but clearly reflected the personal vision of the man who occupied them. Each object had a story and she wondered if she touched his things what they would reveal, perhaps the secret of Porter's choices. How had they come to be his? Were they gifts and why? How had the lovely blue carpet woven on the other side of the world come to rest atop wood beneath stone in a small unheard-of state in Mexico?

She had to see his private rooms; she wanted to see him. Being in his home was like sitting next to him without talking. His voice was being used but she couldn't understand him. She opened the one door he had managed to close and saw him asleep on top of his bed, his shirt unbuttoned and unruly beneath his back. His arm rested inharmoniously above his head, his breathing quiet and restful. She listened as if he let out a song and tipped-toed across his room, stooped down to smell him, and sat next to his legs near the bottom edge of the bed. He stank.

In his room, she couldn't see anything else but him. She couldn't manage to look up and see the color on the wall or whether there was a dresser or a painting. He stirred and she jumped and made for the door, caught herself, and turned around. Maybe she should stay. Maybe she shouldn't. Making up her mind was a damnable business. An impasse ought to possess a hint of the consequences, but making a decision was arriving at an intersection in the dark with neither turn remotely visible.

She wanted to trace his lines with the palm of her hand, hold the shape of his jaw in her hand, and imprint him as she would a memory of twelve or after. She couldn't face him so much as try to memorize him. She had always been more comfortable sifting through memories than days. If she could put Porter in her memory, he might come out and she could touch him with familiarity, like something she had long been used to. But here, overlooking him like a cliff, ready for all the rocks, dirt, and grass to fall, something dangerous might happen. With the safety of memory abandoned, she felt loose and untethered, waving in the air—a stringless kite.

She wanted to shake Porter awake and start.

Aware that putting the present in her mind could amount to putting it into a bottomless pit—to surface only when needed and she would not necessarily be the arbiter of this need. Come when it may or will, she hadn't exercised any control over her memory which had never worried her before. Remembering something from one day to the next had not necessarily been desired, until now.

Slowly, she reached into her pocket and found the pen that she generally carried but rarely used. With a black indelible marker, she lifted Porter's hand and drew a small circle. The circle would be an aid to memory, a guide for tomorrow that would bring her right back to the moments of today. Afterwards, she left Porter's apartment.

18

Coming Apart for the Very First Time

Mexico

Alana guided Thrace to her small exquisite cottage that sat on a corner of land that once belonged to the former El Presidente. She explained to Thrace that her story was a very long one and that her home was a "statue of their relationship" which was based on the father-daughter paradigm more than anything else. Her mother had been his mistress, but she was not his daughter. She told him life could be a bunch of ever "smallening" concentric circles and that she was appropriately overlapping at this time in her life.

Thrace didn't care if she always made sense. As long as he could be near her, her theories didn't matter. He hadn't even bothered to tell her that "smallening" was not a word in English and that he didn't know what she meant by a "statue" of a former relationship. He hadn't told her anything because he had learned to love listening to her thickly accented English. He had never even admitted that he understood and spoke Spanish because he preferred her translations. His affection for Alana cost him nothing, no elaborate emotional constructs. She was entirely self-sufficient, free of odd attachments. He could love Alana lazily and not worry about her in the world.

The four of them returned to the dinner table, Porter with ever-increasing odd markings beneath his clothing. Mrs. Thrace marked him anew every time she spent time alone in his company.

Almost thirty days of bliss were split between the four adults in Michoacán State, Mexico. Candy production launched without a hitch and the four of them celebrated their gift to the world. The candy sold quickly, and they were already planning for increased production. Together, they enjoyed a special dinner and drank toasts to the candy factory they called Cadmus. Alana shared her secret recipe for liqueur with Thrace, and they spilt her syrupy warm liquid, and then drank it.

Porter and Mrs. Thrace talked. Porter expressed himself in ways to help her remember. She tried using his skin as a mnemonic device, drawing pictures on his body that would connect them to the stories he told her but the next day, she didn't care about her own artistry; amused by her depictions, she wondered how long Porter would let her use his right thigh, or arm, chest, or near his knee, as a canvas.

"That's so you'd remember yesterday."

"I remember," she said. "The pitchers and the cow are because you grew up on a farm."

"It wasn't really a dairy farm."

"But a farm?"

"Yes, if you think of a farm as a house with land around it," Porter said.

Each day he told her a story that he hoped she'd remember, and she tattooed him in a way she wouldn't. Porter let himself be decorated. He, too, scanned her body seeking explanations for the scars that were already there. Mrs. Thrace had few scars without the memory of how they arrived, making the injuries seem unreal—surreal. Porter touched her scars—one a day, a day at a time—placing them in his own memory. As he touched them, they slowly began to come alive for her, but never in his presence. Always after she left him, the story returned.

And then she began to draw differently, not what she wanted to remember about Porter, but what she wanted to remember about herself. White skin, like unlined paper, made a good surface, and Mrs. Thrace began to draw a map, from memory, a map to her own beginnings.

Christmas was coming and Alana and Porter knew and expected the Thraces to go home.

Sadly, they did travel back to the States, but not before Mrs. Thrace asked Alana to take her to the post office.

Christmas on the Mountain

Because Max the Black had never before received a box this close to Christmas, he was sure that the box was a present from his mother.

"Grandma, can I open this one on Christmas? It's from my mother."

"Is it addressed to you?"

"It's from Mexico again. Look how big it is." Something about size seemed to make Max the Black irrational.

Grandma was regularly in her Thrace-built house now; she had even used the kitchen once or twice. At night, she went home. But she had been in the house when the package arrived. She came into the room with the very large box and wondered if her daughter had finally sent herself home. She looked at Max the Black and then at the box and sighed.

"You know, son, reality is available if you want to live in it." Max the Black felt his bubble deflating. Instantly, he knew she was right. He was almost grown and hadn't had a Christmas yet.

Aberdeen didn't think she'd ever had a Christmas, though Selsie loved celebrations. She might not have even believed in Jesus. Aberdeen imagined her grandmother saying she was going to celebrate the birthdays of people she knew and loved and that didn't include Jesus, whoever he was. But, Max the Black surprised her with his intense desire to celebrate the holiday.

She and Dag mulled over the idea. Aberdeen believed

most surprises were Dag's fault, especially since they always came from off the mountain. Dag had been the one who talked her into sending Max Thrace to school. He had hit a home run when he told her that Max should be "equipped" to live off this mountain if he chose. "Equipped," she would say to herself and smile. Dag must have gone somewhere off that mountain to get that word and came back. He had convinced her and every morning, in the beginning, Dag walked that boy to school. School was where he got all sorts of notions that would have been fine if he'd stopped bringing them home; but he hadn't. Christmas was the one he didn't let go.

"You want to give that boy Christmas?" Dag had prodded her, and she knew it was coming.

"No. You know I don't do just to do."

"School's out, everybody celebratin'."

"That's to be celebrated. Maybe we can be 'new notion' free for a time or two. That'd be a vacation for me but nothing to celebrate."

"We can celebrate what we want to," Dag said.

"Then it don't have to be Christmas."

"How about Aberdeenmas?" Dag laughed.

"Aberdeenmas ain't in December."

They could have gone on arguing and never gotten anywhere. Even Max marveled at their stubbornness—and the lengths to which they could go. With Christmas, he knew they could spend the whole season arguing, so he took Christmas on himself. He picked a tree in the woods and decorated it. He'd made presents for both his grandparents. He'd made one for Jessup, too, but he wouldn't let Jessup help him with Christmas. He'd drawn his grandparents' portraits with his pencils. He'd drawn one for Jessup, too, but wouldn't give it to her until after Christmas with his grandparents. One thing school had helped him discover was that he could draw exquisitely, almost anything.

From then on, school made sense to him. School unearthed things in him and Max the Black figured there might be more; he was willing to find out. He told himself that he was going to get as much schooling as possible.

He hadn't figured how he was going to get his two grandparents out in the woods where he wanted to lead them. He wasn't even sure whether Dag would still be around. Nobody could keep him around all the time. Max the Black wondered if Dag might not be celebrating Christmas somewhere else. He'd have to if he wanted Christmas, but he didn't seem concerned about it either. Max knew that some of the arguments that Dag got into with Aberdeen were for his sake.

He toyed with taking one of his mother's packages and running up into the woods. Maybe Aberdeen would chase him to get it back and Dag would follow her. Even though they were ageless, he still couldn't picture them chasing him into the woods. Aberdeen wouldn't have needed to run after him anyway. She could use her will to make him come home. She always made him and Dag do whatever she wanted. Dag told him he'd better ask himself if he were walking 'cause he'd wanted to or if his Grandma weren't making him move. She'd probably done the same to his mother.

Maybe it didn't work on everybody. Maybe it only worked on the people that loved her back the way he and Dag did. Max the Black truly loved his grandmother, loved her in a way he'd never been allowed to love anyone, and he appreciated her willingness to let him love her so. He thought it was the one thing that was going to help him become a man like Dag, the man he most wanted to be.

He had a bunch of ideas about how to get his grandparents into the woods, none of them good. He even thought that if he went and howled near a big old tree, or the one his grandmother named for him that they'd think he was hurt and come running.

He decorated the tall tree closest to his great-great-grandmother Selsie's kitchen library. Then he decorated the kitchen library. On Christmas Eve, he framed the entire thing in blue lights, the slightly peaked roof, the two windows, and even the door. When he finished hanging the

lights, he plugged them into the generator behind the building. Dag had brought light to the kitchen library years back.
He had put it there without telling Aberdeen and waited for
her to discover it.

"It took her about a day. That place is her inside mind; if
something changes, she'll know."

On Christmas evening, when he saw his grandmother
stirring, he raced up in the woods ahead of her. Because it
was headed toward evening, he guessed Dag would follow
her, and he'd guessed right.

He was waiting and ready. When they stepped into the
clearing, he heard them and pushed the generator on. The
blue lights clicked on with a sound like a horn, electricity
firing up at once, muffled by trees.

Aberdeen and Dag simply stood still with mouths hanging open until she looked over at her husband and tapped
his chin closed. They giggled at one another until Max the
Black came from around the house. His grandparents barely
noticed the tree except as a backdrop to the kitchen library.

"Merry Christmas!" he yelled over to them and came
running. "I'm not finished. Come inside for your Christmas
presents."

"Boy, did you tie the sky down or put mirrors in them day
lights? They the same blue. You got us here at exactly the
right moment, the right blue." Max the Black kept trying
to get them inside, but they wouldn't budge. The kitchen
library looked frozen in blue time, a suspended piece of
magic, and Aberdeen and Dag wanted to see the entire act.

"Come on, come on inside," Max insisted. "Come get your
Christmas presents!"

Finally, Max the Black went to the back side of the house
and unplugged the blue lights, which reanimated his grandparents.

"Come on," he pushed them. Once inside the library he
handed each of them their gifts. He had to tell them to unwrap them. "Tear off that paper."

He gave them each a portrait. They held their pictures out

in front side by side, each looked at their own and the other's. They automatically switched them without saying a word.

Then Aberdeen explained to Max the Black, "I already got me. If you don't mind, I'll take Dag." Max thought she meant she already had a picture of herself.

"I carry me around all day, every day in still form and now I got Dag through your eyes, boy. You see him beautiful too. It's a fine thing, a fine fine thing. Now it really is Aberdeenmas!"

"And Dagmas! Thank you, son. Thank you, Max." He was glowing. Max was shining in their love and appreciation, their gift to him. This was about as Christmas as his grandparents would get and Max thought it perfect, especially after they all wrapped their arms around each other and stayed.

Christmas in Washington, DC

In Washington, on Thursday, December 23rd at dusk, the sisters were together in Alley's bedroom.

"Mother was a directionless walker," Alley declared.

"Just because we didn't know where she was going didn't mean she didn't have a destination."

"She walks aimlessly no matter where she is. She lives aimlessly."

"She disappeared off the streets. First, we were behind her and suddenly she's gone. She must have gone somewhere," Mirella said.

"That's not necessarily true. If she was going somewhere it would have been easier to track her. Aimless walking doesn't have to get anywhere."

"For hours, every day, she walked," Mirella said exasperatedly. "How is that possible?"

"All right, you tell me what she was doing," Alley waited.

"I think she was meeting someone."

"In a country where she didn't speak the language and didn't know anyone?" Alley sighed. The suggestion was improbable.

"You don't need too many words to ..."

"So you think our mother had lovers in every city she visited, including this one."

"You used to see that old man, didn't you?" Mirella spit out.

"Not lately."

"Precisely. You don't see her either. I'll bet as soon as she comes back so will he," Mirella went on.

"Oh yes, he's been waiting for her to return, his heart in his hands, ready to give to her. She ignores our father, her perfectly youthful husband in exchange for an old man who can barely put one foot in front of the other. A white old man!" Alley snorted, "Our mother, the love maiden. She barely knows that she exists in the world, the world where people live. She may be more able to talk to you about the 1890s and *that's* when she's in the mood. It's easy to lose someone when you're not going any particular place. If she were going somewhere, we'd have been able to pick up the trail—if not in the beginning, maybe in the middle but somewhere the path would repeat itself—even at her lover's front door. We could have waited there."

"She was doing something with someone!" Mirella screamed.

"She was. She was walking with herself and frankly with our mother, that might just be two or three people."

"What is that supposed to mean?" Mirella asked.

"Oh, so you never noticed how different she can be."

"So she's moody. So are *you*."

"Well, you won't see me walking along perfectly content with one of my moods."

"Who could see you doing anything considering you only move in the dark like a resident mole or other night creature?" Mirella teased her sister.

"Well, it's better than walking aimlessly about in the day for everyone to see. Like mother, like daughter."

"I'm not our mother. I go to school. You know where I am, each and every day."

"Barely. For all I know, you pretend to go to school; really, Mirella, maybe you spend the day with your lover."

"He gives me the homework assignments that you do."

"He could be a teacher. Maybe you are literally the teacher's pet." Alley thought she was being funny.

"If you'd have bothered to come, you'd have noticed that there aren't any male teachers at Mrs. Wallace's."

"Who said the teacher came from Mrs. Wallace's?"

"Oh please, Alley. I'm going to bed."

"You can't make Mother make sense, Mirella."

"She doesn't have to. So what? We didn't have a traditional upbringing."

"I'm the one who's accepted that, you're the one still imagining good tidings."

Mirella got up and left Alley's room. A short time later she came back.

"Okay; it doesn't have to be normal, just understandable." Alley reached out, Mirella came close, and she hugged her little sister.

On December 24th, Mr. and Mrs. Thrace came home sometime in the wee hours of the night, Christmas presents, and a fake tree thrown in with the luggage. They took the trouble of setting it all up in the living room so that the girls would find Christmas when they awoke the next morning. But the girls slept late and when they did awaken, neither of their parents were available. Their father had gone into the office on a day that he knew he'd be alone and Mother, well surely, she must be scattered about her bedroom.

Mirella went downstairs first and immediately ran up to get her sister.

"They're back."

Alley put on a robe and followed her sister.

Some of their mother's things were hanging on the tree along with the rest of the ornaments and both girls wondered if they'd ever be spared the Calamity of Mother.

"Wouldn't it be nice if every once in a while, she would come in and say hello like a normal human being?"

Christmas with Memories from the Mountain

Once again, they were being summoned and both listened for a long while before their mother's voice lured them up the stairs and into her room. Her voice was so garbled that neither girl could make out what she was saying. Alley was thinking that nonsense finally sounds like nonsense and what a welcome change that was. But then she noticed that the storm windows were up in her mother's room as Umm II had had them put up around the entire house for warmth. Their mother's voice was caught in between the two panes and Alley started to leave it there and then walked over and lifted the window a fraction so that her mother's voice could squeeze in from outside. She wondered if her mother's voice always being outside had anything to do with the things she said. Maybe it was easier to make up stories from the outside in, or was talking so difficult that she had to distance herself from the things that she said?

Mother was simply strange.

Her words came on in and joined up with her lips which were laying smack dab in the center of her face. As she spoke, she gathered herself together a little and by the time she was finished talking she seemed rested and peaceful atop her colorful spread.

"The first time I left home, I followed my father because I wanted to know why he always went away. I didn't think I could get lost in the woods, but I did. I was the only child and for me the woods were my brother and sister and I thought I knew them. But my father was always leaving, and though my mother was fine, I wasn't. It seemed to me that there was something somewhere else in the world that he was concerned about and I wanted to know what it was. I was twelve, I think. He left and I followed behind him. My mother never seemed to notice as she never said anything to me when I returned."

Alley noticed that her mother's voice was deeper and heavier, and she wondered if Mirella noticed too.

"My father never took the same route twice and he lost

me every time I followed him or maybe I lost him. Since the trees were my family, he might have had another family too. Maybe my mother and me weren't enough, maybe he didn't feel needed because my mother didn't need him or me or anybody. I used to think she was teaching me all kinds of things like how to pull sap from trees, how to feed myself well when the creek was dry and when it was wet, how to hear what the trees were saying, what their silence meant. Then I realized that all her lessons came to one meaning—she was teaching me how to be alone—the thing she knew and maybe liked best.

I discovered the mountain had an end and that I could walk to it any time I wanted to. One day, I was going to step off."

The girls stopped listening to their mother's gruesome cartoons of the past. Thinking her own thoughts, helped Alley not listen.

"Malton McIntired Jessup," Mother whispered, and if her daughters had been paying attention, they would have noticed the convulsion that began at the top and slowly snaked down her entire body.

Finally, a memory restored with all the bite with which it began.

"We were in Malty's barn that day, playing the touch game. Each of us won five spots on the other's body and we could touch the spot for the count of ten. You could choose five different spots for ten or you could leave your hand in the same place for fifty counts. Malty always tried to leave his hand on my breasts, but I wouldn't let him. I was still stronger and bigger than he was, and I wanted to touch him in lots of places. I always had to control the game or Malty would ruin it. I let him touch the middle of my chest in between where breasts would eventually be if I turned out to grow them. Then I let him touch me just beneath my navel for twenty-five counts and I did the counting. I wanted to touch his joints, the places where one thing changed into another. Malty was so angular, I always placed my hand in the turn of where something was going, the place in the road that led to somewhere unexpected. For five counts, I put my hand where his back met his behind. For another five, I molded my hand beneath his armpit with his arm stretching away from his body like a tree branch. Then the door banged open and Malty's father walked in, dragging a little girl behind him. She was younger than us, Malty's second sister, not the oldest and not the youngest.

She was crying, "Please Daddy, please Daddy, don't hurt me, don't make me. I'm yours, Daddy, don't have to prove it. I'll always be yours, Daddy, please."

"You will be mine first," he said, "and I don't got to prove it to nobody."

"Please, Daddy," she cried.

Malty shrank up and though he was next to me, he seemed a million miles away. His father took his sister and tied her hands with the horse reigns. They didn't have any horses. He tied her arms around a post at the bottom and he wrapped one leg, so it was kind of stretched away from the other one. She was curved sideways, and he pulled her clothes—dress up, under things down. She twisted and pulled until she froze. A still little bent thing. Their father took off his pants and spread her little legs and kneeled around her. He fit himself between her legs, raised his chest. He rose on top of her, and then he was taking all of her, everything she ever said, everything she was, and he was stuffing it back inside of her with his grunts and shoves. He moved on her for a long, long time. The longer he moved the quieter and smaller she became. Her and Malty shrank. Their father was shrinking them. I knew I should do something, but what didn't come.

God should have made girls father-proof. God should have made it impossible for men to take what could be beautiful and leave destruction in their wake. When Malty's father got up, a stick hung from his navel. He mumbled a lot of things, but all we could understand was something about smearing his baby girl on their mother. He got up and walked out of the barn towards their house, as he was.

Shrunken Malty climbed down from where we were and unwrapped his sister, he lay behind her and they curled up like they were two spoons used to fitting together, familiar with one another. She sucked one of her thumbs and he held her in his arms. He told her everything was alright, and she reached back behind her, holding him.

Mixed up squalor shook that barn like a wet dog. Afterwards, for a long time, I used to dream over and over again that me and Malty dug a hole for his father until we actually did. Malty tricked him into the woods. We recovered the hole. After that, I never got to touch the rest of the places where Malty curved. I reached for him, but my hand fell off my wrist and the rest of me came apart in pieces, dripped all over the dirt, mixed up with the dead leaves and shrubbery. Picking me up and putting me back together seemed impossible, 'specially to put things back where they'd been. Pieces went to different places and the memories went with the pieces.

Everything had a first time. My mama said that. That was the first time I fell apart. That was the first time that I knew another part of me might arrive just in time to help with the awfulness. Mama said we could bury things, but it didn't always solve the problem. Things had to be properly put in the ground."

Mirella had been imagining herself as the belle of the ball. She also found herself wondering what her father would contribute to school this time as his parting gift, and she didn't mind if her mother went back with him. She and Alley had a routine. When they weren't arguing, life was just fine. They had parents for presents and special appearances.

For the life of them, neither Alley nor Mirella could remember having ever celebrated Christmas. This year, they had everything: lights, decorations, presents, and a great big dinner prepared by Umm II. Neither of them knew what to make of their gifts. Candy, colorful blankets, hats, and wooden painted figurines of strange people, and each of them was given a striped poncho. Their father said they were little token gifts, tokens of love, all they could pick up on their way back in time for Christmas day.

The Thraces stayed a couple of weeks in Washington, DC Selma pulled herself apart and put herself back together again at a far faster pace than ever. Some days, she summoned her daughters twice. She changed her clothing several times a day. At night, she and Mr. Thrace headed out or went to bed early. The commotion that their parents brought home unsettled the entire household.

Neither of the girls knew how to accommodate their parents. They mostly tried to keep out of the way and in the end, longed for the peace and quiet of their lonely and solitary home. Wishing for parents was better than having them. Thrace was all platitudes and their mother either monologues or silence. Both Mirella and Alley found life easier when they were home alone imagining their parents' return. The actual arrival had the girls standing outside on the front sidewalk watching a tornado blow through the house.

The night before they left, Thrace mentioned college and their futures. College was more than half a year away and Alley wondered if he were bringing it up now as a way of saying that he would see them after they had graduated. Advice was beyond their mother, however, as she was wearing flowers and of late seemed to have adopted a kind of commodious outer countenanc. She was all attempted hugs and kisses.

Off they went to Mexico, to candy making and waiting lovers.

Alley and Mirella got their peaceful household back for a month or two before the arguments began anew and continued intermittently over the next year even after Mirella graduated from Mrs. Wallace's and decided on a college major.

"Mother wasn't really able to be a parent," Mirella stated calmly.

"She didn't want to be a parent. She just didn't decide that until after she had two children," Alley corrected her sister.

"Three," Mirella corrected right back.

"Three then," Alley concurred.

"But do you ever think that having a brother was in our imagination?" Mirella asked, honestly unsure whether they had a brother or not.

"No."

"Well, do explain what happened to him," Mirella asked.

"He ran away and didn't come back," Alley told her sister.

"That's the obvious part, but where was the grief, the profound sorrow for losing your only son?"

That was in the heart that she left under the bed," Alley laughed.

"No, in the closet!" Mirella laughed too. "She left her heart in the closet in Cairo."

"Or no, where did they live before Cairo? In Atlanta," Alley concluded for both of them.

"Imagine how difficult it would be to live without so many things," Mirella softened again.

"Don't start again." Alley chided her; she could feel a fantasy coming.

"Don't start what?" Mirella knew.

"You know exactly what I'm talking about." Tracing their mother's whereabouts was a variation between an argument and a game that they had been playing for years. "I'd be willing to say that Mother hadn't had her heart for years before she had us."

"You'd say anything, the worst about Mother. Mother gave us so many things," Mirella started in. "We have her eyes, her skin, her hair, a love of walking."

"To follow her or get where we're going?" Alley teased.

"Even now, I still love a nice long walk."

"You like to leave your senses behind and these days, your legs too," Alley answered. Mirella hadn't walked anywhere in ages.

"Mother taught us many things just by example, and honestly, if you love yourself, you'd have to love our mother."

"What has one got to do with the other? So, by accident of birth we've some of her features. If we're lucky, we'll have none of her personality. Oops, I mean *personalities*," Alley added.

"But, you're like Mother in many ways." Mirella goaded Alley. She did resemble their mother more than Mirella.

"Frankly, I find myself quite a bit more charming than Mother. At least with me you'd get some interaction."

"Charm wasn't really where I was focusing."

"Surely not," Alley answered.

"Mother was never mean," Mirella went on.

"Not particularly sweet either."

"Don't you ever wonder what father saw?" Mirella asked.

"No."

"She must have seemed so bewildering to him. Can you see her standing amongst the trees on their mountain? He must have fallen for her at first sight." As Mirella spoke, Alley began humming a musical.

"Oh yes," Alley sang, "Lovely, flimsy, indecipherable and compelling, fruit from a tree, fish on a stick—oh my, I see my wife."

"It was enough."

"It wasn't anything really, accept your imagination."

"Do you ever wonder what she may have left behind in her childhood home?"

"No. Where was she from anyway? What was it? The Hill between Two Towns, The Town between Two Hills? The name is preposterous. She probably made it up with all her other stories." Alley snorted when she laughed.

"Where was father from?" Mirella asked.

"Which father?" Alley asked, "Pretend father or real one? Or do you mean the one who bought this house, paid for us to go to college, and makes it so that life is still comfortable now? Your job can't afford your life."

"Not yet maybe but wait and see."

Alley had absolutely no qualms about being supported by an absent father. He was paying for all the things that he cost them by moving away. Sure, they had come home quarterly in the beginning, less after that, and then never at all. They were grown now, and it had happened primarily outside their parents' watch. She and her sister were still tied together through habit and emotional necessity—ropes both real and imaginary. They fought constantly. The arguments were the paste that mashed them up against one another. Maybe they'd get to the bottom of their mother, maybe they'd understand why she had been as she was, but in the meantime, they'd reached a kind of détente.

They would not argue until one of them was angry, but rather just enough so that no one would get angry. Their emotional attachment to the data had waned over time. They were young, but in mannerism and dress, they were two spinsters—one nocturnal, one diurnal. The only time that the neighbors could have seen them together in public for longer than a moment was at dusk when they'd both come out to sit in their backyard.

No one had had more than a glimpse of day-lightened Alley in years. It wasn't that she never went out, because she did. She had gone to Mirella's graduation from Mrs. Wallace's and her graduation from college. Each time, Mirella had publicly presented Alley with the diploma or degree, which she had earned as much of as Mirella had. None but the two of them knew a truer statement as Alley had never stopped doing Mirella's course work. Mrs. Wallace's audience had been most gratified to have turned out such a lovely lady and of course, there may have been a sorrow or two about the lack of gifts that they would receive now that their most giving family had graduated.

At her college graduation, Mirella had received high honors and spent a little more time on the stage than any other young woman. Alley stood when asked and had taken her own bit of applause as the supportive family. Afterwards, they treated themselves to a fine dinner.

"Well, dear, dear daughters. What marvelous, marvelous daughters you are!" Alley raised her glass, doing a credible impression of their father.

"Why, yes. Professional, marvelous daughters, what a proud, proud father you've made me!" The two toasted themselves and smiled. "What was it father had begun to repeat over and over again in that funny little Mexican accent he acquired?" Both daughters could do an exact imitation of their father's speaking voice.

"Which things, as he always had plenty of . . ."

"A man can plant plenty of seeds in his life, sprinkle them about, let them sprout here and there, but the success of his children? Well, it's his children's successes that solidify his contribution to the world." Mirella had interrupted her sister.

"Proper first action prevents later forced reaction," Alley too imitated their father.

"Oh yes, and prosperity is truly sweet."

"A man's daughters can civilize his prosperity, turn it to sweetness and beauty. Daughters, prosperity does not only stand with money, but love and family," Mirella added her father's gestures.

"I wonder how he knew." Alley did truly wonder.

"Warm Mexicans and sweet candy must have made everything bearable."

"Except for missing his dear, dear daughters until he erected their two life-sized peppermint statues." Alley pictured their father sitting with their likenesses in his Mexican house.

"He did used to say one day we'd see ourselves, our likenesses in candy. You think we've been divvied up and eaten?" Mirella asked.

"Probably. Probably started a whole new business venture—your likeness in candy! We were his contribution to the world when we were still teenagers, maybe now we're his window on the planets." Alley wanted to add, "He can look through us, not at us," and then modified her thinking—father could look at us from a distance, through a telescope, but couldn't see us close-up. She laughed again and her sister joined her, rather warily as the unfunny would come next.

"Shape and mold everything you put your hands to," Alley sighed with the words.

"Sugar is paramount to syrup. Great syrup is tantamount to great candy. But the magic is in the stirring, the heating, and the mixing!" Mirella raised her water glass.

"A true secret can only be kept in a man's mind, not on paper, not in a whisper. Girls keep your own secrets," Alley quoted her father. "He practiced what he preached."

"All platitudes, maybe that was father's secret," Mirella claimed. "He had no secrets."

"Well, at least he didn't make them up."

"Don't start," Mirella warned her older sister. "Mother practiced transference."

"What's that supposed to mean?" Alley was genuinely curious.

"She tried to transfer her secrets to us."

"How exactly?" Alley was genuinely and momentarily curious.

"When she used to hold us, I think she held us so long because she was trying to tell us something she couldn't say."

"You mean like all the crazy stuff she did say," Alley put in.

"Are you ever going to give her anything?"

"Are you?" Alley answered.

"Some days."

"Would this be one of those days? You can give her a little credit on your graduation day when you're particularly happy or because you've excelled?"

"No, on the days when I pretend we had a different kind of upbringing."

"Why can't you just be nice to the woman in your imagination?" Alley answered.

"You know, I can't really imagine another mother. I take the same one and make her a better mother in small ways," Mirella answered.

"If nothing else, you give her credit for bringing us into the world?"

"No. I mean, I pick a moment and alter it."

"Please be concrete with our Mother. She was diaphanous enough without your imaginings," Alley said.

"Remember how she'd suck on pumpkin seeds for hours, leaving a mound of empty shells on a plate at her feet?"

"Yes."

"She used to call it something, she named it but I'm not sure..."

"Dumping. Salt absorbed and dissipated the ugliest memories, swallow the center, leave the empty shells, all the empty shells were a sign of newness, space to use. She always connected memory to salt, salt to tears, tears to memory, her favorite circle."

"I pretend..." Mirella attempted to begin.

"Remember how strange she used to look, squinting; her mouth pursed to kiss something ugly, probably from all the salt burning up her lips and mouth."

"I pretend that instead of ignoring us, she shared her seeds. I know they used to burn her," Mirella added quietly.

"I know you know. We tried it together. We ate twice as much as she did."

"I barely remember us eating any," Mirella said, surprised at herself.

"That's your problem. You're so busy trying to re-remember Mother that you forget yourself."

"Oh and not getting out of bed for years has given you marvelous things to remember," Mirella chided her sister.

"To tell you the truth, bed is very time consuming. It gives me plenty of time to practice not thinking about our Mother."

"Did practice make perfect?"

"Mostly, except when you drag her in," Alley was lying. "There must be thousands of other things to talk about."

"She is a thousand things, a million things. You ought to admit it."

"It doesn't matter as there are still a million other things that have nothing to do with her. Why not live on that other side?" For a moment, Alley let her plea stand.

"Why don't you?"

"I live in my mind and it travels."

"You've barely been further than the H in the front yard."

"See how you come right back around to where you've always been."

"Because I mention the yard?"

"You mention the one thing that you don't understand that's in the yard which is symbolic for not understanding Mother," Alley pointed out.

"And you do."

"She's all nonsense." Alley was not sure she could convince her sister.

"That's what you pretend."

"Maybe you ought to pretend, Mirella."

"That is what I'm doing. That's what I was trying to explain to you."

"For Christ's sake, Mirella, you want to pretend our mother was nice and sweet, sharing and caring. Why not use your wishes on yourself? Pretend you're a successful lady graduate, secure out in the world."

"I don't have to pretend to be that."

"Yes," Alley paused, "you do." Alley said it with such surety that Mirella was quieted.

Alley liked her bed. She just didn't discover this fact until she'd lain in it for months in hope of attention or possible rescue. She should have known that her reclusion from the world would not have produced the desired results. Her mother welcomed her to her bed and her father hadn't crossed the threshold of her bedroom since he'd had the furniture delivered and arranged. She had been forced to stay abed in defiance, stubbornness, and mental exhaustion too. Not so much for all the thinking she had done, but for the thinking she had refused to do.

In bed, where she had mostly spent the last seven years, she discovered herself. She had spent herself cheaply and only now began to wonder if being born to a woman with multiple personalities meant that she'd been left without a personality at all. She had no pressing reason to get up.

She hadn't felt any particular way about anything. She argued with Mirella because she had always argued with Mirella, but as far as feeling possessive or proud of any one argument? Frankly, she did not. Generally, she occupied the stance that Mirella hadn't. She wanted Mirella to accept their parents and it wasn't an argument so much as a standard. Be clear. All attempts to muddle met with the wall that Alley had sturdily built. Her conversations with Mirella were not arguments so much as corrections.

Their parents had abandoned them, and they'd done so even when they still lived together. This was the sum total of things and Alley had no compulsion to do anything other than host facts. As a matter of record, she had no compulsion to do anything whatsoever, so far. She knew that one could always eventually get to anything—or not. Strangely, she was more energetic than quite a few people who spent a fraction of the amount of time she spent in bed. If she had been compared to her sister, she may have come out on the upper end of energy and ability as though Mirella had collected all the assignments to and for school, Alley was the one who had made them a fait accompli.

She spent her mornings listening to the repetitive music of an awakening house and that was only after she had felt the slight temperature fluctuations of night turning to day. Alley would have known the time without a clock as she had learned to feel the coolest point of night when absolutely still, turn toward the infinitely slow surge of warming light. The house creaked at first light, caught by the subtle deprivation of constant cover as night pulled away.

19

The Family Boxes

Unbeknownst to his children, Thrace did think of them, allowing himself a moment or two here and there. He did so in his office in Mexico surrounded by things he loved—small bronze statuettes, used soft leather, and polished stone. In the drawer to his left amongst other papers, were letters he had started to his children, old bills that resisted itemization, repairs that needed inspecting, and his carefully wrapped copy of *"The Curiously Successful Negro."* They were together in his drawer of to-dos. He thought of his son more often than his daughters and wondered if he had turned out a Thrace after all—tall, fairly handsome, accomplished, and even tempered. He wondered if he was proud of himself and whether that was justified. Was he self-contained and without need, restrained, forward thinking, and emotionally intelligent? No one could contest his love for his son. Love between father and son, as he knew, was an incorruptible thing that didn't require nearness or conversation, threading or stitching, it was whole cloth. An unbending, unchanged line followed his grandfather to his father to him on down to his own son. Yes, he'd certainly love to see his son and prove himself right.

He hadn't put together a consortium of successful Negro families as his father and grandfather surely wished. He hadn't discovered if the "bank" once founded and protected by the families continued to function. He'd joined two families on the list, his own and his wife's and he'd leave his son to perhaps meet his own father's wishes. Many of the families may have resisted change, wedded as they'd always been to backyard accomplishment and quiet accumulation. A factory may have been far too conspicuous an enterprise for some of them, even in Mexico. Others probably still had a small fortune. For them, a bank was not a building with a vault, but rather an umbrella for a hundred small enterprises, not only a collection of currency, a collection of workers, able strong men, some highly skilled, builders, glass workers, distillers, electricians, designers and most, literate and papered. Old Lady Jack had told him that it all began with a chance meeting, like most things. She said something about Lloyd Earl and a blacksmith. Macomb was not the start. He was nearer to the end.

Clifton Maxwell Thrace, III hadn't done his research. His preoccupation with the daughter of the family had gotten in the way. For if he had known about his wife's family, he'd have known that he had married into a dynasty greater than the dreams of both his father and grandfather. If his wife hadn't appeared like an ancient temptress, taking over all with her beauty.

Indeed, Lloyd Earl had collected and amassed a fortune. As he walked and pushed and pulled his wares from town to town under the protection of the "ubiquitous old darkie with a broken-down wagon" and the easement of the white man that he had invented, he put together a portfolio of real estate and other goods.

Lloyd Earl's father had known a Lord Earl and named his son after a man that he'd eased to his death. He hadn't helped him die, he'd eased his path with a bed, food, and his ability to listen. Lord Earl died after telling all his stories and left his bag. Lloyd Earl's father had come across a deed in Lord Earl's bags and spent his time learning to copy it exactly. He'd let his little son, Lloyd Earl watch and trace and create many more. He'd let Lord Earl teach Lloyd Earl lots of things before he died. Comebacks was one of the things Lord Earl liked to talk about. He said banks and royals were thieves but in different ways.

"After you spent your life paying for something, the comeback was when it went back to the family you'd bought it from in the first place. That was the difference between here and where he was from. He'd told Lloyd Earl, but when you've loaned someone the funds to get something, when they finished, they need to give back and the comeback ought to come back to you."

Lloyd Earl found another version of a deed in one of the books he'd collected to shore up Selsie's big table. Unbeknownst to her or anyone else, Lloyd Earl could read and write. He had read every book, piece of paper, sign, dollar, or letter that came his way. His father had taught him both reading and writing and by example, had shown him the pleasures of an erudite man who kept his learning and pleasure to himself. Lloyd Earl had started the family trait of walking.

He had walked way further than when he used to follow Selsie up into the woods.

Lloyd Earl walked in his own shoes over his lifetime from South Carolina to Tennessee, Alabama to Mississippi, and even Kentucky. Surely, he'd first walked all over the state of Georgia, his birth state. While he was walking with his broken-down wagon and white man sanctions, he bought up land, houses, and livestock. He even owned a hotel for a time. The Dumas Hotel, in Washington, DC, where black folk migrating up north used to stay, where white folk lodged their darkies when they traveled with them. He had tried to get Selsie to move but that was generally when she made him some "change his mind" sausages. He had had to walk away from Selsie many times in their married life. He always came back. He had a house over in another Georgia city, where he had bought the land patents straight from the government and paid good money too. He had bought most of his land with cash, saved from all the jobs of his endless amount of industry and most of the time, if he were going to live in his house, he'd built it partly with his own hand and partly with the same group of men and their sons who always built everything for each other.

He'd resisted when the Freedman's Savings Bank came along, wanting to hold onto Negro money. The bank he used with his other colleagues had no name, place, or building that anyone knew except for the gentlemen who had added their skills or funds, whichever they could spare. Lloyd Earl had been the founder. Sometimes, he double deeded his property to protect it from the white men who might want to take it. After he bought property, he'd save the original and do up another deed. The first Lord Earl, a white man come over from England, sanctioned by the queen, had decided that his darkie had earned a parcel. Sometimes, it'd be left to Lloyd Earl by the original Lord Earl's wife after they both died. He could sign Lord Earl's name the same as he had.

Lloyd Earl knew that whites had a special place for more uppity whites. Once, he was even asked if he'd taken his old master's name to which Lloyd Earl answered "absolutela" so proud that the white man asking him laughed, shook his head, and gave him back "his right to be walking around as he pleased" papers.

When he was older, one of the last things Lloyd Earl did was buy up the land under the darkies that lived in Georgia in the town closest to him and Selsie. He bought up the land for the church and the cemetery and nobody minded 'cause it was him and Selsie, trustworthy darkies that they already knew.

Lloyd Earl put his deeds and whatnot in a box and put them in the corner of the kitchen/library that he'd built for Selsie. He told her that if ever there was a good man to enter this family, the box was for him.

"She ain't gonna marry," Selsie told him about their own daughter.

"Maybe her daughter gonna marry a man, gonna walk around, gonna understand my box."

Selsie laughed. "You ain't nothing but an ole box yourself Lloyd Earl."

"Box within a box, just you remember to tell somebody, somebody right. Just 'cause you can cook don't mean you a good judge a character."

"Got you, didn't I?"

"That was more my doing than yourn."

"Lloyd Earl, I been poisoning you toward love since I saw you looking at me when I was slaving up to Scilla Landry."

"That's when I vow not to eat your food 'til I know you loves me, but I already knew how I felt. I was waitin' for you."

"Lloyd Earl, I snuck some weeds down your well." Selsie laughed and smiled her under smile, the one with her head down and her eyes up, concentrated on his face, over at him.

"I ain't never used that well, so somebody else use to love you besides me."

"You mine. Don't care how you believe it happen."

"You ought to want to know somebody love you you can't control."

"You ought to eat some of this food and keep on doing as you doing."

Selsie never gave Lloyd Earl's box to anybody. She couldn't give nothing Lloyd Earl ever touched to anyone. Everything she knew about she kept until she died, wearing his boots, asleep in their bed, probably a hundred years old. She joked that having Lloyd Earl's things all around was like sleeping with a skinny uncomfortable ghost. She used to make Aberdeen get off Earl's side of the bed.

"You settin' on Earl," she'd say. "Can't nobody set on Earl but me." She seemed to think this was particularly funny and would laugh herself on into the evening, thinking about Lloyd Earl. "Lloyd Earl gonna ease me out this earth."

Somebody did ease her, but not from the bed. Selsie walked out of the house and never returned.

Henry Olmstead Dagomire Macomb got the box, right after he got Aberdeen and she decided to give it to him. She wasn't moving off the mountain either. He walked the path Lloyd Earl created, checking on his property the way a good son should, collecting rents, making repairs, putting the earnings away for his family, spending what was needed, never telling a soul. When his daughter followed him, he thought he'd found the next generation, but she wouldn't listen whenever he tried to talk. He told her about her legacy, but she didn't care. Maybe it'd be her husband, maybe not. The issue had remained unsettled for him until his grandson came home. Max the Black would get the box and know what to do. He'd give him Lloyd Earl's original notes and Dag's too.

It would always remain a close argument between the sisters as Alley's ability to hear the voices of the house certainly surpassed her sister's. Though she could have told her when a mouse crept through the basement, Mirella happened to be passing through the front of the house on route upstairs with a glass of juice from the kitchen which gave her the vantage point of being able to see out the front door and clear to the sidewalk. She saw the man with the suitcase loitering out in front of the house, but it was also true that Alley heard the first footfall of his boot on the porch before her sister. When the stranger knocked, each of them peeked, retreated, and said nothing to the other.

Over the course of a day or two, the stranger had knocked, waited a while, left, not given up but had come again and again, knocking a little more insistently and waiting for longer periods before he went away which afforded the sisters more opportunity to get a look at him. A neighbor had assured him that they were at home, which didn't mean they would necessarily answer the door.

Alley believed that the stranger's very steadfastness proved that he was her suitor sent by her father.

Mirella used the hours to stick the idea into her head that

her father had sent her the patient and quiet type of man that he would want for her husband.

Each hour, the sisters embellished their conclusions without the slightest support from reality.

On day one, both girls suffered the simultaneous kismet of discovering their father had not only thought of them in a touching and intimate way, but had provided them the cure to the loneliness that neither of them had registered suffering. Their father thought of them personally and must have sorted and sifted through many young men to find the most suitable husband. Alley remembered her only dance with father at Mrs. Wallace's long ago, when he had put her hand in the hand of another man. Was it a prelude to now?

Alley had known that it was purely the work of her father, but Mirella believed that Mother had also gotten involved with such a very special choice and together interviewed potential gentlemen over dinner and various other social rituals to determine utmost suitability.

Tall, broad, and reasonably well dressed, the man could be expected to work very hard while being very gentle. Broad arms meant he would support his wife and free her from her father. He'd be a man who'd love all his, perhaps many, children and always be near.

Alley felt a tickle in her legs and when she was sure her sister wouldn't notice, she held up her dresses and danced around her room, pretending to hear music with her fiancé. In her fantasy, he put his hand in the curve of her back and whispered not too closely into her ear. His plans were concrete, and he discussed them with Alley before putting them in place. He thought the wedding should be small and Alley would make it beautiful.

Their suitor moved his right leg onto the porch first which clearly stated that he was meant for Alley who was right-handed. He carried his suitcase back and forth each time. He was strong and only a physically strong man would do for Mirella. He wore a hat which covered his head, 'sensible as can be' suited Alley. His eyes were probably brown.

Mirella had instantly known that she was the chosen sister as she, at least, had some sense of the world. Surely, both their parents had found her the easier bride. She was well educated, young, professional, and when she realized that all the same adjectives applied to her sister, she began to think of attributes which would distinguish her. She believed she had done a little more thinking about cooking than her older sister. She found herself better at forgiving, more easily disposed to happiness. She felt she had the more modern ear when it came to musical tastes, and companionability as she mainly kept normal hours. She didn't imagine much but when she did, could not imagine being second in her parents' thoughts.

The gentleman seemed quite tall and as Alley was the tallest sister when they stood together, they would look better. She was the oldest which of course followed tradition and though her sister had been out in the world she had warmed the hearth so to speak; clearly, she was more open to a husband.

Finally, each sister imagined being courted in their equally fantastic ways, but they hadn't ever been without each other, so each pictured her gentleman taking her to the cinema and bringing her sister along. The courting sister would sit between her fiancé and her sister. At the moment, both sisters were exceedingly happy. They had indulged themselves long enough to abandon the fear of their fantasies not being true.

Alley dug through the crust to find her heart. The crust had built up a silent layer of indifference that, until now, had blanketed her undisturbed flesh. Now, freshly awakened, Alley begin to consider the nightly duties of a wife and felt certain that she could pay. She'd give herself freely and outdo her sister who probably imagined being coaxed rather than swept away.

Mirella, too, had been examining her own flesh and its appeal to a man. The value was hidden, waiting to be discovered like an unfolding mystery. Mirella would outdo her sister by holding onto her secret until it was wrenched away piece by tiny piece. She felt herself falling over before falling asleep.

In the morning, they each went on with their regular day. Only Alley had grown far more used to the imaginings of nights and while Mirella slept, she used more time to prepare herself for a man in their life.

After a couple of days of having a stranger appear, disappear, and reappear at their door, the sisters were ready to answer. When they arrived at the threshold at the same moment, each registered the other's alarm but opted for full speed ahead, satisfying themselves that everything would all be sorted out properly when the courtship began. They opened the door together and both stood expectantly on the other side waiting to be chosen.

"Abigail? Tremaine?" Their gentleman had brown eyes, luscious lashes and a very slim gap between his two front teeth. Neither of them had imagined the first words and neither of them knew what words to say back so they didn't speak.

"Abigail? Tremaine?" They each wondered if he had been clever and thoughtful enough to have already known their names. Still, neither said a word. Then finally, Alley put her hand out and Mirella immediately followed her, not wanting it to appear that she hadn't thought about extending her hand in welcome at the very same moment.

"Allerima"

"Mirella," each curtsied almost imperceptibly.

"Surely, you've stopped the ridiculousness of those names?" The gentleman reached out his hand, returning first one shake and then the other as he spoke, half incredulously.

"You're not still the backwards and forwards twins of one another with those ridiculous names, are you?"

Suddenly, he looked not so handsome and quite odd. Both sisters had the passing sliver of an idea that he may be more suitable the other.

Furthermore, his voice was a little higher than expected

and neither of them understood what he kept saying.

By now, Umm II had heard the commotion and appeared in the front hallway from wherever she generally lurked when she was in the house. Alley and Mirella were slightly annoyed that she had insinuated herself into such an intimate situation. But Umm II saw instantly what neither of them could imagine. She could see the similarity between the three people standing in the hallway.

"The boy, your missing boy," she whispered, realizing she could not recall his name.

"Maxwell Clifton Thrace, the Fourth," he extended his hand to his old housekeeper. The girls were even more astonished, and strangely, very angry.

When he realized that neither of them seemed inclined to speak nor was the least bit ashamed of not wanting to speak, he thought he ought to say something. He turned and pulled his bag in from the front porch.

His sisters' faces blanched, and they stepped back in an odd unison.

Umm II reached out, welcomed him in and promised to make him something to eat. She disappeared and Alley and Mirella were disturbed at her exit as they had been at her entrance.

"Please call me Max," and once again he reached for his oldest sister and then the younger one. "You must be Tremaine and you're Abigail." Again, they made no response. "I'm Max, your brother."

Finally, Mirella felt she understood something that her sister didn't. He was naming them, calling them by the names that he remembered from their childhood. He told them that they weren't twins and Mirella, ahead of her sister, realized that he was talking to himself, attempting to explain things to himself.

Curtly, she answered, "No, we are not." They had never been twins.

"Surely, your names?" Again, they were both mystified and reverted to silence.

Some Questions Just Don't Get Answered

Perhaps it was the distance—the journey traveled backwards from the brink of love—but neither Alley nor Mirella made easy transitions. Umm II saved the day by readying the proffered meal and guiding their brother into the kitchen. Each of them retreated to her room not to reappear at all that evening.

Nor did either of them make an appearance the next day, nor the one after that. They heard him creeping around. He seemed to have picked the most suitable place in the house to camp himself, down the hall in the direction of their parents' bedroom. Neither of the girls spent much time at that end of the hallway. Alley disliked his intrusions and the noises he added to the house. He used bathrooms no one else did and walked around in places where no one had for years.

Mirella and Alley were used to tolerating unwanted guests. They began to take their meals alone again in Alley's bedroom.

The idea of being unwelcome by his sisters hadn't occurred to Max the Black. He thought he remembered them loving him, he thought they would want to know everything he had come prepared to tell them. Most excruciatingly of all, he remembered what it was to be ignored by everyone in the house. Fortunately, feeling sorry for himself redoubled his desire to get to know his sisters and for them to know him. He had a need to share, and they were the only other adults he'd presumed would be interested.

From the living room, he started calling their names, or at least, the names he knew were originally theirs, "Abigail and Tremaine." He began to change the cadence with which he called and where it began as a chant, it turned to music and when nothing worked, Max the Black called them by the names they called themselves.

"Alley, Mirella!"

For reasons that he couldn't understand, they marched down the stairs and into the living room, summoned as they had been to their mother's bedroom. He had so much to tell them he didn't know how or where to begin. Before he could decide, he blurted out the facts. They tumbled out, one over the other, causing only confusion.

"I visited our parents in Mexico." Max said and his words to his sisters, would release his mother's words in his head.

"There was a monster on our mountain. Not an ordinary creature, a compilation of cruelty, death, the things that happen in families, meant to be secrets that hide until they can cause the most harm. For us, my family, I guess it's the things that we refused to leave to God. Vengeance and such. In every case," She never finished her sentences, he remembered.

"I went to Mexico, sat with our parents." he smiled, "They were quite formal, but seemed very happy. Mother was completely changed, and they were very happy that I had come to see them and asked about you, if I had been back to see you too." He paused for a bit, trying to gauge their interest.

"For them, it almost seemed as if it were an ordinary day. A son they hadn't seen since he was ten knocked on their door."

"I wanted to prove that I was intelligent, talented, and capable of being a successful man. Show them myself . . . I told them I was headed to law school." His sisters' odd and distant behavior made him a little boy again. "I . . . anyway."

"The strongest things that linger in memory begin with acts of cruelty. For our family, the beginnings were long ago with Grandmother Selsie. Like me, she had a hard time accepting the world as it was, and she needed help carrying the weight of awfulness. It wasn't just the things she saw but truthfully what she did. White men's cruelty started it and we didn't have to follow suit, but we did. We were vulnerable in ways that we didn't understand. It connects us. This story starts with burying things and will end that way too. But son, I am whole now, and all the memories are here, in my own heart and mind. I can put them away properly now, like my mother, finally, like Selsie," Mother told him in Mexico.

He began again.

"Our family's not large but is very wealthy and very secretive. We own a plantation in Georgia, all the land where the black folks live and more down from The Hill between Two Towns, even the property underneath the church and the cemetery. All the documents are on the mountain. I grew up with our grandparents and . . ." Max kept talking.

He seemed to have found a rhythm. But for his sisters, he was speaking a foreign language. If he got everything out, they might pick up a strain and he could go from there, but they seemed uninterested in anything he had to say. They had already convened, ruled, and decided the matter. Then it hit him. His sisters had been summoned; they expected a story, not a dialogue. He would provide one as soon as he figured out where to start.

"Our mother ran away from the mountain. She often did as a young girl. I ran away too. But our mother wanted to know where her father, our grandfather went. She thought he had another family where he fathered other children or had something that pulled him away. I think I ran away to find somebody to raise me. Anyway, she used to send

packages back home—pieces of herself that our grandmother never opened, keeping them for when our mother
might come back to claim them. When I came, after a while,
she gave them to me. I opened our mother's packages."
Their expressions had not moved.

"Well, first, maybe I should tell you some things about our
ancestors. Our grandmother and our great-great-grandmother between them did what they had to, to protect what
was ours. A building, a legacy that our great-great-grandfather
built for our family."

The sisters' practiced ritual came into play. Right at the
word "ancestors." They stopped listening and if their brother had stayed around for the rest of his childhood, he, too,
would have learned the art of tuning out their mother's
voice, the same skill they now employed on him. A small
part of them may have wanted to know what he had to say,
but instead they sat there, honestly wondering how long he
intended to stay.

So what if there mother ran away and sent packages
home? 'Was it our mother or our grandmother who smokes
and killed a man?' They wanted to know but didn't have the
stomach for someone rearranging and fragmenting their
history. Truth or not, it would only alienate them from the
life they had so carefully put into place. In Alley's bedroom
later, they laughed and reaffirmed their togetherness.

"Was our grandfather a bigamist?"

"Maybe more long-lost brothers will show up." They each
felt the other's very cold shiver and made a lousy attempt to
laugh some warmth back into the room.

"One murdered for property, the other for—what did he
say?" Alley asked.

"I didn't hear him say, but if there is so much property down
there perhaps, he has a place to live and is only visiting."

"Did you hear him say something about visiting our parents in Mexico?"

"Perhaps we should ask about the statues?" Mirella wondered.

"Did you hear him say they welcomed him? No apologies.

They have absolved themselves of abandoning their three children." Alley wasn't surprised.

"Goodness, you heard a lot more than I did," Mirella noticed.

"Just dribbles and bits," Alley said.

Max the Black sat in the living room wondering what went wrong. He had imagined them surprised, happy, and anxious to see him. He thought they would be terribly interested in all he had learned and could tell them about their family, though he had promised not to tell them about Mother's surprise.

"My own son, "she gently reached for and held his hand. "I'm going to travel to Washington, DC, soon. I'm merely gathering myself. I can only imagine how my own children couldn't have any feelings or understanding for me. I'd like to explain but more than that, I'd like to bury the past and start anew. I'm sure it's possible—maybe I should say hope—I hope it's possible. I think I know how to try. You being here makes me want to try. Thank you, son. Thank you for coming."

Then he remembered how shaken he had been by his parents' attitude. He was the one who had realized that they had absolved themselves of abandonment and he hadn't liked it either. They were so easygoing and happy, his mother fully conversant, friendly, easily given to laughter. She acted as if she'd only seen him just the other day and all four of them—the Thraces, Alana, and Porter—sat around the table focused on him. He could barely tell which two were a couple. They almost made him doubt his own memory. The woman was his strange, package sending, inaudible mother? He remembered the largest packages, the last ones she sent were empty.

His grandmother had been the one to recommend his visit. Somehow, she knew that when his mother stopped sending pieces of herself, she'd finally ordered enough of the past to live with a future. His grandmother told him that his mother had found a way to put all the memories in place. Aberdeen told him that, "Somewhere within the disease, generally lives the cure." She'd told him that one couldn't survive without the other.

He'd made a mistake with his sisters, telling them something that no one would want to know. Maybe he should have started with Aberdeen. But they hadn't been interested in him, their parents, or their grandparents. He sat in the living room wondering how in the world to reach them.

What could he say that would spark something in them? He had tried too hard to tell them all the things that he had wanted to know. He had been with them for days now. Looking out the windows of his room, he remembered how he had stalked his own mother, following behind her in Rock Creek Park. He chose to watch her from the woods and treetops, while she walked along the trails. Up in a tree one morning, watching her pass beneath his feet as he gazed downward, he suddenly knew that he'd never find out anything, following her. She was a sealed entity. In the tree, he had decided to run away, to find his grandparents, to stalk his mother from a distance.

He'd never told anyone, not even his grandmother, and it was a funny thing now to admit to himself. Once again, he felt that he needed a conduit to get him the thing that he most currently desired. He wanted his sisters' attention, their interest, to have picnics, sit around together, eating, and laughing. Maybe he should start with today and move backwards, tell them about himself first and then wait until they asked before he went anywhere else.

The next evening, he summoned his sisters again, calling out the ridiculous names they used for themselves.

"Congratulations to you both. I heard you graduated from college. I did as well; in fact, I'm headed to law school now. Our grandparents were very kind to me, uh I mean well, nice things have happened for me too," he practiced.

At least his voice came from inside his body instead of outside the window. Alley had the feeling that he wanted to tell them something he wasn't saying. He kept calling them and when they came, he began to mumble stuff that no one wanted to hear. He wanted something he didn't know how to ask them. Alley decided to help. Being continuously summoned by him was frankly a little too strange.

"What is it that you're having so much trouble trying to say?" She politely asked him. Once again, he blurted out, not the words he wanted to say, but the ones that found their way fastest.

"I have a small son; would you like to meet him?" He turned redder and flustered, "He's hardly any trouble but I need well..."

"Yes, we'd love to meet him. Where is he?"

"He doesn't really have a mother. It's been all up to me. I haven't told anyone. His mother left. She just disappeared. It would only be for a time but..."

"Go and get him." Alley stopped him, understanding now why he had seemed so strange. He needed them.

For some odd reason, he wanted them to understand his circumstance. He was a veritable font and once he started on himself, had a hard time stopping. Mirella and Alley glanced between one another, deciding to listen a little.

"Had you ever heard our mother speak of another family that lived in the woods. Their name was Jessup. I ran away with a Jessup daughter. I knew it was wrong before I even left the only place I'd ever loved in my life after Egypt." He heard himself talking.

"Jessup and I grew up together..."

And not saying... "In bed how I prayed she wouldn't come, or that I'd sleep through the signal, or my grandfather's words would still me. One night, I ignored her. She came again and again. When she was around I—I lost. I could do things, things that wouldn't ever enter my mind. It didn't start that way but... Anyway, I was headed to college, I was headed off the mountain. Our grandparents had done everything to help me go to school and Jessup promised to take care of everything if I took her with me. She needed to get off the mountain and she would have done anything to leave ..."

He kept telling his sisters the mundane, easy to say details of his predicament, his mind wondered over the other, the details that couldn't be voiced. She had put her arms around him and moved him into her. She wore those flowered dresses, and she could awaken and stir him from across the room. She was beautiful, she had grown into her beauty, startlingly, one Wednesday or Tuesday, after school. He lost himself in it, in her, left consciousness, only to open his eyes lying next to her curled up like a spoon with her hand reaching behind her body, holding him like he was hers.

"I don't know how to travel home or what to bring. Beauty gives me strength. Maybe just some Mexican flowers. Would your sisters love Mexican flowers?"

After that, he followed her easily as if pulled by an invisible noose. Fortunately, she had led him to school and in the beginning, she had kept her word in the small room she kept immaculately, cooked, cleaned, and gave him leave. She stayed under him until she became accustomed to the city and then she began to stray. She covered more and more territory and stayed away for longer and longer periods of time. She claimed to walk all day. Max the Black went to school without worry and excelled. He had begun to recover, freed from her bonds, and happy to be alone. Then she would return and take possession of his will.

During one of her reclamations, she had declared herself pregnant. During the pregnancy, she stayed away so long that Max would start to forget. She came back for the delivery, behaved as a mother would for a few months, and then changed. Her dress was different, and she wondered aloud why anyone would ask two college students to keep a baby in their care. He told her that she wasn't a student, and no one had asked. She'd stop for moments and then become even more estranged from him and the baby. She was so unrecognizable that he wondered why she came home at all.

Then she stopped. He hadn't seen her in quite some time. An old neighbor had come to his rescue.

Anyway, here he was. But he didn't plan to stay. He only needed some time, long enough to get adjusted to law school, find a place to live, a job, and someone to help with his son, Dagger. The boy was named for their grandfather.

He retrieved the little boy from his old neighbor, helped settle him into the house and went off to school. His old neighbor would have taken care of Dagger forever if age didn't prevent it. She had lost most of her sight and her hearing.

Dagger was an odd, two-year-old sad little thing, standing around in a way that could only be described as "factual." He simply existed without explanation, and yet something was so recognizable in him that his aunts, first one and then the other, fell for him with a passion that they hadn't ever known. He looked just like them. He was unformed and innocent, yet concrete enough in his little ways to wholly submerge them. He had their skin and coloring, a few freckles and crazy hair. Tiny little perfect teeth could be seen if they could get him to smile. He didn't speak much.

"He has my hair." Alley peered down at the top of the little boy's head.

"Uncombed yes, but," Mirella gently tugged a few strands, "same color and texture as mine."

"He's too quiet, we'll noisy him up," Alley said.

"Maybe he's a contemplative little boy and needs to be," Mirella offered.

"He doesn't know what he needs and neither do I," Alley said, looking over at her sister with a funny smile and waited.

"You're," Mirella paused, "right," slipped out.

"Let's find out what children like to eat, and then we can figure out what it is they need to eat." Alley walked down the hallway into their father's study. Mirella followed her.

When Alley opened the door, Mirella looked around for the first time in years after she'd stopped sneaking in and using his chair. She had spared herself the memory scents of him and clearly, needn't have bothered. Alley had taken over and rather than their father's old leather and whatever the smelly stuff he used to use on his small metal creatures was, the room smelled like Alley.

"The books are all in here."

Alley noticed that if she left the room, Dagger followed her wherever she went. Sometimes, the two of them would just walk around the house. Alley called herself getting him used to his new home. After a bit, he caught up, reached up, and held her hand.

They fixed their brother's room for the boy, turned it into a playland. They couldn't bear to let him sleep alone, so they took turns having him one night with one aunt and the next night with the other. Dagger was a dry thirsty sponge even at the tender age of two and happily soaked up any and everything that came his way.

Alley didn't bathe until her sister came home because Dagger didn't like to be alone.

Aunt Alley and Aunt Mirella began to form plans around the thousand things they now had to do. Dagger needed everything, clothing and lessons, food and school, cars and college funds, and above all, the love his two aunts had in them. Once corked, it now spilled out all over him.

"Dagger, you don't want to go anywhere, do you?"

"Dagger's going to stay with his aunts forever and ever."

"Dagger has two moms, Auntie Mirella and Auntie Alley."

"Auntie El and Em" was all Dagger could manage and that was enough. His aunts had invited their brother to stay in school, study hard, and leave Dagger to them, an easily accepted proposition. Auntie Em worked outside the house and Auntie El worked within it, and together they were an obsessively happy family.

They used Dagger to give themselves the childhood they had wanted. They doted upon his every expression, loved him in a big noisy obvious way, telling him all the time so that he couldn't forget.

Dag ran through the house yelling Auntie EmanEl, Auntie EmanEl! He awakened one morning in Auntie Em's room and the next in Auntie El's. If he awakened before his aunts, he'd run downstairs, make as much noise as he could and then hide. He always hid in the same place, under the cushions in the window boxes where unbeknownst to him, his grandmother used to hug his aunts and daddy. Auntie El and Em would pretend they couldn't find him and would be forced to cry through breakfast. Auntie Mirella was better at the fake wailing than Auntie Alley. Her moaning sounded anguished, and she could produce real tears. Auntie Alley always ruined it because looking at Auntie Em made her laugh.

"We'll have to throw all the ice cream and toys in the backyard."

"All the clothing and trucks, the blocks and coloring books too. What about the crayons and paper?"

"Oh, what a strange tree we might grow, but Dag won't be here to see our tree made of him." They'd both start to cry and then Dag would pop up by the windows.

"Don't make me a tree, I want to be a boy."

They'd hug him and promise. Kiss him and skip around the kitchen hands in hands.

It wasn't the least bit difficult to decide what to do when another stranger came knocking. They didn't even have to talk about it. First, Auntie El and Auntie Em dug a hole in the back of their consciousness to have a place to put unwanted things where they belonged, in holes covered over with dirt, shoveled in a most particular way.

They behaved exactly as they had the first time a stranger came to the door with one important difference. On the second day, they gave Umm II approximately a week's vacation.

This stranger wore a dress and had a suitcase too but rather than carry it away, she left the case on the porch on the first day. No heave-hoeing back and forth.

After a day or two, Mirella and Alley lifted the suitcase into the house, hopefully making their own statement to the stranger who must have noticed the disappearance. They went through the case, nothing but dried up flowers, a sweater, and a dress that seemed more suited to an older woman. The flowers had a cloying floral sent as if baked in in a tropical place. There were a few other oddities, as well. An empty box, a prescription that described the drug but not the name of the person who needed the medication. A smallish pair of old mountain hiking-looking shoes.

"Who could it be?" Mirella asked.

"Do we really want to know?" Alley made her think.

"This stuff doesn't prove anything. There's more dirt and dried flowers in the bottom," Mirella showed Alley.

"It's not as if she'd pack her identification. You need it to travel around," Alley answered.

In the evening, they peeked out the window and each took a long look at the woman, but it was dark and she was hard to see. They didn't want to turn on the porch light or whoever it was would know that they were watching. She was stately, and of indeterminate age. Truthfully, she was beautiful in a rather insensitive kind of way; she could hold her superiority over lesser lights. Certainly, she would be easy to dislike, and the sisters decided not to bother at all, to never answer the door. They extended Umm II's vacation another few days in the hopes that their caller would simply stop calling.

Then, they went out back together, took up shovels and began to dig a hole in the backyard without uttering a single word. Simply, Alley started on one end, Mirella on the other. Every night, after singing Dag to sleep, they went out back and dug deeper and deeper.

"What if we find treasure?"

"We already have the most amazing treasure we'll ever have."

"Is it six feet by six feet?"

"Deeper. Let's make it ten feet deep."

Perhaps she wanted her bag back and that's why she wouldn't go away. They would return the bag but she'd have to come around back in the evening to get it. They didn't put all these details in the note. They knew asking her to come so late seemed silly, but they had confirmed that her bag and "all" of her belongings would be waiting. Furthermore, they wanted Dag to be firmly asleep.

There was no reason for him to see any strangers. If indeed, she came back that evening as planned, small direction arrows would be waiting. She'd have to come all the way to the door to see the note.

"The front lock is broken, please come to the back door."

Two arrows, one on the door, one on the side of the house lead their knocker around back.

Auntie El and Auntie Em waited in the dark kitchen after having tucked Dagger into bed. They left him in his room on the other side of the house, promising that they'd both check on him later. He was a good hard sleeper like any two-year-old after a long day.

They heard the sounds they expected—fumbling, tripping over clay pots, and one final thud. They waited for silence and then stepped out the back door with shovels in hand. They picked up the soft dirt edging their fresh deep hole and the suitcase with its dried flowers, sweater, oddities, mountain lint, and mountain shoes and dumped shovelful by shovelful back in the ground. In the dark, they buried their hole.

"Did you try the shoes on?" Alley asked.

"Why would I do that?"

"You and Mother wore the same size, I just thought of it."

"What?"

"They looked about your size," Alley said, smirking.

"Don't be silly? And what would make you think of Mother?" Mirella asked her sister.

"Truthfully, I have no idea."

As they worked, odd things loosened and unyoked from around them, things they'd probably held too closely for too long. Alley and Mirella couldn't quite tell what they were covering in dirt. With one thing, came others—good and bad memories unconnected to things they could under-stand; ties that they may have honored; arguments about the woman who had them—and they cleared a pathway to the future.

Burying things was enormously freeing.

At first.

Acknowledgments

Without my friend and walking partner, Dr. Debony Hughes, I wouldn't have known about Bold Story Press! Clearly much appreciation is owed to her and, of course, thanks go to the team at Bold Story, including Emily Barrosse, Karen Gulliver, Julianna Scott Fein, and Laurie Entringer, who made the process a very good one. Salimah Perkins was the most fantastic editor that anyone could have. Her attention to detail, persistence, and understanding were essential. She made this story better.

This book has been a long time coming. For that reason, there are so many people over the years who broadened my horizons . . . The Holey Roaders was my first writing group and the memories of our times together, their helpful criticism, and culture stays with me. And I've been breaking bread with the Dreamy Dining Divas (Sonio Ali, Nicole Blake, Tracene Davis, Debony Hughes, and Sheila Williams) once a month for more than twenty years. These dinners and our friendships sustain us!

And there is always family. My mother, who took forever to read my first book (some time ago), regularly pressed me to know when she would receive this one. I'm so very lucky in the sense that all of the people I love know that I love them. I'm the better for it!

Finally, dear reader, should you have the desire, ability, and kindness, please take a moment using your words of mouth and your favorite pens to review this book, send a copy to friends, and add your review to Amazon! These days, one needs quite a lot of help getting the good word out!

From me . . . more is coming your way.

Vailes

Vailes Shepperd grew up with a love of words: Words first, then stories, and inevitably books. Thank goodness for her grandmother's library. She is happiest in her reading chair, enjoying one story with two new books waiting in the wings. Shepperd is one of the founding members of the Washington Independent Review of Books and a former senior features editor. She grew up in Washington, DC, and after moving around the world, returned home and lives there now with her husband and sons. *A Good Ending for Bad Memories* is her first published novel.

Bold Story Press is a curated, woman-owned hybrid publishing company with a mission of publishing well-written stories by women. If your book is chosen for publication, our team of expert editors and designers will work with you to publish a professionally edited and designed book. Every woman has a story to tell. If you have written yours and want to explore publishing with Bold Story Press, contact us at https://boldstorypress.com.

BOLD STORY PRESS

The Bold Story Press logo, designed by Grace Arsenault, was inspired by the nom de plume, or pen name, a sad necessity at one time for female authors who wanted to publish. The woman's face hidden in the quill is the profile of Virginia Woolf, who, in addition to being an early feminist writer, founded and ran her own publishing company, Hogarth Press.

CPSIA information can be obtained
at www.ICGtesting.com
Printed in the USA
BVHW070424060921
616119BV00003B/15